Praise for *Th*

'*The Short Straw* is an intensely re[...]
turns tense, shocking and moving [...]
cut with a knife'

'An addictive read that takes place over one unforgettable night, where one family's secrets rise to the surface – Patricia Highsmith meets Shirley Jackson'   **Gillian McAllister**

'Deliciously creepy, and a fascinating study of the complex, often toxic, relationships within families'   **Sharon Bolton**

'Utterly gripping and unputdownable'   **Jane Fallon**

'Having three sisters, I could relate to the sibling dynamics … It's twisty, gothic, and with a heartbreakingly shocking reveal'   **Lisa Hall**

'Holly creates such exquisite tension that you really can't put her books down … I felt the sense of place, the weather, the cold in that house in my bones'   **Emma Curtis**

'A spectacularly dark, eerie, and haunting mystery. Should come with a "do not read before bed" warning'   **Sophie Flynn**

'Gripping, creepy and drenched in atmosphere'   **Catherine Ryan Howard**

'*The Short Straw* practically pulses with foreboding and menace. Get ready to stay up all night! Fans of Shirley Jackson and Ruth Ware will love this. No one writes of family dynamics quite like Holly Seddon'   **Jack Jordan**

'A highly enjoyable, many-layered mystery with a masterfully handled sense of foreboding … Ending was by turns terrifying, suspenseful, and heart-breaking'   **Melanie Golding**

'Three sisters find themselves stranded at the gothic manor house that dominated their troubled childhoods. This irresistible slow-burn thriller is as much a study of family dynamics as it is a creepy & suspense-filled spine-tingler'   **Fiona Cummins**

'*The Short Straw* is creepy, twisty and more than a little Gothic'   **Sarah Hilary**

Holly Seddon is an international bestselling author and one half of the popular Honest Authors podcast. After growing up in the English countryside obsessed with music and books, Holly worked in London as a journalist and editor. She now lives in Kent with her family and writes full time.

You can find her on Twitter @hollyseddon, and on Instagram and Facebook @hollyseddonauthor.

Also by Holly Seddon

Try Not to Breathe
Don't Close Your Eyes
Love Will Tear Us Apart
The Hit List
The Woman on the Bridge

THE
SHORT
STRAW

HOLLY SEDDON

ORION

First published in Great Britain in 2023 by Orion Fiction
This paperback edition published in 2024 by Orion Fiction,
an imprint of The Orion Publishing Group Ltd.,
Carmelite House, 50 Victoria Embankment
London EC4Y 0DZ

An Hachette UK Company

1 3 5 7 9 10 8 6 4 2

A CIP catalogue record for this book
is available from the British Library.

ISBN (Paperback) 978 1 3987 0952 2
ISBN (eBook) 978 1 3987 0953 9

Typeset at The Spartan Press Ltd,
Lymington, Hants

Printed and bound in Great Britain by Clays Ltd,
Elcograf S.p.A.

www.orionbooks.co.uk

For my sister, Cristabel

'Those who cannot remember the past are condemned to repeat it.'

George Santayana, *The Life of Reason*, 1905

In Ancient Greek mythology, the Moirai are the three daughters of Nyx, the goddess of the night. You may know these sisters better as the Fates.

1

EDEN VALLEY, CUMBRIA
September 2023, 8:07 p.m.

And now they are completely screwed. They just don't know it yet.

Nina had left the motorway earlier, just before it became impassable, a slick pool of rainwater spilling out across four carriageways where workers had already downed tools to flee the sudden storm. Taking the exit had seemed the right thing to do. So much so that Nina hadn't discussed it with her two sisters, just indicated and swung the car. A unilateral eldest child decision, the latest in a series of many.

Then Nina had nudged her snub-nosed Mini Clubman onto an almost equally busy A-road. But then, buoyed by familiarity, she had escaped that traffic by slipping away, onto the lanes that had criss-crossed their childhood. Burrowing through smaller and smaller roads that began to curl around each other like the inner workings of a shell.

Lizzie, the middle child, watched uneasily as they surged further into the darkness, leaving behind the reassuring twinkle of hundreds of headlamps. For a while, she could still see them in the mirrors, strung along the horizon like fairy lights, growing fainter.

They're long gone now.

Now the sisters are well and truly corkscrewed into the remote Eden Valley. The black, spiky trees on either side of the lane seeming to draw together like a zip behind them. As if the rest of the world was never really there.

When the sisters started this journey from their dad's house in Cheshire several hours ago, at least the rain had a perkiness to it. A sense of occasion as it teamed up with the late afternoon sunshine to become a rainbow.

But the energetic rain was followed by a sudden blackening of the evening sky that snuffed out the stars, one, two, three, like the cheap candles their father blew out on his birthday cake. The cake he'd bought for himself and presented to his guilty daughters over lunch.

Now the sky is black and the water sprays chaotically all over the car as if someone is standing above it with their thumb over the end of a hose. The thunder booms erratically and lightning cracks through the now starless sky like the whip of a madman. The thick trees on either side of the winding road sway, loose and dangerous. On this dark night, they are just shadows and suggestions, nothing is solid here.

Condensation runs down the inside of the windows as if the car itself is sweating. The overworked heater smells of burnt dust and headaches. There is no reception; the maps on their phones are empty spaces with spinning wheels. Nina taps her phone, snug in its dashboard cradle. Nothing. She tries to ignore the tiny shiver that runs down her arms. Flexing her hands on the wheel to expel it.

The car radio splutters in and out again, bringing only snatches of bad news. High winds, flooded roads, grounded planes, bad people. Overhead, a lattice of lightning cracks through the sky and thunder rolls lazily behind it. Now there is only static. Nina snaps the radio off and rubs her forehead.

Neither Lizzie nor Aisa seem to have noticed how low the petrol gauge is, and Nina is chewing over how best to tell them. It's been red for a while and if she's not quick, it'll start beeping.

'Are you sure you know where we are?' Lizzie asks gently. She knows they needed to come north from Cheshire, through Cumbria where they once lived, but the map is hazy. She knows too, that whenever she questions Nina, her older sister grows defensive, as if the worst accusation in the world is to not be fully in charge of a situation. Lizzie shrinks pre-emptively.

'Don't you recognise it?' Nina says. 'We actually used to live just down the road, this is—'

'Moirthwaite?' Lizzie says, peering nervously into the gloom. 'Gosh, is it really?'

'Yes, well, near to it anyway. The village is just a bit further along, but I'm low on petrol, so I need to go to the old garage. It'll be fun, reliving our childhood and—'

'What old garage?' Lizzie asks.

Nina swallows. She was sure there was a petrol station around here somewhere. She used to go there with Dad to fill up the car sometimes. She'd push the hose in for him and he'd get her a secret pack of Smarties from the little shop. Though perhaps that was the other side of the village. Or somewhere else entirely. *Shit*. 'You know,' Nina says. '*The* old garage.'

'How low is the petrol?' Lizzie asks.

'We'll be fine,' Nina says, trying to ignore the pounding in her head.

'It's been thirty years since we lived here,' Lizzie says nervously. 'Are you sure you know the way?'

'I absolutely know the way,' Nina lies. 'And we get a bonus trip down memory lane, to boot.'

'It's just that, Aisa's flight is—'

'Aisa's flight is what?' a voice says from the back seat. Aisa sits up and squints out of the window. Her chin-length dark hair is tousled, her Stevie Nicks T-shirt crumpled, as if she's just woken up on the set of a music video. Two white AirPods hang like speech marks on either side of her face. She tugs them out. 'Where the hell are we?'

'We just need some petrol,' Nina says.

'Can you get me some sparkling water?' Aisa mumbles, sliding back down in her seat. 'I feel a bit car sick.'

'Maybe you shouldn't have had so much wine at lunch,' Nina says.

'I had, like, one glass.'

'Sure you did,' Nina says. 'If by glass you mean one of those giant Toby jugs.'

'Oh, piss off.'

Aisa rolls her eyes and puts her headphones back in. She's anxious about making the flight, but that plays second fiddle to the other thing. The thing she struggles to name. The way her family makes her feel. Small, sad and difficult. A more acute alienation since their mother died.

A wave of nausea radiates from Aisa's stomach. She did drink too much wine, but she's damned if she's going to admit that to her know-it-all eldest sister. Instead, she closes her eyes, turns up her music and tries to tune everything out.

They shouldn't be here together like this. They're out of practice. And it really was a long, awkward day. Was their dad always such hard work? Or has he got worse since their mother, Rosemary, died in spring? It's not a topic they broach often. It's too raw, even now.

But still, they did their duty today, cake and cards for his sixty-eighth birthday and lunch in a place of his choosing – a Harvester, much to Aisa's distaste. 'You used to love Harvester,' he said, looking hurt. 'I used to love Little Chef too, but it's hardly...' She'd withered under Nina's gaze. After lunch, they spent the requisite amount of hours stifled in the too-warm house. Then they fled.

Lizzie was looking forward to catching the TransPennine Express from Manchester Piccadilly to Carlisle. A single window seat from which she would watch the viaducts and city bric-a-brac rush past, gradually replaced by little towns and bright green Lancashire countryside. And she had her book ready in her bag for when the sun slipped out of view around Morecambe Bay, leaving her with nothing to look at. A thin tea from the trolley, a pack of toffees. Or a chocolate bar. Maybe both. No finer way to spend some time.

Aisa was supposed to be getting a flight back to Paris from Manchester Airport tonight, but the plane was cancelled due to extreme weather. She is looking after an artist's cat. She put a few extra handfuls of dry food in its bowl when she left before dawn this morning, but she was supposed to be with it the whole time she stayed. ''E 'as a stress problem,' the artist had explained when she first arrived last week, with perfect Parisian pomposity. 'Poisson needs company.'

'I won't leave his side,' she said, before leaving to hook up with someone she'd met at the airport almost as soon as the artist left the apartment.

'Doesn't *poisson* mean fish?' Nina had asked last week, when Aisa called, trying to get out of Dad's birthday on grounds of feline mental health.

'Yeah. It's a cat called Fish,' Aisa replied. It's the kind of wry joke you're not supposed to laugh at. But Nina laughed anyway.

And then said bollocks to Aisa missing the celebration. The compromise was flying here and back in one day. Which worked out terribly.

Still, Aisa had managed to find a seat on the first plane out of Newcastle first thing tomorrow, preferring to sleep at the airport than spend the night in suspended animation at her dad's house, the missing shape of her mother looming too large for her to handle.

They should have kept the change of flight plans to themselves, because the whole incident set their dad off on one of his almighty flaps and before they knew it, he'd railroaded them into a complicated and unnecessary plan.

So now, instead of having three peaceful journeys home, they're jammed together in Nina's Mini in the middle of nowhere, swinging up and down hills, sliding around severe bends and skimming black lakes that draw poets by day and, by night, ghosts. It's just like when they were small and Nina was de facto babysitter, her little sisters like ducklings, waddling behind her everywhere she went. Tonight, Nina is supposed to be dropping Lizzie home on the Solway Coast and then cutting across the top of the Pennines to drop Aisa at Newcastle Airport, before driving herself back to Edinburgh. Which would be straightforward if her car wasn't on the brink of wheezing to a stop, and if she'd admitted, just a little sooner, that she couldn't remember exactly where the—

'Garage!' Lizzie says, pointing at the horizon.

'I know,' Nina says, biting back her relief. 'Right where I said—'

'But it's closed.' Aisa slumps back in her seat.

It's not just closed. The garage shop is boarded up and the pumps have been vandalised. Nina switches off the engine to save fuel, feeling at once exhausted, guilty and annoyed.

'We need to find another garage,' she says, hoping that a take-charge attitude will pre-emptively nix any criticism. 'Do either of you have reception?'

'Nope,' Aisa says tersely, her phone still glued to her hand. Lizzie fumbles around in her big fabric handbag, pushing books, gloves and dog treats out of the way.

Nina grits her teeth. 'Come on, Lizard.'

When Lizzie finally pulls out her phone, it's switched off.

'Sorry,' Lizzie says, turning on her phone and wondering why any of this is her fault. When the screen eventually lights up, the five-year-old phone can't find a network. 'Do you have a road map in the car?' she asks Nina, who shakes her head.

'A paper map? To go with her monocle and penny farthing?' Aisa says, rubbing her eyes and switching off her music. 'The signal will be back soon, Nina, just keep driving until it comes on.'

'I don't have enough petrol to just keep driving.'

'Well, you know you've not passed a garage yet, so there's no point going back that way, and as we can either go backwards or forwards, let's just go forwards. Jesus.'

'Thanks, Aisa, remind me how long you've been driving?' Nina says.

'I don't need to know clutch control to work out that if we've not passed a garage the way we came, there's no point going back that way.'

Nina is breathing heavily through her nose now, which Lizzie knows very well is a precursor to a shouting match. 'Please,' she says, 'fighting isn't going to help anything.'

'You sort it out then,' Aisa says, pressing play on her music again and closing her eyes.

So far, it's as if they have skimmed along the edge of the storm, but stopping here has allowed the weather to catch up with them. A frantic shard of lightning appears right above the garage, then the thunder claps so loud it could split the sky.

The Mini sits useless on the potholed forecourt, like a toy in comparison to the hugeness of the electrified sky. In the back, Aisa keeps her eyes shut, fully checked out again, but Lizzie and Nina stare at the boarded-up little shop.

'I think there's a house behind, I should see if there's someone there,' Nina says. 'Or at least a payphone.'

'Draw straws?' Lizzie says, but Nina shakes her head. She reaches into the back and pulls at a raincoat that's been caught under Aisa, who lifts her leg with a grunt to release it.

And then Nina is out of the car, using her phone as a flash-light while Lizzie marvels at her bravery.

Nina approaches the little shop with rising panic. Could there really be someone out here to help them? She looks back just briefly at her sisters, sitting vulnerable in the car she's stupidly allowed to nearly run out of fuel. Two grown women, but not to her. To her, they will always be her soft middle sister, frightened of her own reflection. And little Aisa, so determined to be fierce that she'd run headlong at danger just to prove something. Nina takes a deep breath and walks on.

The shop is so much smaller than she remembers and the bulk behind it is just an old outbuilding, not a house at all. But maybe there's a phone on the forecourt somewhere. As the rain thumps on her hood and rushes down her face, she runs the light along the wooden boards that cover the windows, then turns the corner and sees a payphone attached to the wall. She dashes to it, lifts the handset and hears nothing. It's dead. Of course it's dead. She can't see the Mini from around this corner and allows herself to shed a couple of frustrated tears, cuffing them quickly on her jacket. As she turns to walk back to the car, something grabs her shoulder.

2

8:25 p.m.

Nina screams, and then freezes, eyes screwed shut.

'Oh my God, are you OK?'

Nina opens her eyes, lifts her phone cautiously and illuminates Lizzie standing in front of her, holding her own phone as a flashlight.

'I thought I heard you scream. Oh, you're tangled.'

Nina turns carefully, finally daring to breathe again, and sees that it is just a mess of overgrown brambles snagging her, not a person. The ends drape over her shoulder like fingers.

'Yeah,' she manages to say, allowing the breath back into her lungs.

Lizzie carefully teases away the brambles and Nina notices that her sister has rushed out without stopping to get her coat. She is soaked, and Nina's chest rolls with an emotion she can't fully articulate. Gratitude, irritation, care and guilt, stirred unpalatably together.

Back in the car, Lizzie shivers in her baggy T-shirt as she pulls off her jumper and lays it along the parcel shelf to dry.

'That smells like a wet dog,' Aisa sniffs.

'Hey,' Lizzie says, pointing at Aisa's phone. 'Don't you need 3G to listen to music?'

Aisa looks at her as if she's mad. 'Um, no. I'm listening to my downloaded songs?' Her inflection rises in a way that reminds Lizzie how much younger Aisa is than her. 'And it's 5G now, Lizard.'

Just as she starts to feel stung, Lizzie catches a slight smile from Aisa as she turns away. Aisa has always made Lizzie feel old, even when she was a teenager. It's only been in her thirties that Lizzie realised she rather likes being 'old'.

Nina stares out at the empty road ahead. This was once the main road between a string of tiny villages and sparse towns, but then the bypass came and sucked all the cars away like a big magnet. No wonder the garage closed, it was probably struggling for business when they lived here. Nina closes her eyes, brings up a patchy mental image of a map, then gently starts the engine.

They crawl along. The sky is the blackest Nina has seen for years, stars chased away by the storm, tucked into some secret pocket of the sky like precious coins. Even in the car, they can feel the temperature drop as they drive near the river, as if the water is draining something from them.

A tiny junction appears, bolstering Nina's developing plan. Yes, she knows where she is. And she knows where to go for help. She swings for the junction without indicating and ignores Lizzie's questioning look.

The ornate old white signpost catches the headlights as she turns: 'Moirthwaite – 5.'

Five miles? *Christ.*

It's much further from here than Nina thought. She looks at the petrol gauge, beeping occasionally but softly, like it knows it's pointless. Can she make it another five miles? Nina looks in the rear-view mirror at Aisa, either asleep again or pretending to be. She looks back at Lizzie, clearly trying to hide her worry behind a thin-lipped smile. 'This'll be fun,' Nina says brightly.

At first, the lane slopes gently upwards, but it quickly drops down again. Nina slips out of gear into neutral and lets the car coast, picking up speed. OK, this could work. As they roll along, the headlights pick out a slight rising slope ahead, which she thinks is then followed by another downhill slope. The narrow road is marked by a tough little stone wall on each side. Yes, that's the hill where she used to put it in third gear for Dad.

Momentum carries the car upwards and Nina sighs in relief, perhaps they can make it after all. The car skips over the brow and then free-falls.

It all happens so quickly. The lightning, the thunder. The puddle of water so black it's like antimatter. She brakes, jamming the car into gear to try to get more control. But it's too late. The Mini plunges into the water at the bottom of the hill. The engine cuts out but the wheels keep moving, the silent car like a headless chicken, completely out of control.

They glide through the water and settle against a thick, curved tree, which has broken through the drystone wall and now leans into the road like a pregnant belly.

Nina scrabbles to free herself from her seatbelt and pushes her door open. The air is freezing out here, the wind and rain so wild that her hair is plastered to her face before she can even get out.

Her legs are swallowed up to calf-height and in the shock of the cold gritty water, she slips awkwardly.

'Shit!'

Lizzie's door is trapped by the tree, so she shuffles across to the driver's seat to follow Nina out, while Aisa pops the back door cautiously open.

'Oh my God, Nina, are you all right?' she calls to Nina, who is now sitting in the road, near the edge of the puddle, face twisted into a grimace. Her hands are clutching her right ankle.

'Obviously not.'

Back in the car, Nina is now claiming to be fine. But the pain is written across her face as she sits in the driver's seat, door open, twisting the key. The engine clicks drily, like a tutting tongue.

'We can't stay here,' Lizzie says gently to Aisa, as they stand in the dark behind the puddle, lashed by rain and staring at the stranded Mini.

'I know,' Aisa says. 'But she can't exactly walk far.'

'I heard you and I can!' Nina calls out, but when she tries to step out and put her weight on the damaged ankle, she buckles backwards onto the seat.

The others rush into the water to help prise her out of the car.

They flank her, their arms around her shoulders, as she hobbles from the Mini, locking it pointlessly. Who could steal it? Car thieves don't tend to carry spare fuel.

They pause a moment, letting the layers of silence peel back until they can just make out the sound of the wind and the rustle of animals hiding from the storm.

'Why don't we try Jane's house?' Lizzie says suddenly. 'Moirthwaite Manor, it's just a bit further along from here, I'm sure it is.'

'Good idea,' Nina says.

'Isn't there anywhere else?' Aisa says quickly. 'I hate it there.'

'How do you even remember it? You were, what, four when we moved away?' Nina winces, hopping slightly on her good leg.

Aisa opens her mouth, ready to keep it going, but Lizzie gives her a pleading look to stop before this descends into another row about semantics and memory. Always the peacekeeper. And besides, if anyone remembers Moirthwaite Manor, it's Lizzie.

*

Their mother, Rosemary, had worked at the big house for years as a housekeeper, often taking Lizzie with her to play with Jane, the little girl who lived there. Sometimes Nina and Aisa came too, when their dad, Bob, was in the pub or working odd jobs. But it was usually just Lizzie, and that's when she liked it best.

Memories gather. Of whispering secrets, hide-and-seek, playing in the woods. Of kindred spirits, unspoken understandings. Of, probably, her last proper platonic friendship. Something she's not really missed, but still.

'Yeah,' says Nina. 'Good idea. We can use their landline and call a breakdown service.'

'And an ambulance,' Lizzie says.

'Over my dead body am I calling an ambulance for a sprained ankle. Paramedics are busy enough, trust me.'

'You're a midwife, not an expert on every medical situation,' Aisa says, then her voice softens. 'And we're just worried about you.'

'They might even have some petrol there,' Lizzie says, changing the subject. 'For their ride-on mowers. Remember how big the grounds were?'

Aisa stares up at the sky as if hoping for some god-hand to scoop her up. She shakes her head just slightly, but the others don't notice.

'Yeah, I remember the grounds,' Nina says, a strange look passing briefly over her face. 'Hopefully the water's not borked the engine and we just need a bit of fuel.'

'We should just walk back to the motorway and hitchhike,' Aisa says.

'Nina can't walk that far, Aisa,' Lizzie says.

'And it doesn't matter how far I can walk, hitchhiking is mental.'

Aisa scowls, her fingers gripping the fabric of her sister's jacket. 'I don't want to go to that house.'

'Why not?' Lizzie asks gently, but Aisa just stares down at her wet feet.

'I don't … I don't know, but I just—'

'Oh, enough of this,' Nina says. Then she adds softly, 'Please, I'm in a lot of pain.'

3

8:59 p.m.

There is water in their ears and the seams of their wet jeans have savaged their inner thighs and behind their knees. Lizzie's jumper is still wet, and it's true, it does smell like a damp dog. So *she* now smells like a damp dog.

Nina winces with almost every step, and the others' shoulders ache under her weight.

Conversation had stilled first to grumbling, and now to nothing at all. It's bleak and dark, they are three lone women in the middle of nowhere. None of them want to let on to the others that they're scared, so each nurses their private fear in silence. They slowly follow the narrow lane up over the brow of a little hill and then down again until they reach a driveway, framed by two huge pillars, carved from the same red stone as everything else around them. On top of each pillar sits a stone fox, their tails and noses chipped away. A sign clatters in the wind. As it briefly settles, they can make out the name with their phone lights. So many letters have worn away that it now reads MOIR AI.

'This is it,' Lizzie says, but they knew that already.

In the far distance, a few lights now sketch the outline of a village. A couple of hours' walk in normal circumstances. They turn into an unlit driveway, scattered with gravel and rife with potholes. Nina cries out when her bad leg slips sideways into a dip.

'Are you OK?' Lizzie asks softly.

Nina nods and Aisa squeezes her arm.

Either side of the drive, the trees are layered like spools of lace. Lizzie and Aisa use their phones in their free hands to cast enough dim light to see a little way in front of them.

'I wonder if Jane will be there,' Lizzie says, knowing it's unlikely. She's the same age as Lizzie – thirty-eight – and even she has left her parental home.

The long driveway winds upwards, then down, following the contours of the land, and they shiver even in their coats. Summer has not long ended, but they'd forgotten that the seasons do what they like up here.

'I think I've got trench foot,' Aisa says.

'Hopefully they'll let us dry our socks and shoes on a radiator,' Lizzie says, trying to remember if there even were radiators. There were fireplaces, she knows that. But then, it's decades since she's been inside and it's probably changed beyond all recognition.

The storm is still behind them, but every so often the sky lights up, and on this most recent flash, they finally see it. Moirthwaite Manor.

The unlit building is about a hundred metres away, matte black as if someone has cut a square out of the navy sky.

'Maybe they've had a power cut,' Lizzie says. 'With the storm and everything.'

Aisa looks behind her from where they've come. Just more layers of dark things. Trees, a squirming black sky, the driveway, the roads behind it. Like some kind of gothic papier mâché. She feels a tingle in her feet, fight or flight activated. She hasn't felt such a visceral fear since … well, since she was last here. *Where did that thought come from?*

'I don't like this,' she hears her voice saying, childish and high.

'Yeah, there aren't any other house lights around here, so all the power must be out,' Nina says, ignoring Aisa.

'There are no other houses,' Lizzie says. 'Don't you remember?'

'There must be some,' Nina says. 'Between here and the village.'

'No,' Aisa says, looking behind her just briefly. 'They were completely alone out here, and so are we.'

They look up, eyes adjusting slightly, but find little reassurance. Moirthwaite Manor is the shape and – in this light – the colour of an ink pot. Solid, unwelcoming.

'I thought it was bigger,' Aisa says.

'Yeah,' Lizzie says. 'I remembered it being more like … Downton Abbey or something.'

Moirthwaite Manor is big compared to normal houses but dwarfed by its surroundings. Trees so tall they must have seen dinosaurs. Or at least, Lizzie thinks with a shiver, the Black Death. She doesn't remember them being so massive. But then, in her memory, this place was a living, breathing monster, needing constant tending. Now, it lies still as a corpse. Where is everyone?

Nina starts to shuffle forward, jostling her sisters. 'Come on,' she says as Aisa and Lizzie get pulled along with her.

As they edge closer, more of the house becomes clear. A large front door is set deep into the stone frontage, with big picture windows on either side. The next floor up, three large windows are spaced equally along. Lizzie has a sudden memory of looking up at that right-hand one, where Jane would sit watching, waiting for her to arrive.

A crack of lightning fizzes through the whole sky and every-thing is suddenly, grotesquely, lit. The stone of the walls, a palette of blood and rust. The smashed fountain, green with slime. The circular gravel end of the drive with space for several cars, now empty, save for tufts of long grass and tangles of thorns. A slab of wood has been tacked on to the roof, like a dog with a patch of lighter fur. Graffiti snakes around the corners of the building, the competing designs and clashing colours like tattoo sleeves.

The moon has peeped out from behind a black cloud, bleeding light into the sky. Against that milky backdrop, it is clear that the house has been long abandoned.

'Gosh,' says Lizzie. 'I wonder what happened.'

'Does it matter?' Nina says, her voice hoarse and face slick with rain. 'The point is—'

'There's not going to be any petrol or a landline,' Aisa says. 'So there's no point going any further.'

'We have nowhere else to go though,' Nina says, her voice almost lost to the wind.

An ornate arched lintel over the doorway has crumbled away at one end, like a droopy eyebrow. The windows are thick with dust and grime and there's a security sign stapled to one of the window frames with a silhouette of a German Shepherd.

Nina leans against the front wall and reaches for the door handle, but Aisa knocks her hand away. 'What the fuck are you doing?'

'Going inside, at least it'll be dry.'

'You can't go in, it'll be locked and—' As Aisa protests, Nina twists the handle and pushes the door open.

The first thing they notice is the cold. Somehow, it feels colder inside than out. A frozen silence, years in the making, is embedded in every crevice. This place is a stranger to sunlight.

They run their phone flashlights along the floor cautiously, the terracotta tiles now a uniform dust-grey.

They shuffle further inside cautiously, waiting for an alarm to sound or a German Shepherd to come barrelling towards them, but nothing happens. They try to ignore the scurry of things hidden by the darkness.

Although seemingly intact, the building smells earthy as they walk deeper into it. As if the ground has reclaimed it and is just biding its time before swallowing it whole.

A staircase rises up out of the darkness, slivers of its ornate balustrade lit briefly in the light.

Lizzie remembers her mum cleaning that staircase. Eschewing the vacuum cleaner and rubbing at the carpeted runner with a thick wet rag, dragging out every speck of dirt carelessly crushed there by Jane and her father. And others? Were there others? She tries to picture this place as it was, but reality gets in the way.

Some of the treads now have holes in them and the demarcation of paint along the edges is the only hint that a carpet was once in situ. How lightly Jane would skip down these steps to greet Lizzie, who had to stand in her socks so she wouldn't leave a trace of herself and her ordinariness in this extraordinary space.

All that work keeping this place polished and shiny, and now look at it.

Lizzie flicks a light switch near her shoulder, but nothing happens, of course. She sweeps her phone light around the hall and finds another switch, an old-fashioned chunky nobble of a thing. She tries that too. For a moment, she imagines hearing a whirr of something, a crackle, but it's wishful thinking; they remain in the dark.

Still using phone flashlights, they check the first room on their right – the library – but aside from the dusty bookshelves and an armchair, there's not much else. Just a few old books, rotting to mulch.

Lizzie feels a pain in her chest at the waste, but doesn't risk ridicule by saying so. She had borrowed so many books from here. Jane's mother had once collected them and they'd been untouched since she died. 'No one will care if you don't bring them back,' Jane would say, but Lizzie always did. With one exception, *The Secret Garden*, still a favourite, sitting on her own double-stacked shelves back home.

'This is like a bad film,' Aisa says behind them. 'Siri, show me a stereotypical horror-film setting.' No one laughs.

They back awkwardly out of the library and then check the room on the left. It's in better condition, dusty but fairly neat. Two giant Chesterfield sofas are pushed together into a V surrounding the fireplace, which still has a pile of wood next to it. Their phone lights pick out matches and candles on the mantelpiece, even a couple of woollen blankets on one of the sofas.

'The door was unlocked,' Nina says. 'How was all this not ransacked? There's not even any graffiti inside, it's crazy.'

'Maybe no one knows it's all here,' Lizzie says, helping lower Nina onto one of the sofas.

'Maybe it's usually locked,' says Aisa, quietly, before lighting the candles. A fizz of burning dust making her jump.

The room is at once huge but cramped. The sofas are at such a strange angle, it's as if they've dropped from the sky. Near the window, in front of thick velvet curtains, a table lies on its side and a bureau is askew towards the back of the room, empty drawer open like a lolling tongue.

'Shall we close the curtains to keep the cold out?' Lizzie says, but Nina shakes her head.

'Any moonlight is more useful.'

Lizzie squats down in front of the fireplace and shines her phone light cautiously up the chimney.

'Looking for Father Christmas?' Aisa says.

'No, birds' nests. But it's OK, it's clear. Somehow.'

The sisters' socks dangle like Christmas stockings in front of the now glowing fireplace. Their shoes steam slightly on the hearth. As they sit exhausted on the sofa, Aisa's heart rate is rising. 'I have to catch that flight, Lizzie,' she says.

Lizzie isn't paying attention. She's looking around at the extra slivers of the room now illuminated by the fire's glow, snatches of memories dancing in the light. There's a certain pride that she built that fire, but a greater unease that they shouldn't be sitting here in front of it. They are intruding, no question, but there's no one to ask for permission.

'Nina,' Aisa says sharply, turning to her other sister instead and pushing the dusty blanket back off her jeans. 'We can't stay here.'

'We should at least see out the bad weather,' Nina says. 'Even if you get a later flight, the cat'll be fine.'

Lizzie stirs then, her heart always prone to animals in need. 'How much food did you leave him, Aisa?'

'Enough for the time I was away. I just didn't think I'd still be stuck here.'

'He'll be OK for another day,' Lizzie says. 'He'll be a bit hungry and need a lot of cuddles but—'

'But what if he shits everywhere? Or rips the place to shreds looking for food?'

'He'll probably just sleep,' Lizzie says. 'He'll be OK, try not to worry.'

'I'm not worried about the cat, Lizard. I'll lose my star rating on the pet-sitting site if his owner complains and then I'll only get rubbish jobs in future. Looking after pet rats in some sinkhole of a town.'

'Maybe you should just stay in one place for a bit then, how about that?' Nina says.

'Maybe you should just mind your own business, Nina, how about that?' Aisa stands angrily and pulls her damp socks back on. 'I've had enough of this bullshit. You two can sit here in the dark if you like, but I'm not waiting around for Dr Frank N. Furter to appear.' If the others get the *Rocky Horror* reference, they don't react, which winds Aisa up even more. Mum would have liked it.

'Hey,' Lizzie says quickly. 'Don't be silly. Let's talk about this.'

'What's to talk about?' Aisa says. 'I need to get to the airport and are you planning to just leave your car floating around in the lane, Nina, or what?'

Nina frowns. 'We'll go and move it tomorrow, we can—'

'What will be different tomorrow?'

'It'll be daylight.'

'And? You still need to get a breakdown service out and—'

'OK, fine,' Nina says, trying to free herself from the blanket to stand, but then sitting back down in pain. 'Look, why don't we walk to the village and find a phone somewhere, call a breakdown service.'

'You can't walk that far,' Lizzie says. 'You know you can't. Me and Aisa will go.'

'And leave her here alone?' Aisa says, pointing to Nina, who glares back. 'No offence, Neen, but whether you admit it or not, you're pretty vulnerable here all alone with a smashed-up ankle. No, you two stay here and I'll go,' Aisa says. 'I'll call the AA and then I'll walk on to the main road and hitch to—'

'Are you mental?' Nina says.

'That's the second time you've used that word today, it's really fucking problematic—'

'I'll go,' Lizzie interrupts. 'I'll go to the village, call the AA and then come back.'

Aisa looks at her older sisters. Imagines being stuck here with old bossyboots while clueless Lizzie wanders around out there, getting lost. 'Just let me go,' she says.

Lizzie looks at her little sister. So small, so feisty. Always taking unnecessary risks and spur-of-the-moment decisions. 'I'll go,' Lizzie says.

'I said *I'll* go,' Aisa says, tugging her damp jacket on.

'No, I—' Lizzie starts to say softly, but Nina eases herself to standing with a wince and hobbles to the fireplace. The others watch as Nina lifts the found box of matches Lizzie used to light the fire. She doesn't need to explain. Ever since they were little, this was a way to settle arguments. The only way.

'Fine,' sighs Aisa.

'OK,' says Lizzie, uneasily. 'I guess.'

Nina teases two matches out of the box, snaps the end from one and tosses it into the fire. Turning awkwardly away so her hands are out of view, she arranges them to appear the same length between her fingers.

She thrusts out her hand.

'Whoever gets the short straw goes for help.'

4

NINA – 9:35 p.m.

Nina stands at a diagonal, leaning most of the weight on her good leg. A wave of nausea sweeps over her. She always feels sick when she's hurt, but she hardens her face to not show it. The last thing the others need is her falling apart. A leader needs to be decisive, make decisions. She stands by that, even after everything.

She thrusts the matches towards her younger sisters. 'Go on, take one then,' she says, more snappily than intended. Lizzie's eyes grow watery in the flickering light of the dismal fire. Hopefully Lizzie will get the short straw and then Nina can fix it when she's gone and won't be offended – the logs are stacked up all wrong and it'll peter out in no time. But then... the thought of being stuck with Aisa in this mood...

Lizzie pinches one of the matches with her fingertips. Aisa snatches the other one.

Nina sits back down heavily, a little plume of dust dancing up around her. 'Let's see who got what then.'

Lizzie and Aisa have their matches in their palms, held out like offerings. In Lizzie's palm, a full-length match. In Aisa's, a ragged short straw.

'I don't think this is a good idea, Nina,' Lizzie starts, coming forward as if approaching a judge's bench.

'Fair's fair,' Aisa says, already pulling her shoes on.

It's funny, thinks Nina, how fairness isn't a concept that makes a regular appearance in her adult life, unless she's with her sisters. Then fairness – or the lack thereof – is a guiding principle and constant source of acrimony.

'I don't think you should go alone,' Lizzie says, turning to appeal directly to Aisa.

Aisa scowls. 'Don't you trust me?'

'It's not you,' Lizzie says.

In the dim light, Nina can see lines on her sister's face that weren't there before. Thirty-eight, but she always seemed so young. So immature. As a child, Lizzie would grind to a halt in almost all situations, overwhelmed and in need of rescue by their parents or Nina. Even by Aisa, despite her being so much younger.

It boggles Nina's mind that Lizzie is a living, breathing, autonomous person. That when she is under her own steam in her own house, she makes adult decisions and does things for herself. Lizzie, who used to cry under the pressure of choosing something to spy in I-Spy, somehow pays bills and cooks dinner and has a job. God, and has sex. Has she ever had sex? She must have ... but, how? With whom?

Nina wouldn't have been surprised to learn Lizzie just powered down and went to sleep when she was out of view, like a Furby. Although Furbies don't shout and lash out in their sleep, and Nina distinctly remembers that side of Lizzie.

'I just don't like you being out there by yourself,' Lizzie says, and Aisa laughs then. An actual belly laugh, not the sardonic gunfire she normally peppers them with. A laugh that splits her face in two, revealing her beautiful sharp teeth.

'If you could see the places I've been by myself,' Aisa says.

And so they wave her off from the front door, her narrow shoulders and angry stomp soon swallowed by the darkness.

'Are you sure we should let her do this?' Nina says to Lizzie.

'No. But you try stopping her.'

Nina makes her way back to the living room, leaning on the wall for support. Lizzie trails behind her.

'I hope she's OK,' Lizzie says. 'Do you think she knows how to call the AA?'

The things that Lizzie worries about... Nina shakes her head.

'No?' Lizzie says, her voice higher and shakier than before.

'No, I wasn't... Oh God.' How long will they be stuck here like this? 'Yeah, I think she'll be fine, Lizard. It's one phone call.'

'But she doesn't drive, do you think she'll understand their questions? Maybe I should go after her.'

'You don't drive either,' Nina says, sitting back down with a sigh. 'I really think she'll be fine.'

Not that she'd admit this to Lizzie, but Nina is worried about her car as well as her sister. About the hassle, the paperwork, the cost. About what happens if water has got in the engine and wrecked it. Will the insurance cover it? Will she get a courtesy car? She can't remember what her insurance policy says, but she can't do her patient visits on a bloody bicycle like she's in *Call the Midwife*... In the middle of the night, in Edinburgh, chaining her chopper to the fence. That's if they let her have access to patients again. *Don't think about that.*

'Everything will be fine,' she says firmly.

'I hope you're right,' says Lizzie. 'How's the ankle?'

'Better, I think. I managed to put more weight on it just then. Hopefully by the time Aisa gets back, I'll be up and dancing.'

Lizzie clearly isn't listening. She's staring around the room, squinting into the corners.

'Weird being back,' Nina says.

It was meant as a statement. But Lizzie answers as if it was a question just for her. She was always proprietorial about this place. And about their mum. 'It is a bit, yeah. I'd like to have a look around actually, do you fancy it?'

Nina nods, and gestures for Lizzie to help her move. 'Why not.'

They're in the hallway again, pointing their phones into the next room along, in the middle of the house. It's smaller than the front rooms.

'His office,' Lizzie says, without elaborating.

Nina sniffs the air from the doorway and instantly regrets it. Something has died in here, a rat or a rabbit maybe. The sweet cloying taste of rot hangs heavy in the air, waiting God knows how long for someone to come along and smell it.

This house is surprisingly cluttered considering it's been completely abandoned. She'd have expected it to be picked clean by now. From the doorway to the office, they can see an old metal filing cabinet and some tattered cardboard boxes that they dare not disturb.

Still in the hall – ducking under the lazy twirl of a spider's legs, much to Lizzie's distress – they shuffle into the dining room. There was once a huge antique table in here, with paintings on the wall and a big glass chandelier. Now there's a couple of dining chairs with their seats missing and not much else.

They move on to the kitchen at the back of the house. The floor is more ragged in here, a few floorboards at angles like pulled teeth. There's a huge stove, which used to steam and clank and fill the whole place with noise. The inside of the old fridge, with its Bejam's logo hanging by a thread, is coated with black mould and dusted with rodent droppings. An image of her mother on her knees checking the cupboards springs to Lizzie's mind. What would she have been doing? Writing a list, a shopping list, that's right. She did all the family's shopping for them.

'It's bigger than I remember,' Lizzie says.

The kitchen *is* huge. Lined with great wooden worktops leading to a vast larder in the corner. How many people lived here? Nina only remembers it being Jane and her dad, though they did have other staff. From here, she can see a few tins in the larder and her stomach growls, though they'd presumably be decades out of date.

'I can't believe this place is empty,' Lizzie says. 'Looks like it's been this way for a long time too.'

'Maybe they couldn't afford to run it,' Nina says. 'What did Jane's dad do?'

'I have no idea,' Lizzie says. 'I can't even picture his face, it's really weird.'

They head towards the stairs, testing the first tread in case it gives way.

'Do you really think Aisa'll be OK?' Lizzie says.

'Of course, I told you that already,' Nina replies, hoping her voice doesn't give away her own worries. Aisa has always been a mouse who acts like a lion, it's amazing she's not been in more scrapes. Or maybe, Nina thinks with a pang, Aisa just tends her scrapes in secret. She's always been like that, ever since she was little. 'Ow, God.' Nina catches her bad ankle awkwardly on the next step. 'I need to sit down.' She perches on the second step and looks up at the ceiling, checking there's nothing ominous about to drop on her head from the darkness. As she looks around, a tiny light catches her eye in the corner of the hallway. 'Maybe there is electricity after all,' she says, pointing to it.

'What?' Lizzie says, hovering in front of her with her back to the door. She turns round quickly, confused.

'There was a ...' But there's no light in the corner. Nina blinks and rubs her eyes. It's not the first time she's seen floaters, usually at the end of a very long shift. And this has been a very, very long family shift. 'Don't worry, it's nothing.'

5

ROSEMARY – 1973

No matter how wide I open them, my eyes can't take in the whole house. I feel like an ant.

I'm sweaty from cycling here, my uniform soured up, and the mascara I sneaked on is probably halfway down my face. I'm half an hour early because Mum was so sure I'd be late, and I have no idea where I should put my bike. Its rusted body and wheezy old wheels feel obscene here and I flush guiltily like I've been caught smoking or I'm wearing frilly knickers on my head. Everything here is so … grand. So … proper.

And then I feel guilty all over again for thinking bad thoughts about the bike. Dad's bike. The seat lowered as far down as it'll go to accommodate me when I stop, I can only press one foot to the ground at a time, like a see-saw. My sole, treasured inheritance. This bike and the wristwatch I'm wearing, even though I can't fully trust its timekeeping.

As I stand, staring gormlessly up at the windows and fanning my sticky face with one hand, I remember my mum's words. Her prophetic, philosophic, wise guidance. 'Don't cock this up, it's your last chance.'

My other chances, of course, are left behind to gather dust

30

along with my 'bloody expensive' uniform that Dad had to do overtime to afford. Poor Dad.

I could try to come up with a decent excuse, or blame friends, or boys or ... I don't know, Edward Heath. But the simple truth is that everything was going OK. I wasn't a straight-A fifth-former, but I was clinging on. And then Dad died just before my mock exams, I went bananas, and everything else slammed into a wall.

My mum could barely look at me when I was expelled. 'First of the family to go to grammar school,' she kept saying.

'First of the family to get booted too,' I'd said, and she walloped my legs.

So now I'm staring up at my last chance, hands slick on the handlebars, half-hoping they made a mistake and don't have a job for me here, and I can go home and back to bed. Lick my wounds and work out what to do with my life. Then the front door opens, a woman in a black uniform comes out. She's shaped like a Scotch egg and her grey hair, whipped up in a neat bun, frames her face, which is as red as a postbox.

'Whut yer djarn standing there like that?' she says, bustling over, and then looks behind her quickly and tugs my arm. 'Rosemary?' she asks and I nod. 'Stash your push iron there, lass, and then we'll get t'work.'

6

LIZZIE – 9:55 p.m.

Lizzie has helped Nina back into the living room – an ironic name given it feels like a mausoleum – where her sister now lies on one of the sofas, near the fire. Lizzie has packed her in with both the blankets, shaken again for dust (and spiders), which Nina grumbled about but allowed to happen. It's the best place for her. Not just for Nina's sake, but for all of them. If Aisa gets the AA to come and fix the car, Nina needs to be able to drive it.

Lizzie has had driving lessons. A lot of them. More than she'd admit. But she always felt like she was being asked to ride a bucking metal bronco through streets surrounded by soft, vulnerable humans. It just felt like a bad idea, something that should never be allowed. In the end, she realised that driving wasn't the problem, she was. It was a relief to let her provisional licence expire.

Aisa, on the other hand, has not had any lessons as far as Lizzie knows. Yet she would almost certainly seize the keys and attempt to drive the car if Nina was out of commission. So yes, Nina recuperating in front of the fire is by far the best plan.

Lizzie has made her way carefully up the stairs, testing each tread in turn. They used to run up and down these steps, Jane and her. 'I'm not allowed to run up the stairs at home,' she remembers saying giddily, a rule and a conversation long ago archived. And that feeling, God yes, she'd forgotten that feeling. That when she was here, she was in Jane's jurisdiction. That Lizzie's mother, Rosemary, 'the help', had to adhere to those rules too.

At home, their mum tucked kitchen roll into their necklines when they ate their tea so that they wouldn't spoil their clothes after just one day's wear. When Lizzie had first eaten in the kitchen here, she'd asked her mum for the kitchen roll out of habit and been passed a fancy-looking napkin instead. Jane just shook her head when Rosemary held one out to her as well, and food had dripped from her chin onto her dress. Lizzie remembers looking nervously at her mum, but her face remained neutral. Later, she realised that Rosemary couldn't tell Jane what to do, she just had to clean up after her.

How must that have felt for their mum? But she never complained. Perhaps that's why she was kept here so long, way beyond Jane's dad really needing a housekeeper three days a week.

The light on Lizzie's phone illuminates a space in front of her that's about the size of a small dog, nothing more. She has to sweep it constantly to get a sense of where she is and where to tread. The floor seems intact, but who knows. It creaks and sighs as she steps along, back in her damp shoes and coat.

A crack of lightning and boom of thunder startle her, rattling the roof and windows. She can't remember a storm ever being this close; it's like it's chased them here. She hopes Aisa is all right out there, but at least if the storm is dancing around them here, her little sister is walking away from it.

The house settles again and Lizzie realises she'd been frozen still, breath held and jaw locked as the sky crackled over her.

Gosh this is strange, she thinks, trying to come back into her body and move normally. *Take a breath, take a step. Come on, Lizzie, it's just Jane's house.*

That one summer holiday she was here more than she was at home, and then never again. Her friendship with Jane switched off like a tap. Did she even say goodbye before they all moved down to Cheshire?

She stops suddenly, winded by a memory. Dad driving a van up ahead, Mum grinding her teeth with tension in the Mini as they followed. They were moving house, that's right. Moving from Cumbria to Cheshire, completely out of the blue as far as Lizzie remembered. At first, they'd stayed with a great-aunt who looked like Miss Marple, then moved to a rented place that she can barely picture anymore, and a few years later bought the house in Northwich that her dad still lives in now. Nina and Aisa were sulking about not seeing their school friends again, and Lizzie had asked quietly if they could stop in to say goodbye to Jane. 'She'll be home, she's always home.'

Lizzie hadn't let it drop. Unusually for her, she'd carried on pleading, moaning, until her mother turned slowly from the front seat, eyes red raw from crying. A look that Lizzie couldn't read. 'I'm afraid you won't be seeing her again,' she said. 'But I'm sure she'll be OK.'

Lizzie steps into a back bedroom. She'd often played hide-and-seek in this very room. Jane loved that game, almost as much as Aisa did when she was younger. Lizzie found it very high stress. The pressure of someone else counting down, trying to stuff herself into nooks and crannies that Jane – who, of course, knew the house best of all – would rumble almost immediately.

What's left here today is a skeletal version of the scene from that memory. A bare metal bed frame still set up in the middle of the room, an empty picture frame on the wall, a dusty bulb that doesn't work. A cold feeling runs through her and she rushes back out onto the landing to try to shake it off.

Even though it's unnerving to be alone up here, it's nice to finally have some thinking time. It's been tough, spending a whole day with her family. Her dad trying to take an interest in her job, asking about career progression and whether she'd thought about opening her own 'doggy daycare'.

'They seem to do a roaring trade around here,' he'd said, sitting in the same old recliner he'd had since he retired. 'People who work, leaving their pets and all that.'

'I work in an animal sanctuary, Dad, not a kennels.'

'Come on, Lizard. Don't you want some of those doggy day-care big bucks?' Nina had joked, sitting in their mother's chair.

'Don't you want to be the top dog?' added Aisa. That glint in her eye, the pleasure she got from winding people up. Adorable cheekiness when she was little, it was much more annoying in adulthood.

And it *had* lightened the mood, but did her life and choices really have to be fodder for them like that?

She wonders what Jane went on to do. Jane had loved animals as well, although ... An image flutters just out of reach. Something about animals. Something weird. No, the memory is gone.

The next door opens onto a large bathroom, and she teases it open cautiously, suspecting it to have been taken over by hideous spiders. 'Attercops', that's what her mum called them. Nan too. Lizzie still chuffing hates them, whatever their name.

The clawfoot bath is in surprisingly good shape. Heavy brass taps peer over one end, a black plug sits squat near the plughole, making her jump.

This must have been where Jane had baths. Unlike the Kelsey sisters, who only had a bath and hair wash on Sundays back then, Jane probably soaked in here daily. Her dad had enough money not to worry about the immersion heater.

Lizzie thinks of her own little tub at home on the Solway Coast, the Radox she still uses, just like her mum. Washing away the mess of the animals. She has to use strong, squeaky shampoo that strips the dog smell from her hair but also the lustre, so she just wears it pulled back. She reaches a hand up to smooth it. Maybe it's lucky Jane isn't here to see who she's become.

The only person who ever seemed pleased with who Lizzie had become was her mum. Eventually. 'Reach into that drawer there,' her mum had said in one of their final hospice conversations.

'Which one?' Lizzie asked, scanning the two bedside drawers and dreading what might be in there. Her mum's fingers were too thin for her rings by then and she pointed her bare fingers at the top one.

'Read it when I'm gone,' she added, the exertion wrinkling the paper-thin skin of her forehead as Lizzie pulled out the envelope.

And Lizzie had just dried to a crisp in that moment. Unable to cry. Unable to swallow. Her mouth sealed shut. *When I'm gone.* She'd not said that before.

And, weeks later, she had finally opened it. Steaming the envelope as if she was in a mystery novel, not wanting to tear through the seal her mum's dry lips had managed to make. The card inside had a picture of a dog on it, and was filled with a shakier version of the handwriting she'd grown up with, and tried to adopt for her own.

The last lines were the ones that meant the most.

Every choice you've made has been your own, even when the others took the mickey. So, you're exactly who you chose to be, and exactly where you belong. And I'm proud of you.

I'm quite proud of me too, Lizzie had thought. Still thinks. Something she wouldn't dare utter to her sisters, living – in their various ways – bigger lives. But Lizzie loves her job and her little house. She likes the time she gets to herself, without having to apologise for reading on the sofa and not wanting to go out. The people she works with respect her, maybe even like her. And her secret, the cherry on the cake. She finally has that, after all these years of believing it was out of reach to her.

Lizzie wonders where Jane is now, whether she has lots of friends, a big life, a family of her own. Where might she live? She wasn't born here, was she? Her mum and dad had moved here when she was tiny, but Jane never had the accent. Her dad, still faceless in Lizzie's memory, didn't have it either. How does she know that? She can't picture him, can't conjure up his voice, but somehow she knows that.

Wherever they came from, perhaps they had returned there. She feels strangely more alone at the thought.

7

AISA – 9:45 p.m.

They would deny it, but her older sisters definitely shared one of their looks when Aisa drew the short straw. It's not the look itself that boils her piss the most, although it *does* boil her piss, it's the fact that they think she doesn't notice. That she can't read the little message that fizzes between the older two. Nina making her judgements and Lizzie absorbing them, never speaking up for her little sister.

Aisa is too young to understand, Aisa is being a brat, Aisa needs protecting, Aisa is making up stories.

Well anyway, bye.

She'd assured her sisters that she had enough phone battery to call the AA if she found reception before she reached the village. In reality, she's barely got 30 per cent, but she wasn't about to tell them that. She snaps the flashlight off to save power and takes a sharp breath.

God, it's dark. She feels swallowed up by it. A shiver runs up her legs and across her shoulders, even colder in her damp clothes after the brief respite by the fire.

She pictures a warm airport lounge, curling sandwiches and a coffee machine. Not long now. Aisa has no intention of going back to that house. And why did they have to stop there of all places? After all this time?

She'll call a breakdown service when she gets to the village, as promised, but then she'll get a taxi to Carlisle railway station, where she can get a train to Newcastle Airport. She knows the northern train networks backwards, ingrained during her younger years. Every step, she tells herself, is a step towards escape. Hopefully the smelly old phone box is still there, but if not... God, whatever. She'll bang on doors if she has to. She's not going back to that house.

Something flickers in her memory. A sliver of the red of the phone box they could see from their old shared bedroom. Pulling the fairy-patterned curtains to one side. Dark skies lit by village lamp posts. The squeak of the phone box door. Mum.

Why would her mum have been using the phone box? They had a landline; it wasn't Victorian times. Maybe they'd not paid the bill. Yes, that's probably it. When Dad lost his job. The recession, the great unmentionables.

She just worked and worked, their mum. Every uniform pressed, every meal cooked from scratch. God, exhausting. Never her, never Aisa. She laughs a moment, actually audibly laughs into the cold, dark air. She doesn't even have her own place, just a suitcase. It's probably not possible to find a more polar opposite lifestyle.

'I envy you so much, my little Ace,' her mum had said. It was one of their last conversations in the hospice, Rosemary talking painfully slowly, while Aisa scrabbled to try to escape. 'You're the biggest person I know, you make the whole world seem small.'

'I don't feel big,' she'd managed to say, before pulling her hand away and almost running out of the room. When she finally went back, buoyed by two rancid coffees from the machine, someone else was visiting. Not a back of the head she recognised.

Dark, slightly curly. Her mum knew so many people. Behind the stranger, the indignity of her mother's bald head, peeking from her headband, crushed Aisa to pieces. What a waste. She'd left without saying goodbye, feeling a coward.

On the next visit, the final visit, her mum told her to pull an envelope from the top drawer of her bedside table. 'Read it when I'm gone,' her mum said, avoiding her eye.

'I don't want you to go,' Aisa had managed to say, before burying her head on what was left of her mother's narrow lap, and crying like a child.

Aisa left the funeral barely a week later, before either of her sisters. She handed in her notice on her flat, quit her job and fled. Head down, running straight into the house-sitting, freelance-working, credit-card-stretching life she lives now. But the more she travels, the smaller the world still seems without Mum in it. The only scrap of her she has left is the still unopened envelope tucked in the passport holder, its corners grey and softened.

Above, the air feels swollen with threat, the gods of thunder sucking in air and preparing to bellow. The moon is barely visible and the whole sky squirms with dark clouds, only a few stars able to peep out from behind the velvet curtain. She focuses on the brightest one. God knows what it's called, or which constellation, but it's the one she always sees as brighter than the others. The one she pictures her mum peeking through. She doesn't believe in God, ghosts, fucking horoscopes, none of it. But she desperately wants to believe her mum is watching, keeping her safe.

She will never admit this to anyone.

She has reached the end of the long driveway and turned towards the village. Her phone battery has dropped to 29 per cent, but she puts the flashlight on anyway and points it back along the lane they had driven down to get here. The car is still there. She heads towards it. Water pools around the Mini's tyres, rain bouncing off its roof. Maybe the engine has dried out though? Aisa doesn't have a clue how cars work, but she's always felt she'd be a natural driver. She trudges up towards it, but as she gets closer, she realises she doesn't have the keys. Oh well, fuck it, it probably wouldn't have started anyway.

As she turns to go, her phone light catches the mud around the bank they'd scrambled up. Their footprints almost washed away. Jesus, Nina has big hooves, she thinks. Then she looks again. Counts. Swallows. There are four sets of footprints here, aren't there? One bigger than the rest.

She turns round suddenly, but of course she's alone. It's a sign of life, isn't it? Someone has been around here, someone must have squeezed past in their own car and then stopped. Come back and investigated the car, peered inside to see if anyone needed help. Maybe they've taken note of the registration plate and gone off to call for help themselves? Maybe help is already on its way, and Aisa can concentrate on getting to Carlisle station, getting to the airport and getting back to Paris and that ridiculously needy cat. Oh God and the bath, the clawfoot tub sitting in the window looking out over Montmartre like a perfume advert. The thought of opening a Burgundy and pouring it straight down her throat as she soaks, it's enough to make her run.

But would someone really call for help like that? Would they bollocks. She sighs and looks again. Her imagination is playing with her. It's so muddy, it's hard to make anything out. And those bigger prints could be from their trainers slipping and sliding earlier.

Aisa turns round, but she's still completely alone. And when she lifts her head to the sky, even her mother's star has disappeared.

8

ROSEMARY – 1974

'Don't you fall for one of those borstal boys,' my mum warned when I first took the job here.

'It's not a borstal,' I argued. 'That's just a nickname.'

'If the nickname fits…' my mum said, turning away before I could argue.

I don't know what you'd call it here. Depends who you ask. A tight ship, the Brigadier might say – not that he'd ever talk to me. He's in charge of the boys and has nothing to do with household staff. That's the lady of the house's domain, Mrs Proctor. This place is a second chance for poor unfortunates, Mrs Proctor would probably say. Though she's like one of the horses when they're out on her runs – blinkered.

I don't speak much to the boys themselves, so I don't know what they'd call it here. I imagine, at first, it must seem like Shangri-La. A bed and food, no questions asked. I take them glasses of water when they're working outside, I wrap their sandwiches in paper in the mornings and wash their bedding – which is even worse than cleaning the toilets – and sometimes, I find a stray boy loosened from the pack. He'll be thinking – I can always see them thinking – about running. 'He won't come after you,' I always tell them, but they don't always believe me.

And I've heard whispers, things the other staff say when they think I'm not listening. About punishments, equipment, 'the Brigadier's funny ideas'. Things they think I'm too young or squeamish to hear about. And maybe they're right.

Well, anyway, I haven't fallen for a borstal boy, I've fallen for a Brigadier's son. (Who, for what it's worth, would call what the Proctors do here 'a misguided social experiment'.)

William has just finished university, spending the summer here before starting a job in London. When I heard from the staff that he was coming, I assumed he would treat me with the same quiet contempt that his mother did, adopting a begrudgingly patient, patronising tone that I imagined they called 'dealing with the natives'. But he didn't. From the day he arrived, he got involved with the 'boys', joining them for their manual work and even eating with them in the kitchen while his parents ate later in the silent dining room. And he was kind to me. Praising my work as if it mattered. And I swelled with pride.

He arrived with floppy dark hair and a CND badge, which the Brigadier ripped clean out of his T-shirt and crushed under his riding boots. Now he has a haircut like the rest of the boys – 'a man's haircut', according to his father. One of the house rules: women's hair is long and tied back, men's is a regulation short back and sides.

It's a rotten job, mine, but it's been enormously enriched by the time William carves out to see me. It was, I'm more than happy to admit, an infatuation. At first. But it wasn't entirely unrequited. He wasn't *infatuated*, and it took a while for him to stop talking to me in a kindly older brother kind of way and take longer looks, flirt a little, but it did happen.

When I admitted I'd been expelled from grammar school, he said he envied me for going in the first place – he was home-schooled by the Brigadier and would have loved to have been expelled from that. For the last three years, he's been studying in London. He laughed when I asked if he'd seen the Queen, I think he thought I was being ironic. 'You'd love the galleries,' he said, 'and the discos.'

'I'd love to see *Grease* in the West End,' I said. 'Or *Joseph and the Amazing Technicolour Dreamcoat*.'

He gave me another look like he did about the Queen, but I think he could tell I was being serious. 'There's something for everyone,' he smiled.

Then he suggested I sign up to that new Open University. I won't, I'm not old enough and, to be honest, other than doing the village panto and listening to music, I have no idea what I want from my life. But I'm flattered he thinks I could.

We sneak away on my break most days now. At first, we'd just walk around the grounds. Then we'd sometimes sit on the soft grass up near the stream where the garden becomes a fairy-tale wood. Now we just run straight to the wood, no time to waste, to lean up against a big fat oak that shelters us from eyes and ears. The whiff of escape is as powerful as any pheromone. Because I know he's moving to London, I know boys like him don't stay around here, but maybe … maybe a girl like me could also leave.

9

NINA – 10:05 p.m.

Where will Aisa be now? Nina tries to picture the journey she'll have taken. Back out of the house, down the potholed drive and then onto the lane. Will Aisa pause to get her bearings? Has she ever paused?

I hope she's OK.

Overhead, the thunder taunts her. A sudden stalactite of lightning appears like a distress flare, colouring the dirty glass window bright white. Shit, Aisa is surrounded by trees. Does she know not to touch them when there's lightning? Does she know not to lean wearily on their bark, not to shelter from the electric rain, her size four feet standing on the roots. The same way she used to stand on Nina's bigger feet when they were kids, Nina walking around and Aisa screaming with laughter. Nina should have warned her about the trees. Nina and all her Duke of Edinburgh treks and survival weekends, and she didn't think to check if her sister knew the basics.

Is anyone safe being outside in a storm? At least no one else will be out in this, no one … bad. It's funny, of course, that when Aisa is off living her own life usually, Nina doesn't worry like this. She doesn't even know where her sister is most of the time, her transient life leaving metaphorical snail trails all over the world, while Nina has stayed firmly put, roosting. Or helping other people to roost.

For all Nina knows, Aisa could spend her time running around bad neighbourhoods in the early hours of the morning, wearing a 'rob me' sign and throwing bundles of cash around. She didn't even know Aisa was in Paris until her little sister tried to use it as an excuse to get out of seeing Dad. But now that Nina knows precisely where Aisa is, knows the big swampy nothing she's navigating on her own, she can't put it out of her mind.

With a grunt, she eases her sore ankle off the sofa and wrestles the dusty blanket off herself. The fire wasn't great to begin with, now it's dwindling to nothing. Has Lizzie ever built a fire before? Nina camps so often that it's second nature. As a Girl Guide, she was a natural at learning these skills. Signing her up was one of the first things her mum did when they moved to Cheshire. They were all signed up for a bunch of stuff, thinking about it. In Cumbria, the Kelseys had never been ones for extracurricular clubs and costly hobbies, but in Cheshire they were hurtled into a programme of swimming, trampolining and art club. Maybe, looking back, it was an attempt to ensconce them in a new life, with new friends, as quickly as possible.

Lizzie soon dropped out and retreated to her books, and Aisa just wanted to play with the kids who lived on their new road and then, as a teenager, smoke and listen to music. But Nina carried on with the active stuff. Girl Guides became Rangers and Duke of Edinburgh. Then there was orienteering and mountain climbing and long blistered treks through the Highlands throughout university and right up to the present day. Relishing being the one to hold the ropes, to administer first aid, to build a life-saving fire. If only she still had her camping stuff in the car, but she'd cleaned everything out last week, anticipating having to hand the work car back if things don't go her way.

Don't think about that. The investigation, the angry family...
not now.

The soft thud of a door closing somewhere in the house makes her spin awkwardly around, but there's no one there. It must be Lizzie exploring. Or the wind, maybe. Though this house is surprisingly sure and true, even as a storm buffets it.

Nina inches painfully towards the hearth. God, Lizzie has made a pig's ear of this.

Nina uses one of the logs to pat what's left of the burning logs into a base and then starts again.

She pulls a nearby book towards her, checks again to see if Lizzie is watching, and then tears out the brittle pages. It's some old children's book, *The Coral Island*, and there sure as hell aren't any kids around here, but seeing it still makes her feel creeped out. The illustrations don't make her feel any better as she balls up the pages. Wild weather and shipwrecks, is that so different to tonight? And then three lads, young men maybe, clinging together. She bundles them all briskly onto the embers, where they fizz and spit as they catch alight. On top, she places the thinnest of the logs, wincing a little as she has to crab around on the floor, leaning on the fireplace for balance.

She used to read books to Aisa. A regular occurrence filed away in her memories, catching light as she twists more of these old pages for burning. She used to read to her all the time. Curling up to her sister's little body on her half-sized bed, kissing the top of her head and reading page after page until she fell asleep. She would have done anything to protect her. A little pinball that ricocheted into Nina's life. But now, she sighs, now she's letting Aisa traipse around in the back of beyond, during a storm, miles from anyone she knows. How could she explain that to Dad, if... She doesn't finish the thought.

This is ridiculous, she tells herself, struggling back to the sofa and sitting down heavily. They're all grown women, even Lizzie with her deer in the headlights approach to modern life. But Nina will always be an older sister, always be the one blamed for not looking after the little ones. And, she allows just briefly, tonight's fiasco was her fault. If she'd just stayed on the M6, she'd be through the roadworks by now, have swung into a service station for petrol and probably be dropping Lizzie at home. And then it would have been her and Aisa for the last leg. She's learned nothing.

'You have to let other people help sometimes, love,' her mum had written in a card, a picture of a rock climber on the cover, given sealed to Nina on the instruction to read it after Rosemary had died. Nina had opened it that same day, sitting in the car park of the hospice, unable to stop herself. 'And you deserve to be as happy as anyone else. But you're always so busy worrying about others, you're missing out on living your own life.'

Nina had wanted to go back inside and argue. To demand that Rosemary explain exactly how Nina was supposed to do any of this. To undo these hardwired habits. It wasn't fair. Had her mum forgotten that she was expected to look after her sisters, expected to be the eldest?

And besides, she was in this now. Her life, her career, it was all based around worrying about others. She can't even remember having a passion for midwifery, it was more pragmatic than that. She was unflappable, good at biology and couldn't wait six years to qualify as a doctor.

'Do you even like this job you're choosing over me?' Tessa, her last girlfriend and a disillusioned paramedic, had asked once. She'd not said anything because she didn't want to lie, but she didn't have a good answer to the obvious follow-up: then why do you do it?

Her mum was right, that was the worst part, and she realised too late to tell her. Too late to ask, what the hell should I do then? How do I let other people in?

She wondered if the others had been given deathbed advice like this. They didn't talk about it. She didn't dare ask in case they did, and it was kinder. She regretted opening that envelope more than anything. It had left her cross, and she still felt indignant even when it got to the funeral. Digging her heels in, becoming even more isolated, even more bossy.

You don't have to fix everything and you're not responsible for everyone.

Her manager had said something similar, multiple times. It was the reason she'd not progressed higher, an inability to delegate. Which was ironic, or maybe just irritating, because her ability to 'work under her own steam' was seen as a strength when she first qualified. Whatever people say they like best about you will always end up being the thing they end up hating. She said exactly this to Tessa's back as she was leaving. She had paused, as if to argue, but then just shrugged. 'I'm not coming after you,' Nina had muttered, then prayed Tessa would come back. She didn't.

Another memory starts to form. Here, right here in this house. She and Aisa. Aisa's skinny little shoulders, those tatty denim shorts she always wore. Her little fingers curled around Nina's. That little hand slipping away…

But why would they have… Mum, of course. She'd brought them to work and, as usual, left Nina in charge. Lizzie and weird Jane had wandered off and Aisa had immediately run amok. Where had she gone? Was it hide-and-seek? Oh God, Aisa loved hide-and-seek. How could something so fundamental about her have been forgotten?

But she'd hidden too well, and Nina had started to panic.

Nina must have looked for her in this very room, but that

part of the memory is missing. Just the feeling remains. Fear. The knowledge that Nina had to find her, that she couldn't admit what had happened to Mum. Nina feels her chest grow tight, and throws the blankets back off her legs, breathing deeply.

She wonders if Lizzie or Aisa remember that day too, though she has no idea what day it even was. It was summer, she knows that. Warm enough for Aisa's shorts, warm enough for... Yes! That striped Tammy Girl dress Nina loved, picked up from the church jumble sale.

If you'd asked Nina this morning about playing hide-and-seek in Moirthwaite Manor, she'd probably have drawn a blank. If you'd asked her to describe her favourite childhood dress, she'd have told you she never wore them. A tomboy, through and through. But oh, she loved that dress. And she loved Aisa. And she was absolutely terrified about what had happened to her.

Has she made the same mistake?

10

LIZZIE – 10:15 p.m.

There are nine doors up here, all branching off from the long galleried landing. The central nervous system of the house. Lizzie leans against the wooden balustrade for just a moment before pulling herself back. It could have been riddled with woodworm, ready to crumble like a Victoria sponge, but it feels as rigid as a spine.

Alongside the bare-bones bedroom she'd once hidden in are two mirror versions along the back wall, plus one on the corner at the back of the house, which she doesn't remember going in. She steps inside now. The identical metal bed still has a thin, old-fashioned mattress on it. Striped, impressed with buttons, like a child's seaside dress. An old towel folded at its foot.

She remembers now why she wouldn't have gone in here before, it belonged to the groundsman. What was his name? Lizzie can picture him now, tending the tomatoes in the greenhouse or pulling up weeds. He had his work cut out, the surrounding woodland belonged to the house too and there was once a beautiful lawn, plenty of bushes and flower beds. But he was devoted to it, she remembers now. Devoted to the grounds and to Jane's dad. Her parents used to talk about that in hushed, sometimes sardonic, voices.

He can't have been that old, maybe younger than she is now, but he seemed ancient to them. He'd shout at Jane and Lizzie for trampling through his fresh beds, then chase after them and apologise. Lizzie would glow hot with shame and pity, but Jane seemed to enjoy this moment of awkwardness.

'He knows I'm in charge,' Jane said once. 'I just click my fingers and he does what I say. He's like a dog.'

And Lizzie's dad had said similar, that's right. Called him an oddball with nowhere else to go, like some kind of stray. But it was affectionate too, like he worried about him. And it's not like Dad had many places to go either – he seemed to exist almost solely in the pub back then. Though she had a vague sense of Dad and the groundsman being friends. What was his name? A... Al... A-something, anyway.

A door clicking shut somewhere downstairs snaps her back to the present. Nina just cannot rest, can she? Lizzie just hopes she's not making her ankle worse.

She looks around. This is a tiny room for a whole grown man, she thinks, looking at it now. Room for a single bed, a narrow wardrobe and not much else. Why did he put up with it?

Between the four back bedrooms is the bathroom – which she doesn't dare visit again in case of spiders – and another separate toilet which sits by itself in a room little bigger than a cupboard. Although she can feel a prickle in her bladder and hasn't used the loo since Dad's, there's no way she's going to squat over that. God only knows what's living in it.

She walks along the landing, elbow grazing balustrades that look down over the stairs. Along the wall, there's a thin door that gives her a sudden rush of déjà vu as she teases it open. It's an airing cupboard, still containing a few greying towels in surprisingly good condition and a boiler that is stone cold and long dead. Classic spider territory, so she kicks it closed with her foot.

The landing coils round to the front of the house, where there are two more rooms. She knows one of them intimately; the other is a complete mystery. It always was. She reaches for its handle now, feeling guilty and on the brink of huge trouble. Jane's dad's room, access as strictly forbidden to her as his office. Did she ever make eye contact with him, or did she have to stare at her shoes like a subordinate?

She remembers only his shadow. A solemn man with sloping hunched shoulders, walking slowly but emphatically so you simply moved out of the way without thinking. But when she tries to picture his head, all she can picture is the back of it. Dark, messy, grey-flecked hair. For his face, nothing. A migraine aura, a glowing absence.

And she cannot picture him existing anywhere but right here. As if he and the house were part of the same organism, he the house's lungs. And now the house is dying without those organs, just a skeleton of its old form. Did he ever leave here back then? Did he go into the village to collect newspapers and milk? What about the school?

Their own dad only ever came to their village primary school if their mother was laid up ill, which was – back then – incredibly rare. Their dad did come to get them while their mum was in hospital once, though. But he was smiling, it was not a sad thing. A warm waft of celebratory beer circling him. Yes, Aisa had just been born. Lizzie would have been four, but she's staggered by the detail she can remember. The little wall along the front playground that the children lined up against at home time. A tiny school building, kids in ragtag uniform that the Kelseys barely stuck to. An intake so small that there were only two classes: infant and junior.

Yesterday, she couldn't have answered questions about that school if her life depended on it. Now she could draw a blue-print to where the overhead projector was kept and remembers the very precise smell of the school dinners cooked on site in the tiny kitchen.

But while she can picture her dad's occasional, chaotic home-time collections, she can't ever picture Jane's dad there. In fact, she can't picture Jane there. *Because, of course, she didn't go to our school.*

She takes a deep breath, flashes her phone light behind her, to check for goodness knows what, and then shoves the master bedroom door open. She steps inside, sweeps the light over the room and gasps. Of everything she's seen in this house, this is the most unsettling.

There are no pieces of furniture, no carpet or curtains. No boxes or books, no rubbish. There is no wallpaper, every scrap of it peeled off, leaving bare plaster, pocked with age. There is not even any dirt, just the faintest tides of dust at the edge of the walls. It is as empty as Lizzie's memory of its one-time occupant's face.

Did someone come in and steal everything? Strip every scrap like a colony of termites? But why would someone clean it too? Out of respect? By way of apology? Lizzie wishes she'd never seen it; it throws up questions she can't really make sense of, let alone answer. She pulls the door shut again, heart thumping.

Outside the big landing window, the wind shrieks and Lizzie shivers, wrapping her coat tightly around her body. Her jumper is still slightly damp, and she can smell the musty wool mixing with her own sweat.

It's a relief to push open Jane's old bedroom door and find the room almost intact.

As Lizzie steps inside and moves the phone light through

the room, she pictures young Jane in here. As if watching a memory from a new angle, her one-time friend waiting at the window with her knees on the seat and her elbows on the sill. There are shelves on either side of the chimney breast which at one point were filled with dolls. Collector's items from Jane's dad that they weren't allowed to play with, inherited from his family. None of them are here – she wonders if Jane still has them. Perhaps she has passed them down to her own little girl. A ripple of jealousy catches her breath. *Am I jealous of Jane for being a mother, or her imaginary daughter for having one?* She thinks it's probably the latter.

There's the little desk that Jane sat at to do her work. Homework? Did she go to private school? There are some posh ones around here, their exact details missing from Lizzie's mind because those were worlds to which she and her sisters would never have belonged. But... Lizzie stops and closes her eyes for a moment, feeling the room and its memories crowding around her.

No, Jane didn't go to any school. She was home-schooled by her dad. Lizzie shudders at the thought but can't work out exactly why.

Home-schooling isn't wacky these days, is it? Especially since the pandemic. It sounds pretty nice to Lizzie now, who never fully relaxed around all those other kids. But back then in the early nineties, it was the preserve of crackpots, hippies and the ultra-religious. Was Jane's family religious? It doesn't ring any bells, but maybe they followed one of those discreet faiths...

No wonder her mum brought Lizzie here so often. She must have seen Jane as an ideal friend for Lizzie, someone who had no other options. How lonely Jane's life must have been outside of her visits. Everything about the room makes the girl in her memory seem even smaller, even more alone. The double bed, something that to Lizzie was the preserve of adults, seems somehow monstrous. It's made from brass, dulled by age but obviously expensive. It's high off the floor, and she remembers her and Jane jumping from the rug onto the mattress and down again.

She realises she's almost doing it now, bouncing on her toes on the dusty rug and springing backwards to sit on the bed. The bed springs groan as she lands. Its mattress is covered with a sheet, but she can feel the buttons through it, hard as spinal vertebrae. In the corner of the room, an eiderdown is slumped like a body, but she can make out a familiar floral pattern. How can any of this still be here? Aren't abandoned buildings normally smashed to bits, at the mercy of the weather and looted down to their pipes?

Lizzie perches on the edge, glad of the softness, but alert, ready to run. She sweeps the light around the room from this new angle and something in the corner makes her jump off the bed in recognition. A doll's house sized replica of this house. She remembers it now. Remembers with a shudder what Jane kept in it. Surely *they* are not there anymore? She creeps closer and as she does, she hears a footstep behind her.

11

AISA – 9:58 p.m.

Her phone is now at 26 per cent, but she can't bear to part with the light again. The sooner she can get off this lane, through the village and away towards civilisation, the better. As she tramps along, the very distant hum of the M6 calls her. She's doing sums. Trying to work out the latest time she can get to Newcastle Airport and still get her flight to Paris. What time is it now? Coming up for ten o'clock. Even if she walked at top speed, she couldn't possibly reach the motorway on foot and thumb a lift in time. And though she'd deny it to her clucky sisters, she's too scared to do that anyway now.

No, the best plan is still to get to the village, find a phone and call a taxi. Even if she has to wait a while for it, so long as she gets to Carlisle by the time the last train leaves, she'll be fine.

She says it out loud to herself, 'I'll be fine,' and tries to believe it.

Aisa will cycle drunk through Berlin late at night and think nothing of it, jog in Central Park with headphones in and go home with whomever she chooses in any city, but it's here she feels scared. It's too empty, too black. If a tree falls in a forest and all that.

She knows she'll be in trouble with her sisters for ditching them, but when isn't she in Nina's bad books for some bullshit or other? Or treated to Lizzie's sad old teddy bear eyes? Besides, she has to get back to that bloody cat, who has probably long eaten through the extra food she put down and is clawing the furniture in retribution. She should have stayed there instead of coming to a birthday celebration to be pawed at and worried over and patronised.

'You can always stay here,' her dad had said at lunch, apropos of nothing. 'You don't need to stay with strangers.'

'I don't stay with strangers, Dad,' she said, necking another glass of wine, at which Nina frowned.

'Just strange animals,' Lizzie said, nervous of her own joke until Nina joined in laughing.

'I don't like you having to rely on people you don't know,' Dad had carried on, somehow managing to eat a soft potato so loudly, so annoyingly, it rattled right through her. 'Not when you've got a family.'

'I've not been taken in like an old stray,' she'd snapped. 'I'm a professional house sitter. This is my fucking job.'

'Aisa!'

'What, Nina?'

They'd stared each other down until Lizzie had practically squeaked in distress. 'I'd love to have you to stay sometime, Aisa. If you ever have a gap in bookings, I mean.'

'Thanks,' she'd managed. *Over my dead body*.

While she fumes, churning over a greatest hits of Kelsey jokes at her expense, she hears a twig break behind her. Aisa freezes.

She stands still now, imagining someone rushing up on her, seizing her neck. But nothing happens. No more twigs break, no more footsteps. She swallows, breathes again and turns around slowly. Her phone lights up a useless little pool in front of her and she lifts it higher, hand shaking. All she sees is black on black. Black trees, black road, black rain, black sky.

It has been a while since she heard thunder. She turns back around and walks shakily on. As if summoned, the sky suddenly cracks open, purple and blue, a sonic boom. She spins around to make use of the light, just in time to see something tuck into the hedge a little way behind her. Jesus Christ. Jesus fucking Christ. She walks faster, swallowing, not sure what else she can do.

Maybe one of her sisters decided to come after her. Maybe they don't trust her. She'll be blind with fury if they have, and so relieved she could throw up. But right now, her neck and back are sweating, her pulse is loud in her ears and her vision is blurring with fear.

Because if it's not one of her sisters, who is it?

12

ROSEMARY – 1974

He leaves tomorrow. William. London, a train ride that may as well be a rocket to the moon. I asked to go with him. This afternoon. My stomach rolls at the memory as I pedal home, remembering his shock.

'I can't,' he spluttered. 'I mean, I'd love to bring you but ...' and he talked about shared houses and single rooms and work and my family here and our lives and ... and ... and ... I hadn't cried, but he stroked my face and pulled me in as if I had. Afterwards, it struck me that he'd said 'bring' not 'take'. That, in his mind, he was already there.

'I mean it,' he said. 'I'd love to, it just needs a little planning.'

'OK,' I said.

'No.' He lifted my chin up and forced me to face his sincerity. 'I mean it, Rosemary. I've never felt like this about anybody, I was dreading leaving you, but I can't stay here, not with ... them. I didn't dare hope that you'd leave your whole life to come with me. Just give me some time and I'll be back for you.'

I said nothing, but he saw my silent question.

'I promise,' he nodded.

13

NINA – 10:27 p.m.

'Gosh, you made me jump,' Lizzie says, turning around.

'Sorry, Lizzie.' Nina hadn't been thinking. She should have called out as she came up, she knows how skittish Lizzie can be. She's standing like a frightened rabbit in the middle of the room, unfashionable jeans spread slightly apart, arms with their thick grannyish coat sleeves too long over the hands, holding her phone out in front of her like a gun. Or maybe more like a white flag.

Nina leans on the door frame for support, her phone light pooling with Lizzie's so she can see a fair bit of the room. Like the lounge downstairs, it's strangely intact. A big brass bed with a mattress on it, the kind of bed she's helped many rich women in Morningside deliver home-birthed babies on. The loose sheet has no obvious holes or even marks. The thick velvet curtains hang either side of the big window, whose window seat still has a cushion in place. Empty shelves sit either side of the chimney breast and in one corner sits a small desk.

Nina was never invited into this room when they were children. The three of them would be brought over in the back of their mum's car, but once they arrived, they split into two: Jane and Lizzie, Aisa and Nina. Rosemary was gone, busy until

61

lunchtime, and it was Nina's job, as ever, to keep Aisa out of trouble. Whether she succeeded on those days is neither here nor there, but no one succeeded overall. And her little sister is still trouble. Still sails too close to the wind, has no plan, no security.

Any given day – not that their contact is anything like daily – Aisa could be in Ireland, Indonesia or Italy. She wasn't always nomadic, she went to university for three years and lasted the course, she rented a flat in Manchester and took a job. What was it? Something in marketing, something... Nina shakes her head, it didn't matter how many times Aisa explained it, it meant nothing to her. Something about influencers? Social media... something. It sounded like selling snake oil to her.

Anyway, that's a thing of the past. Not long after their mother's funeral in November, Aisa quit her job, left her flat and started house sitting and doing weird online freelance work. The first she heard of it was when Nina texted the family WhatsApp to say she'd be in Manchester for a work course and did Aisa want to meet up.

'Can't,' she'd replied. 'I'm in Barcelona for a month.'

Aisa continues to live a life that makes no sense to Nina. She's flummoxed on an emotional level, like how does Aisa cope with having no space of her own? Nowhere to retreat? But the logistics also blow Nina's brain. Like, where is all Aisa's stuff? Where does she get her post sent? To Dad's? And does her bank know that she's basically homeless? Where is she registered on the electoral roll? But when Nina tried to ask exactly that, Aisa laughed her head off at such limited thinking. 'Who votes anymore? I'm post-political.'

Until last week, everyone knew where Nina was on almost any given day. Delivering babies or checking blood pressure or listening to tiny, rapid heartbeats. And when she's not at work, she's most likely at home in her flat or walking on Arthur's Seat, overlooking the city. Occasionally out in the country, camping with friends from work who know almost nothing about her. *Will they stop inviting me if… Stop it. Stay in the present,* she tells herself.

And when she is out there, lying under the stars next to a campfire, listening to medics share their war stories, Nina feels big and brave. A lioness stalking on the plain as the great sky rolls over her. But really, she's a house cat, with a finite territory. Aisa reminds her of that. Seems to delight in reminding her, mouth twisted sardonically as, yet again, Nina walks into a trap and proves herself old and uncool. Despite that, that old imperative is throbbing ever harder: keep Aisa out of trouble.

She looks back at Lizzie, who seems to be away with the fairies, her forehead crinkled in thought. 'Maybe we should go after her,' Nina says, nodding towards the window. Lizzie doesn't answer, doesn't seem to be listening.

'Is your ankle better?' Lizzie asks, eventually, flashing her phone light at Nina's foot and then looking up with those guileless eyes.

'I got up the stairs OK,' Nina shrugs.

'Oh good.' She pauses, sweeping the light towards something on the floor. 'That's Jane's.'

Nina shuffles closer, trying not to wince as she drags bad ankle with good.

'The doll's house?'

'Yeah. Well, it's kind of a doll's house and kind of a…'

Nina waits, but Lizzie doesn't explain what she means, she just stands there. Lizzie is a complete enigma to Nina, always has been. So still and quiet.

Eventually, Lizzie steps towards the doll's house again and Nina moves closer too, unsure what's going on.

Lizzie stands still for another moment, staring down at the miniature house as if building up the nerve to act. Then she takes a big breath, stoops down suddenly and shines the flashlight of her phone inside.

14

LIZZIE – 10:29 p.m.

Lizzie stumbles backwards so fast that she clatters into Nina, who was hovering just behind her.

'Ow! God!' Nina scoots backwards awkwardly until she can sit on the edge of the bed and gingerly rub her ankle.

'I'm sorry,' Lizzie starts, holding her hands up in surrender, the light of her phone swinging as she moves. 'I just...'

But Nina isn't listening, she's carefully prodding her ankle and turning her foot one way, then another. Her own phone is next to her on the bed, flashlight beam pointing up towards the ceiling so one strange column of space is lit, dust motes twirling.

Lizzie stares in silence for as long as she can and then squats down, knees clicking, in front of Nina. 'Are you OK?'

'Yeah, I'll live. What were you looking at anyway?'

Lizzie sits on the bed next to Nina and shines her flashlight towards the doll's house. 'It's a replica of this house,' she says quietly.

Nina squints briefly, disinterestedly. 'Oh yeah,' she says, and then returns to her foot.

But Lizzie uses her light to study it again, glad of the distance. It's made from wood, about two-foot square, the same ink-pot shape as Moirthwaite Manor. The roof has been painted grey, and the walls have been washed with a sort of rusty red colour to match the local stone, each individual brick picked out with a delicate brown line. The windows have proper wooden frames, but no glass, so little hands can easily open them. Just as Jane's once did.

From here, Lizzie can see the top floor easily, both the front and the side windows. She can make out that the grounds-man's bedroom and Jane's bedroom (this very bedroom) are wallpapered and filled with tiny miniature furniture. A little desk and chair. A tiny wire bed to replicate that on which they now sit.

But when Lizzie lights up Jane's dad's miniature bedroom, it's not empty like its real-life counterpart. Instead, the room has been used for a very different purpose.

Lizzie wasn't expecting them to still be there. She'd rather hoped she'd imagined the whole thing, but no. *Crumbs, Jane.*

Lizzie moves closer, steeling her nerve. The shock has worn off, but it's been replaced by something deeper, something that turns her guts to liquid. Before she realises it, she's making a strange noise, a low frightened moan that's seeping out like air from a punctured tyre.

'What are you doing??' Nina says, easing herself up and shuffling closer, flashlight bouncing all around.

Lizzie opens her mouth to explain, but she can't find the words so instead she keeps shining her light back through the top right window of the house. 'She used it as a display case,' she says, but Nina clearly doesn't understand. 'Look closer.'

Nina grabs Lizzie's arm for support and leans closer to the doll's house, then snaps her head away. 'Jesus Christ. Nina backs away. 'That girl was always weird.'

She was, probably, but something about this sad little collection of animal skulls makes Lizzie want to cry. Each one carefully – lovingly – skinned, cleaned and polished. 'She just liked collecting them,' Lizzie says quietly.

Nina doesn't answer, and when Lizzie turns around, she sees her sister shuffling out of the room, shaking her head.

The skulls are loosely stacked in size order: rabbits at the bottom, their bulging eye surrounds and two thick front teeth looking almost comical. They fill the width of the room and support the next row of squirrel skulls. Lizzie recognises the curious 'pincer' shape of their jaws. Like little ivory lobster claws. Stuffed between a row of squirrels' heads and the wooden ceiling are the odds and sods. Little mice, with cartoon eye holes. Birds with beaks like knives. Other little bones, lying carefully across like rafters. Teeth dotted here and there. Everything is yellow with age but was once carefully preserved. A layer of dust sits over them and Lizzie is tempted to blow it away, but stops at the thought of causing an avalanche of skulls.

Jane only had four of these in her collection the first time she showed them to Lizzie. A rabbit, a mouse, a bird and a squirrel. She'd given each of them one of the bedrooms, tucking the cleaned skulls in the miniature beds, under the hand-knitted blankets. Who knitted those blankets? It can't have been Jane's mum, she'd left when Jane was still a toddler, though Jane didn't like to talk about it often. But the knitting is too rough and the sizes too specific to be shop-bought. Was it... maybe... Yes. She has a dim memory of her own mum knitting little things sometimes. Could she have made them for Jane? Lizzie knew her mum felt sorry for Jane. An uneasy jealousy ripples through her again.

On the miniature version of Jane's bed, the little blanket has flowers just like the eiderdown over there. But Jane didn't put a skull in her own tiny bed in the doll's house, that's right. Gosh, it's all coming back now. Jane's miniature bed was reserved for a doll version of Jane herself. Lizzie looks in the doll's house again, letting the light fill the toy version of the very room she's standing in. And yes, there it is, lying under the bed. Jane. What if…

Lizzie whips around suddenly and drops down until she can shine her own light under the real-life bed. From her awkward squatted position, she can see that there's nothing there. No mannequin, no human being lying in wait. No body.

Why would there be a body?

You've read too many manor house mysteries, she tells herself, dusting her aching knees as she turns back to the little house and plucks out the wooden Jane. It's dressed like she always was. A pinafore dress, a blouse, long socks. Dark hair bunched. Her head is not wooden like the rest of her, it's knitted, the wool rough with age and grey with dust. Lizzie blows it away, gently cleans her old friend and places her back in her bed. *Where are you now, Jane?*

15

AISA – 10:39 p.m.

Every step out here feels fraught, as her city trainers slap the ground, damp and ill-equipped. I'm here, I'm here, I'm here, yells the rhythm of her footsteps, ringing out across the grey countryside. Still no one emerges, but she was so sure she saw someone behind her. The fear builds up like steam in a kettle so she has to stop herself crying out. That would hardly help, but this is unbearable.

The narrow road is made narrower still by the stubby stone wall running along each side, twisting and coiling with the bumpy land like a snake. Lactic acid shoots up her calves and her damp shoes pinch her feet. Her hands, peeking out from her jacket, are bitten by the brutal wind. It feels personal. And there's a lot more of it to come before she reaches civilisation. Did she imagine seeing something hide? Maybe it was a bit of sheeting tied to a gate or something? Maybe.

Aisa looks behind her, squinting into acres of nothing, and then carries on. In the distance, in several directions, lone houses dot the distant landscape. Their dim lights flicker like dying stars, too far to reach on foot. Maybe even cut off by flooding if the earlier part of tonight's journey is anything to go by. Oh crap, could the village be cut off? *No, don't think about that.*

God, who would choose to live here like this? Sitting ducks, alone and vulnerable. She kind of understands why her parents lived nearby; they were born around here and simply lacked imagination. Her dad was from a beer family, several generations working at the stinking brewery on the road to Penrith; her mum was the daughter of factory workers. They were schooled here, met here, married here, had kids here. The real surprise is that they left here.

But some people, they actively chose this place. Some of these houses will be filled with people who have seen other ways of life and yet chose this one. Psychopaths.

The lactic acid has climbed to her thighs, her jeans are rubbing her legs and her coat is wet through. She wonders just briefly if she should ditch it, if its dampness is just making her colder. But she can't bear to peel it off and have fewer layers of protection between her body and this weather.

Her phone now has 23 per cent battery. She'll have to conserve it more carefully soon. She'll have to switch the light off, but the thought of being alone out here in the darkness...

She swallows, her throat dry and stomach aching with hunger. When did she last drink something? There was the wine at lunch. Then a few cups of tea in the afternoon. Was that it? God. And she barely ate her lunch too, just nudged all those carbs around her plate with her fork. She looks at her Apple Watch, itself on the last wisps of battery, and sees that she's blasted through her Move goal on this walk at least. When she gets to the village, if there's any shop still open, she's going to buy a whole loaf of white bread and just bore a hole in it with her teeth, climb inside.

A small stone skims across the road behind her, stopping against her heel. Kicked by a foot? She stops dead, a wave of panic running the length of her body, coating her in a sudden sweat. So there *is* someone following. Oh God. She hears the slightest rustle. Nina? No, her ankle. Lizzie. Please be Lizzie, sent by Nina to bring her back and too nervous to know what to say. Please fucking hell in heaven be Lizzie.

Aisa stays still, listening keenly to every sound which blends into a whoosh of wind and a crackle of leaves and branches. And… and… Shit. And what sounds like a footstep. And another. Treading ever so lightly with painful, cautious care. If it was Lizzie, she would have spoken up. Surely?

Aisa closes her eyes, building up the nerve. She has her light on like a beacon, there's no point pretending she's not here, so she turns suddenly and sweeps the flashlight of her phone around, expecting something terrible.

There's nothing there but the hideous skeletons of the trees, layer upon layer of wooden shadows. Neither of her sisters is here. The footsteps have stopped. Whoever was following is pretending otherwise. This isn't good. This isn't bloody good. Shit.

Aisa always believed she would put up a good fight. She lives out there, unapologetically taking up space and fearlessly throwing herself at life; she always knew she'd be handed a bill for it eventually because that's how it goes. But she never thought it would be here, in the arse end of nowhere, where her worst memories reside.

She runs into the woods on her left, bag clutched tight to her, ducks behind a tree and then turns her flashlight off. She can't hear any footsteps, but she doesn't wait around, plunging deeper among the trees, zigzagging in the dark. If someone is following her, they'll have to track her by sound alone now she's switched off her light. She treads as quietly and quickly as she can, grabbing the thick wet tree trunks to swing herself around, glad of the soft forest floor, robbing her steps of their noise.

A sudden memory. Running through trees, away from something. But what? She shakes it away and focuses on the present. She still has no reception, there's no reception at the house, and she's damned if she'd call her sisters anyway. There's no one she would call. No one she could call.

She slows and clings to one of the trees, trying to keep her breathing steady and inaudible. She curls herself into the smallest shape possible in case whoever is there turns their own flashlight on. Then she inches forward carefully, peering behind the tree and staring the way she just came. She sees absolutely nothing. The stars and thin moon can't reach her through the canopy of trees. She listens hard, but hears nothing useful over the wind.

She's a sitting duck and needs to keep going, so Aisa grips her bag close to her body with her elbow so nothing inside rattles and gives her away. As she has on so many other nights, she teases her keys out of her pocket, a jumble of metal for the apartment building in Paris, a million miles away from here, and positions each key between the fingers of her right hand. Then she brushes her fingers against her passport holder and its precious cargo for good luck. She needs to survive this dreadful night so she can finally read that card. *Yes, Aisa, that's how it works.*

She weaves across the woodland for another minute, aware that a straight line makes her very easy to follow. Then she ducks in behind another thick tree and peers out, trying to let her eyes adjust. She still feels like prey, just waiting to be caught, but she can't just keep running and getting lost in the woods. Especially as whoever is following her must know this countryside far better than she could.

The lightning flashes then. Followed almost immediately by thunder, a short bombastic burst like mighty hands clapping. It's close by, another episode will follow soon. She almost hides from it, burying her head into the bark of this ancient tree. But she forces her lids to stay open, forces herself to keep looking, waiting for the sky to light up and show her what – who – she's dealing with…

When the lightning comes again, she scans as far as she can, scouring the woodland as the sky pulses bright yellow and blue. Just before it fades again, she sees it. Him. Them. The silhouetted figure crouching low to the ground, heading her way.

16

ROSEMARY – 1975

'A flying visit,' she says. There's something in the look that accompanies her words. Or maybe it's in the way she smooths an invisible crease from her corduroy skirt, that makes me think she knows. More than knows. Owns. That she owns William, owns his time, owns his affection. Controls how it is all parcelled up, metered out. She gave me Friday off, which I'd been so chuffed about at the time, and that's when he arrived. Gone by Sunday. She didn't need to mention it, I wouldn't have known, but she did.

'Anything else, Rosemary?'

'No, ma'am.'

I place the tea things on the low table in front of her and scuttle away like the dormouse I am. Gritty-eyed, sweating from my temples, biting clumps from my cheeks, I slam straight into one of the boys standing shirtless in the hallway.

'What on earth?' I say, my voice haughty as if becoming an immediate representative for the household. I can smell him. Ammonia and sweat.

He just stands there, shaking, and I catch up with myself and realise what I'm seeing.

'Kitchen,' I say, knowing it's empty.

He thunders in there, with me following behind, skirt hitched. I point to the larder, grab the mop and bucket I'd filled ready to use and slop the water haphazardly everywhere, slicking the terracotta.

I stand in the doorway, working my mop while the boy is pressed against the tins in the larder, quivering. His pale skin shines like a flare, but when the Brigadier comes marching down the hallway, I look up as placidly as I can.

'Wet floor?' he says.

Well obviously, I don't say. 'I can fetch you anything you need, sir,' I say, hoping the fear-rattle is not as obvious to him as it is to me. 'I wouldn't want you to slip.'

He puts his hands on his hips. He's wearing those awful jodhpurs he insists on, and I see his hawk eyes scanning the floor for footprints. There are none, of course, I wetted it only after the boy's bare feet were safely across, but I find myself following his gaze anyway.

'Very good,' he booms, turning to leave and then looking back, just quickly, directly at my chest. 'Very good.'

I hear the front door and the crunch of gravel, then moments later the engine of his big old car as he goes off to see if the boy has made a break for it on tarmac. I wait until I'm sure the Brigadier has gone and then I call out, 'It's OK, you can come out.'

The boy doesn't move. He's pinned close to the wall, as if the tins of luncheon meat and jars of pickle are his brothers-in-arms and he won't give them up.

'It's OK,' I say, moving closer. As I do, I notice the marks on his wrists. Livid red bracelets, weeping blood in places.

He looks at them now too, as if noticing for the first time. 'Insubordination,' he whispers. 'So I had to do "Reflection".'

He's not the first trembling boy to escape from Reflection, but this one is different. He doesn't live here, he comes by day and gets food and a bit of cash in hand. The Brigadier has probably forgotten that, has seen him as just another head in his cattle drive. But this one has a family, the cook told me.

'Go home, Bob,' I say.

17

NINA – 10:37 p.m.

Nina is sitting on the floor in front of the hearth, fixing the sloppy job Lizzie did with the fire and trying to warm up. Her shoes are steaming slightly to the side of the grate, socks draped over them. It hadn't been nice putting them back on to go upstairs, but they were a form of armour at least. Now she wriggles her naked toes on the dusty rug, one of the old blankets lying over her shoulders.

If she closes her eyes and lets the smell of burning wood flood her head, she could almost believe she was out camping. Somewhere with a crystal sky, surrounded by gently swaying, scented trees, with rain pattering on the roof of her trusty old tent. Nothing fancy, just a classic lightweight two-man, long and narrow with a little porch that makes her feel like she's the hungry caterpillar, all swaddled and fat. She'd give anything to be tucked up in her tent now. Especially with Tessa, exploring the open spaces of the world together, though she'd have never admitted that. Never wanted to be dependent, only depended upon... She stops for a moment and sits up. *A tent*. There was always a tent in the woodland out the back, who did it belong to?

That's right, Alan. Alan the groundsman. A quiet man,

dedicated to the land and the garden, shy around the girls. He would make them little hedgehogs out of teasels, little corn dollies. He must have had a room in the house, all the staff did except their mum, but he preferred the tent. She wonders what happened to him. How devastated he would be to see the ruin that surrounds this place.

Either her ankle is much better or adrenaline has deadened her nerves, but either way, she's glad to be out of that haze of pain. Able to think more clearly. It could almost be cosy now that a proper fire is burning, if it wasn't so dusty and creepy. Even lying down with a blanket, her shoulders are rigid and her nerves are fizzing.

The door opens behind her and she turns awkwardly, but it's just Lizzie.

'Hey,' she says as Lizzie walks over, arms full of the old eiderdown from upstairs. 'Finished in the pet cemetery?'

Lizzie visibly bristles but says nothing. Instead, she walks cautiously over to the sofa and lays the eiderdown gently over it. 'Thought this would be warmer than those old blankets,' she says. 'I've checked it for creepy-crawlies.'

'Oh Lizzie, you didn't have to. I could have checked it myself.'

By the time she started secondary school, Nina had removed so many spiders for her sister that she was immune from fear and would frequently be called upon by other kids to perform this skill. On camping trips, it was she who could clasp any wriggling beast between two hands, no longer needing a cup and a piece of paper. Even now, she's designated bug catcher, taking enormous pride in scooping up insects that make other adults quake. 'You're my Bear Grylls,' Tessa used to joke when Nina removed a hefty moth or shooed a spider outside. God, why is she thinking about Tessa so much tonight? *Move on, Nina. That would never have worked out.*

'It's OK, I just gave it a good shake,' Lizzie says, but Nina notices her peering nervously into its folds anyway. 'Want to share it with me?'

Nina shakes her head but moves a little so she's not absorbing all the heat herself. 'Don't worry, you curl up.'

Lizzie nods gratefully. 'I'm pretty tired,' she says, 'so it'll be nice to just rest a minute. Don't let me fall asleep though.'

'I won't,' Nina says, smiling to herself. 'I just want to keep an eye on the fire so it's still going when Aisa comes back.'

Outside, the storm still ruffles the trees but it's not as violent as it was earlier. She hopes Aisa has escaped the worst of it. Maybe she's somewhere warm and dry in the village now. Even if it's just that little phone box that was outside their old house.

Nina looks over at Lizzie, bundled in her eiderdown like a satisfied house cat. Now she just needs Aisa back, and then she can rest knowing they're both safe and warm. Always the eldest.

She sees it in the families she visits as a midwife, firstborns still in pull-ups themselves being prepared for their new role as big sister or brother. A role that comes with very few perks, but that they generally seem excited for. Had she been excited? She was two when Lizzie was born, no chance of remembering that. But she remembers Aisa. Remembers her growing in their mum's tummy, worrying about the skin stretching too thin so the baby could poke its fingers out. Worried about their mum dying in childbirth like all the women seemed to in old books and films. And then Aisa appeared. Fully formed from day one, a ball of energy and spirit. Nothing like the others, immediately just herself. But always wanting to be in the mix with Nina and Lizzie. Always following them around, glued to Nina in particular. A loyal little puppy, who would snarl and bite if you ever called her cute. Which she was, that much is clear from all the old photos, but at the time she was too much of a pain in the arse for Nina to realise it.

Aisa was a fibber too, gosh she told whoppers. And she was never one for dolls. She was like a little doll herself but hated dresses, choosing to clothe herself in ridiculous ensembles even then. 'Let her choose,' their mum would say. The same mum who years earlier had rigorously reviewed Nina and Lizzie's outfits, liking them to match as if they were from a catalogue, and scouring the charity shops for similar stuff.

And Aisa loved playing hide-and-seek. She's a bit like that now. You never know where she'll be. Never calling for help, never seeming to be without money. Always hustling, a heat-seeking missile for an opportunity.

Maybe everyone would have plenty of money if they didn't have rent or mortgages to pay, or council tax and bills. But the very idea of that life makes Nina cringe. She loves her own space too much. She never breathes as easily as she does at home, with its high ceilings and open-plan main room. The fact that she bought it brand new, and that no one else has ever slept there or washed up in the sink, was well worth chaining herself to a mortgage. A mortgage that will have to be met, come what may.

But Aisa's life is perfect for her, Nina concedes. She was never going to play a straight bat. And good for her, Nina thinks, and wishes they were the kind of family to say that out loud.

A noise from outside brings her back to the moment. A sudden, indescribable noise. Over before she could analyse it. Something falling? A breaking branch? A car door? She didn't grab hold of it in time, but she definitely heard *something*.

Maybe Aisa is back? Perhaps she ran to the village and back, or found a house along the way, used their phone and begged a lift.

Nina hoists herself carefully to standing and heads to the

window. Lizzie watches her lazily, seemingly unaware of the sound or Nina's sense of urgency.

She presses her nose and eyes to the window. A figure is standing on the driveway, fifty feet or so away, motionless. Could it be Aisa? But why isn't she moving?

She squints and tries to make it out, but the dim light of the fire makes the darkness outside even blacker, less penetrable. She blinks, wishing she'd worn her glasses, but they're in the car. It takes a moment for her eyesight to settle, but when it does, all she can see are the black trees standing like sentries, closing them in. There was no one there.

18

LIZZIE – 10:45 p.m.

Lizzie's eyes keep drooping to a close. But Nina seems to have renewed energy now, pacing around like a guard dog despite her duff ankle. It's making Lizzie feel even more exhausted. Before she came down by train to her dad's house this morning, she'd been at the sanctuary all night watching over a stray dog found with a damaged leg.

The poor thing was so frightened that even with a cast and a cone collar, he was hurling himself into things and making it worse. She'd checked in on him as she was about to leave. She'd been so ready for her bath, a Manhattan in a vintage glass and some lovely, secret company. Instead, seeing how sad the dog looked, she had opened up his crate and let him climb onto her lap as she sat against the wall.

He was some kind of curious mixture of breeds. A smiling husky face, squat little body and solid legs. Thick hair that came off in her hands and coated them like fingerless gloves. He finally fell asleep while she stroked him, his pulse slowing and his limbs gradually losing their tremble. She resolved to stay like that as long as he needed, and ended up staying the night, calling to move her plans to the next day – tonight – just in the nick of time. Not that that's worked out well.

She finally nodded off in the early hours and woke up a few hours later, curled up to the dog's warmth. Her shift should have ended at 6 p.m., and it was closer to 6 a.m. when she left, but it was worth it. Or rather, it felt worth it at the time. Now she feels nauseous with lack of sleep, and even sadder than she expected at missing out on plans. Until recently, Lizzie's favourite type of plan was to have no plan.

When she was still upstairs, she could hear the rain drumming on the black slate roof, but in this front room, you could almost forget the weather. Until the occasional crack of thunder and lightning, at least. But out there, poor Aisa can't possibly forget the weather. She must be soaked. She pictures her little sister, rain running down her perfect nose, hair plastered to her face, and feels sick with worry. Lizzie should have gone. But it would have been futile trying to argue with Aisa. If she'd pushed too hard, Aisa would probably have peeled off her coat and gone out bare-armed just to make a point.

'You'd cut your nose off to spite your face,' as their mum used to say to her, but with affection. Almost as if she was impressed by Aisa's total commitment to being a contrarian, while she – Mum – always did the right thing.

They say each subsequent sibling that arrives has to find a role for themselves, a niche. Like, we already have a Nina, we can't have two people good at building fires and staying calm in a crisis and climbing mountains or whatever it is she does. So Lizzie came along and chose... what? She's not really sure. A small, quiet life. And then Aisa took what was left. A loud, ludicrous life.

Aisa is the coolest person I know, she thinks, closing her eyes and nestling further under the thick eiderdown. *Wonder what she'd say about me?*

*

The fire is roaring now, and Nina has taken root again in front of it, jabbing at it a little with the rusty poker and laying another two logs carefully on top. The eiderdown is surprisingly unmusty. A light layer of dust came loose when she shook it, but that's all. God knows when it was last washed, but beggars can't be choosers.

She thinks of Jane lying under it all those years ago. Her dark hair in bunches, her serious eyes. The way she would smile when Lizzie arrived, but then cover her mouth as if her pleasure was a secret. 'I've got something to show you,' she'd often say, holding out her hand for Lizzie to take it, to pull her into whatever adventure Jane had planned. She always had something to show her, and sometimes it wasn't a nice thing so Lizzie's stomach would clench in anticipation. There were often weeks between visits, and she thinks now how lonely Jane must have been in that time. Lying in that giant bed at night, with just her dad and the hired help for company by day. No wonder she was a bit different. What was Lizzie's excuse?

'You should have been born a century ago,' her mum said once. 'You'd have been happier in the past.' And hadn't she shrunk at that? Yet when something so similar was said to her again recently – 'You're like a gift from a bygone time' – hadn't she just swelled with pride? Tonight, after hours with her family, she feels ever so small again.

As her eyes start to close, she imagines herself shrinking down even more, dissolving away until she is the size of that little Jane doll, climbing into her miniature bed next to a mausoleum of animal skulls. Until finally, she thinks nothing at all.

19

AISA – 11:03 p.m.

Aisa slumps against the tree and tries to picture what she just saw, and how far away he was. It was a split-second silhouette, but he wasn't there before and it wasn't her imagination.

She's not going to run; she refuses to be prey. She looks at her phone, still no reception, of course. And 22 per cent battery. She's all on her own, several miles from her sisters now. If she called out to them, if she allowed herself to admit she needs them and just screamed for them, it would still do no good. Instead, she turns on the flashlight, covering it with her hand for a moment, and then stands and shines it where she saw him, hoping to dazzle his eyes and then run at him with her keys. She bounces on her toes, looking, looking. Where is he?

And then she sees a figure even closer to her. Still low to the ground. This time on all fours. Terrified. A fox. Skinny nose, mangy body. She shudders with relief, a low moan leaving her body before she can stop it.

Oh thank Christ.

'Filthy nasty thing,' she says to the back of him as he scurries away and she picks her way back towards the road. Bring on the hunt, she thinks, and imagines the savaging from the social media dogs if she ever voiced that.

She doesn't really mean it, just that old instinct to be contrary kicking in. She's delirious with relief, her blood spiced with it. She treads harder, with a renewed desire to get to the village and get the hell away from here.

It's far quicker to get through the trees when she's got the light on. It turns out she'd barely even grazed the woods, even though it felt like an entire life had passed in there. In under a minute, she's back on the road.

A fox! Just a fox. And not some crazy killer. And not her sisters either, coming to check up on her. A small part of her is disappointed, but the larger part is relieved. To be self-reliant is a credo she's proud of, and she's managed to slip out of a terrifying situation with it intact.

How much further is the village anyway? The lights still twinkle up ahead, but no closer than before, even after walking for ages. It's like a mirage or something. She plods on, feet rubbing against the thin trainer soles, but so glad to be alive, she could almost start running. Almost.

She tries to remember what the village has to offer but all she can really remember is the phone box, which is hopefully still there, plus snatches of the tiny school and their house. Her bedroom. No, *their* bedroom, all three girls shared a room until they moved to Cheshire. Then everything changed. They stayed with an old relative for a few weeks, a great-aunt who looked like Skeletor, then they moved to a house in Northwich with a bedroom each. Their mum stopped working and took up amateur dramatics, even doing Theatre Studies and Textiles A levels at the local college. Their dad embarked on the job track he would stay on until he retired. Eventually becoming Robert Kelsey, Station Master, Northwich Station.

He would bring home route maps for them to use for

artwork, and she'd study them instead, plotting her eventual escape. She can still reel off the exact route of every branch of the old GWR and LNWR network, should anyone ever require it. Now it's Northern Trains, but it's the same old lines, the same tendrils spilling out across the Pennines, near where she now walks.

Her feet thump along the tarmac, but the village lights stay as far as ever in the distance. One of them is her old house. Number 2, Teapot Lane. A storybook address. She wonders who lives there now, if they're happy. If they have little girls. If one of them is dreaming of escape.

She's still thinking of this when she realises her wrist is vibrating. Her Apple Watch, warning of low battery or ... She pushes up her damp jacket sleeve and sees them in all their glory. Notifications. Notifications!

She stops dead, terrified that she'll chase the reception away as she checks her phone, still being used as a flashlight. Only 19 per cent charge, but good old-fashioned 3G and one little bar of reception. She watches the charge tick down to 18 per cent as everything floods in. Social alerts. Emails. WhatsApp messages. She doesn't know what to check first, and stands for a moment, smiling with relief.

The text message is from the airline. Her flight has been delayed by an hour. It's nearly half-eleven now. She needs to be at Newcastle Airport by 4 a.m. at the absolute latest and she could still make it. Shit. She had all but given up, but she could make it yet. On a mad whim, she opens her Uber app, but obviously there are no cars available.

But there is a car just sitting idle back at the house ... and there's still one bar of reception. She only really has one option. The option she had promised to take all along. As much as it kills her to leave her notifications unread, she saves her battery power to google the number for a breakdown service. It comes up painfully slowly, but she finally calls it, and then presses the phone to her ear and waits.

20

ROSEMARY – 1980

I can feel Bob shaking next to me as the vicar prompts him. 'I do solemnly swear…' Our relatives, in the main, laugh. Maybe thinking of their own last-minute wedding nerves. The mean-spirited among them, especially Bob's parents who we were in two minds about inviting at all, might think he's having second thoughts, that he wants to bolt. But there's no chance. My favourite relative, my dad's Aunt Winnie, clutches my mum's hand in the front pew, but my mum pats her arm reassuringly.

I squeeze Bob's hand and look up. His grey suit shimmers slightly under the dramatic light pouring through the stained glass, and his thin moustache trembles a little as he returns my smile. He has what my mum calls an interesting face. I think he's handsome, but he's not pretty like some men. He's not neat and smooth. He's more… carved from molten rock. His face formed by life, the way a pebble is shaped by the sea. A scar through his eyebrow, a dent on his chin. A slight shake in his hands sometimes. I love him. And I feel sorry for him. But mostly I just love him.

This is not wedding jitters. He was full of nothing but excitement last night when he banged on my mum's door at gone midnight, having necked a happy skinful from his stag do in

The Fox. She'd chased him away up the road, waving a tea towel at him. But she didn't mind really. She loves Bob, was glad to see me settling down. I'm twenty-three, an old maid in the eyes of a woman who married Dad when they were both nineteen.

No, it's not nerves. I cast an eye to the back of the church just quickly, a glimpse of the scrawny blanketed knees and thinning grey hair of the Brigadier in his wheelchair. I'd thought it was a safe bet, inviting them. Never imagined that they'd actually come, not with his condition. I'd hoped they might stump up a good wedding present and, if I'm honest, that was my driving motivation. In the last few years, bemoaning how difficult it is to get good workers 'these days', Mrs Proctor has dropped heavy hints about there being provisions in their wills for loyal staff. It's the main reason I'm still there. Money maintains my proximity to people that cast long shadows over people I love.

But no wedding gift could ever make up for the Darth Vader shadow the Brigadier has thrown over my happiest day.

Alan is here too, wearing a suit that I can only imagine once belonged to the Brigadier when he was still in his prime. Even so, I can see slabs of Alan's scarred wrists, flashes of his ankles. Reflection never worked on him, or maybe it's still working now. He's the only boy left. And certainly not a boy anymore. He's here to push the chair, while Mrs Proctor drifts dreamily alongside. A proprietorial serenity on her face. Her member of staff, her village church, the stained glass paid for, the family crypt in pride of place.

They won't come to the reception, they say, after the ceremony. Relieved, I thank them as they leave. Bob talks in a quiet, urgent voice to Alan, avoiding looking over as the Brigadier grasps my hands. I'm propelled towards him, receiving a kiss on both cheeks. He has an underground river of strength undiminished by age or illness, and I'm carried along it. As I scrabble to free myself, I nearly trip over the train me and my mum spent so long embroidering.

'A lovely ceremony, Rosemary,' Mrs Proctor says, offering me a powdered cheek to graze with my own. In contrast to her husband, she has no strength, no physicality at all. Her hand brushes my arm, and I think that she might think that constitutes affection. For a moment, I'm struck with pity for their only – and long gone – son. 'A little something,' she says, and offers me an envelope. 'Don't open it now,' she cautions, as if people like me aren't used to getting gifts and might not know the decorum.

'Thank you,' I say.

As soon as they're installed in the big car, Alan at the wheel although I'd be amazed if he had a licence, I tear into it. It's a card. *Congratulations on your wedding. Warm Regards, Brigadier and Mrs Proctor.* One crisp five-pound note flutters out.

21

NINA – 11:20 p.m.

Lizzie is snoring on the sofa, one arm dangling free, legs splayed, mouth open. As buttoned up as she is by day, by night she is the opposite. Unfurling and taking up space. Making noise. *So that's all there inside you then*, Nina thinks. *You could be* more. Lizzie claims she's happy with her lot. A tiny, terraced house in a small seaside town, a job looking after waifs and strays, piles and piles of second-hand books and a belly rounded by hot chocolate and doorstep sandwiches. Nina has more than this and she's not particularly satisfied, so surely Lizzie's contentment can't be real.

Tessa once said that Nina deliberately picked other shift workers so she always had a reason to let things fizzle out. *We're too busy... our schedules clash...* 'That won't happen to us,' Nina said, knowing full well it would. Not wanting it to, but too scared to jump in with both feet.

Nina hears another noise outside, close to the house. Was she wrong to mistrust her eyes before? Maybe there is someone there. She tries to tune out Lizzie's snoring and the crackle of the fire. Is it Aisa? If it is Aisa, she'll come inside any moment. But if it isn't... Nina waits, silently, listening hard.

She's still trying to get her bearings, to work out the direction, when another noise reaches her, closer and louder this time.

She gets back up slowly and walks as quietly as she can to the window. Balancing on her better leg and casting a quick protective look at Lizzie, she hides most of herself behind the curtain and squints out. If it was Aisa out there, she'd have her phone flashlight on, but there's nothing there, no light.

Nina squints, trying to make out individual shapes, but it's just one big, dark nothing. No Aisa. No one? Or is someone out there, hiding from her? Overhead, she can hear the trees moving, can hear the static in the sky. The grumble of thunder threatened, but she heard two noises that were distinct from this, she knows she did.

And again now. A third noise. Inside the house this time. Footsteps? The direction confuses her, scrambling as it reaches her ears, so when she tries to place the source of the sound within the house, her mental image of the house spins and fractures like an Escher drawing.

Nina is always level-headed; she has always had to be. Births can spiral out of control and as a midwife she is there to wrestle them back, without ever letting on that she's worried. Pressing emergency buttons to call in crash teams while keeping neutral eyes on the birth partner, whisking blue newborns to get oxygen while the mothers lie panting, endorphins curtaining them from reality. And even when the worst happens, the absolute worst, she is calm. She is the strong oak tree that grieving mothers weep against. Just as she is the one who fixes the ropes on climbing trips. The one who solves colleagues' problems. The captain of the work netball team, rallying and unflappable. She clenches her teeth and tells herself this is still true, despite what happened last week.

There is only one scenario that sends her spine to jelly, and that's enclosed spaces. Sometimes, even getting a hoodie stuck on her head can send her heartbeat rushing up like a rocket.

Traffic tightly wound around a narrow lane makes her breath quicken. Embarrassingly, she would rather lie down and die than get stuck in a tunnel or be shut into a lift. But life is adaptable, and she simply runs up the stairs at the infirmary and everything is fine.

None of that is a problem here anyway. The house is huge, this room is enormous, plenty of slightly dusty, smoky air to breathe. She takes a gulp of it now. She will not let panic grip her. This is a creaky old house and they've already looked through it while searching for blankets, Lizzie more than once. No one is here. No one is here.

It is probably full of rats though. Or mice. Never the twain together, Lizzie told her that. As if they've carved up the world like the Sharks and the Jets. Where did that come from? She hasn't thought about that since ... since Mum.

West Side Story was their mum's favourite, although Rosemary liked absolutely any musical she could get her hands on. The sisters were raised on the kind of content you'd never dream of showing little kids now. *The Rocky Horror Picture Show*, *Little Shop of Horrors*, even *Hair*, for God's sake.

The happiest she'd ever seen her mum was when her amateur dramatics group put on *Oliver!* and she got to play Nancy. Belting out 'I'd Do Anything' and 'Oom-Pah-Pah' to a revolving selection of Kelseys in the audience each performance, to help her nerves.

Nina had forgotten that by the end though. God, she should have played Mum her favourite songs in the hospice. Why did none of them think to bring in her CDs? Make her a Spotify playlist? Why didn't Dad?

Focus, Nina!

Yes, this place is probably full of vermin of various stripes who all hid when the sisters came barging in earlier and have now ventured back out. Maybe even attracted by the heat of the fire, or the smell of human bodies. Nina sniffs one of her armpits. Ripe from the walk, dank from the rain. Maybe some creatures find that heady mix delicious. Either way, it can't be a person. Who would come all the way out here in a storm and not just knock on the door or announce themselves? But still.

She tugs on her coat, still a little damp. Then she teases on her stinking socks and trainers, wincing a little.

Let Lizzie sleep, she thinks, watching her for a moment and then testing her weight fully on her ankle. Much better. Definitely good enough to go and do another recce through the house, just in case. She won't be able to rest if she doesn't check, even though she's probably overreacting.

But, even without acknowledging to herself that she's worried, Nina plucks one of the heavy candlesticks from the mantelpiece with one hand, weighs it in her other palm like a baseball bat. Just in case. Didn't they have some like this, growing up? A pair of them that came out at Christmas ... Probably cheap copies.

With one final glance at Lizzie, scratching her stomach in her sleep and muttering nonsense, Nina creeps out into the hall.

22

LIZZIE – 11:35 p.m.

Lizzie drifts in and out of sleep. Her eyes open for a while, taking in the flames of the fireplace, the grey corners of the room, and then she slides back to the nineties, when she and Jane were eight years old.

She is thinking about the first lunch she had here, a picnic packed for them in the Moirthwaite Manor kitchen by Rosemary, but nothing like they'd ever have had at home. Scotch eggs, ginger beer in glass bottles, paper-wrapped doorstep sandwiches with thick-cut ham instead of Billy Bear sausage. And that Labrador and the smugglers' tunnels ... She opens her eyes. That was *Famous Five on Kirrin Island*, not a memory of her and Jane's time together.

She sighs, stares at the ceiling and tries to picture reality. Did they ever even have a picnic? Yes, yes they did. They'd sat in the woodland out the back on a crochet blanket that left little Os all over their legs.

Her eyes close as she focuses on the details. A heavy wicker basket from the cupboard under the stairs, that Mum had dusted off with a proper feather duster. A flask of lurid Kia-Ora, which they weren't allowed at home because it sent Aisa loopy with the E-number colourings. They did have doorstep ham sandwiches, that was true. And a bag of crisps each, and a thick slice of cherry cake. Jane let Lizzie have hers and she ate both slices and felt sick.

She'd lain on that picnic blanket clutching her stomach while Jane tried to wind her up with scary stories and bad ideas. That's right, she'd forgotten that about Jane. How she would sometimes try to take their games in directions that Lizzie didn't like. How she'd have talked you into something before you realised what was happening. And how Jane could lie, spilling tall tales that even Lizzie recognised as the imagination of a desperately lonely child. How Jane could be cruel.

Most of the time, Lizzie let it wash over her. She herself was the middle child of a bossy older sister and a fibbing younger sister, so nothing Jane did could rile her up too much. Unless she invoked the Rosemary Clause.

Your mum likes me best.

Your mum has to do what I say.

Your mum would prefer to be at my house than yours.

Lizzie feels heat prickle her neck at the memory. She realises she's pressing her nails into her palms now, just as she did then, counting all the kinds of animals she could think of, anything to distract her and stop her reacting. To react was risky. Mum needed the job, more so after Dad lost his, and the Kelsey girls could never risk rocking that boat.

'She's probably a bit jealous because her own mum's gone,' Lizzie's mum would say on the way home, as Lizzie glumly pressed her forehead to the window and let it bash her as the potholes bounced the car. 'You've got to let it wash over you.'

'She was saying mean things about you though.'

'There'll always be someone saying something, and you can't stop that,' her mum shrugged. 'But you can choose whether you let it bother you.'

*

The exact details of Jane's mother leaving were hazy even then. And no matter what Jane did, no matter how much she goaded, Lizzie never, ever mentioned it in retaliation. It was tempting, and sometimes the words would line up in her throat like bullets, but she just had to swallow them down.

The talk in the village was that Jane's mother had run off with a gardener who'd been working there for the summer, although that seems a little cliched now she thinks about it. Maybe she's mangling the memories with something out of a book. Besides, village talk is a cheap commodity, rarely useful in the world outside that bubble. They used to say things about Jane's dad too. *I heard he once killed a man.* She shakes her head, eyes still closed. *You idiot. That's from* The Great Gatsby.

The village did gossip about him, but that was probably because he ignored them. Alan used to pop up there from time to time though. She remembers him walking past and giving her a wave. Maybe he drank with their dad in the pub.

To think of Dad then is to think of another man entirely, and so Lizzie rolls onto her side to avoid doing that. Instead, she teases at the edges of Jane's dad, the cut-out shape of him in her mind. The empty room. Perhaps someone bought this place and started to clear it all out. Maybe you would start there as it's the biggest room? They gave up pretty soon, whoever it was. Or perhaps they'll be back. She shivers, although they're hardly going to show up tonight in this weather.

He always wore dark clothes. Sometimes a black hat too, she remembers that, like something out of a storybook. He seemed older than Lizzie's parents. Slower, a little stooped, very set in his ways. It's hard to picture him as a dad. A father, yes, in the abstract sense, but not a dad like Bob is a dad. She can't picture him ever playing the spoons to make kids laugh, or chasing them around the garden.

Rosemary used to say Lizzie was nurturing too. 'You'll be a lovely mum one day.' She'd stopped saying that eventually. Not because Lizzie wasn't caring, she was frequently laughed at by her family for being *too* caring – the rescued bee, the fostered hedgehog – but probably because everyone thought Lizzie would be alone forever.

As she falls back asleep, Lizzie dreams of overhearing Jane and her mum in the kitchen down the hall. Rosemary using the same soothing voice on Jane that should, by rights, have been reserved just for Lizzie and her sisters. And Jane's voice rising, becoming upset. Tantrumming and stamping her foot. Lizzie having to bite her cheeks so hard that she tasted blood, but never retaliating. As the memory morphs into another dream, the thumping of her foot grows louder and louder, her complaints mutate into screams.

Lizzie wakes again with a start, the voices overlapping her sudden rush of consciousness. But there's no one here and the noise has stopped.

23

ROSEMARY – 1986

'I think we should go to the funeral,' I say, as Bob flinches. 'Well, I should go anyway. As a member of the household staff. But I thought maybe you—'

'If I go, it'll only be to make sure he's definitely in that grave,' Bob says. 'Then I'd like to take a piss on it.'

It takes me and the cook days to organise and prepare all the food. Mrs Proctor has convinced herself that all the 'old boys' are likely to turn up to pay their respects, an idea that is so laughable I can barely repeat it to Bob. 'The grave'll be flooded if they do,' he says.

The manor is filled with flowers, though it's unclear who sent them or if Mrs Proctor called for them to be delivered from the florist she likes in Penrith. They were here when I arrived to work, the day after the Brigadier finally wheezed to a stop. Mrs Proctor had glided down the stairs dressed head to toe in black, a veil over her thin face. It was not just for show, I'm certain of that. She looked genuinely lost without him. 'I'm so sorry for your loss, ma'am,' I said, bowing my head a little.

'It's all of our loss,' she said, her voice barely above a whisper. 'The world's loss, really. He changed so many lives.'

*

On the day of the funeral, I leave Nina and Lizzie with the childminder and dress in the closest thing I have to mourning clothes. My black work skirt and shoes, plus a black satin shirt I found at the church jumble sale. I put my make-up on in the bathroom, going heavy on the mascara in full confidence that I won't shed a tear, and then go to see if Bob's made up his mind. He's sitting on our bed wearing his wedding suit, which strains a little at the waist and is totally the wrong colour.

'Are you sure?'

He nods, unconvincingly. 'Want to check he's actually dead and this isn't one of his lessons.'

The church is patchily filled. Far fewer people than when my own dad passed away, and considerably drier eyes. Aside from Bob and Alan, I see no former boys and I'm glad of it. At the front, Mrs Proctor is flanked by a man and a curly-haired brunette, the woman is wrestling with a dark-haired toddler about Lizzie's age. The man is clearly William. I haven't seen him in over ten years, but I recognise his posture. It's the opposite to his father's, a deliberate stoop, an apologetic rounding of the shoulders. And I recognise his head, the hair that I once wound my fingers through, a million years ago. He's grown it longer again so it scuffs the nape of his neck, and a little thrill goes through me that he's not cut it military style for the funeral. It's his equivalent of pissing on the grave.

I feel briefly strange and warm and I look at Bob, guiltily, but he is staring at his shoes. His six-year-old wedding shoes.

The funeral is, as funerals are, full of descriptions of someone no one in the congregation would recognise. Except, perhaps, Mrs Proctor with her dreamland view of her late husband. I watch William and his wife intently. If it were Bob and me, we would pass the fractious child between us to try to distract her, but that would certainly not work with Mrs Proctor sitting between them. I'm tempted to go over and offer to take the poor little thing for a walk around outside, show her some flowers and let her have a run out, but I can't do that to Bob.

Afterwards, Mrs Proctor and William stand in the church doorway as the rest of us file out, mumbling our condolences. 'Thank you,' they each say in turn. But then William seems to wake up and realise who I am, and I see him smile, just briefly.

'Rosemary,' he says, his voice barely audible. I nod. And then get jostled from behind by the sub-postmaster from the village, clearly keen to get to the food he knows is laid on at the manor.

'We'll talk later,' I say lightly.

Outside, I see William's wife and daughter walking around the graveyard. She's pointing to the flowers, and then squats to blow a raspberry on the little girl's neck so she dissolves into giggles.

Back at the manor, I swing between being staff and guest, funnelling empty plates into the kitchen, topping up glasses, but making small talk too. Bob swings between drinks, growing pinker and louder, talking boisterously to anyone who'll listen about absolutely nothing.

I don't get to speak to William again, but I introduce myself to his wife and am surprised when an American accent replies. 'I'm Selina,' she says. 'And that little rugrat you saw earlier was Jane, but she's having a nap now.'

A ripple of excitement runs through me. Foreign accents always have that effect on the rare occasion that I hear them in real life.

'Is it your first time at the manor?' I ask.

'Sure is,' she says. 'Not for want of asking.'

'Mrs Proctor can be like that,' I whisper, feeling reckless for saying so.

'Not her,' Selina says, a little louder than I would like. 'She's been begging my husband to bring us up here. Was appalled we didn't want to marry here, even. Can you imagine?'

'Yes, I can,' I say, my expression grim. We both laugh and are shot an angry look from the lady of the house, her arm firmly wrapped through her son's, her pale face anguished.

'No, it was all William,' Selina says quietly. 'He would never have come back here if he could help it. Like, never ever. I thought he might do a moonlight flit last night.'

He's good at that, I want to say, but that's hardly fair. And not exactly current.

'Hopefully we can put in our time today and then get out of Dodge tomorrow,' she says.

I'm about to say something back when I hear a little squeak from Mrs Proctor across the room. We both turn again and Selina gasps as her mother-in-law folds over on herself, one arm still clutching her son, the other her heart. William, grey with shock, helps lower her into a seat.

Within five minutes, she's dead.

24

AISA – 11:36 p.m.

Aisa has been on hold for five minutes when a real human finally answers. After hours by herself, save for that horrendous fox incident, her mouth feels dry and unwieldy, as if it has forgotten how to form words.

'I need help, our car broke down, well, it ran out of petrol—'

'So you need fuel?' the woman cuts in with alarming good cheer.

'Yes, but we also hit a tree. So that needs dealing with.'

A pause. 'Are you OK, madam? Do you or does anyone with you need medical attention?'

'No, we're all fine,' she says, surprised by the wobble to her voice. 'But I'm running out of battery and I really need you to send someone to help. Please.'

In the background, a clatter of keyboards and the hum of voices speak of call centres with strip lighting, a vending machine, a smoking room. Having never made it past a week of working in such places while at uni, Aisa suddenly feels a roaring nostalgia. She shakes her head to get rid of it.

'OK, so your car hit a tree and is it damaged externally or internally?'

'Externally? No, I don't think so. And internally, you mean like the engine? Yeah, I think … who knows? If I was a mechanic, I wouldn't be calling you.'

'Madam, please—'

'Sorry, sorry, I'm just really cold and really hungry and I need this car fixed.'

'Can I take your membership number?'

'I'm not a member and I don't know if my sister is—'

'Your sister?'

'The driver. But I'll just pay whatever, I need this sorted. Unless … How much is it likely to be?'

'I really couldn't say, the towing costs will be a fixed amount, but the actual repairs—'

Aisa sighs and closes her eyes. What difference does it make, they still needed rescuing.

'Can I take your name?'

'Aisa Kelsey. A-I-S-A, not Asia.'

She's standing as still as she can as the wind buffets her and her knees knock into one another. She daren't move, as a milli-metre either way could nix the reception. She doesn't know if she'd have enough battery for another five minutes on hold if this whole circus started again.

The woman continues to pepper her with questions that she can barely answer.

'Yes. No. Yes. Mini of some kind,' she says, her jaw juddering in the cold, making her voice sound strange, like her jaw is wired. It *feels* like it's been wired, aching from the bitter chill and from gritting her teeth through the awful muzak. 'Please help, I'm freezing my tits off here.'

The woman at the end of the line laughs, as if in surprise, and then collects herself with a cough. 'And what's the location of the car?'

'Moirthwaite Manor,' Aisa says, flattening her vowels as she always does when she deals with sunshine southerners.

'Moirthwaite Manor? Wow, that's a little bit hard to say, isn't it? Like a tongue twister.'

'Sure,' Aisa pinches her nose with her free hand.

'And what's the postcode there?'

'I have no idea.'

There's a pause long enough for Aisa to do a full body shiver.

'No matter,' says the woman at the other end, her accent one of those vaguely south-eastern ones that could be from anywhere outside of London. But not London itself, which is only full of other accents in Aisa's experience. 'Could you give me the rest of the address? The street name, maybe?'

As she speaks, Aisa imagines her micro-bladed eyebrows, the sheen of her skin, her neat high-street clothes and sighs. *Why am I like this? This woman's not done anything wrong.*

'I don't know that either. Look, I really don't mean to be shitty, and I know you're just doing your job, but I'm running out of time, so can you just google it or something?'

The pause is as good as a sigh, then the voice comes back even higher, exasperation masked with squeaky practised professionalism. 'OK! No worries! Can you give me any more information so I can make sure I send the van to the right place?'

'It's in the Eden Valley, in Cumbria. Not far from Penrith, but I don't remember any more than that and I've got hardly any battery left.' Without thinking, she pulls the phone from her ear just briefly and winces. 'Seven per cent actually.' She snaps the phone back, glad to hear that the call hasn't cut off.

'Oh fiddlesticks. OK, I'll be quick.'

Aisa looks down the empty lane, grit glistening from the rain. She feels no closer to the lights of the village than she was earlier, but at least she can go back to the house and pretend this was her plan all along. No need to mention she was intending to ditch her sisters and find a taxi. She only hopes the mechanic will come quickly enough that Nina can get her to the airport.

Aisa can hear the tapping of a keyboard and drums her own foot impatiently. 'Will they bring petrol with them then? Actually, I don't know if the car's petrol or diesel.'

'Can you ask the driver?'

'She's not with me at the moment.'

'Oh yeah. Well, they'll bring a bit of both, enough to get you going again. Oh, I think I've found the address, but, Miss Kelsey, are you *sure* you're at Moirthwaite Manor?'

'Yeah, I mean I will be by the time—'

'Moirthwaite Manor on Black Tree Lane?'

'Black Tree Lane, that's it.'

'And you said it's an abandoned house, is that right? It's not your property?'

'Yes, but I'm sure no one will mind if—'

'Miss Kelsey, are you and your sister by yourselves? It sounds a bit... weird.'

'What?' *How would she know that?*

'When I was googling it for the address, there were some funny results. Some reports from urban explorers—'

'That doesn't surprise me, but can we just—'

'Should you really be in there, I mean, it sounds—'

Aisa's pulse starts to beat through her scalp. 'Sounds what?'

'It's just that they say—'

The phone dies in Aisa's hand.

25

NINA – 11:35 p.m.

Even with her ankle still sore, it's easier to scan the house properly by herself, without Lizzie and Aisa. When they first looked around this place, newly arrived and wet through, it was a cursory glance for firewood, for signs of something helpful. A quick check for danger, from holes in the roof or tilting walls and not… whatever she's looking for now. Now she can take the time to check this place properly, find the source of that noise and make sure there isn't someone here with them.

It was almost certainly the wind, but it sounded too much like footsteps to rest easy. And if Nina doesn't take care of this stuff, who will?

There are rows of books still in the library, an old armchair whose fabric has split, the meat of it springing out. A book lies open on its arm, was that there before? She doesn't remember it, but it must have been.

Heavy velvet curtains cover the library window and she holds her breath as she pulls them open, but no one is there.

Too many horror films as kids, she thinks. What were her parents thinking? She was often allowed to take a quid and a note from her mum to the post office and select from its ten or so rental videos. She'd grab the scariest one she could find, thrust the money and the note over the counter and then she and her sisters would watch it on the TV that had been lumped upstairs by their dad. She recognises now that this was to keep the kids out of the way so their parents could either argue or 'have an early night'. The sisters wouldn't sleep properly for weeks after watching the 'video nasties'.

Out in the hall again, Nina pokes her head round the front room door and sees the reassuring, quilted mound of Lizzie on the sofa, still fast asleep. They shared a room for the whole of Nina's childhood, but she'd forgotten what a noisy sleeper Lizzie was, her nose snuffling into the pillow like a truffle pig. She'd forgotten the sleepwalking too. Waking up to find her banging around in the wardrobe, or trying to get down the stairs. Getting clobbered for trying to help her without waking her. 'You shouldn't disturb a sleepwalker, it could give them a heart attack.' A myth she believed until A-level Biology.

Nina treads carefully down the hall, her ankle clicking a little but the pain reduced to a dull throb now. As she shuffles, a draught bites at her feet and she shivers. Where did that come from?

She moves away and hovers in the doorway of the old office, muscle memory preventing her from going inside. She – well, everyone – was banned from that room. She remembers the arch of Jane's dad's back sitting in the chair that was slightly too small for him, bent over his desk. Remembers the fear that ran up her legs when she thought he might see her and question what she was doing. Just to hear his voice was enough to turn her to jelly.

She steps inside, one foot, then the other. Pauses, heavy candlestick dangling from one hand, phone in the other. Nervously waiting. As if the ceiling might collapse in outrage, or Jane's dad might appear suddenly and boom at her.

The desk is still here, pushed to the back of the room behind some boxes. The old metal filing cabinet is on the floor, its drawers hanging out like someone's emptied its pockets. She steps closer, the air unpleasantly sweet, and dreads finding the source of the rot. A dead rabbit or rat probably. She thinks of the little skulls upstairs and shivers despite herself. *Freak.* Then she sees them. A row of hooks, and three straggly birds' bodies hanging from them. Pheasants, or maybe grouse. Christ, how long have they been there? They look ragged, but not mouldy. Has the cold preserved them?

The dining room next, where, in the centre of the ceiling, an ornate rose swells and intricate cornicing skirts along the edge of the room like fancy icing on a wedding cake. Nina pictures her mum, tiptoed on a chair, dusting along the edge. Rosemary was strong and lean. A wiry kind of strength that came from constantly moving. Here, in this house, it's easier to remember her at her fullest. By the end of her life, she was a carcass, greying in front of them. But here, God, she must have been younger than Nina was now.

Rosemary wore a black dress with a white trim to work, with a black cardigan and flat black shoes. A bizarre monochrome uniform, but it seemed normal to them back then. At home, she'd scrape her fair hair into a bun and pull on the softest, comfiest clothes she could find. T-shirts of Dad's that draped over her lean frame, tracksuit bottoms and shorts in summer. Nina is the same and can think of nothing worse than hoicking herself into uncomfortable pinched waists and rigid underwires. Out of work, she'll also pull her fair hair into a bun and slip into a pair of joggers and a hoodie. 'You should just cut some arm holes in a sleeping bag,' Tessa said once. It wasn't a bad idea.

She feels a pull in her chest. For Mum. For Tessa. The tugging sensation fades, and Nina rushes back out of the room before it returns.

The kitchen has no blinds or curtains, so the great sheet of glass urgently reflects the flashlight from her phone, stinging her eyes and making her jump. The wooden worktops are still in good nick; she's seen reclaimed worktops like these in fancy apartments when she does home visits. People would spend a fortune to get their hands on what has just been left for dead in here.

Once, this room would have been filled with activity. Cake baking and big suppers being cooked for Jane's dad and whoever might have been visiting him. Who would have visited that man? She doesn't remember any visitors when she was here. But anyway, every crumb has been long picked clean. Now only a line of dust marks where the worktops meet the tiled walls.

Nina's stomach rumbles. Thinking of big suppers, when did she last eat? Lunch at the Harvester with Dad and then a slice of that too-sweet birthday cake.

She's ravenous, but she hadn't realised until now because her thirst was – is – so overpowering.

She steps closer to the big Butler sink that was once kept so clean by her mum's gloved hands, puts the candlestick down and twists the brass cold tap. The pipes chug and whistle a bit, but nothing comes out.

As she stands back up, feeling even thirstier now, a face stares back at her and she jumps in alarm, but it's just her reflection. Still, it reminds her about the footsteps and pushes her to keep checking. Lizzie is lying vulnerable in the other room after all, sleeping soundly because she knows she can rely on her big sister. Everyone can.

*

Nina is upstairs now, walking slowly and carefully around the upper rooms, shining her flashlight into every space. She had plugged her phone in while she was driving and still has an almost full battery now. How much did Aisa have? She should have given Aisa her phone to take. She looks at the time. Aisa has been gone hours. The village was less than five miles from here, although it's awful weather. But she should be back soon, surely?

Nina holds her phone in her left hand, which feels a bit unnatural but means her stronger right arm can hold the heavy candlestick. She feels faintly ridiculous but faintly (yes, she has to admit it, much more than faintly) freaked out.

As her heartbeat races, she reminds herself that she is the trespasser here. She's walking around like she owns the place. But if someone else is here and thinks she's out of line, why haven't they confronted her?

She grips the candlestick tighter and steps into the bathroom. It's three times the size of Nina's shower room at home. A big metal bath with frou-frou decorative feet swims in the middle of it. She peers quickly in it, no one there, then grabs the door and looks behind that. There's something swinging on the back of the door, an old towel or dressing gown, and it touches her as it sways, making her suck in her breath.

Turning back to face the room, it's clear no one is in here. It's surprisingly clear of anything, not really dusty and not as dirty as she'd expect. Even the sink is clean of limescale. These old ceramic sinks seem to stay in good condition though, far better than the basin that came with her new-build apartment, already stained. But it doesn't sit right. Nothing here sits right.

She leans against the basin stand to take the weight off her sore ankle, closes her eyes for a moment. This place doesn't feel like shelter, it feels like a held breath. Her throat tightens.

The water in these taps is probably switched off like down-stairs, but she turns the cold one on the off-chance and nearly laughs in delight as the water flows, no chugging and burping. She puts the candlestick and phone down carefully and, with her hands cupped, slurps the water. It's icy cold but tastes normal. Better than normal, it tastes like heaven itself after all these hours. She feels it cooling her throat, her chest shivering as it rushes downwards.

The flashlight beams from the sink to the ceiling, a great column of light. As she dips back down to scoop more water, she hears a creak. It's an almost imperceptible sound that she wouldn't have heard if she wasn't on high alert. A floorboard maybe ... or a door. It's pitch black behind her. She freezes, replays the sound in her head. It was a door, somewhere down the corridor. No question.

Nina tries to think, tries to plan her next move, but she's still frozen with fear, the water rushing relentlessly, noisily, on.

She feels the air change behind her. Someone has come into the room.

She swallows, her hand reaches for the candlestick, but she knocks it onto the floor and hears it roll away. Fuck. She wills herself to turn round. It must be Lizzie. Or maybe Aisa has come back. But why aren't they saying anything?

Sweat runs down her back, she is still at the sink, water still gushing, the phone still blasting its light unhelpfully into the air. She reaches for it carefully and flips it over to snuff out the light and turn the window next to the sink into a black mirror.

Then she sees it. A face. Just a sliver of eyes in the soupy darkness. Just for a second before fear overtakes her.

Then everything goes black.

26

ROSEMARY – 1987

I got eight hundred pounds in the will and the promise of a job for as long as Moirthwaite Manor remained in the possession of the Proctor family. Neither inheritance thrilled me. The money went on a new Mini. By which I mean a seven-year-old Mini, but new to us.

I had assumed that the 'job for life' would be a moot point, but the manor was under something called a 'fee tail' that meant William was forbidden from selling the house. Apparently, the Proctors' wills specified that it must be held by the living male descendant of the Proctor family. 'If only my husband had been a woman, hey,' Selina said.

At first, William avoids my eye. Then, he simply avoids me. Leaving Selina to handle the household staff, the way his mother once had. She hates it here. Unequivocally detests it. The Californian sunshine she once leaked everywhere has disappeared behind a permanent rain cloud and her sense of humour has become more and more acerbic. When they first moved in, a couple of months after the shock of both deaths, she already had a haunted, drawn look. 'It's like a crypt,' I heard her say, as she surveyed it through the eyes of the afflicted, rather than a novelty visitor. I'd spent days scrubbing and polishing, directing Alan to make the outside as pretty and neat as possible, and felt a shiver of disappointment that it went unnoticed. Or worse, that all my polishing had just made the horror of the house shine that bit brighter.

Although she hates the house, the grounds, the isolation, the village, the mud, the … everything, Selina seems glad to have me to talk to. Our girls are a similar age, and one time I even brought Lizzie over on my day off while Nina was at school. We sat in the garden on an old blanket and ate a picnic I'd prepared the day before and left in the fridge. The girls sat in shy lumps at first, before eventually cautiously bonding over a game of pulling out clumps of grass and sticking their fingers in soil.

'I ran away to London to get the real English experience,' she told me. 'And didn't I just get that in spades.'

William has taken to shutting himself in his office all day, though sometimes when I take him coffee in the afternoon, I can feel him appraise me. I'm embarrassed that I'm still here to be appraised but glad that I don't look too flabby or shabby, then feel guilty for thinking such things.

Selina and Jane spend their days in the living room or the library. I vacuum and polish around them, stopping for a tea while Selina has coffee ('I still don't know how you drink that stuff') and trying to rally her spirits. The more I try, the more irritated she gets and eventually I stop and just let her unload her frustrations.

'I feel homesick for everywhere else I've ever lived,' she says one day, the rain steadily beating on the windows like it wants to be let in. 'I didn't feel homesick for California in London, because I had *London*. Here, I feel homesick for California *and* London.'

'I feel the opposite of homesick,' I tell her. 'Well, I guess I am sick of my home. I've never lived anywhere else and I'm bored to death.'

'Why don't you leave?'

'People like me don't leave.'

'People like me didn't leave, until I just did,' she says. 'Sometimes, you just gotta.'

'If I lived in Hollywood, I wouldn't leave,' I say, and she laughs.

'I lived in a town called Cedarville in Modoc County,' she says, which means nothing to me. 'It was further to Hollywood from there than London is from here. It's beautiful and it's isolated. A huge forest, a couple of lakes ... everyone hunts and fishes, and not much else. It's so fricking boring.'

'Sounds like here,' I say, and she nods, watching the rain out of the window, one hand on Jane, who has curled up next to her on the sofa.

'Yeah,' she says. 'And like I said, sometimes you just gotta leave.'

27

LIZZIE – 12:20 a.m.

Lizzie wakes up with a jolt.

'Oh.'

She's lying facing the other way on the sofa; she must have spun herself round as she slept.

Sometimes she finds herself in the kitchen at home, sometimes on the bedroom floor. And, of course, those other times when she's woken up in the nick of time, pyjamas around her ankles, perched on a dining chair just about to pee.

They all laughed about it when she was little, although she always burned with mortification, how her parents would wake up in alarm as she wandered around the house.

Occasionally she worries: what if one night she just pops her front door open and keeps walking until she hits the sea? She bought a big bolt for the front door, just in case.

She grapples to sit up and pats the eiderdown for her phone, finally curling her fingers around it. The fire is now a lazy orange glow slunk down low behind the grate, the light and heat barely reaching her.

She taps the screen on her phone. It's past midnight. She slept for over an hour and just feels dizzy rather than refreshed. Outside of her, there is nothing. No more thunder, no more anything. She feels a curious sense of loss. That swirling storm had been a reassuring soundtrack, in a way. A reminder of things bigger than her and bigger than the immediate problems to be solved. Now, there is just a distant wind, and inside here there is silence. The kind of silence that begs for sound. A pin dropping, that's the cliché. Or a scratch at the door. A knock from an unknown hand. A breath in her ear. *Gosh, stop it.*

She's never known quietness like this, even in her seaside town that all but shuts down for winter. The crackle of the fire rings out as loud as fireworks in this void. She feels absolutely tiny, like she and Nina are something out of a fairy tale, the two sisters fast asleep in this terrifying house in the middle of the woods. She's amazed, really, that she was able to fall asleep given the gothic surroundings. And even more amazed that Nina must have given in too.

Lizzie's throat is dry, rough with dehydration and probably from snoring. She'd bobbed around through feverish, chaotic dreams, maybe she was sleep-talking as well as moving around on the sofa. Her sisters used to complain about that when they shared a room a million moons ago. Telling her she'd mumbled the names of boys from school, or pop stars, delighting in watching her cheeks glow red. When she got really into *The Lion, the Witch and the Wardrobe*, the television version of one of her favourite books, they told her that she'd been mumbling rude things about Aslan the lion.

Her shoes and socks are still by the hearth, the socks looking decidedly crispy in the flickering light. She wills herself to flip back the covers. She should heave herself up to go and put her socks and shoes on, but it's so cold and she's the closest to cosy she'll get before she's finally in her own home.

Lizzie thinks about her little house; she would be there by now if she'd caught the train like she wanted. Why does she never stand up for herself? She really would have preferred to get the train. A nice cosy window seat, reading her Agatha Christie, buying a warm drink and a Flake from the trolley.

'Neen?' Lizzie rubs her eyes and looks around the room. The receding light of the fire has returned the corners to a chalky darkness. On the other sofa, a mound of blankets hides Nina's sleeping body. At least her poor injured sister is finally getting some rest.

Lizzie reaches for her phone again and puts the flashlight on, sweeps it around the room. She frowns and sweeps it back again, slower this time. Something isn't right. She scans again, trying to work out what's missing.

The shoes.

She points the light back towards the hearth, where it illuminates a single pair of shoes, her own. She flicks it back to the mound of blankets and finally heaves herself up, the chill of the room coiling around her. She shuffles to the other sofa and pushes down softly on the blanket. 'Nina?'

Her hand meets no resistance, sinking onto the sofa cushion beneath the pile of fabric. When she peels back the layers, no one is there.

Maybe Nina's gone to the toilet. Or she's patrolling around again. She'd need her shoes to wander around in this cold, dark place.

Lizzie climbs back under the eiderdown and listens, but the house is silent. Even the thunder seems to have stopped, the pattering of the rain is taking a rest. How long has Aisa been gone? Lizzie does the maths on her fingers, but doesn't know exactly how far past the five-mile sign they drove, so the equation dies in her hands.

Maybe Aisa already came back and she and Nina are both waiting outside for the breakdown people. Better them than her, it's so cold. And yet, those old green bubbles of sibling envy start to rise in her gut. If they are together, they were probably glad she was asleep. Probably out there taking the mickey out of her. Out of boring old Lizard. *Stop it, that's not what's happened.*

She thinks about calling out, but stops herself. Regardless of where the others are, Lizzie is still sitting in the middle of an abandoned lounge in the heart of a derelict house in the middle of nowhere. Crowing like a big hen and drawing attention to herself is not the smartest move.

For a whole minute, Lizzie just sits still on the old sofa and listens. It's exactly how she handles a new animal in the sanctuary. Sit back, give them space, watch what they do. Listen to their sounds, look into their eyes. Animals will tell you who they are in sixty seconds; people aren't much different. Houses... well, let's see.

She tries to ignore her nagging worries and closes her eyes, shutting out anything but the noises that might tell her whereabouts in the house Nina is moving. She counts in her head, but by fifty-eight, fifty-nine, sixty, there's been no sound. Just a void.

With a deep breath, she swings her legs out from under the covers again and paces quickly to the fireplace. She tugs on her now scratchy socks, stuffs her feet into her still-damp trainers and then dumps a couple of extra logs on the fire. Oops. A great cloud of ash jumps up and scatters the floor. The already limp fire now looks suspiciously flattened.

She looks around, expecting to see Nina rolling her eyes, but Lizzie is still alone. She kneels down and blows a little to get the dying orange glow to spark and catch into flames again. It doesn't play ball.

Using her phone flashlight, she picks carefully through the stack of logs for a few smaller, drier pieces to stuff into the grate, bracing herself for an onslaught of spiders. OK, that's the best she can do, that should keep things warm while she goes to look for Nina.

Feeling slightly braver after surviving the logs, Lizzie walks to the window and peers outside to look for either of her sisters. But there's nothing but squirming darkness.

There's no way around it, she's going to have to go and look around the house for Nina. Oh blimey, why couldn't she just be on the train home?

28

AISA – 11:44 p.m.

Aisa stares at her phone, now just a useless glossy pebble. She blinks a couple of times as if this will somehow activate night vision, but then she sags in defeat. She can't see shit. It's pitch black, the moon is still being strangled behind layers of clouds, while the village is still twinkling like a mirage, a million miles away.

And what the hell was all that about anyway? There are urban explorer reports about Moirthwaite Manor. Well, so what? It's an abandoned building, it's bound to have been found and photographed.

When Aisa is in Amsterdam, she often hooks up with an urban explorer called Torbjørn. A gentle guy with a very nice beard and the biggest feet she's ever seen. He's from Norway. No, Finland. No, Norway. Somewhere like that. He and his little online group are obsessed with breaking into abandoned places to photograph and film them. When she first met him, he was fresh from climbing out of an old bunker under the Vondelpark, his breath still warm with celebratory beer and strong weed. Anyway, perhaps to someone like the breakdown company woman, those kinds of pictures look spooky. They *are* spooky. Yes, she tries to convince herself, it's just something like that.

'Who are you, Aisa?' he'd asked that first night, over bottles of craft beer (what else?). Not *what do you do*, not *where are you from*, but *who*. She'd faltered. No one had ever asked her that question, and she didn't have an answer. No sarcastic rejoinder ready to shoot from the hip, no borrowed song lyric. She'd kissed him instead of answering, but the question had lain heavily around her neck even when she woke up in his room the next morning.

Torbjørn would have been in that house like a rat up a drainpipe if he was here. Maybe that AA woman was just a bit unadventurous and didn't have any experience of the kind of circles Aisa moves in. *The circles I orbit*. She's not truly part of any circles, not really.

Who are you, Aisa?

She stares at the village ahead, trying again to work out which of those lights might belong to their old house. Maybe their old shared bedroom. If it even faced this way. As her sisters have constantly reminded her tonight, she was only four when she left, she must barely remember it. So why does so much of it feel deadly clear?

Enough of that. The woman said she was sending someone. Didn't she? Aisa runs back over the bizarre conversation again. Yes, she definitely said she was sending someone. Aisa thinks so anyway. Maybe. Did she? Well, Aisa chooses to believe.

OK. She looks at her Apple Watch, itself in desperate need of recharging. It's nearly midnight. *If* she goes back to the house and *if* the mechanic comes and fixes it by 3:30 a.m., and *if* Nina can take her straight to the airport and the roads are clear... she could still make her flight. Just. Aisa could be back in Paris before that absurd cat opens its lazy eyes and all this could be a weird memory.

That's an awful lot of ifs. But it's her best hope. Walking to the village could take another hour or more, and then there's no guarantee there'll be a taxi nearby. Or that the phone box will still be there and still working, and not turned into a sodding defibrillator. But at least if she walks on to the village, she doesn't have to go back to the manor house. She wouldn't ever have to go back. Why would she choose to head towards a place that had turned her blood cold at its very mention? *Because my sisters are there.*

She stands motionless, legs aching from all the wet, cold miles. *Who are you, Aisa? What matters to you?*

They do have a fire at the manor at least. And she would be doing the right thing, a good thing. She sighs, knowing she has no real choice. She couldn't really leave her sisters like that, not knowing where she'd gone. Whatever they already think of her, however reckless they might think she is, she couldn't do that.

By the time she's finished the thought, she's already turned to face the darkness that she's just spent ages walking through.

Aisa *should* be welcomed as a conquering hero, but no doubt there'll be something for them to gripe about. Something to dispute. How long it took, or the great crime of not having enough battery. *Well, at least I went out and sorted it while you roasted yourselves like a pair of pigs.*

That's the lot of the littlest, always having to prove herself, perennially looked down on. Never mind that Lizzie's never even left the country – probably doesn't even have a passport – she still looks at Aisa like a naif.

Aisa who has travelled to more countries than she's kept count of… And OK, she's not had any long-term relationships, but that's a choice. That's a good choice. And relationships or not, she's had a lot of sex. Way more than them, she's certain. Lizzie is probably still a virgin. But Aisa's still the baby? Fuck off.

Getting all riled up helps to distract her from how cold it is. How cold and how scary. *Jesus, this is so fucking scary, it's almost funny.* Middle of nowhere, check. Thunder and lightning, check. Abandoned manor house, check. All that's missing is the escaped maniac from a nearby asylum.

Almost funny, but she's not laughing. She pictures herself from above, seen at a remove. A vague notion she's had since she was a child, imagining herself being watched. Performing to that witness. In her teens, she would imagine her friends or the boy she liked watching her. She would cover her body with her hands when she changed, alone. Or, feeling bold, dance around her room to songs the coolest people at school would approve of, weighed down with affectation and awkwardness. When Rosemary died, if Aisa didn't stop herself in time, her mother would be the imagined witness. Aisa's face wet with tears that she'd try to hide from her. Now, she wants to shrink from view again, imagining that somewhere in this great openness there's a malevolent presence watching her. A dark, unblinking thing. What does it see? *Who are you, Aisa?*

'Oh my God!'

Aisa recoils from something's touch, gasping for air, but when she taps her Apple Watch for its pathetic glimmer of light, she sees it was just a huddle of brambles. She'd veered too close to the hedge.

This is going to take so long. It was bad enough walking along here in a small pool of phone light, but now she's trudging back blind, legs so heavy she can't imagine running away even if danger did strike.

She puts her head down, forces her legs to move faster, and hurries back. She will never tell anyone about this thought, but right now, she just wants her sisters.

29

LIZZIE – 12:38 a.m.

The air in front of the fire is warm, but the rest of the room is so cold that Lizzie wraps herself tightly in her coat and layers one of the old blankets on top, swaddling herself so just her head is poking out, childlike. She looks like she's playing Mary in a school nativity play. Although Lizzie only ever played one of the animals in the manger.

As she scouts around for anything else to ward off the cold, she notices that Nina's coat is no longer drying on the back of a chair. She grips her phone and, using its flashlight, steps out into the empty hall.

'Neen?' she whispers uselessly, too scared to raise her voice.

She creeps through the rest of the downstairs, looking for any sign of her older sister. It's so dark outside of the phone light that she could miss her while being in the same room. But it's not like Nina might be hiding behind a door. Why would she be? And, of course, she isn't.

But Lizzie is thorough, at first for her own peace of mind and then out of astonishment. Surely Nina hasn't just picked up and gone? There is no sign of her in the bathroom, although the tap is now dripping a military drum tattoo that seems to urge Lizzie along. The back bedrooms offer nothing. She won't be in the spider cupboard. Nina probably thinks no one knows about her claustrophobia, but you don't get to keep secrets like that for long in a five-person family in a two-bedroom house. Still, to be thorough, Lizzie pulls the cupboard door open just briefly, peers in and then clicks it shut.

She even goes back into the eerily empty master bedroom, heart thumping as if she'll get in trouble. It's still empty, and even weirder on second viewing. The way it has been picked clean, like one of those little skulls.

If Nina was here, she'd certainly have heard Lizzie clattering around on her search and come to her. Perhaps Lizzie was snoring and Nina had sought peace and quiet somewhere else. Maybe even taken some strong painkillers from her bag – it has been known – and crashed out on Jane's bed. Lizzie lets this hope swell for a moment, but when she twists the handle and pushes open the door to Jane's room, there is no one there.

Of course there isn't.

Nina must have gone out looking for Aisa, it's the only explanation. Not trusting her little sister, worrying about her. Forgetting, as Nina always has, that she has another little sister who might like to feature in her concerns once or twice.

Lizzie paces to Jane's window, kneels up on the window seat as Jane herself used to, cups her hands like a visor and looks out. There is a creaminess to the sky now, a suggestion of moonlight that helps her make out the tall trees and the once-gravelled circle at the top of the driveway. She sees no human movement and no glow of phone flashlights. She looks in vain at her own phone, but, of course, there's still no reception. She can't just call her sisters and ask where they are. She can't call anyone.

She climbs off the window seat and heads back downstairs, legs feeling heavy with the weight of what they're going to be asked to do. She has made the decision before she can talk herself out of it, now she just needs to keep going. She doesn't want to stay here alone and she needs to check Nina hasn't fallen over somewhere out there, overestimated how much her ankle could take, perhaps. But if Aisa comes back and finds them both gone... Lizzie thinks for a moment.

Back in the lounge, she tears a piece of paper from the notepad she keeps in her bag and digs out a biro, dusted with unidentifiable crumbs.

Stay here, I'm coming back. Lizzie x

She sheds the blanket she's been wearing, it's not right to take someone's belongings, and forces herself out of the door.

It's so much colder outside than Lizzie realised. While she slept in front of the fire, a steely bitterness replaced the wildness of the storm out here. Now, the chill whips her face as she steps further outside and pulls the door closed behind her.

The flashlight on her phone seems absurdly dim. The moon has come out a little more, but its light is strangled by trees before it can reach the ground. She stumbles a few times as she makes her way back down the driveway while half-memories flit through her mind. Car journeys from the village, her mum working, Jane and Lizzie running around here, welly boots, tired legs, hedgehogs, puddles.

She reaches the bottom of the driveway and is surprised by the wave of relief she feels to be out of that place and on public ground. It's a little less dark away from those trees, the sky over her a little lighter. Out here offers the hope of other people, of rescue, and of finding Aisa and Nina. Stepping onto the lane, she looks to the right in the direction of the car, and then to the left, towards the village.

The village is still miles away. *What to do? Which way to go? Come on, Lizard, think.*

The car is only a few minutes' walk up the other way, and the breakdown people might have told Aisa to meet them there. Perhaps Aisa came and got Nina to wait there with her and the car keys while Lizzie slept. Perhaps they're both curled up in the car? She feels tears prickle at the thought of it. Her sisters snuggled up together like puppies in a basket while she flails around uselessly out here. *Calm down, breathe.*

It makes sense to check the car first, she tells herself, and feels relieved not to have to trek all the way to the village just yet.

Lazy girl.

It's not laziness, she says to herself, to her mum, to her sisters, it's conserving energy.

She heads up the slight slope and down into the dip, the phone only illuminating her own hands and the empty air she's walking through. After a few careful minutes, she sees the Mini. It's sitting forlorn in a puddle, but it doesn't seem to have drifted further into the road, so at least any other vehicles won't smash into it. Not that there's likely to be any.

She shines her pale light over its front, the little bug eyes and the grille like a mouth, locked in a grimace. 'Oops,' it seems to say. She always loved her family's old Mini, felt terribly guilty when they replaced it with a bigger Ford in Cheshire. She wonders if that's why Nina chose this one, even though she pretends not to be sentimental. *Don't worry,* Lizzie thinks, as she places a hand on its bonnet, *help will be here soon.*

But help isn't here yet and neither are Nina and Aisa, so she'll have to do the long walk after all. Unless she goes back to the house.

Her legs pump a little harder; she sucks in a gulp of cold air as she walks straight past the turning for Moirthwaite Manor. She really doesn't want to go back to the house by herself.

Her shoes are still damp and she can feel blisters swelling on her heels and little toes. Her body is rebelling against her decision to leave, trying to get her to down tools as it so often does. It's not like she doesn't walk anywhere normally, she walks every day. And in these very shoes! Miles and miles, in all weather. Sometimes she takes the better-behaved dogs from the village she lives and works in all the way down to the roaring sea, along the flinty beaches, by the smugglers' coves whose romance she moved for in the first place.

'God, it's grim,' Aisa said, the one time she and Nina came to visit. But it's not grim, it's breathtaking. Just because there are no nightclubs like the European beaches Aisa heads to doesn't make it grim. Although Aisa would probably laugh at that, nightclubs are probably passé now. It's probably all pop-up sex jamborees now or something.

As she walks, Lizzie keeps checking her phone for reception, but it's as dead as a dodo. This old phone struggles to find reception at the best of times, so it's unlikely to burst into full 3G out here, but still. But still.

It's 1:22 a.m. now. She feels like she's been walking for hours, but it's only been minutes. The rain is still drizzling and the lights of the village are as far away as they ever were. She stops for a moment and thinks. *Is this really the right thing to do?*

As she stands motionless, the air grows quiet without the sound of her footsteps, but then other steps fill the silence for just a moment. Then they stop too.

Other footsteps. Oh gosh, *other footsteps*. She's suddenly blind with panic, brought back to the moment with a jolt. She is trapped in the terrible now with no idea what to do. *God, Lizzie, think.*

The footsteps have stopped now and Lizzie looks around, but she still can't see anyone. Despite its weakness, her phone flashlight just seems very good at making everything outside of it look blacker. She slowly flips her phone round and presses it to her body, muffling the light. Her eyes adjust to the thin moonlight, but she still sees nothing, just empty fields, violent brambles and a drenched, potholed lane.

She closes her eyes for a full minute, heart thumping like a mad monkey the whole time, and listens, sniffing the air. She cannot hear anything now and she can't smell anyone. No wellington boot smell, no wax jacket or leather. No other sweat. Just her own.

She takes a cautious step, and then another. Nothing happens. She must have imagined it, she tells herself, as she walks on with trembling legs.

30

ROSEMARY – 1987

They've been arguing again. Selina is snappy and I can smell that William is smoking in his office, something that only happens when he's really unhappy. More than unhappy, actually, terse. Borderline cruel.

'We used to be a team,' I hear Selina cry.

I'm in the kitchen and she's in the hallway outside the office door. Jane is having her nap. I stay deathly still, I don't want her to know I'm here and I feel embarrassed.

'Bill,' she says, a name I've only ever heard her call him. He's not a Bill. 'Bill, please, we can't just not talk about this.'

The door flies open suddenly and she stumbles into the room.

'All you ever do is talk about this,' he growls. 'Can't you understand, I have no bloody choice.'

'There's always a choice,' she says. 'And you're choosing this fucking house over your wife.'

For a moment, neither says anything. In the kitchen, I stand in the middle of the larder, hoping the cook will come bustling back in from the garden and break the spell. Instead, Jane begins to cry from upstairs. 'Mama, mama.' She never cries for her dad, I notice, and for all Bob's faults, the girls love him and he loves them. They cry for me first, but they'll switch to calling Dad if I take my time. That's how it should be.

'Jane wants you,' William says softly, conciliatorily.

'At least someone does,' Selina says as she heads for the stairs.

When I go up later to put the fresh sheets on their bed, I see her suitcase lying open on the floor. I leave the bed as it is and creep back out.

Sometimes, you just gotta leave.

31

AISA – 1:18 a.m.

As she walks, a song keeps running through her head, a remixed, chopped-up version of 'Alone at a Drive-In' from *Grease*. She never liked it, always preferred the others. 'Summer Nights', 'You're the One That I Want'. Silly songs that sounded like nonsense when she was little until she realised – in her teens – that they were all about shagging.

'Alone at a Drive-In' was moany drivel, as was 'Hopelessly Devoted to You'. But the latter was the one that made her mother cry. Said it reminded her of Dad. The former was the one that always got Rosemary riled up, as if it was the first time she'd seen it. 'Danny bleating on about being abandoned when he was the one acting like a knob.'

Am I the one acting like a knob? she thinks, wondering if her sisters were glad to be shot of her. Has she left them back at the house through devotion, or does she abandon people? She abandoned Dad after Mum died. She knows she did. Knows it from the watery look he gives her when she can bear to see him.

The wind is shunting her and the rain starts to spit again. An aftershock of the storm, a final insult. Her bones ache from these miles. *I could have been walking around Paris.* Through the Jardin du Luxembourg where she always feels like an interesting

134

person. Or the Marais, past the Church of Saint-Paul Saint-Louis. Or over the Pont au Change. At that spot, she always thinks of her mother. Of how she would have loved to see the settings of *Les Misérables* in real life, and how such a concept would have seemed absurd to Rosemary. Out of bounds. But it turns out, Aisa knows now, that you *can* just choose to do things. To go places. If only she'd told her mum before it was too late.

The week before last, Aisa was in Amsterdam. And before that, New York. Well, New York *adjacent*, but she'd gone into the city every day. The whole damn place like a monument to her mother's favourite musicals. *Hello, Dolly! Rent, Hair, West Side Story*. She'd practically finger-clicked and jazz-stepped through the Upper West Side battleground of the Sharks and Jets, even after her long journey from the apartment in Westchester County.

If you could see me now, Mum, she'd thought, and then, *Scratch that. If you could see* this *now, Mum. You should have seen this.*

If she gets back to the house fast enough, she could still be back in Paris this time tomorrow, overfeeding Poisson and taking ironic pictures of the Eiffel Tower for Instagram. Caption: Where?

And then on to Marrakesh, where she'll be able to squeeze in a round trip by train to Casablanca, so long as the house rabbit doesn't throw a fit. *Casablanca* is not a musical, of course, but still a Sunday afternoon favourite. Rosemary mouthing along with every line, while Aisa sat on the arm of the sofa playing on her Game Boy, one foot dangling over her mum, who would stroke it absentmindedly.

And after that, she's heading to London. *Mary Poppins. Oliver!* She might even go to see *Wicked* again, which she and her mum watched for Rosemary's sixtieth birthday.

But she's not there yet. Nowhere near Paris or Casablanca or London. She's here, in the rain, in the one place she never wanted to return. Not that she'd thought of this place for a long time. She barely remembered it until tonight. But she doesn't like what she does remember. She wishes she could shove her AirPods back in and listen to music, block all these bad things out. She'd pretend to be listening to something new and interesting, but, as usual, she'd actually be playing the musicals playlist she made for her mum, when she was dying.

'How will they stay in my lugholes?' her mum had laughed weakly, as Aisa held out her own AirPods in her palm, just as she used to hand over crap bits of art brought home from school.

'They just will, Mum,' she'd said, trying to keep the tears out of her voice. Tears that threatened to burst and wash every word away. Tears that made Aisa come to see Rosemary alone, unable to bear the reflected sadness in her sisters' eyes, or their dad's moronic attempts to look on the bright side. There is no bright side of terminal cancer, you fool.

Her mum had smiled so broadly as she'd listened to the tracks that Aisa had spent hours selecting, and Aisa had simply sat watching her, stroking her arm, until she fell asleep. There is no one else on earth she would hand her phone over to like that, just happy to make them happy. Correction, there *was* no one else on earth.

That's enough of that. She chases the sadness with a quick, barking cough and pays attention to her present instead, just like her mindfulness app always tells her while she argues with it.

Aisa's walked the same route back towards the manor. A reluctant boomerang. The journey seems quicker on the return leg, as if she's being winched along by invisible thread. A little moonlight has been swirled into the sky and she can see the surroundings for what they are. Bleak and empty, but benign. No foxes. No people. Nobody is watching her. She's safe. And she's nearly back with her family, some of them anyway.

But then, the big footsteps in the mud near the car. Did she imagine them? Were they just from the sisters' own feet sliding around?

She hurries on, not wanting to be in that house, but secretly wanting to be with her sisters, pretending not to care but desperately wanting the safety of numbers.

Her feet slap the wet tarmac and the steps ring out across the empty fields and up and down the lane. It sounds for a moment as if they're echoing. She stops to check her theory, but the echo has stopped too. After a minute or two, she carries on.

Finally, she reaches the sign – MOIR AI – which swings gently, the metal hooks whistling with the motion. The driveway looks darker than the lane, the tall trees bending over it like a canopy, closing off the moonlight. Sanctuary with her sisters, but at what cost? She doesn't want to be in that house any longer than she has to be.

She walks slowly, treading carefully and quietly up the driveway. When she reaches the house, Aisa stands for a moment looking up at its monstrous facade. When she arrived here earlier with her sisters, her adrenaline was clogging up her vision. But now she is too exhausted for flight or fight, too exhausted for anything. She stares at each of the front-facing windows in turn, a memory popping up for each, like opening an advent calendar. She even dares to look up at the window that somehow she knows was Jane's dad's room even though she doesn't remember ever actually meeting him, just seeing his legs and feet from some hiding place or other.

Who was that other man they used to see here? The one who shot all the rabbits? Some kind of gardener or something? He gave Aisa a rabbit's foot once. The weirdo. Shyly handing it over when he found her once, hiding and scared. Or was it . . . she found him? She frowns, but the memory is gone.

She steps closer to the front door, takes a final lungful of outside air and then reaches for the handle.

32

LIZZIE – 1:30 a.m.

To her right, big empty fields roll away from her, occasionally filled with enormous bales of hay, wrapped tightly in a shiny black coating just catching the moonlight, looking like alien eggs that have dropped from the sky.

To her left, the woodland is dense and layered. Leaves, branches and trunks create a monochrome collage that looks too thick to move through, but she knows – the memory seizes her chest for a moment – she knows that you can weave through all of that, running as hard as your lungs will allow.

An animal.

Something about an animal.

A hurt animal.

She and Jane running after it. Lizzie wanting to help, to look after it. Jane saying she wanted that too, but ...

Lizzie shivers in her coat and plunges on. She didn't dress for this, she dressed for a birthday lunch. A pretty jumper and smart jeans, neither of which have enough give for all this walking. It's easily been a mile now, probably more. She looks at her phone to see the time and notices the bar of reception. How long has it been there? A tiny bar of hope. She stops dead, scared that she might chase this away if she takes another step.

For a moment, she just stands still at the side of the road, surrounded by woodland and empty fields that might swallow the reception up again. Using the flashlight function has zapped some of her battery too. Unlike Aisa, who is always on social media, or Nina who is always on WhatsApp groups sharing jokes and memes with work friends, Lizzie hardly uses her phone. A few texts from friends at work, the odd emergency call when an animal she particularly connected to finds itself back at the shelter. Occasional exchanges in the sisters' WhatsApp group, Made in Kelsey, a name picked by Aisa that makes no sense to Lizzie.

The one person she would love to send a message to, would love to receive a message from, only has a landline.

What should she do? Maybe she should call a breakdown service, but Aisa should have already done that. Aisa might be calling right now from the village, her own phone not finding this tiny hotspot, and if Lizzie calls too, won't that just confuse everything? She doesn't know the number either, and has no 3G to look it up. But mostly, the thought of calling up a busy call centre – as a non-driver with no money – and answering questions about cars and how she'll pay for the call-out simply overwhelms her.

First, she tries to call Nina. If she's out here too, she might also have reception. It doesn't even ring, just goes straight to voicemail. She knows this voicemail well, or used to, but it's changed. She's sure it used to list alternative numbers for reaching the hospital, the maternity unit, the health visitors. It still has Nina's same brisk, bossy tone, but now it says that she's on temporary leave and is not allowed to speak with patients, to call the main maternity unit instead. Temporary leave? Does that mean she's booked holiday time? Nina told them she couldn't stay over at Dad's because she had a shift the next day, but it sounds like she was fibbing.

Lizzie doesn't have time to ponder this now, but sticks a mental pin in it until later. She tries Aisa next, and the voicemail instantly clicks in. A recorded voice – Aisa is too cool to lower herself to record her own message – offering no alternatives.

For a moment, Lizzie wants to let out the tears that are swelling in the corners of her eyes. A desperate pang of helplessness, of worrying she'll do the wrong thing and everyone will be cross with her. Worrying, as she so often does, that she's already done the wrong thing, without even realising it. Of wishing her mum was here to take over, to make things right. The way she always did.

There is one other person to try.

'I'm not a damsel in distress,' she told Rafferty, the first time they met. He'd come to volunteer at the shelter and had rushed over to help her with some big bags of dry food.

'I can tell that.' He'd appraised her from under his long dark curls. There was a glimmer of . . . she almost couldn't bear to believe it, but he'd seemed rather *impressed*. So much so that she'd decided to cultivate this stance of independence, to wear it a little higher like a brooch. When she allowed him to hold the door to the dogs' units open, he'd rewarded the perceived concession with a gallant nod.

And when she passed him, brushing his shoulders with hers and noticing that he wasn't wearing a coat as she'd first thought, but a cape like Sherlock Holmes might wear, her stomach pulsed. A feeling she'd only ever had vicariously, through romantic storylines in books. *Oh dear,* she'd thought, *I'm in trouble here.*

They were supposed to get together last night, but the stubby little dog had put paid to that. Rafferty was expecting to have seen her tonight instead, but he will have understood, guessed, she'd been delayed. She calls his number, heart beating faster as it begins to ring.

She'd taken Rafferty back to her house after work on the same day they met, four months ago. She'd never felt so safe with another person, so why not? She'd opened up the front door and saw her house as he was first seeing it. The rows and rows of bookshelves, almost every wall covered. The cosy furniture, piles of throws and cushions. Mismatched but loved. The tea things laid out on the little dining table because it always felt to her like a treat, walking in and seeing it taken care of, the leaves already in the pot ready for hot water.

'I'll get another cup,' she'd said.

Four rings, five. It's well past midnight, he will be asleep. But she hopes...

'I love your house,' he'd said, as they lay in her bed afterwards, him naked and her in her nightie. 'It's perfectly you.'

'You don't even know me,' she'd said.

He'd reached for her hand and kissed it. 'Yes I do, Elizabeth.'

And he does. He understands her every bump and scrape, the life she's carefully created. Two odd socks becoming a pair. Her sisters would certainly call him odd, if they were to meet him. And even though he'd like to meet them, he never pushes. Never pressures her for more time than she can give. She needs some nights alone, spent reading. And nights with him laughing and kissing, those too. It just works. She's so dangerously, intoxicatingly content that she dare not admit it, lest she lose it.

The phone rings out and stops. And for the first time since they met, she feels a grumble of frustration. She'd found it charming when he first explained his stance. He likes writing and receiving letters. He likes handshake agreements. He does not like to feel connected every day, every moment, but sees things like telephones as tools that have become overlords to people. 'So you're off the grid?' she'd asked, smiling.

'No,' he said. 'I begrudgingly have a landline. A lovely old Bakelite that I found in that charity shop and tea rooms near the park, do you know the one?' Of course she knew the one. How she'd not seen him in there was the real mystery. 'So I can't use a mobile phone to shift arrangements all the time and feel like I've fulfilled my friendly obligations with a "like" or something … If I say I'll be somewhere, I have to be there.'

She thinks back to when she called yesterday to move their date to tonight, they'd arranged for him to go to her house. He has a key and maybe … Yes, there's still reception. She calls her own number. It rings, three, four, five times. And then her own voice picks up.

'This is Lizzie, please leave a message and I'll call you back.'
Beep.

'Rafferty?' She waits, hoping she might have woken him, that he will snatch up the receiver. But no. 'Rafferty, it's me. I hope you hear this. My sisters and I ran out of petrol and we're stuck in Cumbria at a place called Moirthwaite Manor. I know it's a lot to ask, but if there's any way you could come here and—' Something doesn't feel right, she pulls her phone from her ear and looks at it. The call has dropped. The reception has disappeared.

She has no idea if any of her message was recorded.

33

ROSEMARY – March 1992

I twist the heavy shafts of the candlesticks so they line up perfectly. I could probably chuck them on the floor or throw one through the window for all the notice that'd be shown. But I can't help myself. A job done well, that's pretty much the only thing I have in my control.

I see it in Nina too. It can seem like fussiness, or maybe bossiness, the way she'll take over a job I've given one of her sisters. Straightening their beds or washing out the milk bottles. She'll wind people up with it, I can't imagine a future husband enjoying her briskly taking over whatever he's doing, but it'll see her true.

Capability, more than anything else, is the key to ... not success, God, I'm not that deluded, but ... survival. Drop me in any town anywhere and I'm sure I'd find a bit of work, a place to wash my clothes, a butcher that'll do me a cheap offcut. Nina is the same, even at ten. Whereas Lizzie ... it doesn't bear thinking about. Drop her in any random town and she'd land on her bum and stay there, stuck like a beetle on its back. Aisa is too little to be tested, but already I can imagine her doing fine. Maybe with her it's less capability and more ... ballsyness?

It's bloody boring being capable. No one would choose it as

143

their top attribute in a lover or, I don't know, a Hollywood star! But it keeps the kids clean and fed and has kept me in work all these years.

William relies on my capability, I know that, but it's an unseen foundation in his life. *I* am an unseen foundation in his life. He will never open a cupboard and not find what he needs. Or ask where his good suit is – not that he's asked that in a long time – and not be told where to find it, slippery in its cover from the dry-cleaner's in Penrith. My capability allows him to drift through life, and in return, I take home £90 a week.

Occasionally, he'll notice extra evidence of effort, or he'll lean on me more than is strictly acceptable and then slip an extra tenner or two into my envelope on the Friday. I've put more sweat into polishing that monstrous mirror on the landing today and put in some additional hours with poor Jane, so I hope that he'll top me up this week. Then I can get the phone switched back on.

I sit for a moment on the sofa, its cushions freshly scrubbed but smelling a little of mildew. I run my hand over the fabric. Checking for lint, smoothing out creases. It's second nature now, so I even do it at home, even though our sofa is 90 per cent lint and 10 per cent crease.

I close my eyes as the blood pools in my legs and the throb in my feet feels almost audible. I've not stopped since I got here and I just need a moment. As pins and needles start to climb up my calves, I stroke the mahogany wood, upholstered horsehair seats and velvet cushions. This sofa was once incredibly fancy. Now it's a museum piece.

William has finally agreed to buy leather sofas. Chesterfields, something befitting a room of this scale. Something easier to keep clean. I wasn't sure he'd heard me, but then the other day he said they were on order. I'm not sure why I care really, it's not my house. But then, spending two decades doing basically the same thing is tragic if you don't even care. I choose to care.

I have the house to myself now. William is out on patrol pretending that he isn't. We're all on invisible tracks, aren't we, repeating the same endless patterns, giving them meaning to justify the waste of time. Alan is doing God knows what in his shed, and Cook has gone into town, mumbling something about catching the butcher. I'm pretty certain she's catching the four o'clock at Newmarket, probably losing the beef money so William will have to have ham hock instead. Unless Alan's caught something edible in the woods.

When I sit up again, an hour has passed. I must have slid into sleep and the afternoon has dissolved behind my back. The girls have long finished school and will be home with Bob by now. Or, more likely, the younger two will be home in the charge of Nina while Bob sinks one (one standing in for any number under the sun) at The Fox and Hounds. 'Networking,' he calls it now, amused with himself as he sways a little in his old work boots. He heard that word on the radio.

I'm lucky to have girls, everyone says, as that way I have ready-made babysitters. I smile and nod, but feel a little sick at this. Not a chance in hell that I'm going to see my girls skivvying the way I do. I'm not exactly sure how, but if I achieve nothing else, I'll make sure they can choose the course of their own lives and not have it handed to them by circumstance. So far, it's not exactly going to plan and Nina seems determined to take on a quasi-parental role despite my best efforts. Trying to cook the dinner or bathe Aisa. Every day, I walk back into the opening credits of *999*. I keep expecting Michael Buerk to pop out with a withering remark.

I do a final scan of the house, straightening things, breathing onto brass and silver, wiping away flecks of human evidence with my sleeve. The dining table has been set up, but William will eat much later when the cook is back, too distracted to notice he's not getting what he's paying for. A cold supper has been set out for Jane in the kitchen: cheese and bread, the last of this year's tomatoes and a boiled egg. This is my favourite part of the day. Seeing it all set right, all correct. Like a theatrical stage before the audience arrives.

William should be back by now though. When I go, Jane's all alone. Aside from Alan, who doesn't count. My own children are probably alone too, but three is a different kind of alone to one. A bubble of guilt slides up my throat, but I swallow it back down.

There is another set of candlesticks here – there are sixteen in all, dotted around various mantlepieces and in cupboards. Almost all of them never used. They've been here longer than me, probably worth more than me too, if you added it up. I wonder, as I walk a little closer to the cupboard where the silverware is kept, how much a pair might fetch. I wonder too, if anyone other than me has looked in this cupboard since William's parents died and the estate was priced up by solicitors before being handed over.

I have a carrier bag of Jane's old clothes hanging on my arm, my jacket draped over my shoulders even though it's still warm, and am heading to my car. Now that work is shut away behind that front door, my mind turns – as it often does – to concern for Lizzie. I worry about her meekness. The others have picked on her so much that she keeps it quiet, but I'm sure she's still got that imaginary friend who has bobbed in and out of her life for as long as I can remember.

The gulf between her and Nina is growing ever more

pronounced, despite only a two-year gap. Nina is like a little adult, Lizzie a big bairn. Far more so than little Aisa.

I look up and catch Jane's curtain falling back into place. Another lonely girl I'm failing. If only William would let her go to school rather than teaching her himself. I think he's too terrified that Selina will come back and take her if Jane's ever out of the house without him.

'What you got there?'

I swear Alan is on wheels, I didn't hear his big feet approach. I turn to face him, craning my neck to look him dead in the eye. He's hovering next to the burbling fountain, looking as if he regrets speaking. Poor Alan, never has a big man been less at ease with himself. 'Nosy parker,' I say, but I smile to reassure him. 'It's just some of Jane's old clothes for Save the Children,' I say, lowering my hands gently and making a mental note not to dress Aisa in any of these cast-offs if I ever bring her here.

'And how are your children?' Alan asks, in his soft, stilted voice.

'Waiting for me,' I say, still smiling, but he looks hurt. 'Oh I'm only clarten, Al, they're doing well,' I add. 'Thanks for asking.'

I load the bag into the boot of the Mini, closing it carefully because the handle has a tendency to fall off.

'What time have you got?' I call to Alan, as he heads for the side of the house towards his shed. My dad's wristwatch is for comfort only now, the hands no longer move.

'Five after five,' Alan calls back.

I look up again at Jane's window. I should have left five minutes ago, but she's alone, and she's only a kid. Maybe I should go back inside, read to her while we wait for William. Maybe I should take that time, it's not much to give her. Not after everything she's been through.

The distant rumble of an engine grows closer and I sigh in relief.

'Sorry,' William says as he climbs out of the big old Mercedes, speaking to the top of my head rather than my face. 'Time got, you know ...'

'Away from you,' I add. 'I know.'

'I'll put a little extra in your pay this week,' he says, finally meeting my gaze until I look away.

34

AISA – 1:38 a.m.

The doorknob is still slick with rain when she turns it, half-expecting it to be locked, her sisters shutting her out for taking too long. But it opens silently again, no creaking wood, no squeaking hinges. Last time she came in here, she was mob-handed and they all had lights on their phones, but now she is stepping into total darkness. Alone.

The moonlight of the pale grey sky doesn't cross the threshold and it takes a moment for her eyes to adjust as she steps inside and listens. She can hear the gentle crackle of the fire from the front room but no voices. They're probably asleep.

Even standing in the hall in this swirling darkness makes her lungs feel tight and her heart race. A draught bites her ankles, as if the cold night is trying to swallow her whole. But what alternative is there? If she wanted to wait in the car, she'd have to get the keys from Nina anyway, waking her up in the process.

There's a smell in here that she didn't notice when they first arrived. An iron smell: soil, rusty nails or ... blood? *Stop being dramatic.* But Aisa stays rooted to the spot anyway. The whole house feels like a trap. She tries to tell herself that she's just rattled from the weird reaction of the woman on the phone who was spooked by the very concept of urban explorers, but it's not really that. She felt like this before too. Like she was returning to somewhere she'd successfully escaped.

'Will you walk into my parlour?' said the spider to the fly.

Aisa swallows. It's not like her to dither. Normally, she's made a decision before she even knows there's one to make. Buying a plane ticket. Applying for a ludicrous house-sitting gig on the other side of the world. Saying yes to a date, walking out on a date. Whatever.

In that front room are the two people she should feel closest to in the world. Shared DNA, shared history. But they have never felt like that. It was always Nina and Lizzie – the older, sensible ones – and Aisa, the agent of chaos. The only person who she ever truly felt close to was her mum. A shared look, a quick touch of the hand. They just understood each other. Every adventure, every risk she takes now, she's taking for two. Living the life her mum couldn't. But her sisters would never understand that.

Even now, she's preparing for the criticism from Nina. Never mind that she's called for help, she won't have called for it quick enough. Or she'll have called the wrong person. It should have been Green Flag or whoever. Or she'll be too wet from the rain. Or too ... just too something. Always too something.

She reaches, as she often does, into her bag. Touches the passport holder containing her mum's envelope. *Breathe, stay calm.*

She steps further into the dark and then gently pushes the door of the living room open. It's still pretty dark inside, but the fire is just about hanging on and a yellow glow pulses around it. She steps inside properly and walks towards the sofas, where her sisters lie completely hidden by blankets. For a moment, her stomach flips as she realises just how vulnerable they are, sleeping like this. It was Aisa stepping through that unlocked door just now, but it could have been anyone.

Aisa walks to the fire, tucks her bag safely to the side and then kneels to assess it, on trembling, aching knees. She's rubbish at stuff like this, never one for camping, but even she can tell this fire needs a bit more wood. She teases a few thin logs from the pile and places them carefully onto the glowing embers. She leans back on her haunches and watches. They're not catching. She blows a little, but nothing much happens, just a scattering of twinkling sparks landing on the hearth.

'Neen,' she says, too tired for ego. 'This fire is shit. What shall I do?' She hates the whine in her voice, but Nina hasn't answered anyway. 'I'm back by the way,' she says, louder now. 'Thanks for the red carpet.' Neither pile of blankets stirs.

She blows haphazardly on the fire again and then sighs and gives up, walking over to one of the sofas, which has a big fat eiderdown on it. She pats it, but the mound of fabric just sinks, a puff of dust rising up.

'What the f——?' She pulls it back, but there's no one there, just the sunken old cushions of the Chesterfield.

She rushes over to the other sofa, but she already knows, even before she peels back the blankets, that there's no one there.

'Where are you two?'

She looks at the fireplace again, realises what's missing: their shoes and socks. The coats are no longer drying on the back of the old chairs either. She stands in front of the fire feeling furious. What the hell are they playing at? Did they go after her? But she'd have passed them, surely?

Aisa looks around for any other trace of them, but there's nothing here except old blankets and a dying fire. Weren't there two candlesticks on the mantelpiece before too? She's sure she lit two when they first arrived. There's only one now. Why have they taken a candlestick with them? Perhaps their phones ran out too so they lit a candle for light. And then what? Went exploring like Wee Willie Winkie?

She goes back out into the hall and calls their names. No reply comes, the strange iron smell fills her head.

Maybe they've gone to sleep upstairs, in more comfortable beds. Maybe there's a fireplace up there too. Maybe ... Well, she needs light to go upstairs and look for them, so she goes back into the living room and picks up the other candlestick with its stub of old wax. As she does, a piece of lined paper flutters to the floor, luminous in the firelight.

A note. Lizzie's looping handwriting, not a million miles from the writing on her envelope, but less shaky.

Stay here, I'm coming back. Lizzie x

35

LIZZIE – 1:47 a.m.

Lizzie waves her phone around and tries to find reception again. She walks a little further towards the village, hunting for a pool of connection, but the phone remains steadfastly useless. Oh well, Aisa will have already called someone, there's no real need for Rafferty to trek all the way here in the middle of the night. However much she might have liked him to, however much she might be ready to be a damsel for him.

Lizzie looks up at the mottled sky. After the flamboyance of the storm earlier, it seems to sag with fatigue. A few dogged stars manage to shine through and she's glad of that. It's meaningless, but she can't stop attributing meaning to things since Mum died. Like one of those stars is Mum herself, watching over Lizzie, even though that star has been up there for so many hundreds of years that it's actually already dead. But still, she can't help herself. She doesn't tell her sisters this. She's already a laughing stock to them.

What would Mum have said, if Lizzie had been able to call her tonight? She'd have kept Lizzie on the landline, while calling the breakdown service on the mobile and somehow making up the spare beds at the same time. 'We'll get you back here and then see what's what,' she'd have said. She was so flipping capable, all of the time. Nina has decided to pick up that baton, whether anyone else wanted to make a play for it or not.

Lizzie walks slowly back towards the house, phone held in front of her for light. There is no sign of any more reception, that brief patch seems to have been an anomaly. She shouldn't stay out too long in case the others are back at the house. She wonders if Nina and Aisa are nearby, or perhaps there's another route back. Maybe they've been emboldened by each other's company to go through the woods. Or perhaps Nina didn't even come to look for Aisa and went off to do something else. Or perhaps ... She stops herself. Not that. Nothing could have happened to Nina. Could it?

No, this is just the usual run of play and Lizzie is always the last to know. From the epic to the inconsequential. Because, *of course,* Nina just went off tonight without bothering to wake Lizzie up to tell her. Nina has form for this. She'd not even told Lizzie about Mum's illness for almost a week after the diagnosis. She didn't tell Aisa either. Nina and Dad kept it to themselves, hoarding all that extra time with her. Minutes mattered then, let alone days.

Now isn't the time.

It's never the time, that's the problem. By the time Lizzie has built up the nerve to say something, everyone else has moved on. Like when they got back from Moirthwaite Primary School one day, to that little terraced house down there in the village behind her, to find a borrowed van packed with their stuff, their dad at the wheel. Their mum sat in the Mini behind it, popping the door for them to climb in. Aisa and Nina griped the whole way down the M6, rejecting every point being made – 'We'll find somewhere that you can all have your own rooms and the school has more children to be friends with' – while Lizzie barely said anything. A week later, still struggling to make friends in this new town in Cheshire, at the school with a strict uniform and even stricter teachers, Lizzie finally asked why she didn't get to say goodbye to anyone. Especially to Jane. Her mum had opened her mouth, frowned and said, 'I can't deal with this now, Lizzie.' And that was that. For thirty years.

36

AISA – 1:47 a.m.

Aisa stands in front of the fireplace, Lizzie's note in her hands. Her knees are still trembling, her jeans stuck to her skin with rain and sweat. She thrusts her legs closer to what's left of the fire, chasing the warmth.

Stay here, the note says. But why? And where has Lizzie gone? Where's Nina for that matter?

God, her feet ache. She puts the note back down on the mantelpiece, then leans down and starts to prise off her damp shoes.

She keeps her socks on and kneels down in front of the fire. It's not going to last much longer, but help should be here soon anyway. She puts on a couple more logs, but they just seem to flatten it further. She looks around and finds a mirror wrapped in a few sheets of old crinkled newspaper. She pulls it off the dusty mirror, scrunches it into a few balls and pokes them into the gaps between the logs, blowing until it catches. She spots another newspaper in the corner, but she'll save that for later.

Then she sits down heavily on the sofa, Lizzie's note in her hand, wrapping an old eiderdown around her for warmth. Was this quilt here earlier? She doesn't think so, but she's glad to have it now. Her knees knock together – something she'd always thought was a linguistic myth – and she tucks them under her, folding herself smaller and smaller as the flames finally pick up in the grate.

She's so tired. She can feel her eyes closing, but she shakes herself awake. No way is she lying in this creepy house passed out like some babysitter in an old horror film. Fuck. That.

She tries to replay the conversation with the woman on the phone, but it's all chopped up like a bad poem. Did she say help was coming? Would she have gone ahead and arranged the call-out even after the line dropped? She hopes so.

She's trying not to prod at the other parts of the phone conversation. The strange turn it took. But she can't help it. The fact that there have been urban explorers (hardly urban, seeing as this is in the arse end of nowhere, but whatever) should reassure her. It's not uncharted territory.

But she remembers some of the things that Torbjørn told her, when she asked to go exploring with him sometime. That the minute there's a crack anywhere, a damaged roof or a broken window, the weather will get inside and so will people. People will strip a place down to its pipes and the weather will destroy it. The floors get spongy, staircases collapse and all the paint peels. She'd insisted that didn't put her off, anything for an experience, but then he told her about the shit. If the weather can get in, so can the animals and birds. Pigeon poo everywhere, mice or rats and definitely spiders. Maybe some rabbits, a few animal corpses. Fine, she'd said, I'm not that bothered about coming with.

Moirthwaite Manor isn't exactly squeaky clean, but it's not as bad as Torbjørn made out. Maybe that security sign with the dog on it wasn't total bollocks and there's a firm looking after it, keeping the elements out?

Something else puzzles her too, something from the here and now. She looks again at the note.

Stay here, I'm coming back. Lizzie x

I'm coming back. But what about Nina? If Nina was still here when Lizzie left, she wouldn't have had to leave a note. She would have just told Nina where she was going and that she'd be back. And if Nina went with Lizzie, the note would say 'we're coming back'.

Nina must have left first, it's the only explanation. Maybe she left and told Lizzie to say here, but Lizzie shat herself and ran off after her?

Aisa won't give in to this creeping fear. No. She looks around her, taking stock. No, she'll sit here in this room and front it out. Imagine herself to be an urban explorer, try to see this as an adventure despite it feeling like anything but. *Take nothing but photographs, leave nothing but footprints*, that's the 'urbex' motto apparently. She looks at her dead phone. She won't be taking any photos. The floor is dusty, but she can't see any individual footprints either, just general 'scuff' marks where they've all been moving around since they arrived.

Why would Nina have left in the first place though? Maybe her ankle was better and she decided to head off in a different direction to find reception. Cover all bases. That would make sense, staying still is not really Nina's speciality, even with a busted ankle. Or maybe she came after Aisa. That's even more likely.

There's only one road to the village though. So if Nina was walking along that, Aisa would have passed her on the way back.

Aisa thinks about the figure she thought she saw . . . The crouching figure that turned into the fox. But what if that first glimpse was not a fox but a person, as she had originally thought? She didn't stick around to find out, just assumed it was the fox she later saw.

What if... Oh shit. And Nina is still out there, walking miles to the village unnecessarily on her damaged leg. Not knowing that she can turn back now, that help is on its way. And now Lizzie is out there too. Does she know the way to go? She thinks of clueless Lizzie, at the mercy of the night and whoever else is out in it. Lizzie is not equipped for that. And Nina should be resting. She pictures her mum, finding out her daughters are all scattered around in the darkness.

'At least you've all got each other,' she'd said once, in the hospice. Rosemary knew they weren't close, but the lie had given her comfort, so Aisa had smiled.

'Yeah, there is that.'

Where are my sisters?

37

ROSEMARY – April 1992

It's getting a bit close, this weather. A warm spell. I can feel my skin growing tacky under my clothes, can smell a richness from my body that I woke up with from the warm night. It sets Bob off. He was trying it on this morning before I left. He'd brought me a tea in bed, which he only ever does when he wants to get his leg over. 'Why are you grinning like a chimp?' I said, and watched him wither in front of me. The tea slopped on the bedside table as he set it down and left the room.

He doesn't deserve that. And it's not bad when it does happen. It's better than not bad, and he tries very hard. But it just feels like a chore sometimes. Another thing on the to-do list, and one of the many I'm not paid for. And I hate that. I hate that I feel like this. Bob is the kindest man I've ever met. The most devoted. No one has ever looked at me the way he does, a gaze that seems to whitewash anything I might have ever said or done wrong. Like a priest or something, exonerating me. I can't complain that he'd never go anywhere without me, that he adores me to a fault, when that was exactly why I chose him in the first place. And will always choose him.

I've washed down the terracotta in the hallway, it gets filthy every day, and now I'm watching each tile change colour as they dry like autumn leaves. How many seasons have I watched the trees outside turn from green to red? How many times have I washed these floors?

All these years have slipped past me and I'm still here. Still scrubbing down the terracotta and polishing the silver, only now I slip some of it into my pocket. How is that for personal growth?

There is a sound from the floor above, a door opening – I must get Alan to oil those hinges – and the sound of Jane's light footsteps scurrying onto the landing.

'Rosemary?'

'Coming up, love.'

I have been here for hours now, watching her play with her contraband dolls, listening to her practise French, even though the only French words I remember from school are *piscine* and *boulangerie*.

Only once has Jane seen me looking at my watch, but I felt terrible about it. It's nearly six. Bob will be itching to get to the pub, the girls will be hungry and I want to take this sticky uniform off, get in the bath and drown myself.

'It's a week today,' she says as she rearranges her books, her prim voice without a hint of local dialect.

'Sorry, love?'

'My birthday, silly.'

'Oh yes,' I say. 'I know that very well.'

'I think Mummy might bring me something this year.'

I freeze. The air in my lungs crystallises like ice and my mind jams up. I never know what to say, even after all this time. Jane doesn't seem to notice, carefully reordering her books by height order as she prattles.

'I think eight is quite a big birthday, don't you?'

I nod.

'I think she might have been waiting for a big birthday. I know she thinks about me every day, because you said.'

'She does, I'm sure of it.'

I have painted myself into a corner, but how could I tell her any different? No kid deserves to think their mother doesn't care. Or that she's not coming back.

'Will you be here on my birthday?'

I think, *Will I?* I work here Monday, Wednesday and Friday, so ... and then realise I'm being stupid. It's a week today, so of course I'll be here.

'I wouldn't miss it,' I say. 'And I'll bring you a little something.'

I cannot afford to buy a little something, but Nina is bound to have something she doesn't want anymore.

'I'm sorry, love, I really should go. My girls are waiting for me.'

I realise immediately this was the wrong thing to say because her shoulders slump and her voice quivers a little.

'Will you tell me about them again?'

I'm never getting home.

'Well, as you know, there's Nina, my eldest. She's ten now and almost as tall as me. She's a bit bossy, but she's a good girl. And Aisa is my youngest, as you know' – *because you know all of this and could recite it in your sleep and you're just playing for time, but how can I be cross* – 'and she's very funny and bolshy and can climb like a monkey.'

'Is she your favourite?'

'Mothers don't have favourites,' I say quickly. 'And then piggy in the middle is Lizzie. She's your age and she loves books and animals.'

'I love books and animals.'

'Yes, you're quite similar really.'

'Is *she* your favourite?'

I smile. 'I've told you a million times, mothers don't have favourites. Unless they only have one child.'

'So I was my mother's favourite?'

'Of course.'

'You were friends, weren't you?'

I hesitate. 'We were. I liked her very much.'

'I think she's going to come this year,' she says firmly. 'And I think she's going to bring me a really big present. I didn't get one from her for—' She counts on her fingers. 'Five years, so five years' worth of presents adds up to a big one.'

I feel uneasy. This is snowballing and when the day comes, and her mum is a no-show, Jane'll feel all the worse for it.

'I hope I get a doll's house,' she says. 'One with little tables and chairs, a bed like mine, sofas and a kitchen, everything this house has. Daddy always buys me books and thinking things, but I'd like something to play with as I'm not supposed to play with these.' She looks down at the antique dolls on the bed next to her. 'Maybe Mummy could bring me a doll's house, what do you think?'

'Would you like me to bring Lizzie to play here sometime?' I say, desperate for all this talk about her mother to end. Lizzie could do with a playmate, one that actually exists.

Jane spins around then, a smile on her face. 'Yes, please,' she says. 'I'd love that. We can talk about books and animals.' I breathe out slowly, glad to have found a diversion. But she continues. 'And if Mummy buys me a doll's house, we can play with that.'

I rush down the stairs, now over an hour late leaving. I hear William finishing up a phone call in his office and wait.

'Yup, yup,' he barks. 'And you.'

The phone lets out a little bleat of a ring as he puts it down, hard. I hover closer, thinking, and then I knock softly.

'A doll's house,' I say, and he raises his eyebrows. 'For Jane's birthday next week, she'd really like one. Maybe Alan could…' I trail off and head for home.

38

LIZZIE – 1:57 a.m.

The lane seems to twist and dip far more on the way back to the house and Lizzie can feel every individual stone through her thin trainer soles. These are the same shoes she uses for everything, and they're normally up to any task. In the summer, she switches to a fresh pair of flip-flops that she gradually destroys throughout May to September, dropping them in the bin just as the weather turns. She smiles for a moment, thinking about the summer just gone. Her first with Rafferty, taking a stroll together with ice creams. Walking up to Silloth Lighthouse. A life together that could skim each season, bouncing from year to year. What a pleasant thought.

This particular pair of trainers are fraying at the eyelets, but they've done her well for several years now. Walking the dogs, cleaning the kennels, doing home visits to check prospective 'pet parents' out. A part of her job that terrifies and fascinates her. She never knows if the paperwork will match reality as she knocks on those doors, standing alone gripping her clipboard. People pretend to have no children because they've fallen in love with a dog unsuited to families, and then Lizzie in turn has to pretend she's not spotted the little shoes, or the last toy they've forgotten to hide. People can turn nasty when you say no in person, so she waits to get back to work and then emails the rejection.

She has to look out for telltale signs of dog fighters and has to check against the registry of people banned from looking after pets. She has sat in a living room as neat as an army barracks, with a trembling woman who insisted she wasn't trying to adopt a pet for her banned husband. In fact, that she was no longer with him. And please, please would Lizzie just say yes. *Please*.

But, most of the time, she gets to place sweet pets with forever families where they'll be loved, walked and cuddled for the rest of their lives. Those are the placements that make the job worthwhile. But those too are the jobs that used to leave Lizzie sad in ways she couldn't find the words for. The nights after those dogs left for their bright futures used to be the ones spent in the bath until the water got cold. Now they're spent with Rafferty, and that sadness no longer descends.

The empty fields are now on her left as she walks her boomerang route. A scarecrow makes her jump. She glares at it, at its middle-of-the-field audacity and sinister hat. She hadn't seen him when she first walked past and imagines that he grew up out of the earth after the downpour. She doesn't look at him any longer than she has to, her imagination making him move, talk, walk towards her. She rushes on.

Her phone battery is at 50 per cent. She knows she should probably turn the flashlight off to conserve energy, but she can't bring herself to do that. It's dark and scary enough without navigating this journey blind.

The woodland is now to the right as she walks back. The trees here have grown so high that the pale moon is lacerated by them, appearing only in lines like a barcode.

The wind is still wild and unpredictable, but the storm seems to have passed. It's raining lethargically, there's no real gusto, but her hair is still wet from earlier, hanging in a limp ponytail that drips down her back. Wrapping her coat tighter around her, she tries to start running but stumbles within seconds, immediately out of breath. Gosh, she's so unfit. She used to run through these woods for hours. Whipping in and out of the trees, hand in hand with Jane. What she wouldn't give for little-kid fitness.

Legs pounding.

Mouth twisted in horror.

Fingers tangled, pulling each other along.

They were chasing a rabbit that had been badly hurt by a bullet. By Alan's bullet. He was obsessed with the rabbits trying to eat the fruit and vegetables he grew. Obsessed with catching them and 'teaching them a lesson'. His voice so soft, she'd had to lean in to hear it, but the meaning as sharp as a blade.

They'd been trying to catch the rabbit before he could. Trying to mend its mangled paw, to bandage it so Lizzie could take it home with her, planning to ambush her mum when she finished work.

They'd followed it all through the woods, adrenaline letting it run and run despite its leg being barely more than a stump. They'd kept up with it as it flew through the undergrowth, right by Alan's tent like it was marking it with its scent. Alan's tent, that's right. He had a bedroom in the house but often chose to sleep out in the woods instead. 'He means no harm,' said her dad. 'But best not go in that tent, he's very protective of things.'

They'd followed the rabbit past the greenhouse and then into the potting shed, where they thought they had it cornered. The memory makes Lizzie feel colder, more vulnerable. She doesn't keep prodding at it, just doggedly walks on. But there's no way on earth she's turning off this flashlight.

Almost there now. The thin grey road winding back towards

her sisters. She can tell them that help might be on the way. Maybe. How will she explain Rafferty to them?

She finally reaches the driveway and looks past it up the road towards the car. It seems like a joke that there's a car right there but they just can't use it. This whole night seems like a prank. Some kind of elaborate hoax being set up by an unseen puppet master. Come on – a storm, then a closed garage, then a car running out of petrol and then a spooky old house ... it's almost too perfect. She seeks comfort in this as she pushes herself up the drive and finally reaches the front door. She is just in a story. A nice cosy mystery.

As she steps inside, the door to the front room opens and Aisa steps out. 'Thank fuck you're back,' she says. 'Where's Nina?'

39

AISA – 2:28 a.m.

'I thought Nina went to find you,' Lizzie says, stepping back in surprise. Her voice is so quiet and slow, so apologetic, that Aisa's usual irritation thaws. It's not Lizzie's fault she's a dial-up connection in a 5G world. 'Didn't you see her out there then, Aisa?'

'Well, no, because ... I mean ...' Did she? It was too dark. But that figure ... the footsteps ...

'Did you follow the road?' Lizzie asks softly.

'Yeah, of course I followed the road, Lizard.'

Lizzie looks down at her feet, which spill out of the kind of knock-off trainers that make Aisa almost nauseous with melancholy.

'Sorry,' Aisa says, 'I didn't mean to snap.' Her sister is too gentle for any kind of confrontation and Aisa can't handle someone else's tears. 'It's a relief to see you,' she adds and Lizzie smiles. 'Look, come into the living room and we'll work out what to do,' Aisa says. 'I've got the fire going again.'

Lizzie trails silently after her, like she's nursing a wound. The front door closes behind them and they shuffle down the dusty hall and back into the living room. The fire has picked up and Lizzie flops onto the floor in front of it, unbuttoning her coat and peeling her fake Converse off her feet. She holds out her palms and rubs them together in the heat and then heaves herself back up to sit on the sofa that Aisa was just sitting on. By the proprietorial way Lizzie is wrapping herself in the eiderdown, it must have been her who found it.

Aisa perches on the other sofa and wraps herself in one of the nasty thin blankets, unsure what to say. Aisa is closer in age to Lizzie than Nina, but they have never paired off, never found any middle ground to occupy. Although 'middle ground' is exactly how Aisa would describe Lizzie, were she feeling snide. A middle of the road, middle sister. Aisa looks at her now, at her pale skin and frizzy hair, her badly fitting charity shop clothes, and wonders, where is the rest of her?

Lizzie was always an oddball, more content with animals' company than people. Except for weird Jane, and that probably wasn't a good thing.

They stare at the fire in silence, exhausted. It feels like hours since they were all here together. Two isn't enough.

It's like one of those stocking-filler puzzles where you had to move the pieces around one by one until the numbers were in the right order. Or, in Aisa's case, you pulled the pieces out in a rage and got told off. Lizzie would get her puzzle close enough and sit back satisfied. It was only Nina who would work and work at it until she'd solved it. She was never going to sit here and wait, was she?

Lizzie looks across at Aisa, her mouth opening just a bit, but she snaps it closed again, her eyes filling with tears in the flickering firelight. It's like dealing with a paper doll, Aisa thinks. Lizzie is too fragile for this world, like a skittish animal.

'Oh!' remembers Aisa. 'I saw a fox out there.'

Lizzie brightens then. 'Oh wow, aren't they gorgeous?'

'Yeah, I guess,' Aisa says. 'It freaked me out a bit.'

'Whereabouts was it?'

'On the way to the village.'

'I wonder if Nina saw it too,' Lizzie says, with that exhausted, dreamy voice. 'Although I don't know which way she went.'

Aisa frowns. 'You don't know? Didn't she say where she was going?'

Lizzie looks startled. 'No, she left while I was asleep. I assumed she was going after you.'

Aisa flinches. Leaving without waking Lizzie, that doesn't sound right.

'But Nina was still here when you fell asleep?'

'Yeah,' Lizzie says, rearranging the eiderdown around her as she lies down on the sofa, her face sagging like a loose mask. She looks like she could fall asleep again. 'We were both in here, waiting for you to come back.'

'Did Nina go to sleep too?' Aisa asks, sticking her own feet closer to the fire but still aching with the cold.

'No,' Lizzie says, yawning until her eyes run. Or maybe she's crying again as her voice is trembling now. 'She said she'd stay awake to tend the fire but—'

'But she was gone when you woke up?'

'Yeah.' Lizzie sounds uneasy now, guilty even. 'And the fire was nearly out by then.'

'Does that make sense to you?' Aisa snaps and Lizzie looks down, every move like a timid animal.

'No,' she says eventually. 'No, it doesn't.'

40

ROSEMARY – April 1992

'Lizzie!' I shout up. 'We need to go if you're coming!'

I hear a thud as she gets down off her bed. This is an old house, wedged between other old houses, and it tells tales. She's been sneaky-eating again, her footsteps are heavier than ever. I know it's boredom, I know it's loneliness and I sympathise. But we also can't afford double helpings at the moment.

She plods down the stairs and into the living room, a nervous look on her face. She's wearing her good blouse, which strains a little, and Nina's old jeans.

'Lovely,' I say, and her tense shoulders drop a little. I look around the room. 'Where's Aisa?'

'Dunno,' says Nina.

'Have you seen her, Lizzie?'

'She wasn't in our room,' Lizzie says, in her soft, slow voice.

I look around again. 'Aisa, where are you?'

There's silence but for the prattle of Australian kids' TV from the corner.

'Aisa?'

I hear a giggle. Her distinctive little laugh, like delicate rain, the top notes on a piano... it melts my heart to soup.

'Where are you?' I smile and listen again, then follow the

noise to the window, where I find her curled up on the sill, hidden by one of the curtains. I scruffle her hair – which needs a good brush – and kiss her on the nose. 'You'll be the death of me, you little monkey. Be good for your sister.' I cringe at how easy it's become to say this. I hear Bob's slow steps as he lumbers out of bed, followed by a pause as he scratches his arse, and then a few more plods as he makes his way downstairs for a wee. 'And be good for your dad,' I add.

It's tipping it down, but yesterday it was sunny. So bright you couldn't see straight. You never know what the weather will do in this valley. The only time there's a guarantee is winter, when it's just plain freezing. The little Mini is sitting in a big puddle like a rubber duck in a bath, and I unlock my door and slide in, popping open the passenger door from the inside. Lizzie climbs into the front, vibrating with excitement. I don't send her to the back seats, let her have this moment

'Are you feeling all right?' I ask. She's never been invited to a friend's house before and never asked to have anyone over at ours. Unless you count the friends in her head. She's eight years old and I suddenly wonder, *Does she know how to do it? Does she know how to play?*

'Looking forward to meeting Jane,' she says, softly, oblivious that they met as tots. Of course she knows how to play, she has two sisters and goes to school every day. If there was something wrong ... something missing ... the school would have said. They're quick enough to tell me that Aisa plays tricks on boys who aren't nice to the others. I smile, I can't help myself. She's my sunshine. My naughty little sunshine.

We drive through the village, dodging puddles, and out into the countryside. Some days, most days, I don't really see it. I don't see its scale, its drama, its beauty. I grew up here, next village along, I know it like I know my own body in the bath.

I'm as bored of it too. I certainly didn't think I'd still be here, but then… where else could I go? But sometimes, I recognise it for the marvel it is. Sometimes, like when my body produced these whole human beings, I recognise its power. And today, the sun shining through the rain, the slick roads like veins of silver through these epic hills and ancient woods, I recognise its beauty.

'Isn't it beautiful,' I say to Lizzie and she nods.

'Breathtaking.'

It's such an adult word for such a little girl and I'm tempted to laugh, but I don't. Poor old Lizzie, she's got an old brain in a young body, that's all it is. Same as Jane. Sort of.

We climb the last hill and see Moirthwaite Manor on the right.

'Foxes,' Lizzie says happily, pointing to the pillars of the arch and two statues I've never paused to look properly at before.

I swing the Mini onto the drive and as we bump our way up to the house, I gently go through the rules. Shoes off. Please and thank you. Quiet voice. Knock before you go anywhere – actually, best not to go anywhere, just stay with Jane or me. And don't disturb Jane's dad while he's working.

'What does he do?'

He was going to be a writer, he said. That summer when I followed him around like a little duckling and he let me eat from his hand when no one was looking. His parents didn't approve, his father in particular, so he'd been strong-armed into studying for a career in finance, but back then, he still had hope.

'He… I don't know. He just moves money around and has a lot of phone calls about it, so you need to be quiet near his office.'

As we pull up, I tuck the Mini to the side of the drive where it's not such an eyesore and yank on the handbrake. It screams and sighs – I need to get it seen to – but it holds. Sometimes, that's all you can hope for.

We climb out and I watch Lizzie take the place in. Her jaw drops slightly and she steps back a little as if unable to consume it all with her eyes this close up. It is impressive. Made from the same red stone that everything around here is, looming tall and wide. Each of these windows is almost the width of our whole house and I'm used to that, but I'd forgotten that Lizzie didn't know. That she'd not experienced this scale of anything before, that she's not had much to compare our lives to. This is the first time that she's seen how small our family's world really is. How it slots so easily into the corners of other lives.

I swallow. Is this a mistake?

'Is that Jane?' she says, pointing up at Jane's window.

'No pointing, love.'

We step inside and I see it as if for the first time again. I was twice her age, but it had whipped my legs from under me, the way it's doing to her. The scale of the staircase, the high ceilings, the chandelier over our heads, tinkling with threat as the wind from outside snakes through the hallway. Its grandeur always seems on the cusp of ruin, despite mine and Alan's efforts.

I close the door and whisper, 'Shoes off before anyone sees you,' but Jane is already running down the stairs. Lizzie tugs her shoes off in the least gainly way I've ever seen anyone do it. Jane stops and waits a few steps up – dressed in a velvet dress with a lace trim collar – and stares down at Lizzie. I have a sudden compulsion to bundle her up in my arms and leg it out of the house, but instead I smile. 'Jane, this is my daughter, Lizzie. Lizzie, this is my … this is Jane.'

They stare at each other, Lizzie like a rabbit in headlights, blinking in a panic. Jane smiles but says nothing for so long, I cough out of embarrassment.

'What do you like?' Jane says.

'Animals, biscuits, books,' Lizzie reels off like she's addressing a drill sergeant.

'Animals? Oh good.' Jane smiles. 'Put your shoes back on, we're going to look for rabbits.'

'Is that OK, Mum?' Lizzie asks and before I can answer, Jane nods.

'Of course it is, it's up to me.'

41

LIZZIE – 2:33 a.m.

Stupid, stupid Lizard. *Of course* Nina didn't go off without saying anything. Even if she was worried about Aisa, she would have said something. She would have woken Lizzie up and told her what was happening. Given her specific instructions for keeping the fire going. For all Nina's bossiness, she wasn't sneaky. She wouldn't just slope off. Gosh, if Lizzie had thought a little longer, hadn't been so addled from waking up suddenly like that...

And if Nina had gone after Aisa, then Lizzie would have seen her out there. She'd have caught her up, as Nina would have been so much slower, and they'd have been walking towards the same spot of reception. Who would she have called? A thought blooms like a headache and she calls out, 'Aisa?'

Aisa is pinching the bridge of her nose, walking up and down in front of the fire with the blanket trailing like a cape. She whips her head round and barks, 'What?'

'There's something else. I... I meant to say as soon as I got back bu—'

'What now?'

Aisa is always so acerbic. Always has been, even when she was little. Or maybe... maybe that was just her way of being heard.

'What is it, Lizard?' Aisa repeats, no effort to hide her annoyance.

She wants to tell her sister that help is coming. But is it? She left a message on her own voicemail, after all. She doesn't even know that Rafferty is there, let alone if he will hear it. He could have been asleep in his own bed. It's a whole lot of nothing, and she can't bear to talk about Rafferty when Aisa is in such a dismissive mood.

'Nothing,' she says.

'What was it?'

'Don't worry. I just wanted to say that...' She gropes for something plausible. 'I just keep thinking how spooky it is here. I hope we're safe.'

Aisa sits down next to her, curling in on herself and looking nervously at the fireplace.

'You're not the only one to say that about this place,' Aisa says, quietly, looking behind her suddenly as if she'd heard something, then slowly turning back.

'What do you mean?'

'The woman I spoke to at the breakdown company, she asked if I was safe here. I don't mean like the usual solo female traveller questions or something. But, like, she had to google the house name to find it 'cos I didn't know the address and some urban explorers' reports came up.' Lizzie must have frowned in confusion without realising it because Aisa tuts. 'They're people who break into abandoned places and explore them. They write site reports for other urban explorers to follow and, anyway, the reports about this place worried her and she said it sounded weird.'

'Did you ask her why?'

'Yeah, but the call cut out,' Aisa says. 'And I just... I just came back and you and Nina were gone and I didn't know where and then you came back and that … that took over my thoughts. I just figured she was a numpty who hadn't heard of …' Aisa trails off and Lizzie feels her cheeks colour.

Lizzie tries to imagine what urban explorers might write. Are they the types to be easily spooked? They sounded pretty brave to her. 'Maybe there is something here we should be scared about.'

Aisa looks up.

42

AISA – 2:36 a.m.

'Something here like what?' Aisa says, dredging as much attitude as she can muster. 'Like a ... like a ghost or something?' She forces a smirk as she says it, tries to break into a laugh, but scrunches up her eyes instead.

I don't believe in ghosts.
I don't believe in ghosts.
I don't believe in ghosts.

'You're mocking me,' Lizzie says. 'But I think you're scared too.'

Scared? I'm absolutely terrified. I haven't felt this level of fear since I was a child and I just want Mum. I just really want my mum.
'I'm not scared, Lizzie. I'm freezing cold and I'm pissed off, but I'm not scared. I just want to work out what's happened to Nina, make sure she's OK and then wait for the mechanic.'

'Me too.'

Oh, where the hell is Nina? Without her, Aisa has had to assume the role of group leader when she's only ever comfortable as a lone wolf. And if she had to put together a team, she would have picked almost anyone else she'd ever met before she'd choose Lizzie. Poisson the cat would show more gumption. But Lizzie is made from cardboard, and the slightest hint of people being fed up with her will crumple her to pieces, so Aisa needs to be nice. Nice-adjacent, anyway.

Aisa pinches the bridge of her nose, trying to make sense of this. She instinctively slides her phone from her pocket, ready to search for these urbex reports herself. Grasp the nettle, see what has been said. Of course, her phone is dead.

But whether they can read them right now or not, there clearly are some out there about this place.

She tries to weigh up the options, picture all the moving parts. A rescue truck could technically arrive any minute, so they can't just go off to the village. And Nina is missing out there, and hurt. Aisa looks out of the window as if she'll see her sister marching up to the house, but no one is there.

'Maybe we should wait in the car?' Aisa says, trying to sound casual.

'But Nina has the keys,' Lizzie whispers apologetically.

'Fuck.'

Lizzie flinches, she's never liked swearing. As far as Aisa knows, she still says 'tish' instead of shit.

Aisa casts around for something to say. Something that isn't fear-based and doesn't involve a Rubik's Cube of a decision.

'I'm freezing,' she says eventually, nodding towards the fire-place. 'It's not kicking out much heat now.'

Lizzie nods and starts prodding about in the grate, sparks flying from the embers that are left. She adds some more logs and then looks around.

'There's paper over there.' Aisa walks towards a slightly dishevelled newspaper stuffed in the corner of the room and barely visible in the light from the candles. She stoops to pick it up and passes it to her sister, who takes it gingerly as if it's made from spiderwebs. It's not as crumpled as she thought when Lizzie holds it up. 'Hang on,' Aisa says, as the masthead glows briefly in the reflection of the fire. 'What's the date on there?'

Lizzie squints and holds the paper up to one of the candles. 'Oh,' she looks up at Aisa, her face flushing. 'Gosh. It's yesterday's date.'

'Yesterday, as in yesterday? As in this year, not an anniversary of yesterday?'

Lizzie nods and drops the paper as if it's contaminated, dangerous. 'Literally yesterday,' she says, and shuffles closer to Aisa, who grips her sister's arm.

'Shit,' she says. 'Someone has been in here recently. Very recently. What if—' Aisa doesn't want to say it and she doubts Lizzie wants to hear it, but it's too late, she has to. They have to face up to this. 'What if they found Nina?'

43

ROSEMARY – May 1992

It feels like these kids are never at school. They go back after February half term and then it's Easter. They go back after Easter and it's May half term. It won't be long until it's the summer holiday and then the whole thing starts again. *I should have been a teacher*, I think, as I scrub the big range with a Brillo pad, trying to move the immovable. What the hell has Cook been doing, grilling the food directly on the flame, like she's living out in the woods with Alan?

I imagine what it's like to look forward to the holidays. To be able to plan a schedule of events, to bundle the girls into the car and take them to Windermere or to play on the beach in Barrow. I smile and imagine packing a picnic in a cool box. And a big stripey bag containing a ball, a windcheater, a bottle of sun lotion. I can almost smell it on their warm skin. To just let each day unfurl in front of us, chips for lunch if they want, ice cream. Me reading on a sandy towel while they splash around. It's not much. Small dreams, but still out of reach. More than anything, I would love to be able to give them my time.

It's getting lighter in the evenings, there's more of the day waiting for me when I get home, and every day, I tell myself I'll keep some energy back. I'll hug them all when I get in and

I won't just immediately start on straightening the house and cooking the tea. I'll just *be* with them. But it never pans out that way. The house is fuller than ever as the girls grow, their stuff scattering. Scrunchies everywhere, Aisa's toys underfoot. And there's a lot more of Bob too. Money is getting thinner and thinner and he's had his wings clipped, having to make do with a couple of skems at home instead of the pub. He plods around like a big dog, getting in my way and then looking chastened.

I've started locking myself in the loo, just to have five minutes, even though I've worked more or less by myself all day. The guilt roaring in my ears. *But it's not the same though,* I think, as I finally manage to move a lump of something black and molten. *It's just not the same.*

Sometimes, when I'm here working away, it's like a portal opens up. A latch slips off the gate and I'm not here but back *there*, in the past. I'm sixteen. Skinny and excited. A new perm on my head and an unbroken heart. The whole world is there and I just have to step into it. Only, the closer I get, the more I realise it's more like a cinema screen. You'll just bang your head if you try to climb through.

I realise I'm being watched at the same time I realise I've stopped scrubbing. I turn, though I know who it is already. No one else treads so lightly, like a little forest fawn.

'Y'all right there, love?' I say.

'Rosemary?' Jane says and I wonder if her vowels will ever flatten, if she'll ever sound like she lives here. That she's been here since before she could talk properly. 'Do you think…'

'What is it, Jane? Don't be shy,' I say, with more patience than I know I'll have left for my girls when I get back.

'Well, I was hoping you might bring Elizabeth back to play with me again soon.'

Elizabeth? For a moment I don't know who she means and then the penny drops. 'Lizzie?'

'Yes, I had such fun with her before.'

'I'm not sure, Jane, I don't want to irritate your dad, bringing people here.'

'I'm sure Daddy won't mind. He knows how lonely I get here, without a brother or sister or...' She lowers her eyes and a cruel thought takes flight before I can stop it. *Is this for show?* 'Or a mummy,' she says.

I think about her birthday. About how disappointed she was when – of course – her mother didn't turn up again. Of how many doll's-house blankets I guiltily produced for her, knitting on my days off. I even got Alan to help me make a little doll version of her, which was a right faff. I'll never attempt to knit a tiny human head again. But she's only eight. It's not for show, she's lonely as anything.

'Of course I'll bring her,' I say. *If you promise to stop pining for your mum*, I want to add. The *idea* of her mother, anyway, as Jane can't possibly remember Selina. Her energy, her wit, her hatred of this house.

Then I think about Lizzie's ravenous hunger and the scrapings of the food budget. Two birds... 'Why don't I bring her over and make you two lasses a picnic?'

44

LIZZIE – 2:40 a.m.

They. They. An unknown 'they' was in this house, coaxing Nina away. *Snatching* Nina away. All while Lizzie slept. Just a great lump, snoring on the sofa, while her injured sister was taken against her will. Stupid, stupid Lizzie. She thumps herself hard on the side of the head. Once, twice and again.

'Hey,' Aisa says, alarmed. 'Don't do that!'

'But someone has taken Nina and it's my fault!'

'No,' says Aisa, shaking her head and frowning. 'No one has taken Nina, don't be silly. I was getting carried away . . . It's all a bit weird, but she's obviously just gone off looking for something. You'd have woken up if something bad had happened, wouldn't you? There's no way you'd have slept through it. Even you.'

'Even me?'

'Even you.'

'But the newspaper,' Lizzie says. 'It's proof someone was here.'

'Yesterday,' Aisa says quietly. 'That's all.'

Oh gosh, why did she have to lie down earlier? She'd felt safe with Nina here, so safe she could just fall asleep. It didn't cross her mind that Nina was vulnerable. Even with her bad ankle, Nina is just . . . Nina. She's always OK. But how well did Lizzie actually check if she was here before dashing off? She only had a quick look in each room, assuming Nina would make herself known if she was in one of them. But maybe she was here and in trouble somehow, or hurt, and Lizzie just swanned off and left her.

'I just feel so bad,' Lizzie says, quietly.

Aisa takes a deep breath and then grabs Lizzie's hands. 'Honestly, I'm sure Nina's fine,' she says, unconvincingly. 'I'm sure she'll be back any minute to tell us off for something. But I think we should have a proper look through the house while we wait, just in case … you know, in case she did just fall asleep somewhere upstairs or …' Aisa doesn't finish the sentence and Lizzie is grateful.

Lizzie shoves the eiderdown away, embarrassed by the way she'd been gripping it. She does her coat back up, stuffs her aching feet back into her trainers and checks her phone for battery. Enough to use the light for a good while, thankfully.

Aisa says her own phone is long dead, so she grabs a candlestick, cupping one hand around it to shroud the small flickering flame. Even though Lizzie's light is stronger, Aisa leads the way. They walk slowly, to keep the flame safe and to scour every inch of the house this time. Neither has said it, but Lizzie knows they're not just looking for Nina, but for signs of what might have happened to her too.

They check out the kitchen first. There's nothing much in here: a disused fridge, a giant cold Rayburn. They look in all the corners, and venture into the larder this time. Tucked on the gnarly old floor just inside the door, there's a bulky blue cool box, the kind the Kelseys used to take on trips to the beach in North Wales after they moved to Cheshire. It's an incongruous shock of colour, almost cartoon-like. Aisa starts to squat down, but the flame flickers wildly as she moves, so Lizzie takes over.

Bending over it, she opens the lid cautiously and is surprised to see long life milk, margarine and a pack of open biscuits, twisted at the neck. The sisters look at each other. Next to the cool box is a small camping stove with a chipped old-fashioned red kettle balanced on it. In the flashlight glow, its bottom is visibly blackened.

'I think someone might have been staying here after all,' Lizzie says.

Aisa gives her the kind of look that means 'no shit' but instead she draws her face into an almost smile and says, 'It doesn't mean anything bad though. You get squatters all over the place, they're usually harmless. The urban explorer I hook up with says people get in these places to strip them and do graffiti, and there was graffiti on the outside, wasn't there?'

'Yes,' says Lizzie. Relieved also that maybe the only reason Aisa has heard of urban explorers was because she's romantically involved with one.

'And graffiti artists are harmless, OK?'

'OK,' Lizzie says, and then she realises she'd been rude not acknowledging the nugget of personal information out loud. 'So, is he your boyfriend, the urban explorer?'

Aisa pauses. 'Sure,' she says.

Lizzie opens her mouth to add that she's not the only one with a beau, but Aisa turns away and the moment is lost.

They check the rest of the downstairs rooms and then climb the stairs. Aisa opens the bathroom with a bang and Lizzie cringes.

'There's a loo roll under there,' Aisa says, pointing to the U-bend behind the old toilet. 'And some bleach. God, this is almost civilised.'

The discoveries seem to be awakening something in Aisa, some sense of adventure or some kind of compulsion to explore.

For Lizzie, every tiny sign of life unpicks a nerve, one by one. Do graffiti artists and thieves bring newspapers to read? No, someone has been staying here, she thinks. This is someone's territory, and they've barged into it. Did Nina pay the price?

They look in the back corner bedroom. 'Alan's room,' Lizzie says, and Aisa stops moving.

'Alan,' she says. 'Yeah, that was his name, wasn't it.'

Lizzie looks at her. 'You remember him?'

'Yeah,' Aisa says. 'A little. Strange bloke.'

Lizzie nods and then shakes her head. 'I always thought he was more sad than strange.'

They walk out quickly and check the other back bedrooms. Aisa calmly moves out of the way when a huge spider comes barrelling towards them like tumbleweed. Lizzie scrambles back onto the landing, brushing herself as if covered in them.

Aisa looks at her but has the kindness not to comment.

They open the master bedroom. It's absolutely pointless, Lizzie knows it's horrifyingly empty, but they must look, if only to be doing something.

'One room left,' Aisa says, as they close the master bedroom door. 'Let's hope she's in there, curled up.'

'I checked it thoroughly,' Lizzie starts, but does she hope she checked it properly or that she missed her sister? 'But yeah, you're right. She could be in there.'

They look at each other and then push the door. Aside from the lounge, this is the most cluttered room. The one with the most hiding places and corners.

'Nina?' Lizzie says and they stay deadly still to listen for a reply.

Nothing.

'Nina, stop dicking about,' Aisa calls. She's trying to smile, but her eyes look wild with fear.

They check under the bed, then Lizzie pulls up each sheet and blanket.

'She's not Flat Stanley,' Aisa says.

The thick curtains still hang either side of the window seat and they tug them at the same time, fanning them like a mother's dress, like the black skirt their own mother used to wear here.

She is not here. Not one trace of her is here. There is no sign of ... anything. Nothing to suggest a struggle. *No blood.* Nothing. But Lizzie runs her light along every wall and surface anyway, because to stop looking is to admit something she's not ready to admit.

Lastly, she runs her light over the doll's house.

Aisa bends down, accidentally snuffing her candle, so Lizzie walks closer with her light to compensate. 'Bloody candles. Hey, are those ...?' She snaps back and crawls backwards on her hands.

'Bones,' Lizzie says apologetically. 'Yeah.'

'Jesus fucking Christ,' Aisa says, standing. 'God, Lizzie. I can't ... I can't put a brave face on this. This is really, really creepy. This isn't ... this isn't right.'

'I know,' Lizzie whispers. 'I thought they were Jane's from when she was a kid, but maybe someone ... someone else is ...' she trails off. The light has settled on the lower part of the doll's house and she spots something she didn't notice before. Or forgot. The floor of the miniature lounge is visible through the window, and it's set a few inches higher than the bottom of the doll's house. Lizzie gets onto her knees to look closer, pressing the lower part of the wooden wall carefully, tenderly.

Aisa shoots her eyebrows up in question, but Lizzie can't say, not yet. She needs to check. Her fingertips work their way gently around, as if feeling for a tender spot on a dog in pain, until eventually, at the back of the house, she finds it. A gentle push reveals a barely visible hinge, and a small panel flips open.

'Another level,' Lizzie says, turning to look at Aisa. 'Underneath.'

'I know,' Aisa says, her voice distorted as if her teeth were chattering. 'I know.'

Lizzie sits back, awash with memory now. All the missing pieces tumbling at her so fast she can't focus on any one of them. The day they followed the injured rabbit into the shed. The place Jane wanted to show her. *Oh tish*, she should have remembered. She really should have remembered. The extra rooms, window-less, under the main house.

Aisa runs out of the room, navigating the dark, her dead candle swinging in her hand as Lizzie follows behind with the phone, its light bouncing erratically. As they start to climb down the stairs, Lizzie stops. 'Aisa,' she says, 'look.'

Aisa turns from a few steps below and sees what Lizzie is pointing at. From this angle, they can both see that the tides of dust on the stairs carpet have been disturbed, as if something has been dragged through them. Or someone.

45

ROSEMARY – June 1992

My feet are killing me before I even start work. Five miles, walk, fuelled only by tea. I'd woken up early to drive out to the garage and fill the car with the last of my wages, which I'd left on my bedside table the evening before. But when I reached for them first thing, I found an empty brown envelope.

I'd gone to sleep while Bob was at the pub last night, spending the fiver I'd pulled out for him. He must have come back, grabbed the rest and snuck back out. When I saw what he'd done, I had to run downstairs to the loo. A sudden rush of nausea swept over me from toes to gut and I only just made it to the back door and threw up outside in the yard instead. Then I had to boil a kettle and wash it all away. All the while, Bob slept on up there, snoring like a drain, sweat on his temples and beer breath filling the room.

'How could you?' I said to him as I rushed up to chuck my clothes on, no time for breakfast, no time for anything. I am never late, I hate to be late. I am capable, dependable, I have to be. 'There's no bus, Bob, how could you?'

He sat up, groaned in pain and lay back down. Without answering me, he fell back asleep, mouth open like a fish.

'I hope you choke,' I said to him, but then silently took it back.

'He's not well,' that's what my mum says. 'It breaks a man, losing his job. His way of life. It's an illness.' She doesn't know the half of what's troubling Bob, but my dad lost his job in the biscuit factory just before he was diagnosed, and my mother has long conflated the two. I'm not convinced it had anything to do with Dad's cancer, I think it just shakes down that way sometimes, but we've never had the same outlook.

It preys on my mind as I approach the age he was and wonder. Some nights, I lie awake and run through all the things I've not done with my girls, and the experiences I've not given them while I tread water to earn money that doesn't even stretch. If cancer took me now, like it took my dad, what would they remember of me? My back as I left each morning? All the things I had to say no to. Holidays and sports clubs and days out. But what good is that way of thinking? There's no other option, I'm unqualified and Bob is out of work. When those worries well up inside me, I have to tell myself that one day there will be a way out of this, a way to give them everything they deserve. I just don't know how yet.

I kissed the girls goodbye this morning, whispered to Nina to make sure they had their breakfast before school, and then dashed off. Maybe I could have called in sick – our line is cut off, but the phone box is right by our house – but William keeps me on because I'm dependable. It's certainly not out of any residual feelings or even loyalty. If I cease to be dependable, what am I? And besides, I'd lose the wages from today, or have to make up the time tomorrow, and I've got envelope stuffing to do.

*

When I get to the front door, there's a moth lying dead on the doorstep. I pretend I haven't seen it and rush round to the back door instead. Round here in Cumbria, moths are a sign of death or letters. But dead moths... that can't be good, can it? I think again of my dad and blink rapidly to wipe the image. It helps no one to think like that.

I struggle through the day, dodging questions from Jane about when Lizzie can come back. I had to go and get her from school on Wednesday and bring her back here to 'play' for my last few hours. Using up precious fuel and not even giving Lizzie a say in it. She'd come out of Jane's room pale-faced when it was time to go, unable, or unwilling, to tell me why.

My feet hurt, my back aches, I still feel sick, as if I absorbed Bob's hangover while I slept next to him. I even told William about the car not being available, hoping he might give me a lift home, but he turned his attention back to the papers on his desk before I'd even finished.

While William was teaching Jane this afternoon, I managed to sneak a bit of rest on one of the new sofas that finally arrived this week. They're not as soft as the old one, but I was too tired to care. I managed a kind of one-eye-open dog nap in case I was caught, but luckily I wasn't disturbed. I can't make it a habit, but I feel like every day takes a little more toll than the last and the thought of carrying on like this for another twenty years crushes me. I need a way out. We all do.

I open the front door of Moirthwaite Manor ready to leave, relieved that the moth is gone, when I hear Jane behind me. I muster every bit of energy left not to sag my shoulders in despair. I don't want to bring Lizzie back here, I don't want to feed her to the lions, to assuage guilt, to prop up another kid. But I know I'll have to. I wait for the inevitable questions, but instead, she says, 'Rosemary, can I show you my artwork?'

'Of course you can, love.' I turn around with a smile that fades as I look down. She holds up a piece of wood that she must have found. Pinned to it, with needles from the sewing basket, is the moth from earlier. It's splayed, as if in flight, its furry little body with a needle through the middle, its wings intact and beautiful. My breath catches in my throat and I lose control of my smile for just a moment.

'You don't like it?'

'No, no, I do. It's very… scientific.'

'I did it for Lizzie. She says she likes moths and butterflies. Everything except spiders, she said.' She thrusts it towards me eagerly. I take it – what else can I do? I take it and carry it straight out in front of me, like a tea tray. 'Make sure you give it to her,' she says.

I've just finished stuffing the horrible gift into the hedge down the driveway when Alan catches up to me. I just want to get home, but I've been too brusque with him recently and Bob always reminds me to be kind to him, they used to be close and I know Bob worries about him, so I manage to dredge a smile up.

'Bob not picking you up?'

'Not today, Al.'

'That's a shame,' he says, his voice so soft I have to step closer to him to hear. He smells… sour. 'I wanted to ask him about doing some work. A lot of the bushes need taming and it's a two-man job really.'

God, we need the money. But I shake my head. Bob hates coming back to the house, the cost is just too high. 'Sorry, Al, he's tied up at the minute. Doing some stuff up in Penrith.'

He frowns, and I feel awful because I know he's trying to help.

'Sorry, Al, I really need to go, but thanks for the offer.'

I walk away as fast as my aching arches will let me, and

when I look back, he's walking slowly back to the house in his lolloping way.

Bob needs a purpose and we need the money. Something to get him out of the house. He wants to work on the trains, he always has, but he hasn't gone to ask at the station. Too worried they'll say no. I'll talk to him later, encourage him again. He'll be full of apologies about the petrol money, and I'll have to forgive him, because if I don't, he'll feel guilty. And when he feels guilty, when he feels anything, when he remembers... he drinks. And when he drinks, clearly, he runs his mouth. This time, he's obviously told Alan, or someone who knows Alan, that we're skint. Next time...

46

AISA – 2:57 a.m.

Lizzie stays swaying on the landing, her mouth open in horror, but Aisa's not messing around. She rushes down the stairs to the hallway, getting swallowed by the darkness now that her candle has gone out. As she reaches the bottom step, she can't even see her hand in front of her. She swallows, waiting for Lizzie to catch up, looking wildly around into nothing. She steps down into the foyer and looks up towards Lizzie, still aglow at the top of the stairs, gripping her phone.

'Come on,' she hisses.

Then she sees it. A thin ribbon of light just underneath the bottom step in front of her. Confirmation.

As soon as she saw that miniature house, the extra rooms, it all came back to her. The space beneath the house. She and Nina had been playing hide and seek, and Aisa had found that little door under the stairs. It must still be there now, a few feet away from where she stands.

Back then, she'd climbed into the cupboard, found the trap-door and climbed down a few steps. All she was thinking about then was hiding.

Lizzie lumbers down the steps as Aisa feels her way to the cupboard under the stairs. 'Over here, Lizzie,' she calls, pulling the door open. Back then, it was filled with bric-a-brac, picnic baskets and wellies, ideal for a little body to weave through and hide. But as Lizzie shines her phone's flashlight inside, they can see that the cupboard is now empty.

It's wallpapered with roses – a pattern Aisa suddenly remembers but couldn't have described if you'd asked her. It's not as dusty in this cupboard as it is in the rest of the house, but it's still grubby. Footprints are visible on the bare stone floor and there's a section in the middle where the dust has been mostly rubbed away.

With Lizzie hovering behind her gripping her phone and pointing its light at the floor, Aisa stoops into the cupboard. She could almost touch the furthest wall just by reaching up a hand, there's nothing in here blocking the way.

But when she squats down, she can see that the slabs of stone are not all the same. Most are sealed together with concrete and dirt, but one has a clear gap around it. She remembers this, remembers finding the trapdoor, and feels around.

The ring is still set in the stone floor slab, just like it was back then. It had been partly open when she found it as a little girl, just a chink of light visible in the black of the cupboard. She'd expected it to be difficult to move, but when she wrapped her little fingers around the metal ring and pulled, it slipped up easily. And now, as she does it as an adult, she can see why. It's hinged with some kind of spring mechanism to make it quiet and quick. And the light is on down there now too, just like it was then.

'If that leads where I think it does,' Lizzie says, 'there's another way in too.'

'What?' Aisa looks around at her sister. 'You knew all along?'

'I'd forgotten,' she says. 'But I was there too. Remember?'

'I—' *Jane* was there, Aisa remembered that. But Lizzie too? If Lizzie was there, why did she let Jane…

Lizzie looks at her, as if waiting for a reaction.

'I'd forgotten,' Aisa manages to say, as her memories shuffle like a pack of cards yet again.

'It's amazing what you can forget, isn't it?' Lizzie says, her eyes seeking Aisa's. 'It's even more amazing what you can convince yourself of, even when the evidence is right in front of you.'

Aisa stares at her sister's back as she turns away again. *What evidence is right in front of me?*

47

LIZZIE – 3:00 a.m.

They both peer down at the wooden steps, which are lit by bare bulbs hanging from a long wire which seems to run along the wall and along the passage. So there *is* some electricity here then... What else is still here? *Who else?*

She'd known this all along, but she'd forgotten. And it seems Aisa had too. What else have they pushed out of their memories?

'You go first,' Aisa says and Lizzie blinks in surprise. Aisa is usually the first to barrel into any situation, to heck with the consequences. Lizzie looks at her, so much smaller still, even though they're both adults. Her shoulders have hard little knots on them, her elbows as sharp as knives. Lizzie looks at her little sister's face and sees a brief hint of confusion and fear, which washes in and out again like a tide.

If Aisa is scared, things must be really bad. And yet, Aisa's reticence stirs something in Lizzie. If her little sister needs her to step up for once, then she'll do it. She'll flipping well do it.

'Of course I'll go first,' she says, as boldly as she can manage.

Each light bulb flickers as they brush past. Lizzie heads down carefully, her knackered grey trainers testing every step, gingerly at first and then with something approaching confidence.

The stairs curl in a dog-leg and then land in a dark recess, the light not quite reaching here. She rushes through a brick archway and comes out in a kind of foyer. Behind her, she hears Aisa take a sharp breath.

In her memory, sketchy as it is, this underground foyer was huge. It's actually barely bigger than her dad's little living room. There are several closed doors to the left of them and only one to the right, which is open and leads to a long passage.

'That's the way that leads to the shed,' she says.

Aisa stares up along it and then back at Lizzie, a strange look on her face. She was so little, of course she can't remember any of this. But Lizzie and Jane had come down that passageway all those years ago. It was horrible, filled with spiderwebs that Jane had destroyed one by one with her fingers.

'Oh,' Lizzie says, bending a little at the knees.

'What?'

'I just … I just remembered something, it's OK.'

The spider. The spider that Jane caught in her hand and chased Lizzie with, when they first came down here.

Why did she do that? It was so mean. Lizzie remembers the surge of anger that she'd had to swallow back down.

'You remembered something about down here?' Aisa's eyes are wide, the whites of them looking almost orange in this weird light. She looks terrified, something Lizzie can't remember seeing for a long time.

Get it together, Aisa needs you.

'No, nothing like that.'

Aisa had needed her then too. She was here, alone, a little four-year-old crouching in the dark by herself. Where was Nina? She was above them still, clattering around in the hallway cupboard they'd just been in tonight. That's right, the Kelsey sisters had split up when they first arrived. Aisa and Nina had been playing hide-and-seek while Jane and Lizzie went off on their own. Then they'd eventually made their way under here and found Aisa hiding. Jane had spoken to Aisa and calmed her down while Lizzie had called up to Nina in the cupboard. 'If you're looking for Aisa, she's down here.'

But why did she and Jane make their way into this place before that? Lizzie closes her eyes and tries to remember, but the mental film just spools back to the beginning. Running through the woods, wild, exhilarated and terrified.

They both look up the long passageway now, which is also strung with the same kind of bulbs, each illuminating a little patch. As far as she can see, it looks surprisingly clean now, no spiderwebs nor mouse droppings. Someone has cleaned it recently, Lizzie can see tides of dust along the edge, as if the middle has been brushed.

The end of the tunnel is too far and too dark, despite the light. The whole thing must be a hundred metres long and change, the floor is flagstone and the walls are brick. However old Moirthwaite Manor is, this section looks like it's been here the whole time, so it must predate the electricity. Maybe little candles once lit the way for the servants who lived down here. Lizzie imagines a gust of wind blowing them all out, and shudders at the idea of being plunged into darkness. What if the lights go out suddenly now?

The thought makes the back of her neck tingle and she turns quickly, but no one is there, and Aisa is still in front of her.

She reaches into her pocket for her phone, grips it like a gun in a holster, ready to pull it out and switch the flashlight on again.

She glances one more time up the passageway that she'd come down all those years ago, with Jane, and then back up it with her sisters afterwards, Nina and then Aisa. Jane hadn't been with them. Jane had stayed here. It was the last time Lizzie saw her. They moved so soon afterwards that she never even said goodbye to Jane, let alone had another glimpse at her house.

What happened to Jane?

48

ROSEMARY – June 1992

'Nan brought a book round for you,' Nina shouts from the kitchen as I walk into the house. 'It's on top of the telly.' The telly that is blaring, with Aisa sitting right up in front of the screen. Lizzie is lying on the sofa with her head in a book. I think it's one borrowed from Jane; it looks prehistoric. Most worrying, I can smell burning.

'A book for me?' I say. That's my mother in a nutshell, even managing to use inanimate objects to judge me. When do I have time to read a book? 'And have you been cooking, Nina?'

'Just toast,' Nina says, sliding some plates into the bubble-filled sink as I walk into the kitchen.

'How much washing up liquid did you use? That's expensive, Nina.'

'Not much,' she says quietly, plunging her hands into the sink so the bubbles slop over onto the floor.

I close my eyes and pinch my nose to stay calm when a thought strikes me. 'Did Nan come in?'

'Just to drop off the book,' Nina says. 'She said she didn't have time to stop.'

I look around at what my mum would have seen – and judged – on arrival. The floor is covered in bits. The vacuum broke last year and we've been using a carpet roller, but it's a losing battle and the carpet is visibly waving a white flag. Or a dirty grey one. I keep the house relatively tidy, but there's not always time for a full scrub and polish.

There's a full laundry basket next to the washing machine, which is itself full of clean washing that should have been hung out today. A basket of ironing sits in the middle of the living room like a marooned shipwreck and all the boxes from my envelope-stuffing job are stacked against the wall.

'Lizzie!' I shout, before I can stop myself. 'What are you doing just lying there like a lump?'

Lizzie looks up from the sofa, stung.

'How can you just sit there reading while I'm working and Nina is looking after Aisa and Dad is …' I waver. *Doing some cash in hand that it's best not to know about.* 'And Dad is out. You're a big girl now, you need to pull your weight.'

She looks down at her tummy.

'No,' I say, kicking myself. 'Not weight, like … just *helping*, Lizzie. Without being asked.'

'What shall I—' she starts and then runs aground. 'Can I ask just this time?' she says quietly.

'Just, look. There's that washing in the machine, that could go out on the whirligig.'

'OK.'

'Did I do something wrong letting Nan in?' Nina asks, rinsing the last of the plates and stuffing them on the draining rack as Lizzie plods into the kitchen and starts yanking the washing out of the machine and into a basket.

'No, no, none of you have done anything wrong, I just … I'm embarrassed that she saw—'

'Us?' Aisa says, jutting her chin out at me and glaring.

'No, God no, not you, sweetheart. Not you three.' I sag against the wall. I've not even got my shoes and tights off and I've fudged it all. 'This house is a mess, that's all. And I spent all day polishing someone else's house and I just … I'm tired. I need a bath.'

Nina cringes.

'What is it?'

'That was the last of the hot water.'

I say nothing. I sit on the dip of the sofa that Lizzie has vacated and close my eyes tight for several minutes. When I open them, the girls have all tiptoed upstairs and the whirligig in the yard is tipping sideways with the clothes Lizzie has hung up.

After the girls are fed, again, I'm looking forward to a cup of tea in the bath now that the water has finally heated up again. Bob will put the girls to bed, a gesture he's made a few times recently as part of his ongoing apology tour for taking the petrol money. Then I remember what day it is. Friday. He gets his pay packet today. As a reward for his efforts this week, he's going to the pub after work, as per our new arrangement.

'Girls,' I call. 'Brush teeth and bed!'

'All of us?' Nina calls back. 'Or just Aisa?'

'All of you need to get ready for bed, but you big ones can read for a bit.'

I kiss them all goodnight and head back downstairs, flopping on the sofa. And then begins the review of the day – the mistakes, the regrets, the to-do list that has grown like the magic porridge pot. My mum, dropping off a book she seems to have bought from the library clear-out called *The Seven Habits of Highly Effective People*. It has a sticky note on it in her large writing, all capitals.

I THOUGHT THIS MIGHT BE HELPFUL TO YOU.

For a long time, she acted like I was nothing but a disappoint-ment – the once golden girl who could have gone on to A levels, maybe even university, and instead became a 'scullery maid'– so it's nice that I've been promoted to a disappointment who may yet have the potential to become highly effective.

I toss the book onto the pile of paperwork and bills I'm yet to deal with (even in a minimally effective way) and think of Lizzie. I was unfair to her earlier, cruel even. I know she'll still be awake up there, reading. I should go up to see her, give her a cuddle and apologise. She's eight, why would she think to put the washing out? Do I even want an eight-year-old – or any of the girls – to feel obliged to hang out washing? No. If I achieve nothing else as a mum, I want them to have higher hopes and expectations than me.

'Mummy?'

Aisa has crept back downstairs, her long-loved, straggly teddy under her arm and her nightie dragging on the floor, a hand-me-down from Jane that makes her look like a Victorian ghost.

'Are you OK, Ace?'

She shakes her head and then takes a running jump, landing on top of me. She wraps herself around me and I kiss the top of her head.

'I'm scared,' she says. 'But don't tell them.'

'Them?'

'Nina and Lizzie, they'll laugh at me.'

'Is it because of that film again?'

'If I say yes, you'll say we can't watch those films again and they'll blame me.'

I sigh, because she's right, I already don't want them watching those films again as this is the third time Aisa's got back up this week, and last week was no better. But I don't want this little weight off my lap. I don't want to lose these little arms around my neck. I know it won't be long before Aisa is as hands-off as the other two – or, even worse, I'm as hands-off with her as I am with the other two.

'Let's watch *Grease* together and then you can sleep in our bed just this once,' I whisper to her. 'But don't tell the others.'

49

AISA – 3:06 a.m.

Aisa looks at Lizzie's back. She's taller than Aisa, but hunched over a little, her body forming a question mark. Her hair is pulled back into a ponytail, a mousey brown that might have bits of blonde in, but it could just as easily be grey. Aisa wants to ask, 'Don't you care?' but she fears the question says more about herself than Lizzie.

But just look at her. She wouldn't hurt a fly. And yet, Lizzie was the last person seen with Nina earlier today, and the last person seen with Jane all those years ago. And let's not beat around the bush, Aisa thinks. Let's not bother to pretty up the thought, because it's not for external consumption anyway: she is weird. Lizzie is objectively different. And sometimes, that's enough.

Lizzie takes a step forward, and Aisa follows. This atrium area is a kind of L shape. The passageway running behind them, and then four doors in front. One of them is barely visible around a slight corner.

It's almost a mirror of the top floor of the house, but without the bathroom, loo and airing cupboard. They approach the first door.

'Open it,' she says, and Lizzie spins round to look at her.

'Me? OK, yes, OK.' She reaches out for the doorknob, twists it and pushes the door cautiously open. It's black inside, but when Lizzie sweeps the phone flashlight around, it's just a disused cupboard. Same as it was all those years ago.

Aisa exhales.

They stand in front of the next door. Aisa looks up at her sister for signs of … what? She's not really sure. Maybe signs that Lizzie has done something terrible, or that she plans to do something terrible.

Lizzie scrunches up her eyes, reaches forward to turn the knob, but Aisa stops her.

'Did you check down here when you woke up earlier and Nina was gone?' she says.

Lizzie frowns. 'No, you know I didn't.'

'So you just suddenly remembered that this whole layer existed?'

'You know I did. Same as you.'

'You never actually said that, you just ran off and then pointed to the light.'

'Don't you trust me?' Lizzie says quietly.

'I don't trust anyone.'

She wants to ask if Lizzie really left the grounds earlier. If she even went to look for Nina or just hid somewhere and watched Aisa return. But to do so crosses a line. It would either break Lizzie's heart or crack her veneer. And what might be behind that surface? What might have been behind there all this time, hidden just below but reliant on no one being interested enough to look?

Because what happened to Jane back then? And what happened to Nina tonight? And does anyone else know about this secret layer? If the mechanic knocks on the door, there's no chance the sisters will hear it down here. Rescue could have been and gone already, if it's even coming at all.

Lizzie seems to be waiting for her to say more, but instead Aisa reaches suddenly for the next doorknob and shoves it open. It's dark again and Lizzie switches her phone flashlight back on. She seems to know what she's looking for, has an air of ownership, as if this is her domain now.

It's a bigger room this time, more like the back bedrooms on the upper level. An old brass bed lies on its side without a mattress, a dry old water jug sits on a dusty side table and there's a tall wooden wardrobe shoved against the wall. A servant's room from long ago, perhaps.

'What was that?' Lizzie whispers, looking around.

'What?'

'A noise,' Lizzie says, pointing towards the wardrobe. 'I think it came from in there.'

'Open it then,' Aisa says, backing away slightly. She didn't hear anything. Nothing at all over the rush of her own blood through her ears.

In her hand, the candlestick feels heavy and slick with sweat, despite the cold. She lifts it slightly, holding its end in her other palm, readying herself. Is all of this a trick?

Lizzie approaches the wardrobe like she's walking to the gallows. A small brass key sticks out of one of the doors and she turns it, looking back at Aisa just once before pulling it open. Then the other door. Nothing. An empty wardrobe, no hangers, no clothes, nothing. Aisa breathes out in relief.

For a moment, nothing happens and then a small black shape flies out from underneath the wardrobe, zigzagging through the room. Aisa recoils, but Lizzie stands stock-still. 'It's a mouse,' she says, the corner of her lips twitching in a half smile.

The little body bashes into the bed frame and then slips behind it, out of view.

50

LIZZIE – 3:10 a.m.

'Oh my gosh,' Lizzie says with relief, her hand on her heart. 'Reepicheep the Mouse,' she says, 'from Narnia.' She smiles but Aisa doesn't return the sentiment. Chastened, Lizzie leads the way back out into the foyer.

'Come on,' Aisa says. 'Open the next door. Please?'

Impatience and fear are radiating off Aisa. Lizzie can hear her sister's breath, can tell from the way she's shuffling her feet on the stone floor that she's fed up. The glow that Lizzie warmed herself with earlier is fading. *Come on, get yourself together.*

Lizzie closes her eyes to collect herself, takes a deep breath and then opens the third door briskly. At first, she can't make anything out. It's just a squirming pile of darkness. But then her eyes adjust, and her flashlight catches them and she slams the door shut.

Spiders. So many spiders, crawling over a pile of charred logs and charcoal. Lizzie loves every single living creature, except them. She hates them in fact; she hates them so much and she can feel them on her. She pats herself down and shakes her hair, tears at her coat to pull it from her.

'There's nothing on you,' Aisa says crossly and louder than Lizzie would like. But she can still feel them on her skin, under her skin, in her ears. She can feel their webs around her throat, feel their evil lightness, barely there but there nonetheless as they move around inside her sleeves.

She throws her coat on the floor and then starts to pull at her jumper.

'Lizzie, get a grip! Jesus Christ!' Aisa grabs Lizzie's arms and pins them to her side. 'There's nothing on you,' she shouts, pushing Lizzie away in defeat and then picking up her coat. Aisa shakes it firmly, turns it inside out and shakes it again. 'Put this back on and pack this crap in.'

It takes all of Lizzie's effort to squeeze out the images, to accept what Aisa is saying and to keep her clothes on. She tentatively pushes her arms back into her coat sleeves and ignores the itching on her scalp.

'Sorry, Aisa, you know how I get.'

'Yeah,' Aisa says. 'I know. You wouldn't hurt a living thing, would you.' It feels more like a statement than a question, and a strange one at that.

And now they are standing outside the last door that Nina could be behind. This is the last chance before they accept that Nina really isn't here.

51

AISA – 3:12 a.m.

The final door. A black hole in her memory for all these years is suddenly filled in, rich with garish detail and alive with fear. She feels it like electricity across her back, her scalp. She has woken from nightmares on the cusp of pushing this door open, yet all the time she'd forgotten it was real. Can there be anything more frightening than realising that a bad dream was actually a memory, and then finding yourself back in it?

She and Nina had been together, playing hide-and-seek in the house. Lizzie and Jane had been somewhere else, they'd paired off as soon as Mum had brought them here. But they'd met back down here, by accident or design, she doesn't remember. And then the four of them had faced this door.

Aisa draws a deep breath, puffs her chest up and juts her jaw like she did thirty years ago, on this spot. When Jane asked who was brave enough to go through the door with her.

'What's in there?' eight-year-old Lizzie had asked, backing away slightly.

Jane had smiled, but not a nice smile. Not a menacing smile though, it was more … sad. Nina hadn't wanted to go in. She was already sweating in the enclosed foyer, already uneasy and making noises about leaving.

'One of you has to go in, fair's fair,' Jane said. It was classic kid logic. Because no one *had* to go in, why should they? But none of them said that.

They decided to draw straws. Where did they even get straws from? Nina had them, that's right. They used some candy cigarettes, warm from her pocket, the little card with a footballer on still inside the box. They each had great stacks of those little men back home, fought over them even though none of them followed football.

They fought over everything, Aisa and Nina loudly, but Lizzie through watery eyes and pleading to their mum. Which sister would go first on a swing or sit in the front seat of the car or choose the first Quality Street at Christmas. It drove their parents bonkers. So their dad had taught them about drawing straws. And they'd taken to it with such gusto, refusing to do anything without drawing straws, that *that* had driven their parents bonkers too. But that day, down here, it was still a novelty. One Jane had adopted as her own too.

Nina had passed the pack over and Jane had teased three candy cigarettes out. Three, not including herself, because Jane was going in regardless. Aisa had puffed up with pride. She, Aisa, was to draw a straw alongside her much older sisters and their friend, to do older girl stuff. Brave girl stuff.

Jane had snapped one of the candy cigarettes, the sudden violence of sound cracking through the dusty passageway, then turned her back to arrange them.

The sisters lined up as if preparing to take medicine, and then each pulled a candy cigarette straw.

Why didn't Aisa remember this earlier? Why didn't her memory plunge her back here as she'd pulled the broken match to go out on that wretched journey to the village. The outcome was the same: Aisa's small hand holding the short straw and her sisters immediately panicking and petitioning for a redo. And the fury, the outrage of that. 'No,' she'd said, her little voice ricocheting off the stones, 'I'm going in.'

'Why won't you ever back down?' her mum used to say, but a thread of affection ran through the complaint and always seemed to Aisa like tacit encouragement. So she wore it with pride, her bravery, her boneheadedness. She may be smaller, she may be younger, but she's braver than the other two put together. Brave to the point of recklessness, but there's a cost to everything.

And that day, nearly thirty years ago, she was damned if she was backing out. Even as her knees quivered beneath her shorts, as her heart banged so loudly she thought the others might hear, she still stood stiff next to Jane as the bigger girl put her hand on the doorknob. The same doorknob that juts vulgarly out at them in the dim light now.

Jane had paused for effect, and Aisa had watched her intently. But the pause had grown, and Jane had sagged a little, the moment trickling out of Aisa's grasp. 'Are you sure you want to go in, Aisa?' Jane had whispered. 'It's OK if you don't.'

But Aisa had protested. Of course she had. 'I want to go in.'

Behind her, Nina and Lizzie had been whispering about something and when Jane opened the door and Aisa followed her in, the older sisters had run off laughing. But Aisa stood her ground and stayed. She had stepped in, matching Jane's stride, ignoring the retreating footsteps behind her, the wild laughs.

Footsteps... Lizzie *had* run off. She wasn't lying about that. Aisa closes her eyes with relief. Lizzie wasn't lying, and she couldn't have done anything to Jane – she had fled and left Aisa with Jane. And she surely didn't do anything to Nina earlier tonight either. Of course she didn't.

Aisa turns to Lizzie now, haunted and pale in the light from her phone. She is limp, weak, watered down. She is good. She is kind. She is Lizzie.

'Lizzie,' Aisa says, nursing the return of that peculiar but reassuringly familiar mix of pity, irritation and affection that Lizzie always generated. 'Let me go in first, OK?'

Lizzie could never hide her reactions, and right now relief washes through her face. 'Are you sure?'

'I'm one hundred per cent sure.'

52

ROSEMARY – July 1992

The girls are with me at the manor again today and my nerves are on fire. I have spent nearly twenty years calmly keeping the cogs turning without so much as a squeak. Now, every sound I hear, I imagine it's them smashing something ancient or bursting into William's office. They've paired up and run off, Nina with Aisa and Lizzie trailing around after Jane. It was so much easier when we could still afford a childminder.

At least I can feed them a big lunch here. Since Cook had her win on the horses and quit, it's fallen to me to prepare meals when I'm here, and I know there's always more than will be consumed. Then I can just do buns for dinner. I wonder what it's like to not measure out your life in meals and money.

I'm hanging out the sheets, usually my favourite task. There's something incredibly satisfying about pushing dirty, smelly linen into a washing machine and pulling it out a few hours later with all human traces washed away. Hanging the washing out on a warm day, the air scented with the lashings of fabric conditioner I'd never use so liberally at home, the fabric fluttering gently in the breeze. But today, I'm distracted, watching as at least some of the girls leg it around the garden chaotically, voices a bit louder than I'd like. Then I hear the shot.

It's like in a film. The sound cracks through the sky, the birds flap up like they're on fire and in the corner of my eye, something thumps to the floor. I drop a sheet in the basket and scan the garden for a clue to what has just happened, reassurance that the girls are OK. My pulse beats in my ears and my eyes take nothing in.

'Nina!' I call, my voice sounding outside of myself in the panic. 'Aisa! Lizzie!' I see the blue of Lizzie's T-shirt first, then her legs sticking up from the ground like two chipolatas. I gasp and then I'm running, and Nina is running from somewhere else, and Aisa is running from behind a tree and I get there just as Jane, who was God knows where, is yanking Lizzie up by her arm, laughing.

'I panicked and fell over,' Lizzie says, blushing the colour of a phone box.

For a moment, I can't speak.

'Lunch in ten minutes, Jane,' I say, unable to look my own girls in the eye for reasons I genuinely don't understand. As I turn towards the house to start preparing tea, I slam into Alan's chest; two pheasants hang limp in his hand.

'What the f—'

'Rosemary, you can't keep bringing your girls here like this,' he says, looking to the side of me, struggling to make eye contact, even when we were teenagers.

'Excuse me?'

'It's not safe, Ro. I'm shooting rabbits and birds, and I'm not looking for little girls running about.'

'It's only occasional,' I say firmly, although the thought of what might have been is still stirring my guts with a spoon. 'So why don't you tell me when you're planning to go on a shooting spree and I'll keep them home.'

'It's not like that,' he says, his gentle voice more urgent than usual. 'I'm reacting, the shooting's not planned.'

'Don't react then,' I say, and I can see him suck in air to reply when the doorbell rings out from the house. I'm glad of a reason to storm off.

The man at the door is a bit older than me, as narrow and bent as a banana. He's wearing stiff clothes that must be boiling him, and giant sunglasses. He clears his throat but waits for me to talk, squinting behind his brown lenses.

'Can I help you?'

He's carrying a battered briefcase and I expect he's trying to sell something, but he might be here for William, who does occasionally get visitors, so I need to be polite. I look him up and down and my heart sinks as I realise that this strange creature could be yet another private detective. They're all shifty and they never find Selina, nor give William reassurance that she won't sneak back and swipe Jane.

'I'm, um, well, I was hoping ...' he dries up and looks at me desperately. His face looks familiar, but I can't place him.

'Are you here to see someone?' I prompt, peering round him to see if there's a company name on his car, but I don't see any vehicles. I am using what Bob refers to as my Hyacinth Bucket voice, something learned from the long-gone housekeeper whose footsteps I now walk in.

'Well, not a person, I'm here to see the house. If I may?'

'The house?' I look behind me, heart cantering suddenly. Is William selling the house? But no, I remember, he's not allowed.

He wipes his forehead with a very bright white handkerchief, stuffs it back in his pocket and scrunches up his eyes. 'I'm sorry,' he says, 'I'm not explaining myself well.'

'Would you like to come inside and have a glass of water?'

'Thank you, I've had a long walk.'

'You walked here?'

The man nods, looking embarrassed, but I can hardly judge him, I was on foot twice last week and have the blisters to show for it.

William was absolutely adamant he wasn't to be disturbed today, so I quietly encourage the man into the library, where no one goes anymore. When William first moved back, he and Selina stocked these shelves together. Removing most of the traces of the Brigadier's collection and filling it with their own. It was the happiest I ever saw them, even though they must have been filled with dread about their new lives. I think they used the books as a kind of language to each other, choosing titles and holding them up and laughing, or smiling while I slid a tray of tea and coffee in and asked a few inane questions. I've never been much of a reader.

William had long stopped claiming to be a writer by then, but he still made noises about being a reader. As far as I know, he hasn't picked up a single book since the separation. I could probably get away with not dusting them at all, but I will. I always will.

Once through the door, the man swallows so hard that I hear it through his throat, and grinds to a halt in the centre of the room.

'Take a seat, I'll get you that drink.'

In the kitchen, I peer through the windows as I run the tap, but I can't see the girls now. I tiptoe past the office, but the door is open, the room empty. At the foot of the stairs, I can hear William moving around upstairs. As I slip back into the library, the man shoves a book back onto the shelves and gratefully takes the glass.

I wait for him to drain it and then he hands it back, his

sunglasses now pushed up through his hair and his darting eyes more visible.

'Thank you,' he says, 'that was very kind. I was flustered and ... it's taken a lot to come here.'

'Are you here to see the master of the house?' I ask.

'The Brigadier?' He stands up straight and looks around as if expecting him to walk in.

'The Brigadier died, I'm afraid, a few years ago now.'

'He did? And his wife?'

'Her too.'

He smiles, then immediately covers his mouth. 'I'm sorry. I'm very sorry.'

I look at him closely. 'Don't be,' I say. 'You stayed here didn't you? I thought I recognised you.'

'Rosie?'

'Close,' I say. 'Rosemary.'

He looks at me with pity now. At least he got out.

'You haven't changed,' he says and we both smile awkwardly, because he has changed beyond recognition and I should have. I should have moved on long ago. 'I've come to make peace with it,' he says, then takes a long gulp of water. 'It's bigger, in my memories. It's ...' He grapples for the word, his sad face suddenly screwing in on itself and turning red. 'It's worse,' he says, 'in my head.'

'I'm sorry, I don't remember your name, I think you were here when I was really new.'

He starts to pace, one finger tracing the titles, frowning as he clatters into the edge of the shelves like a daddy-long-legs.

'It's Daniel. Daniel Pettyweather.'

Daniel. Those eyes. I see them now, see him, as he once was. A timid boy who struggled to keep up with the physical demands of the work. I remember seeing two others helping him, and them getting in trouble too. *He won't learn. He won't grow strong.* And I remember the three of them going for Reflection. Slipping in each other's wake like minnows.

It was worse, Bob told me, for the last one in line. He'd have to watch it twice before it was his turn. But I don't want to think about that. I never want to think about that.

'Is this a … normal house now?'

I nod. 'No boys,' I say gently. I know the memories are painful and these men need handling softly. 'Those days are long gone.'

The door opens and Alan comes in, looking at the man as if I'm not here. 'I think you need to go,' he says, and then they face each other and flinch. Were they here at the same time? It's too hazy to remember the specifics, and William had all the records burned when he first moved in.

Alan is a foot taller than Daniel, who shrinks away and looks at me for help.

'It took a lot to come here,' he says to me. 'I just wanted to see it. I don't want any trouble.'

'You'll get no trouble,' Alan says softly. 'But it's time to go.'

53

LIZZIE – 3:14 a.m.

Nothing happens.

The door doesn't budge.

Aisa's arm falls back to her side.

Lizzie can hear her own heartbeat roaring in her ears and exhales more breath than she thought possible. 'She can't have gone in there if it's locked,' she says, only briefly relieved. Because if Nina's not down here, where is she?

Aisa says nothing. Not even the F-word. Then she grabs the door handle again, as if sneaking up on her prey, and twists it urgently, shoving the door with her shoulder.

Nothing.

She sags then, but starts feeling around the door, growing more frenzied as she moves. 'Lizzie, light,' she snaps, and for a moment, Lizzie doesn't understand, but then she holds her phone up, following Aisa's movements with the beam. 'Look,' Aisa says, nudging Lizzie's hand up higher so the phone light picks up the detail of a heavy metal bolt across the top of the thick door. A detail the dim bulb lights did not reach.

'Shouldn't we—' Lizzie starts, but it's too late. Aisa has drawn it back and twisted the doorknob again and this time it opens with a creak.

Aisa pushes the door and makes to step in, but stops suddenly and takes a big gulp of air. 'It looks the same,' she whispers.

Lizzie puts a hand on Aisa's shoulder, but she shakes it off and steps inside. Lizzie follows, cautiously, with the phone held aloft, but it's not totally dark in here. A few more of the bulbs are strung along the wall and she can see and hear how they're powered now – a generator buzzes softly in the gloom.

This is not an empty room, it's filled with bric-a-brac, as if someone had scraped all the left-behind mess from over the years and chucked it here to be dealt with later. A couple of wooden chairs that she remembers belonging to a full set in the dining room. Old gardening equipment, a big watering can, a length of hose. There's a sickly sweetness in the air. Rot?

The door closes behind them and Lizzie rushes to it, props it open with an old paint can. The bolt ... If that fell across, they'd be screwed. Why would there be a bolt on the outside, anyway?

'It doesn't look like anyone is here,' Lizzie whispers.

Where on earth is Nina?

They stand still in the centre of the room as their eyes adjust, and the shadows take shape. There is another source of grey light, which makes Lizzie jump. It's a boxy old TV on a trolley, with a video player underneath, the kind they'd wheel in at school to show an old Disney film on the last day of term. A cord runs from it to the generator and the screen is on, flickering but soundless. Who was watching it? Aisa looks at her, but she has no answers, and she returns her eyes to the walls.

When Lizzie looks closer, she realises with a jolt that there is a pale picture on the screen, it's not just a grey blur. She's looking at the very passageway they just walked down. Then the screen jumps, changes, and now it's the foyer they were just in, with the doors they just tried.

'Aisa, look.' Lizzie points at the screen. 'Just watch.'

Aisa squats down in front of the TV and her mouth drops open. She looks up at Lizzie, who nods frantically, and then back to the screen again.

They watch, transfixed, as it jumps from one scene to the next. Living room. Library. Dining room. Office. Kitchen. The outside of the house now, the untidy once-lawn and the scrubby drive. Now the back, the old shed and the old door to the kitchen.

Someone was watching them? A security guard? Why wouldn't they come and speak to them? Help them?

She hears something behind her and turns to look, startled. There is still no one there. But by the back wall, there are more signs of someone. The someone who must have set this monitor up. The someone who must have watched them come in. The someone who... who hurt Nina?

There's an old-fashioned camp bed on the floor, a blanket on it. They both stare at the same time, squinting to make out the shape. Because it's not just a blanket, it's not limp, it's bulging. It's...

Aisa is running over and tearing back the fabric before Lizzie can stop her.

'There's someone there!'

54

ROSEMARY – July 1992

I rush to open the front door, dumbstruck by Alan's never-before-seen strictness. A gentle giant, I've always called him. 'A woolly woofter,' says Bob, though I know he cares for him deeply and would do anything for him. But I wouldn't cross Alan right now. His eyes fix on the man, his spine straightened to its full height so he fills up the hallway like a T. rex.

'OK,' Daniel says, looking between Alan and the open door. 'I just wanted to—'

'Daniel?'

We all turn and stare up the stairs, where William stands at the top, gripping the banister tightly.

'William?' Daniel says finally. '*You're* here?'

'I am,' William says, 'for my sins.' He takes a few steps down. 'Are you leaving already?'

Daniel looks at Alan, and then back at William, who nods.

'I see.'

Alan's cheeks flush and he stoops again, reduced back to his usual shape. 'I thought it was best...' He grinds to a halt.

'No matter,' William says, taking the rest of the stairs slowly. He pats Alan on the arm, who then scurries away without another word. 'He is very protective,' William says, 'don't mind him.'

William and Daniel stare at one another for a moment, their eyes glassy and wide.

'Rosemary,' William says, without breaking Daniel's gaze. 'We'll take tea in the front room, please. Or coffee?'

Daniel swallows again, a noisy, ragged journey up and down his neck. 'Tea,' he croaks. 'Please.'

The tray clatters as I carry it through to the living room. William is sitting on one sofa and Daniel on the other. He has taken his suit jacket off and folded it next to him, but his face still looks like boiled ham.

I was due to polish this afternoon, so I'm conscious of the fine dust beginning to tide at the edges of the room. I don't know if William ever notices such things, or if he ever comes in here. He just seems to bob between his office, the kitchen and his and Jane's bedrooms. It's not like at our house, where there's always some or all of us jammed on the sofa, arguing over what to watch and who has to get up to change the channel. Our front door opens directly onto the living room, the stairs run up the wall and it's the only route through to the kitchen. 'It's like Piccadilly Circus in here,' Bob says at least once a week, even though he's never been to London in his life.

'Can I help with that, Rosemary?' William says sharply and I realise I'm just standing in the doorway like a lemon.

I snap to and shake my head, carrying the tray to the coffee table and placing it carefully.

'Shall I pour?' I ask, but William waves me away.

I pull the door closed behind me but stay where I am, ear to the wood, trying to shut out all the other noises in the world. I don't know what I'm expecting. There are no voices coming through the door and I'm about to walk away, assuming the wood is too thick, when I hear Daniel speak.

'I heard your parents are dead,' he says, and my eyebrows shoot up to my hairline. As opening gambits go, this one is bold.

'Thankfully so,' William answers.

I walk away, my nerves failing me.

Half an hour later, William and Daniel appear in the kitchen, where I'm sorting through the larder and making a list. Daniel pokes his head into the room and mutters something about having bread and milk in here. 'Sometimes that was all,' he added. 'All day, I mean.'

'I know,' William says.

'Until you came back, anyway.'

They go out into the hall and hesitate. I watch from the doorway of the larder as William soothes Daniel in a low, quiet voice. After a minute or so, William asks, 'Would you like to see…' but I can't make out what he says and Daniel is shaking his head emphatically.

'Everywhere else,' he says.

I hear them mount the stairs, a stilted pattern of sounds as if they're stopping to catch a breath every few steps.

When Daniel finally leaves a little later, William marches into his office and I hear the bolt slide across. I make a strong coffee, put a biscuit on a plate and knock on the office door.

'Yes?'

'It's me,' I say, uneasily. 'Can I come in?'

I wait, about to give up when I finally hear the squeak of the chair, his footsteps and the bolt.

The door opens suddenly inward.

'Coffee,' I say, and push past him before he can protest. He needs it, I know he does. I put it carefully on the desk, not touching any of the paperwork – bills and something about stocks and shares, as far as I can see. I don't see anything about Selina, but I know it's there somewhere. The latest pointless report.

He's been crying, there's no mistaking it. His eyes are fringed in purple and his nose is runny.

'And a biscuit,' I say, placing a hand on his arm just briefly as I put the little plate down. The touch feels unnatural and I look away, a sudden rush of guilt and embarrassment. It's been so many years.

'He was one of the boys then,' I say, although I know. 'I vaguely remember him.'

'You would have been very young,' he says.

'So were you,' I say. And for a moment, I wonder if we're still talking about Daniel. 'He'd come back to—'

'Make peace with his memories,' he says, his voice thick. 'No one believed him, he said, so he started to think he'd imagined it.'

'That would drive me mad,' I say. 'Knowing things had happened and no one believing me or not being able to tell anyone.'

'Well, yes,' he says, and I regret crossing that line. I don't hold it against him for ending a summer fling all those years ago. If anything, I'm cross with myself for giving it so much credence.

'Do you think it helped him?'

'What?' he says, throwing back some coffee as if it was a shot of whisky.

'Coming here—'

'No, God no,' he says. 'That didn't help any of them, did it.'

I shrink at his expression. 'Sorry,' I say quietly. 'I meant, coming back here now. Proving to himself it all existed.'

'I don't know; it looks different now, and my parents are

long gone. The worst of it, the Reflection stuff, that's not there anymore is it.' It wasn't a question, but I shake my head anyway, the back of my neck prickling at the thought. 'At least I could tell him he didn't imagine it, though,' William says. 'But he seemed quite surprised that I'd come back here.'

He wasn't the only one, I think, but I say nothing.

'Rosemary,' he says quietly, putting his coffee cup back down. 'I really did try to help them.'

How? How exactly did running away to London help them?

'I should crack on,' I say, stepping away and closing the door behind me.

Back in the hall, I press myself flat to the wall, eyes closed, and catch my breath. I don't want to hear it. It's not my job to absolve him and his family.

I think about Daniel. About how old he must have been when he arrived. They were supposed to be sixteen, but some of them lied, hearing there was a place that would take them in no questions – or very few questions – asked. I was sixteen when I first arrived; it's easy to spot the gradients of your own age. A few of them would definitely not have been sold fags.

It must have felt like a sanctuary at first. Free food and lodging. Just a bit of labour to pay their way. Tops off in summer, roasting themselves golden as they trimmed hedges and picked fruit. Huddled in winter, sharing a jar, boys in a barracks. The mandatory lessons from the Brigadier might have sounded curious, but just something to roll their eyes through. Same for the benign-sounding consequences when expectations of behaviour weren't met. Thinking about what you've done. Growth through reflection. God knows where he picked this stuff up, as he was certainly not a certified psychiatrist.

These were boys with nowhere else to go, boys who clung to

one another and tried to make it work, this last resort. But one by one, they all cracked. All except Alan, who outlasted everyone.

I am suddenly acutely aware of my girls. Of their soft little bodies. Their trusting brains, their open hearts. Of them here, in this house, swallowed up by what looks, at first, like a benevolent beast but can turn itself into a malicious monster. I want them with me. I think again of school holidays spent with them rather than *coping* with them, of paddling in the sea and sitting at the table helping them do art, or taking Lizzie to the zoo. One day, I tell myself, for what must be the thousandth time.

One day I'll give them everything they deserve. But right now, I want them in our little car, driving away. I don't want them treading on the same stones that poor Daniel trod. The same stones that my Bob once trod. Briefly, but enough to create ripples that we all still live with. God, I want to get away from here. Where the hell are the girls?

55

NINA – 3:10 a.m.

Nina wakes up with a start. Is that a voice? Maybe even voices? They sound far away, maybe even imagined.

And where am I? Why am I in pain?

Nina blinks, sits up a little more and waits for the dizziness to settle again. It's gloomy in here, wherever she is, but not pitch black. Bulbs dot the walls, casting a thin yellow light. There's no one else in here, that's clear. *Wherever here is.*

Gingerly, she tests her arms, her hands, tensing and turning them until they click. She's very sore, but nothing is broken there. Her back feels unbearably tender, as if she's been punched and kicked all over it, but her spine allows her to sit up, to twist around. She swallows, readying herself. She leans over, at the cost of her aching spine, and feels all the way down her left leg. It feels bruised in spots, but nothing is sticking out or broken. And now the other. Even before she reaches her ankle, it's screaming in pain. It hurt before she passed out, or fell asleep, or whatever, she remembers that, but not the how or the why.

It's dark here, no light, no windows, no fire. She's alone, she can tell. Alone, with a busted ankle and bruises all over her and a brain that feels like a battered pea rolling around her skull.

Nausea sweeps over her and she lies back down, then rolls onto her side and throws up over the side of her...whatever this is. A camping bed. Wet chunks of birthday cake land on the floor. When she's done, she feels better but more scared.

She has no idea how much time has passed or what happened. Her thoughts are scrambled and her memory is fuzzy. The car broke down...and she was looking around a house. A cold and empty place. Is she still in it? Did she hit her head? But she's on a bed, she didn't hit her head on a bed and then cover herself with a blanket, which she can feel slipping around as she moves.

Someone.

Someone else did it.

Someone else did all of it.

A shiver runs up her bruised body and chatters her teeth. It's dark in here, dimly lit by a few old-fashioned bulbs and the distant grey glow of some kind of screen in a far corner. No windows. The camp bed she's on is the old type, a metal frame, an austere piece of stretched canvas held in place with serious looking hooks. Her eyes adjust, and despite the distracting pain, she can see more now. No windows, one door. Her chest tightens. A tall ceiling, with old hooks hanging from it.

She eases herself to sitting and tries to remember what happened. Her sisters were with her. Did they put her to bed? Did they...did they leave her? Did she leave them? Something stirs. She left...one of them. They were in a room, weren't they, she and Lizzie in front of a fire. Lizzie was sleeping and Aisa had gone for help. That's right, and Nina came up to look for...She remembers that bathroom. A hood. Eyes. Oh fuck!

Nina doesn't know what to do. Nina always knows what to do, but not now. Her sisters are in danger, maybe already hurt

234

by the person who hurt her. She's the oldest sister, *in loco parentis*, the buck stops with her. Just like it did in the delivery suite, when she made a catastrophic error with her last delivery. And now she's out of ideas again. And she's scared. And she's in a ton of pain.

For the briefest of moments, she wants her mum and dad. She'd wanted them back then too, hadn't she, when she was far younger? That day. That last day, when they came here while their mum worked and she was in charge of Aisa. And of course Aisa wanted to play hide-and-seek, she always did. But she'd hidden too well, for too long, and it hadn't felt like a game.

And where are her sisters now? Aisa was out in the storm, traipsing around in the dark, did she come back? And Lizzie was asleep in front of the fire. Asleep and vulnerable. Oh God, what the hell has happened?

She hears a noise. Footsteps outside. Whoever put her here, whoever scraped her off the floor of the bathroom, is back. Fuck. She lies back down and pulls the blanket over her head and tries to stay still.

The door opens with a crack. Two people come inside. She can tell from the footsteps, and the whispering. The whispers sound female, but she has her arms over her ears, her head muffled by a blanket. And female doesn't necessarily mean safe. She knows that, though she hates to admit it.

If these are the people that put her here, they know full well where she is anyway. But they might believe that she's still sleeping. Still knocked out. Maybe they think she's dead?

More whispering. She strains to hear, catching only wisps. It sounds like someone said, 'It doesn't look like anyone is here.'

But I am here. You put me here. Unless...?

Still she stays quiet, motionless. It could be a trap.

More whispering, almost audible but not enough. She swallows, hears footsteps coming closer.

'There's someone there!'

Is that Aisa?

Before she can react, the blanket is pulled back from over her and she scrunches her eyes up in fear and balls up her fists protectively.

'Nina!'

'Oh, thank God it's you,' Nina says, sitting up and immediately reaching for her aching head, eyes filling with a sudden shock of tears. Aisa sits down next to her, rocking the camping bed and then wrapping her skinny arms around her. Nina's bruises hurt so much under the pressure that she feels on the brink of vomiting again, but she doesn't want to stop her little sister. 'Aisa,' she manages.

Lizzie rushes over. 'Thank goodness, Nina,' she says.

'What the hell happened to you?' Aisa says as she kisses Nina's face, just like she did as a little girl. 'You smell of vom.'

'I think someone hit me,' Nina says slowly, the words feeling misshapen in her mouth. 'And then I woke up here. And I was sick, be careful where you tread.'

'We need to get out of here,' Aisa says. 'Can you walk?'

'I don't know.'

Her own voice sounds odd, as if she's speaking through water, or she's drunk. Seeing her sisters has rooted her to the spot, a wave of exhaustion following in the slipstream of relief. They need to get out, they have to get away, but she really wants to fall back asleep.

'Come on,' Aisa's voice is insistent now as she and Lizzie help Nina to stand. There is a searing pain in her ankle, not to mention her back and head.

They start to shuffle through the room towards the door, pain pulsing with every step. As they pass a damaged section of wall, Aisa flinches and stops for a moment. 'I was looking in the wrong place,' she mumbles.

'What are you looking at?' Nina mumbles, but then she catches sight of the boxy old television screen in front of her. 'Oh God, look.'

56

ROSEMARY – July 1992

As I comb the house for the children, I whisper the prayer my mother used to say with me when she was putting me to bed. It probably doesn't sound that comforting, what with the clanger dropped in line four, and I don't think it's even a proper prayer, but a bastardisation of something she heard on TV. But it's comforting to me. She even said it the night my dad died, her voice catching in a way she's not allowed it to since.

Watch over us, watch over us.
Tuck us safe to bed.
Watch over us, watch over us.
'Til we're all long dead.

Although if there is someone watching over us, he or she has really dropped the ball. I don't lie safely in bed at night, I lie there listening out for signs that the landlord has come good on his threats and is going to turf us out. Or that our car is being towed away. Or I lie there and imagine how things could be. I walk myself through a day in my perfect imagined life, from the moment of waking until falling asleep. The breakfast we would eat, the house we would have – a room for each of the girls – the way I would fill my time and theirs if it was up to me. Sometimes, this is a comfort. Other times, more often, it feels so far removed from my real life that it becomes a self-flagellating whip in my hand. I don't want much, that's the saddest part of it. I don't want much and it's mostly for them, but it's still out of reach.

I check the front room, leaving the tea tray at first, but then think better of it and gather it all sloppily. The still-full pot weaves around and knocks over the milk jug and the drips beat onto the floor as I rush into the kitchen. I slide it all onto the sideboard, making even more of a mess. This is not like me. Bob jokingly calls me Cool Hand Luke because I can hold a hundred things in my hands at once, and often have Aisa climbing up me at the same time. Although I don't think Bob has seen *Cool Hand Luke*.

I check the larder in case the kids are on some kind of food raid, but they're not here. I pause and breathe, in and out as slow as I can manage. There is no need to worry, they're just playing and having fun.

They're not in the library either, where Selina's books lie accusingly on shelves, no longer read. I rush upstairs, listening for signs of life but hearing none. Aisa is obsessed with hide-and-seek at the moment and the disused bedrooms at the back are full of ideal crawl spaces, but she's not here. None of them are. Nor in the bathroom.

Alan's room on the corner is next and I wince as I open it – expecting to find a dead raven in his bed or something – but there's nothing here. No sign of the kids. Nothing weird either, and no real sign that he ever sleeps here. Bob told me that he still sleeps in his clothes, in case he has to leave in a hurry. He's been here for years, longer than me, and he is absolutely, almost frighteningly dedicated to William and this place, but he's still expecting to run. I can believe it, there's nothing here that couldn't be scooped into a rucksack in less than a minute. Poor Alan.

They're not in the linen cupboard, so I rush on to Jane's room, which is the obvious place really. It was once William's room, from childhood through to his early twenties. He had the same bed that Jane has now, the same bookshelves were then loaded with hardbacks and poetry books, which were eventually absorbed into the library. Even in my panic, my mind conjures up a memory of William and me walking around the woodland behind the house, him quoting Wordsworth as I swooned. Idiot.

The girls aren't here, but I can see the detritus of their earlier games, which reassures me a little. Jane and Lizzie ran straight up here when we first arrived, and the doll's house has been pulled out into the middle of the room, so they must have played with that for a while. Alan did a good job on it, the delicate attention to detail brings a lump to my throat. It is a perfect replica of the place he loves, despite no evidence it has ever loved him back.

The curtains in each window are the correct colours, made from scraps of fabric we scratched together that were pinned up carefully by his giant fingers. I tease the windows open to look closer and gasp as a tiny skull rolls out. What the bloody hell?

'Lizzie!' I shout, standing up and running back out of the room. 'Nina! Aisa!' William must be able to hear me. For years, I have perfected the silent creep-around, but now I don't care. I rush down the stairs and out the front door, listening for their voices as I stand in the middle of the gravel turning circle, fighting nausea. I should have found them by now.

'What's wrong?' Alan says, appearing from the side of the house.

'Have you seen the girls?'

'Your girls?'

'Yes, my girls, not that little weirdo, Jane,' I say, before I can stop myself, the image of the skull rolling around my mind.

Alan flinches as if I'd slapped him. 'Don't say that,' he says quietly. 'She's not had it easy. Neither of them have.'

'No, I know, I'm sorry. You know I love Jane to bits, but have you seen the kids or not?' I say and he shakes his head.

As I rush off, he calls after me, 'I'll look too.'

57

AISA – 3:17 a.m.

'What?' Aisa asks, punch-drunk from relief that Nina is alive but nauseous with fear knowing someone really did attack her and drag her here.

And this room... it *is* the one she saw all those years ago. Those were not nightmares, they were memories.

It was just her and Jane then. Jane was Lizzie's best and only friend. Aisa knew her too, but they had never been alone together. Yet she followed Jane into this room. She trusted her.

In her memory, the wall was dead ahead when she first entered the room, which would make it the back wall that Nina's camp bed was pushed up to, but now she knows why she had it twisted. Thirty odd years ago, she'd actually walked in sideways, crab-like, with one ear to the door, listening as her sisters legged it and left her. So she was facing the side wall, Jane to her left, tugging her in further.

'I was the one who found them,' Jane had said proudly, the excitement rattling her breath a little. She'd grabbed Aisa's hand then, her palm unfamiliar after holding her sisters' hands, like wearing someone else's shoes. 'No one else knows,' Jane had whispered.

The room was full of junk then too, Aisa thinks, and there

were some tools on the floor near the gap. A tiny little shovel, and a blunt knife like you'd use to ice a cake. A small pile of stones had been stacked neatly.

'I've been coming down here while Daddy works upstairs,' Jane said. 'On the days your mum isn't working.'

Aisa hadn't known what to say. She had stared and stared at the gap in the stones, trying to understand what she was looking at.

'I have to be really careful,' Jane continued, her hand growing damper against Aisa's own. 'I can't let it just… fall out.'

'Let what fall out?'

'Look closer,' Jane said.

And Aisa had. Pulling her hand from Jane's and stepping closer to the wall, pressing her nose to the cool black gap between the stones and squinting.

'Fucking look!' Nina's voice cuts through Aisa's memory, snapping her back to the present so fast she feels sick.

Nina is leaning on both of them for support, pointing at the boxy old TV.

'Oh shit, it's gone.'

The screen shows the empty living room where they'd set up camp hours ago. It's barely visible, more snow than detail, but they can make out the sofas where they'd spent their time earlier.

'Was someone watching me sleep earlier?' Lizzie says.

Nina shrugs, her voice slurs with exhaustion. 'Probably. Keep looking.' Lizzie and Aisa stare at the screen.

'What are we looking for?' Aisa asks.

'I thought I saw someone.'

'The one who hit you?' Lizzie whispers.

'I don't know,' says Nina, her voice smaller than usual. 'I need to know. We need to know so we can work out what to do.'

They stand in silence, Nina's weight dragging the side of

Aisa's body down, all their faces glowing like black-and-white photos in the silvery-grey light of the screen. The screen seems to change more slowly now they're watching intently. Showing the empty hallway for an age and now the library, lounge, office and dining room. Now the kitchen, the big disused fridge looming uselessly in shot. Time ticks, but still they stay. Watching the screen change to show a bedroom. The big empty one, scraped clean of any traces of the past.

Still they wait, Lizzie clearly itching to get out, fidgeting on the other side of Nina. 'We're not safe here. We really should—' But as the shot changes again, Aisa sees what Nina must have seen. In the middle of the screen, now showing Jane's bedroom, a figure sits on the bed. A small doll in their hands, the doll's house on the floor and something on the bed by their leg. Their face obscured by a hood. They stare, each trying to recognise, trying to make out the details.

'Is that a fucking gun?'

The camera cuts away.

58

ROSEMARY – July 1992

I've checked the whole house through. Well, everywhere except William's office, but he's sealed in there like an iron lung, there's no one getting in or out. My head swims, when did I last see them? Lunchtime, or … Yes, Aisa snuck up on me when I was stretching to reach something in the larder. I snapped at her. My baby.

Nina can't have been far behind because Aisa said she was going back to her. But maybe … I told them not to roam too far, but it's all relative. At home, 'not too far' is the patch of green opposite the house that all the neighbourhood kids play on. Not too far here is … the horizon?

I go out the front first, check they're not waiting by the car. Wishful thinking, there's no one there. I check the old fountain – Aisa is small and silly enough to have climbed into it – but it's just full of rainwater and a faint trace of green slime.

The trees mask the driveway, so I pace down it a little way, but I don't think they would have come here, there's nothing but miles of fields this way, it would take them hours to walk home.

These trees must be centuries old. They've barely grown in the twenty years since I first gaped up at them, yet they're hundreds of feet high. I wonder, just briefly, if Daniel paused to look up at them. I wonder how far he's walked since he left. If he ran as fast as he could to get away, or collapsed against the pillars of the gate, catching his breath or vomiting. Did he see the girls?

A thought punches me in the stomach, but I talk myself down almost immediately. He couldn't fight his way out of a wet paper bag and my girls aren't stupid, they'd not go off with someone like that. He doesn't even have a car to bundle them into. Still, I can't shake this ominous feeling.

I wonder if Bob would remember Daniel. Maybe there's more to him than his frailty suggests.

I peer around the right-hand side of the house, fringed by blackberry bushes that would take the whole place over if they were allowed. Alan hacks them down every autumn, and they climb back more aggressively than ever, thriving on their own destruction.

No one is there.

I cross in front of the house again, peering in the windows just in case, but it's dead inside. I skirt the left-hand edge of the building, brushing against its cool red stone as I go. I stop still and scan the grounds, squinting as if that will help me see through the trees that pepper the garden and then take over the land behind. I don't see anyone.

At the back of the house, the greenhouse is empty of people, full of tomato plants and bags of iron-rich soil that smell like blood.

I stop and listen, hoping that Aisa's loud laugh will ring out, but there's nothing, a void. Even the wind is still.

'Nina?' I call, gently at first. 'Aisa? Lizzie?'

Nothing.

'Nina!' I shout now, a Plimsoll line of panic reached, a point of no return. 'Nina! Where are you?'

I feel sick. How can all three of them – no, all four of them

– be gone. I imagine telling William that Jane has gone too. The thing he's spent years panicking about, building a bunker around her and refusing to let her live out in the world. Only for her to leave him just like Selina did.

I rush towards Alan's tent, the flaps still staked open like a smiling mouth. I can see already that there's no one there, but I have to check. I know Alan, I care for Alan, but sometimes it's the quiet ones. And he's troubled – the gods can strike me down for saying this, but all those boys were troubled. You never really know how trouble will re-emerge later on.

I poke my head inside. It smells of his sweat. There's an earthiness in my mouth, like I'm tasting him. He's been sleeping out here, a jug of water and a flannel sits in the corner, a pile of clothes neatly folded next to it. That old book he carries around, the one he used to read for comfort when I first met him. *The Coral Island.* I'm looking for … I don't know what I'm looking for. I don't want to admit it to myself. Evidence of something bad. But there is nothing here that is not his. No clothes, no shoes, no signs of – as they say in the paper – a struggle.

I crawl back out and collide with something hot and warm. As I cry out in surprise, it says, 'What are you doing in my tent?'

I stand up with a start. 'I'm still looking for the girls,' I say, 'have you seen them?'

'No, I looked everywhere but…' he stops. 'Why would they be in here?'

'Hide-and-seek,' I say, aware that I'm blushing.

'This isn't a good place for children,' Alan says, his voice almost lost to the warm air.

'That doesn't help,' I say. 'And you were a child when you first came. As good as.'

He says nothing.

It was a cruel thing to say, and it doesn't undo his point. It wasn't a good place for him either. I've pieced together scraps from what he, William and Bob have variously said. Alan *was* a child – fifteen – running from home and pretending to be much older. He'd been in trouble with the police, I never knew what for, but Bob does. He was supposed to go to a borstal – a real one – only he got away. And he's been hiding ever since.

His big size was misleading, but as soon as he opened his mouth it must have been obvious he was underage. Still, they invited him in. He worked harder than anyone, but he still messed up. Got in trouble, was punished, but begged to be allowed to stay.

He was made to sleep outside, but he liked it so much that it wasn't a punishment and was moved to isolation somewhere else. Somewhere dark and frightening. When William came back after university, only twenty-one himself, he begged his father not to do that to Alan. Not to do it to any of the boys. Several times, he rescued him and brought him back out to his tent. But then William left, and the others did too. But still Alan stayed.

'I'm sorry,' I say, as he snatches up the book and hugs it like a baby. 'I just need to find them.'

59

LIZZIE – 3:21 a.m.

'We need to go,' Aisa says, tugging Lizzie's coat.

The paint can is still propped in the doorway and a small breeze slips in from the passageway and nips at Lizzie's skin. She pokes her head out, just quickly, but no one is there. Whoever was sitting on the bed is still there. Or at least, not down here. Yet.

'Will you be able to walk with our help?' Lizzie asks Nina, who nods, no longer arguing.

It's disorientating to see Nina like this. She's always been so strong and capable. Always the older sister who Lizzie was happy to hide behind. And even though Nina clashed with their mother so much as a teenager, rolled her eyes behind her back, tried to rally the sisters to gang up on her, Nina looks so like her that perhaps Lizzie was happy to let her act like a surrogate parent when Rosemary wasn't around. Same fair hair, same strength, same sharp nose and full-lipped smile. Nina was *almost*. Almost Mum. Almost enough. Until there was no Mum and no one could take that place.

'We shouldn't just rush out there though,' Lizzie says, finding that she has more of a voice now Nina is so quiet. 'They could be on their way down here, we should let the camera do a sweep again and check.'

'Fuck that,' Aisa says, casting a look behind her at the wall. 'We just need to go.'

'Lizzie's right,' Nina says, her voice wavy and depleted. 'I'm not in any fit state to leg it if we cross paths.'

'Fine,' Aisa says, and Lizzie tries to hide the pride flushing through her despite everything.

Even though there is an armed gunman upstairs, sitting in wait on the old brass bed. Even though they're stuck here in a deadly situation. Even though someone clobbered her sister and dragged her into, effectively, a dungeon, Lizzie is still *thinking*. She is still breathing. Still putting one trembling foot in front of the other. Still speaking up and being *right*.

You can keep being you through anything, she realises. *You can stay awake through any nightmare.* It's a thought she files away for the future.

'Let's watch it through one more time,' Lizzie says, 'and check they're not on their way to us. Then we can go.'

60

NINA – 3:26 a.m.

They stare at the screen, huddling together like they used to when they watched horror films as kids. Only this time Lizzie and Aisa are flanking Nina, where it used to be Aisa in the middle, pretending she wasn't scared.

'I don't even know how you two found me,' Nina says, keeping her eyes on the screen. 'Or how I got in here.'

Aisa pulls away slightly and looks at her, head cocked to one side in a way that is so reminiscent of their mum. 'We found you 'cos we both remembered... stuff. Remembered that this was down here and we'd looked everywhere else.'

'You searched the whole house and... and it was empty?'

'Yes,' says Lizzie. 'We looked everywhere.'

'And then we came down here,' says Aisa. 'And this room was the last place we tried.'

'So that person up there—'

'Was either hiding or had gone away and come back, yeah.'

She thinks of the hood and the eyes. Who is it? Why are they still here?

'Maybe they wanted to pick us off one by one,' Nina says.

'We have to stay together,' Lizzie says.

Their eyes fix on the screen again. The image flicks to the empty kitchen.

'Was this door locked?' Nina asks.

Aisa nods. 'Bolt,' she says. 'On the outside, obviously.'

'Jesus, we need to get out of here,' Nina pants.

'We still need to check where the gunman is,' Lizzie says.

'It won't be long, Neen,' Aisa says.

Aisa is talking, but the words are receding, breaking across the surface as Nina sinks away from them. She can feel her sisters' arms around her aching shoulders. In the space between the bulbs, darkness squirms and sucks up air. The more conscious Nina becomes, the more she grows accustomed to the pain, the less she is able to cope with this enclosed space.

Not now. Please, not now.

But it's too late.

It begins to swallow her. She can't breathe, she can't see properly. She wants to claw her way out, wants to run, but her legs feel like stone and she's stuck to the ground through pain... and panic.

'The door,' she manages to say.

She can feel her sisters' warmth against her, can feel the tension in their bodies as they watch the screen, waiting for it to flip from the empty rooms to the bedroom. But Nina can't stay focused on the screen. The weight of the house smothers her. She scrunches her eyes shut. She feels trapped, the passageway no longer an escape but a snake, winding itself around this room, around her neck. She slaps her cheeks, one side, then the other. But it just makes tears spring from her eyes and that won't help.

'Open it. Open the door more.'

Nina leans on Lizzie, who keeps watching the screen, while Aisa pulls the door open more, carrying an old dining chair across to quietly prop it wide open.

Nina begins to breathe easier, counting her breaths, the way she was shown. Not by colleagues with expertise, but by a YouTube video sought in shame.

'One … two … three …'

'What are you doing?' Aisa asks, aghast.

'Focusing,' Nina manages to say, her voice calmer. Aisa opens her mouth but says nothing and looks back at the screen with Lizzie.

Nina is rarely scared as an adult. Not by heights when she climbs, not by the life-and-death decisions she makes at work. Not by meeting new people or leading training sessions with graduates. Not living alone and scooping spiders out of the bath, nor driving at night. Almost nothing scares her, except closed spaces.

And she was terrified down here in the passageway all those years ago. On that final day when they were still kids. She burns with the shame of it even now, but she'd wet herself. Just a tiny bit. But enough.

It was the fear of losing Aisa, the nightmare places her panic had led her to. Imagining her little sister bent out of shape somewhere, drowning in a pond or run over by a car. Or suffocating. She gasps for air now, the memory operating her body.

Then she'd finally found her down here. This creepy underground layer, the sense of being trapped down here, where no one knew to rescue them. The pressure of being the oldest.

That day thirty years ago, as Jane snapped the candy cigarettes Nina had been saving as a treat for Aisa, the desire to leave had quickly become a drumbeat in her head, then a cacophony in her chest and finally a physical pressure that took over her whole body. Not that she would have admitted it. Not that she ever would admit it.

And as they reached the final door that time, decades ago, the four of them burrowed as far underground as it was possible to be, Nina had felt her heart race even faster, a sickening rush that bubbled down to her guts. Then after Aisa had plucked the short straw, Nina's bladder started to go. She told Lizzie to tell the others they needed to leave and then just legged it. And the further she ran up that passage and out into the woods, the more she laughed. At herself, and then simply in wild relief. Lizzie was in hot pursuit, which for Lizzie was a chaotic stumble, and she may have been laughing too. Laughter is contagious, especially at that age.

Once they'd escaped, Nina had happily peed the rest out behind a tree. That's right, that's what they all did when they played in the woods. Alan had been walking towards his shed when they came bursting out and she remembers being conscious of hiding her bottom as she relieved herself. A new thing, a new way of having to think. And then pulling off her damp knickers and stuffing them in a knotty old hole in the bark, worrying what he would think if he found them.

'Feeling better?' Aisa asks, slipping her hand into Nina's.

'Yeah,' she says. 'A bit.'

Aisa isn't watching the screen properly, Nina realises. She keeps looking at the wall to the side of the TV, squinting in the thin grey light. She feels Aisa's weight shift a little, she's moving.

'What are you—'

'I just need to see, need to check I'm not going mad. Just keep leaning on Lizzie, OK?'

Aisa has split away from them and is walking nervously over to the wall. Nina and Lizzie keep watching the screen as it flips through the scenes.

'Can one of you shine a light over here?' Aisa says, her voice small.

Keeping her eyes on the screen as it shows the empty hallway, Nina turns her phone flashlight on and holds it up so it highlights the wall.

Aisa moves closer to the damaged section and peers in, then stumbles back so quickly she nearly falls over. 'Oh fuck.'

The camera is showing the upstairs landing now, but Lizzie and Nina have shuffled over to see what Aisa is reacting to. Nina peers through the gap in the stones, propped up by Lizzie, unsure what she's looking for until, like the moon emerging from behind a cloud, she sees it.

61

AISA – 3.35 a.m.

Jesus fucking Christ. I knew it. I knew it. I fucking knew—

62

LIZZIE – 3:35 a.m.

Oh my God, it's—

63

NINA – 3:35 a.m.

Shit.

She stares, uncomprehending.

No, she stares with *too much* comprehension. Nina knows exactly what she's seeing – exactly what Aisa must have seen when she was still tiny.

She looks at Aisa, still that same little girl, deep down. That same little girl that was telling the truth all those years ago. Who was laughed at and dismissed, who was told to stop making up stories. Called a drama queen, a fibber, an attention seeker. Their mum even taking Nina and Lizzie to one side and telling them to just ignore it. Not to engage. That Aisa would only get worse if she was encouraged, and they needed to be big girls and help their sister.

But Aisa was telling the truth all along. Sitting at the kitchen table with the Crayolas in the old biscuit tin, tongue peeping out of the corner of her mouth as she concentrated, carefully drawing what she'd experienced. Where did that picture go? That was at their great-aunt's house, of course it was, because they'd left their old home, the one in Moirthwaite. But she clearly didn't forget it.

When did she stop talking about it? Did she carry it all this time or absorb it so deeply even she didn't know it was there?

'Why didn't you say anything?' Nina manages to say. Images of what her little sister must have carried are still clouding her thoughts. *Poor Aisa.*

Aisa's eyebrows shoot up. 'Are you kidding right now?'

'What?'

'Why didn't I *say* something? I said something over and over! You all called me a liar.'

'No, I know, I'm sorry. I know you told us back then, I know that Mum … that we all—'

'Right then,' Aisa says.

'But that was *then* and we were just kids and … I mean, why didn't you say anything *now*? As an adult? Did you remember it this whole time?'

Aisa's eyes blaze and her fists curl, but then she sags and shakes her head. 'Not the whole time, no. It comes and goes, I think. I've had a few dreams about … And then tonight it all, y'know. It's like little bits and pieces were always there, but the whole thing, the whole *memory*, was just out of view. And I never wanted to see it anyway.'

'Oh, Aisa.' Nina reaches to pull her sister into a hug, but Aisa shakes her off. The fire is back in her eyes.

'Anyway, you can talk. Or rather *not talk*. Exactly how and when would I have told you any of this? Either of you?'

They both look over at Lizzie, who stands awkwardly in front of the screen, her palms up in surrender.

'What do you mean?' Lizzie says quietly, her wet eyes flicking between the screen, the wall and her sisters.

'We don't fucking talk!' Aisa shouts. 'We don't know anything about each other!'

259

Nina stumbles back in surprise and Aisa reaches to stop her falling, alarm on her face.

'Sorry, I'm sorry, Neen, it's not the time, I'm just...' She looks behind her at the damaged wall. 'It's a lot. Tonight. *That*. *This*. All of it. But it's not the time.'

'You're right though,' Nina says as she allows herself to be helped to a more stable stance. 'We don't talk, and I'm sorry. I get it. We should talk. I just... I need to sit down.'

Lizzie grabs another old dining chair and pushes it behind Nina. She sits heavily, nausea hitting again.

'Are you OK, Nina?' Aisa says, softly now.

'I'm bruised all over, we've just seen a... I mean, no. No, I'm not. And neither is she,' Nina points at Lizzie. 'And neither are you, Aisa. We're not OK tonight and I'm not OK, actually, in general.' Her sisters look at each other and then stare back at her. 'I made a mistake at work,' Nina says. It's the first time she's admitted it out loud and it surprises her. 'I screwed up, actually. Badly. And the baby nearly...'

'Jesus,' Aisa says.

'Yeah. The baby survived, but it could have gone differently. And if I'd got a second opinion, if I'd double-checked my assumption, it never would have got that far. Anyway, I lied about it and now I've been suspended, and I don't know what's going to happen and I don't know if I'll get to do my job ever again and—'

'You will,' Aisa says, squeezing her hand.

Lizzie nods, 'Yeah, you will. Everyone makes mistakes, you're only human.'

'Yeah, but the thing is...' Nina sucks in a lungful of the stale air. *Is she really going to say this?* 'The thing is that I don't even know if I want to do that job anymore. I don't know what I want to do and I think...'

God, where is this coming from?

'I think maybe I've not been honest about what I want from my life ... avoiding taking risks and, y'know, daring to love people ... and I've been using my job, you know, like an excuse.' She puffs out the breath she's been holding.

'Well,' Aisa says. 'Shit.' She looks behind her at the damaged wall and then raises her eyebrows at Nina. 'Tonight is full of surprises.'

'Um,' Lizzie says, apologetically. 'I'm really sorry to change the subject but ... the camera is going to show the bedroom any second and we need to know if they're still there.'

They stare at the screen. A shiver runs across Nina's shoulders and her vision clouds for a moment. She reaches for Aisa's hand, gripping it in hers like she always used to. She's so grateful when Aisa lets her, that she feels tears on her cheeks.

The screen finally reaches Jane's bedroom. The figure still sits on the bed, but as they watch, the figure slowly stands up.

'Oh shit,' Lizzie says and the others look at her in surprise. 'He could be on his way down here, we have to go. Now.'

64

ROSEMARY – July 1992

I've been outside too long. The girls could easily have made their way back into the house looking for me. The air is sticky and pressurised and I'm acutely aware of the sweat running down the inside of my legs.

'Can you keep looking out here?' I say and Alan nods. 'Thanks, Al.'

I push the back door open and step into the kitchen, shaded and cool, just the gentle buzz of the old fridge in the corner. There's no one in here, but I still call out for the girls, then for Jane.

My voice is quieter now, exhausted by the search. It doesn't make sense. We're in the middle of nowhere and there's four of them, they can't just disappear.

I step into the hall and then look inside the dining room. Nothing. They're not tangled in the curtains or wedged under the huge and largely redundant table.

When I first came, one of my jobs was to set it up for dinner each night. Two places, opposite ends, for the Brigadier and his wife. When William came back with Selina in tow, I did the same. Selina took one look at it and said, 'There's no fricking way I'm going to eat my dinner sitting there like Mr Peanut.' I laughed despite myself and liked her even more. She was never going to last up here, I should have known it then. I should have warned her. Should have warned him. This place will eat your marriage and spit out the bones.

Back out in the hall, I see that William's office door is ajar. I can hear rustling inside and step closer, looking through the gap. He's sitting in his chair, papers strewn in front of him.

The normally untouched whisky decanter that I diligently dust every week is open on the desk, almost drained. An ashtray I've not seen in years sits on the desk, a couple of butts squashed in it. 'It's not enough,' he says. At first, I think he's talking to himself, but then I realise he's aware of me. He's looking straight into my eye as I press it to the space between door and frame.

I straighten up and step inside. 'What isn't enough?' I say, softly, as if approaching an injured animal.

'Everything I've done with their money.' His voice gurgles with the spirit that he must have swallowed far too fast. 'It's not made up for it.' He looks up at me, his eyes wet and red. 'And it's not brought her back.'

Her. I don't react. I can't react.

I walk closer, my palms held up. 'I know Daniel's visit upset you, but it's not your fault.'

'She was right,' he says, to himself more than me. 'I chose this place, I chose their ... bloody legacy and I let her go.'

'You didn't do anything wrong and you tried to ... Look, I'm sorry, William, I want to talk about this with you, but I need to find the girls first. Have you seen them?'

He shakes his head. The one thing he's feared more than Selina never coming back is Selina coming back and taking Jane. But he doesn't seem to realise that I mean Jane too. That she's missing.

'All this money,' he says. 'It pours in, it pours out and it doesn't help.'

I don't know, to this day, how his parents got their money. I'm sure brigadiers aren't paid millions, but there was a title somewhere in the family history, a lordship once removed or something. William's family inherited this house, and money with it. Shares, maybe. I don't know, it's not my world. I don't understand how rich people get their money, or how they keep it. Especially as they never seem to work. William was an accountant in London for a time, but not now... Maybe having money is work in itself.

And now his parents are long dead, William spends his time – and their money – trying to assuage his own guilt. I know he gives a lot to charity. He pays his staff fairly. I mean, it's still meagre, but I earn more per day here than Bob used to in the factory. It's still not enough without Bob's wage, but it's better than I'd get anywhere else around here. William can't possibly imagine, I'm sure, even if he thinks he can.

'I think it helps,' I say. 'I think it helps the charities that you give to, I think it helps the village, 'cos I know you always give generously, church fundraising and all that.'

That long summer that I was sixteen and he twenty-one, we could talk for hours. Anything I said seemed to fascinate him, hearing details of my life that I now recognise as a kind of poverty tourism. A glimpse behind the curtain. And I was fascinated by him. He knew so many facts, could quote so many poems. Now we struggle to say a sentence or two to each other. He's still so raw since Selina left, so bitter and lonely, that I'm scared to make things worse. This is the longest conversation we've had in years.

'And your money helps me,' I say, and he looks up. 'My wages,'

I add, looking down and wishing I hadn't started. 'Me and mine would be even more stuffed without them.'

'I envy you and yours,' he says and I laugh, despite everything. 'It's true,' he says, his cheeks growing red. 'Your lives must be so simple.'

'Right,' I say. Only a rich man could say something so bloody stupid. 'Have you seen the girls?' I say again.

'Which girls?'

'My girls and Jane.'

He frowns and tries to stand up, knocking the desk so that the glass lid of the decanter slides off and smashes on the floor. 'Jane?'

'Don't worry,' I say quickly, bending to pick up the pieces and chucking them in the waste paper bin. 'They're playing hide-and-seek but... I need to be getting home now and I need to find them.'

'Oh, OK,' he says, sitting back down. 'Does Jane play OK? Does she know the rules?'

'The rules?'

'Of hide-and-seek? She's never... I didn't think to...'

'Everyone knows the rules of hide-and-seek,' I say and realise too late that he's not really talking about Jane now. He's talking about himself.

William was his parents' prototype. The success story that buoyed them on to try to model other young men in his image. When he left for university, and his parents inherited this house, they seemed to truly believe that they could turn waifs and strays – as they were known in the village – into young men just like William. If they were taught discipline and self-reflection. If they were educated and exercised. It was, of course, total bollocks. William turned out good and kind and bright despite their coldness, their rules. And William's parents didn't have any of the skills needed to help. The young men and boys coming through these doors were knackered and bent out of shape. Runaways, addicts, drinkers. In need of a bed and a little cash. They were not looking to become an experiment, a Frankenstein's monster.

William is looking up at me now, with wet, worried eyes.

'Don't worry,' I say. I think of the skulls in the doll's house, Lizzie's reticence to come here sometimes. 'Jane plays really nicely with Lizzie. You've done a good job with her.'

For a moment, there's the glimmer of the old William I remember, of the old danger, the dormant attraction. 'Rosemary,' he says softly. 'I'm sorry I just left like that, back then. I was young and—'

'Rosemary?'

We both turn to the noise, outside in the hall. It's Alan.

'She's in here,' William calls, breaking the spell.

'I just saw the girls,' Alan says, appearing in the doorway.

65

AISA – 3:37 a.m.

They shuffle out into the hall, Aisa and Lizzie gripping Nina, half dragging her. None of them are speaking. Flashes of what they've just seen in that room, of what she saw thirty years ago, rush through Aisa's head like a mad zoetrope. By the grey skin and bulging eyes of her sisters, it looks like they're battling similar monsters, especially Nina.

'Are you OK, Neen?'

Nina nods, but Aisa can see the erratic rise and fall of her chest, even underneath the layers of clothing. Her eyes are wide and clumps of sweaty hair are sticking to her temple. She's never known her sister to be vulnerable. To talk like she did back there.

They stagger out into the foyer and towards the passageway, the walls feeling closer than ever. Nina grows heavier in their arms until she stops in the mouth of the passageway, its darkness filing away from them like an optical illusion. Like it goes on forever.

Aisa had come to think she'd imagined it all. That she must have. Because it was so unlikely. If it really happened how she thought it happened, someone else would have known about it. The police. The adults. Teachers. Someone. People always found stuff out in the end, didn't they? She'd allowed them to call her a liar, colluded with them backing down. But now she's here, it feels as real as ever.

Nina stumbles and then stops, sagging.

'Just need to get up the passageway,' Lizzie says, 'and then we're out.'

'Hold my hand, it's OK.' Aisa curls her fingers tighter around Nina's. They're soft, thin and childlike still.

'Come on,' Lizzie says. 'You can do it.'

'I can't,' Nina says. 'I can't go along there.'

'I know you think that,' Aisa says. 'But you can.'

'It's not that simple.'

'But it is.'

'You don't understand.'

'I understand very well, Neen,' Aisa says. She softens her voice. 'It's OK,' she says, squeezing Nina's hand.

Not many people know about Nina's claustrophobia, but Aisa does. Aisa knows so many things about her sisters, about her family, things that they all think they've kept under wraps. The little spy, her mum called her. A little sneak, hiding in tight spots and listening. And always watching. She first saw Nina's claustrophobia years before she knew the name for it. Saw the way Nina would claw at her tight seatbelt in the car, the way she held her breath in narrow alleyways and avoided the water chutes on the rare family holidays to Pontins after they moved to Cheshire.

'You're one of the bravest people I know,' Lizzie says to Nina now. 'We can do this together. We'll be outside in no time.'

They start to move again, Nina wincing with each step, the smell of her sweat, her fear, curdling in Aisa's throat.

When Aisa ran along this passageway back then, thirty years ago, she was alone and – yeah, fuck it, it's not too big a word – *traumatised*. The bigger backs of her older sisters had already made their way up the long passageway to freedom and by the time she had come out of that room, they were nowhere in sight. Had she stood a moment, and got her bearings, or just run hell for leather? She doesn't remember. She pictures herself then. A stripey T-shirt and those denim shorts she loved to wear, both of which she threw away afterwards, stuffing them in the kitchen bin as if traces of the badness had soaked into them.

A gasp of sadness leaks out of her, lost under the thunder of footsteps. Four years old. Running for her life through this horrible pit, out of this dungeon.

Her mum seemed to believe her, but only when they were alone. That night, she'd got back out of bed after the other two were asleep and crept downstairs. Rosemary stroked her head and told her that sometimes we experience things that other people won't believe. And that Aisa just had to keep those thoughts to herself and trust that they were real, but that telling other people wouldn't give her what she wanted. She would never be believed. But that she could always tell Mum. Mum and no one else.

'Not even Dad?' she'd asked and Rosemary's hand had paused on Aisa's forehead just a moment.

'Let me handle Dad,' she'd said eventually.

Aisa looks across at Lizzie, who is gripping Nina with one hand, her handbag under the other arm. It reminds her, 'Nina, I called for a breakdown truck and they could be here any minute, do you still have your car keys?'

They stop and Nina pats her pocket carefully. 'Yeah,' she nods.

'Phew,' Lizzie says. 'Now hurry up. Please.'

They start to move again when Aisa realises. Her legs grow cold, a sudden shiver running down the backs of them. 'Oh no,' she says.

'No, I said I do have them,' Nina says, taking another awkward step, but Aisa is frozen.

'It's not that,' she says. 'I just realised that I left my bag up there in the living room, I have to go and get it, it has everything in it.'

'There's a man with a gun up there,' Lizzie says, more sharply than Aisa has ever heard Lizzie speak. 'There's nothing in your bag worth taking that risk.'

'My passport,' Aisa says.

'You can get an emergency one tomorrow,' Nina says. 'Please, we can't stay here talking, I can feel the walls... I can't breathe properly, we need to get out.'

'It's not that,' Aisa says. 'Mum gave me a card, before she died. It's in my passport holder.'

'Mum wouldn't want you to risk your life,' Lizzie says. 'All our lives.'

'I'm sure you remember every word,' Nina says, an edge to her voice. 'I know I do.'

'You got one too?' Aisa asks.

'We both did,' Lizzie says quietly. 'And mine means so much to me too, but you can't risk—'

'But you don't understand,' Aisa says, a sudden stream of tears sliding down her cheeks. Her sisters stare back at her as she whispers, 'I've not read it yet.'

66

LIZZIE – 3:40 a.m.

'Then we'll all go and get it,' Lizzie says. 'Safety in numbers.'

'No,' Aisa says. 'We can't do that. It's too risky and we'll make too much noise getting Nina up the stairs.'

'You're right,' Nina says. 'I don't want you to go up by yourself, but I'd make everything worse. You should go with Aisa though, Lizzie, I can do this alone. I'm OK, I promise, I—'

'No,' Aisa says, cuffing her surprising tears away with her sleeve. 'You're not fucking listening to me. *I* need to go up, just me. I'll get my bag and then I'll just get out the front door. You two carry on up the passageway and meet me at the side of the house. There are no cameras there, we never saw it on the screen.'

Lizzie looks at Nina, expecting her to take over with a different plan. To pull rank. Instead, she just nods. 'OK, yeah.'

'OK?' Aisa says.

'Yeah, but go quickly,' Nina hisses. 'And be careful.'

'I love you, Aisa,' Lizzie blurts out as her younger sister makes for the steps. There's a pause, and then the sound of quiet laughter.

'Love you too, Lizard,' she replies. And then she's swallowed up.

They watch and listen as her careful footsteps rise up the

stairs. There's a pause, presumably as she opens the hatch into the cupboard, and a few more footsteps. Then nothing.

'God, I hope she's OK,' Nina says. Her voice is still diminished and raspy.

'Well, she has to be,' says Lizzie firmly. 'And we have to be out there to meet her. Ready to start again?'

'Ready,' Nina says, leaning her weight on Lizzie, who tries not to groan under the strain. She heaves dogs around all the time, she can do this.

'I can do this.'

'What?' Nina says, but Lizzie doesn't reply. They start to half walk, half shuffle up the passageway. Hand in hand, fingers threaded together. The light from the bulbs is dim but steady, no flickering, and she can look out for spiders without letting on.

'Watch over us, watch over us,' Lizzie starts.

'Tuck us safe to bed,' Nina joins in.

'Watch over us, watch over us. 'Til we're all long…'

'Christ, that was a dark prayer,' Nina says with a sharp laugh. 'Where the hell did Mum get that from?'

'Nan,' Lizzie says.

'Figures.'

By the time they reach the end of the passageway, they've undone their coats and are fanning their faces. The steps rise up eight or nine feet, cruder and more rickety than the ones leading to the cupboard. Just simple metal rungs set into the stone, more like a ladder than a staircase.

'Are you going to be able to—' Before she can finish, Nina has grabbed the highest rung she can reach and is pulling herself up using just one of her legs, the other dangling.

'I'm used to rock climbing,' she calls down to Lizzie. 'This is the easiest bit.'

As Nina climbs, Lizzie can see bruises blooming on her neck, just underneath her ponytail. What on earth happened to her? Since finding her, they've had one thing after another to deal with and discover, and she still doesn't know how Nina ended up down here.

'I think someone hit me,' she'd said. That was all.

'Nina,' she says, as she climbs onto the lowest rung.

'Yeah?' Nina asks, panting, and not slowing.

Lizzie wants to say that she's scared. That she wants her mum. That she's never seen anything like *that* back there. That she's worried about Aisa. That she's sorry about Nina's job. That she hopes Nina can find the contentment she herself has found. That she loves them both very much but doesn't know, hasn't ever known, if they love her back.

'Nothing,' she says, as Nina pushes the trapdoor up into the shed.

67

AISA – 3:41 a.m.

She shouldn't have laughed when Lizzie said she loved her. It's a Kelsey affliction, laughing at inopportune moments. Their dad was the worst for it, back when he still laughed a lot. Before Mum died. One time, her parents were called into her secondary school after Aisa got in trouble for swearing at a teacher. While the headmaster was droning on about his disappointment, and that calling Mr Bobbins 'Mr Bollocks' was a suspendable offence, her dad had burst out laughing. Seconds later, their mum and Aisa were doing the same. God, she'd forgotten all about that.

But she shouldn't have laughed tonight. It was a surprise, that was all. No one has said those words to her since her mum died, though her dad has tried in his own way. 'Take care of yourself, love,' meaning approximately the same thing. More or less.

She quietly climbs the steps as far as she can before the ceiling gets in the way. The lights flicker once, and she gasps, then covers her mouth. Did anyone hear that? Overhead, the trapdoor they'd come through earlier is back in position and she holds her breath, worried about the noise, but when she pushes up with her fingertips, the square hatch moves upwards silently.

A black hole opens above her head. She stops to listen, then climbs up carefully.

A little of the light from below illuminates the cramped space she's crawled back into, the faded rose wallpaper and the sloping wall and, in front of her, a door. She closes the trapdoor behind her carefully to keep her sisters safe, holding it the whole time to keep it quiet. A shadow of the Aisa she once was is in here with her, scrunched tight. That little girl was determined to do everything by herself. To be big. *I've not changed*, she thinks, with less pride in her stubbornness than usual. She was scared then and she's scared now. But there's no option, she can't leave that envelope up there, unread. The last fragment of Mum.

That figure on screen could have made it down here by now. Could be standing just the other side of the door, in the hallway. Gun cocked. *Oh well*, she thinks, reaching for the cupboard door, *only one way to find out*.

68

ROSEMARY – July 1992

William tips the dregs of the whisky into his tumbler as I follow Alan out, trying not to shove him into a run. When we're finally in the kitchen out of earshot, I grab his arm and say, 'Where are the girls?'

He frees his arm and steps back. 'In the woods. I was heading to check my shed again and I saw them running hell for leather.'

'All of them?'

'No, just your biggest two, I think.'

I rush to the window to look out but can't see them.

'What about Jane and Aisa?'

'I don't know,' Alan says. 'I came to tell you as soon as I saw the first lot.'

I pinch the bridge of my nose and close my eyes. I wish he'd stayed to see if the other two came out, but it's better than nothing. 'Thanks, Alan, I'm sure the others aren't far behind.'

Alan is heading back to his shed as I trudge up through the garden towards the trees. It's cooler here, under this canopy of leaves, and I finally allow myself to feel a little relieved. I can see Nina and Lizzie in the distance. Nina is squatting behind a tree and Lizzie is keeping watch. My mother would call them feral for peeing in the open air, but I see a sister looking out for another sister. That's important. I hope they never lose that closeness.

I can't see Aisa or Jane at first, but as I get closer to the older two, I hear a commotion behind me and turn. Aisa bursts out of the shed and starts running towards her sisters, who then run towards her. I hike up my skirt and run too, desperate to grab them, hug them.

We all reach each other at the same time and I scoop Aisa up in one fluid movement and scrunch her into me.

'Mum,' Nina says, her voice as small as I've ever heard it, but I cling to the littlest one and say nothing, just feel her heart hammering through her thin T-shirt. Aisa is crying – which she rarely lets herself do in front of her sisters.

'Where were you?' I say softly to her, and then more sharply to Nina and Lizzie. 'Where the bloody hell were you?'

Aisa snivels something into my neck that I can't make out.

'Hide-and-seek,' Nina says, her voice cracking just a little. 'Just around the house.'

'I looked everywhere,' I say. 'I was so worried.'

'We were underneath,' Aisa says, pulling back and looking at me. I think of all the blankets I pulled up, the bedclothes dangling down, how did I miss them?

'Where's Jane?'

'She's still inside,' Lizzie says.

I look back at the house, then at my girls. 'Does she know you're not playing hide-and-seek anymore?'

'Yeah,' Nina says, 'she saw us leave.'

Moments later, I see Jane heading to the back door of the house. She doesn't turn to wave.

It's gone five and I've paid more than my dues today. We head to the car, swinging in to see Alan in his shed on the way. The girls stand outside as I open the door and step in, apologising. 'Sorry I was a bit snappy, I was just worried, but I really appreciate your help today.'

He's sitting on the stool, staring at the floor. 'Rosemary,' he says. 'Aisa came out of the passageway. It's not safe down there.'

We were underneath.

69

NINA – 3:46 a.m.

Nina sweeps her phone light around the old shed, looking for the door. It's surprisingly tidy in here, far tidier than the house. Alan's stool is still here, on its back like a dead bug with its legs in the air. But there's a richness to the air. It smells alive, despite the decay. Several sacks of soil are stacked up. The top one has been slashed down the middle, a trowel sticking out of it like a dagger.

Along the length of the wooden shed, an old door is propped across two barrels as a makeshift worktop. Several little plastic pots sit under a plastic lid, presumably to protect them from the weather. They look freshly tended.

They push the shed door outwards, which shrieks in the night air. 'Gosh, that's loud,' Lizzie says.

Nina bites her lip and braces for pain as she steps outside. Her ankles are both clicking and aching, and the damaged one has swollen up like a grapefruit and she's had to loosen her laces so much that the shoe is at risk of slipping off.

The air tastes sweet out here after the stuffy cellar. They pick their way through the trees, the light of their nearly drained phones helping them to avoid raised roots and heavy stones, but making the area surrounding them appear blacker, denser.

'Do you think it's Alan that's still here?' Lizzie whispers. 'Did you see him?'

'I didn't see who hit me, just their eyes ... but they did look a bit familiar. Mum always said he'd never leave this place,' Nina says.

'We were so young,' Lizzie says, as if that explains everything.

Thirty years ago, Alan had been in these woods, walking his slow, loping stomp. He'd had a rabbit slung over his shoulder, twine wrapped around its leg, its ears flopping down his back. Nina hadn't cared about that so much as about hiding herself as she peed. She remembers that Lizzie had flinched at the sight though.

Had Alan seen them that day? She doesn't know. He always seemed to be in his own world, but always there, too. Always, somehow, just round the corner. He can't have been that old. Younger than they are now, but older than them and therefore on the other team. The adults.

He'd headed for his shed, and then ... she doesn't remember. A few minutes later, Aisa had appeared. And the relief overtook everything.

It's rough going, the uneven ground that was once a vast garden has been reclaimed by nature. Clumps of grass and mud, stones and dips. Nina nearly slips and Lizzie catches her with a grunt.

'This is really difficult,' Nina says suddenly, the words coming out before she has a chance to stop them.

'Oh,' Lizzie says, threading her arm through hers. 'But you can do it, you're Nina.'

And of course she can do it, she's Nina.

They carry on carefully until the house looms in front of them. The dark stones bouncing the chilled air back to them, like a slap in the face.

'We should turn this off,' Nina says, snuffing out her light before Lizzie can reply. She does the same. They press themselves to the wall, Nina using it for support as well as hiding. 'Aisa?' she whispers, as they inch their way awkwardly around to the side of the house.

There's no reply.

They lean against the cold wet stone and Nina looks at her phone.

'It's been over twenty minutes since she left us, it can't take that long to get one bag … not unless …'

'This doesn't feel right, does it,' Lizzie says, straightening up. 'You stay here, I'm going to go in the back and make sure she's OK.'

'But—'

'But nothing, we know the man who hit you is inside, whether it's Alan or not. That means you're safe out here, you can rest your leg and I'll go in and make sure Aisa is OK.'

'But, Lizzie—'

'It's not up to you, Nina. It'll be two versus one when I'm in there, right now it's one on one and that's not OK.'

Nina thinks about the card from her mum. *You have to let other people help sometimes, love.* Wherever this new courage has come from in her sister, Nina shouldn't crush it. 'OK,' she says. 'If you're going in through the kitchen, I'll go round the front in case she comes out that way.'

Lizzie starts to move away, but Nina catches her hand.

'Good luck, Lizzie, you're being really brave.'

Lizzie pauses. 'Thank you,' she says, and then rushes off towards the back of the house.

Nina shuffles along the wall, zipping her coat back up, the heat she built up earlier long gone. Either adrenaline or the cold is making her whole body shake, but she keeps going until she reaches the corner of the house and then squats down painfully to creep under the first window. She can't hear anything and lifts her head, but the dusty velvet curtains are blocking most of her view and the dirty glass doesn't help. She can make out the fireplace, part of a sofa and the eiderdown still on it.

Was it really only tonight that they first went in there and lit a fire? Just a few hours ago, but a different dimension. An alternate reality where Alan was a distant memory, and their biggest problem was a lack of petrol and a twisted ankle.

But, of course, that's not entirely true. Aisa clearly has stuff going on, it's not normal to dismantle your whole life and Littlest Hobo it across the world. And Lizzie ... poor Lizzie, always so insular, so alone.

And me, she thinks. *Would the others have ever guessed about my problems if I hadn't blurted them out?* That every night when she should be asleep, she's replaying the birth that went wrong. The decisions. The dropping heart rate. The confusion of her colleagues when she stopped them coming closer, stopped them helping. The tiny cry, the relief that her bad decisions hadn't ... but who knows.

And the biggest secret of all. The one that wakes her up with a start every time she starts to slip under, the one she doesn't let take full form. The relief at not having to do it anymore. The kernel of hope that they'll say she can't return. And yes, the absolute fear over meeting the mortgage, the shame of telling people, the ostracism that always happens when a colleague falls and the world they've left closes up around the exit wound. But the relief, the dizzying relief, of being able to choose a new path.

The bruises on Nina's back and neck throb and her head fogs for a moment. She slaps her face and the sound rings out like a whipcrack in the dead air. Now is not the time for life decisions. All her decisions were made long ago, it's too late for reinvention. It's the time for gritting her teeth and holding on.

She shuffles gingerly to the impenetrable oak front door, pressing her cold ears pointlessly against it. She can hear nothing.

Nina takes a big gulp of air and then, leaning on the facade of the house, starts to shuffle towards the other window to see if Aisa is in the library.

Her progress is slow, but she's nearly at the window now. She turns back, just quickly, to check the front door hasn't opened. No. OK. Another deep breath and then Nina takes a big, painful stride into the dark. Colliding silently with something. Someone. The dim moonlight picks out the hood, the eyes. The same eyes she saw earlier. As she opens her mouth, a gloved hand is slapped across it.

70

ROSEMARY – July 1992

Aisa is asleep in my lap, TV off, big two in bed. On the tape deck, a mixtape of my favourites from the musicals plays softly. But they're not really comforting me tonight.

My tea is long cold and my throat feels like dry straw, but I don't get up to make a fresh cup. I don't want to disturb my little girl and I don't want to break this spell. Her life is going to change so much soon, in fact it already has. Let her have this last little bit of the old one.

Will she ever understand? Will the penny drop when she's older and realises what happened? The thought makes my eyes fill and I pepper her crown with kisses. She smells like baked bread. I can't bear this alone much longer.

It's Friday, so Bob is spending some of his wages in the pub. He's held it together well these last weeks, it's felt like progress. But what's that Bible story about houses built on sand? We've been treading water for a long time, now I need him to swim. Arguably more than I ever have before. Even more than I did five years ago.

The pub is three doors down and I hear the ringing bell, the yells of last orders. Not long now. A few minutes later, the sound of the bar spills onto the streets. It's a male sound, a primeval

284

pack thing, and I can't stand it. I don't imagine William has ever been inside The Fox, or any other proper pub for that matter. I imagine him and Selina went to their fair share of bistros and wine bars when they lived down in London though.

I think then of Jane. I promised Selina I would look out for Jane. I imagine what she would say if she knew I'd just left her today, without checking she was OK. No matter what other people think, Selina adored that child, and that child had been down there, *underneath*.

I make a vow silently. To Selina, to Jane. And then I scoop Aisa up and shuffle awkwardly upstairs as I hear Bob's footsteps outside. I lay her down and take a look at all three of the girls sleeping here, in the only bedroom they've ever known. I've wanted more for them for so long, but this house, for all its faults, had always given them stability and security.

The front door opens and I close the girls' door and head downstairs to survey the damage. Bob is inside and still upright, which is a start. Swaying a little on the mat, but in reasonable condition.

'How do?' he says, looking up as I descend.

'Let me make you a coffee.'

While the kettle boils, I run through it in my head, trying to find the words.

He's slumped on the sofa now and I watch through the doorway as his eyes close and his head snaps back, waking himself up and zonking out, over and over again.

I call out, 'I need you awake.'

He raises his eyebrows in hope and struggles to a stand.

'Come in here,' I say.

He plods through, hands outstretched towards me, but I point to the table. He pulls out one of the dining chairs, its seat covered with socks that I've been meaning to pair up and ball, but he sweeps them onto the floor enthusiastically and I don't say anything.

'You've got plans for me, Ro?' he says, eyes sparkling through their semi-drunken sheen as I pour water onto the milky Nescafé and stir vigorously. He's looking older. Drink and worry have frayed his edges, greyed his hair. But he's still my Bob.

'Drink that,' I say, sliding the mug in front of him and standing back quickly before he can grab my bum.

He blows on it a bit and then gulps it down like medicine, wiping his mouth with the back of his big hand.

Oh, Bob. Always so keen, always so devoted, long before I even noticed him. It's a life sentence, but he doesn't seem to mind. Or hasn't, until now. Even when he must have suspected that—

'What is it, Ro?'

'It's the girls,' I say, and he frowns. 'They found the Brigadier's cellar.'

71

AISA – 3:46 a.m.

The door from the cupboard opens quietly and she hovers for a moment, squatting on her haunches like an animal, ears pricked. It's hard to hear over the hammer of blood in her ears, but she can't waste time. She steps out carefully.

Aisa is alone in the hallway – at least she thinks she's alone. She should have taken one of her sisters' phones for light, but it's too late now, she's wading into blackness, all her other senses heightened.

She can still smell that rich iron tang, tinged with the smell of the kind of wax jacket that her dad used to wear to walk their dog Ralph when they were much younger. Sometimes, she'd go with him to Marbury Park near their house. Happy to have a little time just them, talking about what he'd seen on the trains, spotting squirrels or brainstorming how they would build the perfect tree house, if any of those big park trees were able to fit in their garden. Then she turned thirteen and didn't want anything to do with him. So completely that she'd forgotten that she ever had. Poor Dad.

She crosses the hall and listens at the door of the living room, but there's no sound from inside, so she pushes it open carefully.

The fire is still glowing, just a tiny sliver of orange under the dust and ash. It's a reminder that they really were here earlier. The three of them first, and then in various batches of two. She pinches herself hard on the arm to really underline it. This place she's avoided for so long in her mind, and now she's standing in the belly of the beast.

She just needs to grab her bag and go. But where is it? The light is still navy and grey and the sun not yet up outside. She squints but can't see it and can't remember where she'd slung it when she first came in, looking for Nina and Lizzie. She checks under the eiderdown on the sofa, and then the blankets on the other one. No dice.

It's not on the old dining chair, or near the window. She finally spots it, tucked to the side of the fireplace where she'd put it to dry out. As she goes over, she sees that Lizzie's note is still on the mantelpiece, so she grabs it and drops it on the glowing wood. No need to leave clues that they'd been here. It fizzes and is swallowed into black soot.

Aisa scoops up her bag, breathing heavily with relief, and opens it. She rifles through her tat and reaches the zipped compartment, feeling from the outline that the passport holder is still inside. Still, she has to check. She has no intention of ever coming back here and she's not leaving without that envelope.

But it's there. The edges of the passport slightly wavy from the damp, but the envelope unscathed, as soft and precious as before. She leaves it there, now is certainly not the time to read it, zips the bag back up and hoists it over her shoulder, snatching it to her side to silence its rattle.

Shit, did anyone hear that?

Aisa listens but hears nothing. She just needs to get out the front door now and run round the side to her sisters. Escape is so close she can feel it, pushing her on. She pulls the lounge door handle and it opens wide. Revealing a gun. Held at chest height. In shaking hands. Blocking the exit.

72

LIZZIE – 3:46 a.m.

Lizzie makes her way along the side of the house towards the back, whispering to herself.

Watch over us, watch over us.

Tuck us ...

Tonight, the words circle around her mind, but she can't catch hold of them. Bats, flapping in the corners of her mind. Out of control and scared. She starts again.

Watch over us, watch over us.

Tuck us safe to bed.

Watch over us, watch over us.

'Til we're all long dead.

It's no bloody good. Mum *is* long dead. And maybe they are too, they just don't know it.

She reaches the back of the house and turns her phone light off. The darkness is a shock, but Lizzie shakes it off and peers through the window into the kitchen. It's hard to make anything out, it's just dusty shapes and darkness, but nothing seems to be moving. No one appears to be there.

What on earth would Mum make of this? Her old domain, abandoned and thick with dust when once it shined like a new pin. And inside and all around it, her girls, scattered and vulnerable. And poor Dad, left at home by himself, oblivious in that empty house. What will he do if anything happens to them?

You hardly ever see him anyway, what difference would it make?

She winces. It's true. Before her mum got ill, Lizzie visited a couple of times a month, and stayed the night whenever she could. Sometimes Dad would be away, riding the trains with his retiree's railcard. Mum would cook Chimney Pot Pie or bangers and mash and Lizzie would tell herself that next time she'd admit to being a vegetarian. She's not eaten meat in years, except when Mum cooked it. She never owned up.

Who cooks for Dad now? Every time she visits, they get sandwiches at the local pub and she flees before dinner. He's thinner, she realises. Is he eating? Mum would never let him go hungry.

'I'm sorry,' she whispers to herself. *Tell him yourself, when you're all away from here.*

Lizzie presses her ear to the door, but she hears nothing else. No words, no footsteps, no gunshots.

Gunshots?! What has happened to us?

Anything could be happening in there, but all she can hear is the wind and the distant swaying of trees. If she hadn't seen that gunman on the bed with her own eyes, she'd think she had imagined it. It wouldn't be the first time she'd imagined things.

Lizzie reaches for the back-door handle. Did they check this earlier? She can't remember, but when she takes a deep breath and starts to turn it, she meets no resistance. When it's wide enough to slip through, she listens again, but there's nothing. No one.

She steps carefully into the dark kitchen, the sound of her scuffed old trainers ringing out through the silence. She waits, but no one comes, so she steps further into the room until she feels her way to the internal door that leads to the hallway and stairs. Her eyes are still adjusting, the darkness just a block, but then they begin to pick out shapes. A person, standing in the doorway of the lounge, gun cocked.

73

ROSEMARY – July 1992

Bob has had three more coffees and a huge glass of water while we talked. Or, rather, I talked, he mostly absorbed. He's fully upright now, completely engaged. You'd never know he'd had a drink in his life, let alone six pints a few hours ago.

Whatever anyone may say about Bob, when it really matters, there's no one more reliable, no one braver. It takes me back to that day, five years ago, when the pin was first pulled out of the grenade. He held me together. And I don't deserve him. That is a granite-hard fact. No matter what he drinks, what he messes up, however much he might wind me up in the normal run of family life, I cannot fault him. The man is a hero.

'I should just get it done,' he says, taking the car keys off the hook, but I draw the line there, coffee or no coffee. I can't have him getting pulled over, fingerprinted, shoved in a drunk tank somewhere in Penrith.

'I'll drive you,' I say.

I leave a note taped to the TV just in case one of the girls wakes up and can't find us. I say that we had to pop out to help a friend and to go back to bed. To help themselves to breakfast if we're not back by morning, hoping to God that we will be.

And not to call Nan. The last thing I need is my mother getting a call. The last thing I need is my mother. Full stop.

I drive in silence. It's a journey I have done so many thousands of times, on my bicycle as a teenager, then by car and occasionally on foot. I have done it happy and sad, pregnant and excited, grieving my father, fuming at my mother, worrying about my future, and in relief. I have done it recklessly, feeling I had no choice. And now, this last time, it seems brand new.

I'm glad I'm not here alone, plunging around these tight bends and weaving through giant monstrous trees that sway dangerously even in summer. I wish I was in bed. I wish more than anything that I was back home in bed, the girls in the next room, safe. No, that's not true. I wish that me, Bob and the girls were miles away from here, cuddled together. My family is all that counts now. They're the home, not the house. My auntie said just the same thing when I called her, earlier this evening, asking to stay.

I pull onto the drive but stop about halfway up to the house. We don't want to be seen. The familiarity grabs me by the throat. When I look across at Bob, he seems frozen. I cannot keep doing this to him.

'You OK?' I say as we climb out and he nods, reaching for his little toolbox. But he's not.

He never is when he comes back here.

You'd not know it was July. We huddle closer together for warmth and I reach for Bob's hand. 'We don't hold hands enough,' I tell him and feel him plant kisses on the crown of my head. 'I love you so much,' I say. 'You know that don't you?'

'I do,' he says, his voice muffled by my hair.

'I hope the girls are OK back home,' I whisper, as the big house looms into view.

'Of course they're OK,' he says. 'Because they're together.'

The downstairs lights are all switched off, but I look up and spot that Jane's light is on. I didn't know that she still slept with it on, and feel a sudden stab of sympathy and guilt.

'Wonder if Alan's here,' Bob says and I nod.

'He's always here, isn't he,' I say, more to myself than Bob. 'He's probably in his tent though, so we should be extra quiet around there.'

'Yeah, probably,' Bob says softly. 'Poor bugger.'

We've brought torches, but we don't switch them on – drawing attention to ourselves will blow everything. 'Make sure you're quiet with those tools,' I whisper and he holds the toolbox to his body as we approach the shed. 'I'll wait here and keep watch,' I whisper. 'Not that I can see a bloody thing.' I hug him good luck and then watch as he carefully opens the door to the shed and steps inside. He stands still for a moment and I wonder if he can really handle this. But a moment later, he's disappeared.

74

NINA – 3:51 a.m.

Nina can't breathe properly. She can taste soil and dirt on the thick fabric covering her mouth. She tries to get away, tries to shout out, but it's useless, she's trapped. The pain rising up from her ankle is so intense that for a moment her vision goes. A white heat, radiating from her toes all the way up to her scalp.

Someone huge is behind her, dwarfing her, his arms wrapped around her. She can hear the squeak of a wax jacket against her own puffa coat. She has never felt claustrophobia while standing outside, but she does now. The panic wraps itself around her even tighter than this man's arms.

'Stop struggling and I'll let you go,' the voice says, and the familiarity of it hits her in her bones.

She goes limp. Moments later, she can breathe again. The man is holding her arms, but her face is open to the wind and she sucks in the air as fast as she can.

'Please don't shout for help,' he says, his warm mouth close to her cold ear. She shudders but manages not to make a noise. 'I don't want to hurt you,' he adds. His voice is soft, low, a rumble that passes through her right to the pit of her stomach. He slackens his hold so she can pull away, turning to face him.

That face. The same one that she saw in the mirror moments

before everything went black. There was only one person it could have been.

Alan is massive. Even bigger than she remembers, back when everyone was bigger than her. Now it's more of a novelty. He is twice as wide as her, he looks more like a building than a person. The hood of his wax coat is up over his forehead, but she can see his eyes and that's enough.

'You did hurt me,' she says, quietly.

'I didn't mean to, Rosemary,' he says, one heavy hand landing on her shoulder like a kettlebell.

'I'm not Rosemary!' she cries.

75

AISA – 3:47 a.m.

Aisa's first thought is, *So that's what a gun looks like.* Dark wood, polished metal, a leather handle, it resembles something that might sit on the wall of a naff old pub. Some kind of deadly horse brass.

Her second thought is, *How the hell am I still alive?*

'Don't move,' the voice says quietly.

And Aisa doesn't. She doesn't move her head, or her eyes. She keeps them fixed on the barrel, on the hole where a bullet could come flying out. All it would take is one finger twitch.

The gun is everything, the only thing.

The light is so dim in here, just the disappearing glow of the fire. Yet she can make out the gun's precise lines. Maybe her eyes are just filling in the gaps, drawn from years of ingesting Hollywood films. But everything around the gun is a blur. The person, the door.

Aisa hears their voice as if she's reading it on a subtitled film, fractured and delayed between ears and understanding.

'Aisa,' it says, and then she looks up. *How do they know my name?*

It's a woman. She'd have known that from the voice, if she'd not been too scared to process the information.

A light suddenly comes on, Aisa flinches and for a moment sees nothing. But the woman has lowered the gun so it hangs by her side and has pulled a torch from somewhere. Aisa's eyes ache with the shock of it and she covers them with her hands and bends at the knee, her whole body reacting to the flood of light after hours in a void.

'What are you doing here?' There's a new something in the woman's voice – surprise, but... if Aisa trusted herself and her instincts right now, she'd also say the woman sounded happy. But Aisa is clearly losing the plot in the face of a firearm.

'We ran out of petrol,' she says. 'We just needed to take shelter.'

'Here?'

'Well...' *Obviously.* She fights the urge to be sarcastic to someone holding a gun. 'Yeah,' she says. 'Here.'

'Just randomly here?' the woman says.

'It was a shortcut gone wrong. I'm sorry, but how do you know my name?'

The woman pulls her hood down awkwardly with her torch hand, the light bouncing around the walls and ceiling. A crop of dark wavy hair and a thin face stare back.

'Jane?'

'Your mum—'

My mum?

'She showed me your photo, I recognised you from that.'

'What?'

'Aisa,' Jane says, 'I didn't want to do it like this, but...' She fumbles to get something out of her pocket. As she places the gun down to free up both hands, Lizzie comes pelting down the hallway.

'Lizzie!' Aisa shouts. 'Don't!'

But it's too late. Lizzie is lying on top of Jane, the gun knocked out of reach.

'Lizzie's here as well?' Jane says, muffled by Lizzie's body. Then a shout comes from outside, the fear in it so acute that Aisa feels her blood grow cold in her veins.

'I'm not Rosemary!'

76

ROSEMARY – July 1992

Bob has been down there for ages now. If he doesn't come out soon, the sun will come up and then God knows what we'll do. Alan strikes me as an early riser, and his tent is only fifty yards away, and he has the ears of a hunter.

I don't dare put the torch on, I think its glow would probably be visible through the thin tent fabric. I have nothing to do but worry and seize up, so I walk in small, slow circles to stay awake, keep my legs moving. I'm wearing an old Miller Lite T-shirt, tracksuit bottoms and an anorak, which rustles when I move. I get too hot, so I take it off, and then I get too cold. I won't feel just right until we're well away from here. Away from this house, away from this village. Away from these memories. How I ever thought I could ... we could ... live with them. I really could slap myself.

I wonder how many circles I've done now. A hundred. Three thousand. I have no idea. But I almost wish I could make this harder for myself, leg weights or something, anything to bring it closer in line with what Bob is going through. He hasn't complained. He's just down there, yet again, working away to fix the wall that allowed Aisa to see the—

'Shit!'

I'm on the floor before I realise what's happened, landing with a bump and a grunt. Shit, shit, shit. Did Alan hear?

I sit perfectly still, my legs at awkward angles from the fall, listening hard and trying to control my breathing. Just as I think I've got away with it, I hear the sound of a zip fifty yards away.

My bright blue anorak will act like a beacon if Alan shines a torch around, but taking it off will create a cacophony of swishes. As I hear him bustle out from the tent, his heavy footsteps treading onto the sun-hardened ground, I lie down as quietly as I can, willing myself smaller. There are no leaves to cover myself with, nothing to hide behind. I'm lying on the side of the shed nearest his tent.

He stands still and says nothing. I know he's listening, but I also know there's no reason for him to think I'm here. He's not looking for me. I stay still, scrunching my eyes shut as if that makes me less visible, and I hear him take another step. *Please, Alan,* I think, *just go back inside.*

Finally I hear the jangle of the tent zip as he brushes against it, climbing back in, but I also hear a noise from inside the shed. The rattle of Bob's toolbox as he pushes it up from the passageway onto the floor of the shed. 'Stop,' I hiss. 'Stay there.'

Thank God he must have heard me because the noise stops. We both stay still and silent. The hatch must still be open on the shed floor, but Bob doesn't come up. I barely breathe.

It feels like hours, it's probably seconds, but I eventually hear the steady sound of the zip as Alan seals himself back into his cocoon. I crawl to the door of the shed as quietly as I can and whisper the all-clear to Bob. He climbs up in silence, closes the hatch as if he's handling a sleeping newborn, and then clutches the toolbox to his chest again to stop it rattling.

We don't say a word until we reach the car, halfway down the drive. I unlock the driver's side, slide in and pop his door open.

When he climbs in under the dim glow of the interior lights, I see that he's covered in dust, pale as the moon and trembling. As I lift the handbrake, he stares ahead. I roll the car down towards the road without turning the ignition or putting the lights on, using muscle memory from driving this way ten million times before. As we reach the gates, I turn the key, stare ahead and grope for his hand. All the way home, I only drop it for gear changes, then snatch it back up. It sits in mine, shaking like a little mouse plucked from the wet mouth of a cat, just in time.

77

NINA – 3:53 a.m.

The front door flies open, and Nina can make out the frenetic movements of Aisa, holding a torch that she's got from God knows where. Then she sees the shape and shuffle of Lizzie, holding her lit-up phone in front of her like a taser and someone else, a woman in a hood. The woman stalks towards them, and—

Shit, is that a real gun?

'Get away from her,' the woman says to Alan, lifting the gun to her shoulder.

'That's mine,' Alan says. 'And it's not loaded.'

'This gun belonged to my grandfather, the Brigadier,' the woman says, and Nina feels Alan's heavy hand shake on her shoulder.

'Jane?' Alan says.

Jane? Jane is here?

'It's not really yours, my dad just let you use it. And I found the bullets,' Jane says, jutting her chin up. 'Oxo tin, second shelf down in the shed. Right?'

Alan slowly backs away. Letting Nina slump, he cowers into himself as Jane keeps the gun trained on him. 'Is he . . .' he says. 'Is he here?'

'Who?' Jane says, staring at Alan.

Nina couldn't have described Jane in any detail before tonight. Vaguely dark, vaguely skinny. Eight years old. But seeing her up close, Nina recognises her as clearly as if she was a member of her own family. It's not just that she's still skinny, still dark, it's the essence of her. The sharpness, the grit. The bravery.

'Who?' Jane says again, jabbing the gun slightly forward.

'The Brigadier.'

'He's been dead for fifty years!' Jane says.

'I get confused,' Alan cries. 'I have a note, in my pocket.'

'A note?' Jane says, and then looks round at the sisters. 'What note?'

Alan starts fumbling in his pocket and Jane presses the gun closer to him.

'No tricks,' she says, but he's pulling out a piece of folded paper and offering it to her. She is holding the gun with both hands, so she lets go with one, grabs the note and tosses it towards Lizzie and Aisa. Then she grabs the gun tightly again.

Lizzie catches the folded letter, but Aisa snatches it, holding it awkwardly in the torch light. 'This looks just like Dad's writing,' she says.

'My friend Bob wrote it,' Alan mutters.

'What the actual …' Aisa starts.

'Just read it,' Jane says, the gun shaking just slightly, almost imperceptibly. 'Please.'

'All right,' says Aisa. 'It says, "This is Alan. He means no harm. He gets confused sometimes about what year it is and who people are. He has permission to look after the house. Please leave him alone, he is happy here."'

'I told him to put the last bit,' Alan says.

'Do you mean Dad's been here, like, recently?' Aisa says, looking at her sisters and Jane as if they'd know, then back to Alan.

'He comes every month,' Alan says, looking down at his feet. 'He helps me.'

'He helps you?' Nina says, sounding sceptical.

'Here?' says Lizzie. 'Dad comes back here?'

'Every month,' Alan says again. 'No matter what.'

With their mum gone, and Dad retired from the railways, all he seemed to care about was his girls. And, in response, they try hard not to spend any time with him. If you asked Nina why, she couldn't really tell you, except that being in that house, with all those reminders of Mum, it's too much. It's just too much.

They've tried to get him to join the social club in the town, but he says it's for old people, and besides, he has a friend that he helps out, tidying up the garden and stuff.

'That's enough for me,' he said earlier, or rather yesterday, when they tried again. 'I have my friend.'

'Bullshit,' Aisa had coughed, and they'd all laughed, the three sisters, hiding their hysteria in the kitchen.

'Isn't he a bit old for imaginary friends?' Nina had said, remembering too late that Lizzie also used to make up imaginary friends to stave off loneliness.

But Dad wasn't lying, was he? The truth is standing in front of them. The truth bashed her over the head earlier tonight. Her body still throbs with the pain of it.

Nina can't take all this in. She should be pleased to see her sisters. And pleased to see that 'the gunman' was Jane, who is actually defending her, rather than wanting to hurt them. But she's just so confused. And hurt.

'Why did you call me Rosemary?' she says, looking up at Alan.

'You really do look like her,' Jane says, still holding the gun rigidly towards Alan, but casting a look over her shoulder at Nina. 'The way she used to look.'

'This really isn't Rosemary?' Alan says. 'But she looks just the same, I saw her working here ... the other day, it was—'

'That was thirty years ago! And Mum is dead,' Nina shouts.

'I'm sorry, I forget things these days ...' Alan says, tears clouding his rheumy eyes. 'Rosemary died?'

'Enough of this soap-opera dementia act! You hit Nina over the head and you could have killed her,' Aisa says, moving her own body in front of Nina's. 'Then you dragged her downstairs like a bag of spuds. Look at her!'

Alan is shaking his head. 'No,' he says. 'No, you're wrong. She was looking in the mirror and she saw me and fainted. I think I scared her and I thought it was ... I thought she was Rosemary and then she just—'

'She fainted, so you, what, dragged her all the way down into a dungeon?'

'I'm sorry, I'm sorry,' he cries. 'I panicked. I just wanted to keep her safe until she woke up, it's not safe in the house if those explorer men come in, and they could find my tent. I carried her down as best I could and then I went to the river to get white willow bark.' He holds out something in his hand, but Nina recoils. 'It'll help the bruises,' he says, sounding hurt.

'My dad told me that Alan was looking after the place when we left,' Jane says. 'But I had no idea he'd still be here, or that he was suffering from dementia now and—' The noise of a car engine interrupts her. They all turn to stare down the drive at the bouncing lights, heading their way.

Alan flinches. 'No one should come here,' he says. 'Your dad told me that, Jane.'

78

LIZZIE – 4:02 a.m.

They watch as an old car bobs cheerfully, obliviously, towards them. Lights on full. It bounces over potholes, sloshes through puddles. In this new light, the true horror of the building is lit up like a cathedral. Or maybe it's more like a dilapidated haunted house ride at the fair. Ivy has crept up the sides, poking its green fingers into every hole and gap. The lintels of the window frames are riddled with holes, great chunks missing like someone has taken a bite out of a Cadbury's Flake. The glass is all intact, but it's tinged green, shining like cats' eyes in the glare. The building looks bigger in this light. A great crumbling mountain of a building, floodlit for full dramatic effect.

The Morris Minor pulls up at the small crowd, the handbrake ringing out like a yelp. For a moment, the lights stay at full beam, keeping the windscreen black, the insides unknowable to everyone except Lizzie, who rushes forward.

'It's Rafferty,' she cries out, the silhouette of a man finally becoming visible as the lights dim.

'Who?' Aisa says, looking at Nina, who shrugs.

'My boyfriend.'

'Boyfriend?' Nina says, but Lizzie rushes forward and opens the driver's door.

'You came!'

'The one time you're a damsel in distress?' he says, climbing out carefully. 'Of course I came, it's probably my only chance to ever rescue you.'

For a moment, Lizzie forgets about her sisters. About the fact she is bedraggled and probably smelly. About Jane. About that cellar and its secrets. About Alan and the gun. About all of it. She's just so happy to see him. A relief that she's never experienced before. The purity of the feeling staggers her.

'How long did it take you to get here?' she says, kissing him on the lips and wrapping her arms inside his smoking jacket, limpetting onto his warm body. 'When did you hear the message?'

He hugs her back, their hearts mashed together. 'I heard it while you were leaving it,' he laughs, looking around. 'Wow, look at this place. But, er, problem was I was half asleep, and in my delirium, I thought you'd come home and were talking to me. When I woke up again to use the toilet and saw you weren't actually there, I realised what must have happened and I came downstairs and saw the light on your answering machine.'

'You left *yourself* a message?' Nina asks from behind her. 'When did you do that?'

'When I went out looking for you,' she says, then realises that Nina doesn't know any of what happened while she was missing.

'I called 100 to ask the operator to call you back,' Rafferty says.

'It doesn't work that way,' Lizzie laughs and he smiles rakishly. Oh God, he's just so lovely.

'Well, it didn't, no. So I listened to the message again and got on your computer and looked up the name you'd said. Moirthwaite Manor. Luckily, there's only one.'

'Very lucky,' Aisa says behind them.

'I didn't even pause to get dressed, for shame. And then the old girl got me here.' He pats the bonnet of the Morris Minor, the headlights still shining in a thick pool that they've all gravitated towards. 'Top speed of sixty-five and I did it all the way.'

'Rafferty restored this himself,' Lizzie gushes, turning to her sisters and Jane before she can stop herself. They at least have the good grace to fake interest.

'You know about cars?' Nina says and Rafferty tilts his head modestly.

'A little.'

'Do you happen to have any spare petrol?' she asks and Rafferty nods.

'Elizabeth said in her message that you'd run out, so I brought some with me.'

He walks around to the boot, twists the handle and pulls out a jerry can. She sees that her sisters are thrilled, they're not mocking, even though he's wearing vintage striped pyjamas, a smoking jacket and his old-fashioned boots, such was his hurry. She squeezes him to her again, the fuel sloshing in the can.

Nina, Lizzie and Rafferty climb into the old car to drive down to the Mini, Nina in the front with her seat pushed back and her bad leg – her worst leg – stretched out.

'Hang on,' calls Lizzie through the window as they're about to drive off. 'Where did Alan go?'

'He can't have gone far,' Jane says, speaking for the first time since she held the gun to him.

'I guess he never has.'

79

AISA – 4:21 a.m.

Jane showed her the bullets as soon as they walked back inside, rummaging in her pocket and then furtively opening her hand, that same smile she always had when she did something sneaky. A smile Aisa had forgotten for thirty years.

'I didn't know how to put them in,' she said, her voice quiet and intense as it ever was. A voice Aisa couldn't have described yesterday. 'I was so out of my depth.'

'I don't think any of us knew what we were doing tonight,' Aisa says, a sliver of the old awkwardness, the old excitement she'd felt when talking to one of her older sisters' friends as equals. 'Except maybe Lizzie.'

'Good old Lizzie,' Jane says. 'God, I forgot what she was like. I've missed her, I think.'

Now Aisa sits on the sofa and Jane fusses with the fire before turning to her and throwing her sooty hands up. 'I don't know what the bloody hell I'm doing,' she laughs.

'An absolute mood,' Aisa laughs, surprised to be able to.

'I can't believe you're here. All of you,' Jane says, getting a small flame going and then sitting on the same sofa as Aisa. Her voice has a faint Midlands twang now she's more relaxed. 'And

I'm so sorry I …' She screws up her face. 'I mean, what the hell am I saying, but I'm so sorry I *held you at gunpoint*.'

'You were outnumbered,' Aisa says. 'But I mean, yeah, it wasn't my favourite part of the night. I can't believe I didn't wet myself.'

'This is the most I've laughed in some time, which is messed up,' Jane says.

Aisa doesn't know what to say, so she just waits.

'My dad died last week,' Jane says. 'So, you know, not a barrel of laughs in Casa Proctor.'

'I'm so sorry,' Aisa says, trying to picture Jane's dad but drawing a blank. Legs. Shoes. Adult male. That's about it.

'That's why I'm here,' she says. 'I have his phone now. His old brick.' She smiles. 'And I'd been putting off coming up here, but I got an alert earlier this evening. Someone had triggered the cameras. They hadn't been on for years, but someone had switched them on and … Well, I was worried, to be honest.'

She stretches her hands towards the fire and Aisa notices they're shaking. She wants to reach out and hold them, but she doesn't.

'I was still coming to terms with things, not just Dad but … other things. Things I knew I'd have to deal with, things your mum told me. And then it seemed like someone might get to those things first and force my hand, so I … I just got a train up to Penrith and got a taxi here and—'

Aisa can't keep up with the story. 'Sorry, hang on. You said earlier that my mum showed you my photograph and you just said she told you things. You went to see her at the hospice, didn't you?'

'Yes, just once.'

'So it was you that I saw that time. I'd gone to get some air and when I came back, she wasn't alone.'

'I didn't realise, I'm sorry, I—'

'I just left when I saw you. It meant she had company and running away is kind of my thing. It ... it was hard. At the end. Intense.' Aisa frowns. 'Did you not come to the funeral?'

'I didn't know she'd died,' Jane says. 'I guess no one else knew how to contact me except her. I called the hospice a couple of weeks after I saw her and they told me I was too late. Said she'd left me a card though.'

'You got one too?'

Jane nods. 'I think she meant to give it to me when I saw her, but I ... I was too upset that time, I just left. I regret that now. Anyway, they sent it on to me.'

'Don't feel bad, of course you were upset. She looked so ill at the end, it was hard for us all.'

'No, well, I mean yeah, I was upset, seeing her so ... diminished ... But ... no. The reason I was so cut up that last time was because ...' Jane sighs and turns to Aisa, their eyes locking. 'She finally told me what happened to my mother.'

80

ROSEMARY – July 1992

Bob gets back with the hired van while the girls are at school and we work on autopilot, silently shoving boxes and bags into the back of it. Lifting the few bits of worn furniture we're going to take, not knowing how long we'll need to stay with my auntie in Cheshire and stash it in her garage. As long as it takes to get new jobs and find a house, I guess.

This house looks filthy as we expose its hidden parts. Layers of dirt that have been covered by daily life suddenly revealed. A rectangle of wall that had been hidden by the TV, the original colour, untouched by sunlight. The girls' heights through the years, grooved into the kitchen door frame. Moment upon moment captured in the wood, left for some other family to paint over. I press my palm to Aisa aged three, remembering how she slowly rose onto her toes, thinking we hadn't noticed. I run a thumb over Lizzie when she had that growth spurt at six and went briefly from a broad bean to a string bean. Nina, at the top of them all, almost too old to want to do this anymore. I have a compulsion to kiss every one of these little marks, but I stop myself. There's no time for maternal madness today.

As we do a final sweep of the upstairs, I realise how many of these things were donated in the early days of our marriage and feel a rush of grief and pity for everything we're going to leave. Our bedroom looks smaller somehow, with all our clothes bagged or binned. This bedroom where we barely slept last night, Bob grunting and twisting, working through his hangover prematurely. And me just lying there, planning what I would say, how I would do what I need to do. And thinking about the girls. How we're about to rip their roots up out of the soil, and we'd better bloody make it count.

'If we're to go when the girls finish school,' Bob says, rubbing his hand through his dust-flecked hair, 'you should—'

'I know,' I cut him off with a squeeze of his rough hand. 'You can do the last bits?'

'Yeah,' he says, looking around at the scraps and shrugging. 'There's not a lot, is there.'

I bump up the drive and park in the usual spot, tucked into the brambles where I first took Jane to pick blackberries. Teaching her to choose the sweetest ones just on the cusp of ruin. My little car settles into the grooves in the gravel that it's gradually made over the years. I have the manor keys in my bag, but it's not my usual work day, so as ridiculous as it feels, I walk to the front door and lift the heavy brass fox knocker.

Jane is watching me from her window as I slam the knocker down. I'm trying to act calmly.

Same as ever. Even though nothing is the same.

It takes a long time for anyone to come to the door. I wonder if William is napping. He pretends not to, but I know he likes a nap. I know his daily patterns as closely as Bob's.

Behind the door, I hear the shuffle of day slippers on the terracotta tiles I'd cleaned just yesterday. Another of these spaces that I know so intimately but that were never really mine. The door handle is fumbled and turned, and the door finally opens.

'Rosemary,' he says. 'Is everything OK?'

William's hair almost reaches his shoulders, the back of it curling around his neck like those brambles. It's normally worn slicked back, a look that was bookish, even raffish, when he was twenty-one. But loose and unkempt, it makes him look derelict now. I'm struck that he always has it neat and tidy when I'm here, and as he reaches a hand up to smooth it, something tiny loosens and slips inside me, a pull to him that I've not felt in years. I reach for his hand, which surprises both of us, and then I ask if I can come in to talk.

'Of course,' he says, turning with a slight sigh.

He's aged prematurely in front of me and I hadn't really noticed. He's wearing dark brown cord trousers, and a navy shirt that I washed and pressed myself. His hair is thinning, a few peeks of scalp visible where his fingers have just urgently combed.

He reminds me of someone and it takes a moment to realise that he looks like the Brigadier. I'd not seen it in him before, but it must haunt him every time he looks in the mirror, before he greases his hair back and shaves the grey off his chin.

We are in the hall, and I can't help but laugh when he offers to make *me* tea. But I let him, following him to the kitchen and watching him fill the kettle, spark the hob.

'I came to let you know—' I start.

'Are you leaving?' he says, his eyes meeting mine. I nod. 'You've given us a lot of years, Rosemary. I can only thank you.'

This is not how I had planned it. Not what I was expecting. As he fills the teapot with leaves and reaches for cups, I carry on with my speech, even though it feels redundant now.

'We've got an opportunity,' I say. 'Bob's been offered a job down in … down south.' The lie feels angular, hard to get out of my mouth, but he doesn't seem to notice.

'Good for him,' he says. 'I know it's been hard.'

'The problem is, we need to go today. It's all happened really quickly.'

'Today?' He rubs a hand over his face. 'Jane will, well... you know. We'll both—'

'Me too,' I say, my voice catching in my throat. It surprises me, but I mean it.

He steps towards me but stops. Now he's closer than he should be, yet he doesn't touch me and I don't touch him.

His breath is heavy, equine. I can feel its warmth, just barely, on my face. My chest feels tight, my heart batting up to its edges like a little boat, edging back and forth on its harbour rope.

'William,' I say. The familiarity of that nose. The narrow shoulders. Inheritance is such a curse. 'William,' I say, softer this time. There are things he still doesn't know, things that cannot be taken back if said out loud. That can only be said once, said now.

He looks back at me, expectant but also... resigned, I think. Like he already knows, and I just have to say it. Not Selina. Not that. He can never know that, or all of this was for nothing. The other thing.

'It's just...' I start.

William stares back, his breath quickens. But I think of Bob. His arms trembling with exhaustion as he loaded the van. The care he took over packing up the girls' things: Lizzie's books, Nina's favourite pens, Aisa's special teddy. William could not tell me which is Aisa's special teddy. It's far too late to teach him now. It's far too late to even think about telling him. I step back from the edge. The time for this confession has long passed.

'It's just that... I still have one more favour to ask,' I say, and the moment, the portal to a different outcome, closes.

'One more?' he says, and smiles in surprise. He pours the

tea into the cups as he says, 'You've never once asked me for a favour.'

'Well, I need to leave with no notice, I think that's a favour.'

'You should have left years ago, Rosemary,' he says, handing over my tea. He hasn't made it how I take it. I say nothing and he smiles again, a sort of sad smile. 'What's the other favour?'

'I hate to ask, but I need to borrow some money. I was hoping...' I swallow. 'I was hoping five hundred pounds, which I know is a lot but... It's expensive to move and to start over and—'

He shakes his head and takes my tea, placing it down next to his. Then he puts both hands on my shoulders and pulls me to him awkwardly. Our chests collide, we're out of practice at any kind of proximity and a gasp slips from my lips.

'I can't lend you money,' he says into my hair and my shoulders sag. 'But I have two thousand in cash, give or take.' I don't understand and open my mouth to ask, but he interrupts. 'It's the least you deserve. Just take it. Start again. Somewhere much better than this.'

Our tea sits cooling on the side, but I know we won't drink it now. A full stop has been reached. I feel ancient and exhausted, millennia old. A moment reached, a secret kept. I sag under its weight.

William goes to the safe in his office and I'm hovering in the doorway when I see a movement in the corner of my eye.

'Are you leaving me too?' Jane says, biting her lip. She's holding a French textbook in one hand and a pencil in the other. I must have interrupted a lesson.

'Sit on the stairs with me a sec, love,' I say.

She sits down daintily and I sit flush to her, our hips touching. I put my arm tentatively around her. She's not a tactile child normally, but she leans in to me.

'I'm leaving this job, Jane, but I'm not leaving you. OK?'

'You are, you're leaving like Mummy left, and you always said you wouldn't.'

'I won't be working here,' I say, but I lift my spare hand to my heart and pat my chest. 'But you will always be in here, and I hope I will always be in there.' I point to her narrow chest. 'Just like your mummy is.'

Her chin wobbles, just briefly, and I can see her fighting tears. She almost never cries, but she lets herself now.

'I will write to you,' I say, as the tears slide silently over her sharp cheekbones. 'I promise.'

'Mummy never writes,' she says. 'And you won't either.'

'One day,' I say, whispering as I hear William's footsteps approach, 'I will tell you what happened to your mummy, but you have to know that she loved you with all her heart.' William is in the hall now. 'And I promise,' I say, using my normal voice again, 'that *I* will write. Cross my heart and hope to die.'

81

ROSEMARY – July 1992

The girls are finally asleep in the back of the Mini, exhausted from hours of complaining and questioning. My mother didn't help matters, asking awkward questions right in front of them as we said goodbye. I knew Aunt Winnie would tell her, gloating probably, as there's always been rivalry between that side of the family and this, but I hoped my mum would at least listen to my reasons. The reasons I'd cobbled together anyway.

'I just don't understand why you have to go so soon?' she'd said, clutching the girls to her even though she barely sees them. It's not like she's always on hand for babysitting.

'We just need to get settled before Bob starts the job,' I say, hoping she doesn't ask for more details on this imaginary job, hoping he actually gets one before she comes to visit. William's money won't last long otherwise, despite being so much more than I expected.

I can't tell her the truth. I can't tell anyone the truth. That Aisa saw something in the cellar of Moirthwaite Manor, and if she goes in there again, if she tells a teacher, if she convinces somebody to look ... everything unravels. I have to get her away. If I could get Jane away too, I would. I made a vow to myself, years ago, that I would make sure she was looked after. The best way for her to be looked after is for William to take her far away from this place and start a new life. I told him as much earlier. Only after he'd handed me the envelope of cash, of course, in case he reacted badly. But he didn't, he seemed to listen.

I said that it wasn't the best thing for Jane to stay, but I couldn't tell him the full reason why and so I just have to pray he took it on board. And that, in the meantime, Bob has fixed the cellar wall well enough to stop her getting through it again. Poor Jane. I have to trust that Jane won't tell anyone. That she has no one to tell. If she was going to tell her father, she would have. *I hope.* I wonder if she'll ever realise what she unearthed, maybe when she's a mother and her mind wanders back to her own childhood. God, I hope not. But then, if she doesn't, if they stay there unloved, unclaimed, is that really right either?

ROSEMARY – 1987

Bob is here, right beneath me, in the Brigadier's cellar. The way my belly is churning and my heart is thumping, you'd think he was wrestling a dragon down there rather than performing some basic handyman functions with his friend. But in some ways, both of those things are true.

I've already mopped the hallway floor, now I'm pretending to be dusting the balustrades. Circling the cupboard door like a dog waiting for its master.

I don't like him being here. Not just because it's my domain, a parallel life I've cultivated to the side of him. But mostly because of the effect it has on him. He insisted he was OK right up until we got here, but he's not. He got blotto last night and on the drive over this morning he was shaking like a little terrier.

William wants every trace gone. Of what, he didn't say. I've not been down there myself, but Bob knew exactly what he meant as soon as I relayed the message. Cash in hand. Generous amount. Alan can't do it by himself. It needs to be someone William can trust. Someone who understands. And Bob understands all too well.

Selina is in the office with William, arguing again. Ordinarily, I would discreetly retreat to another part of the house, but I'm rooted here. I need to see Bob the second he's out of there, need to hug him and make sure he feels safe. To throw my body on the bomb.

'I don't care what you say or do,' I hear Selina say. 'You will *never* keep my daughter from me. Never.' She starts to emerge, just her thin shoulder, exposed by the loose T-shirt. Suddenly she's yanked back inside and William emerges instead. I have never seen him look like this. But I've seen this expression before, on his father. It punches the air from my lungs and I stumble in my panic to move out of view.

'You're not taking her anywhere,' he shouts. I rush into the library, my duster in hand. William storms up the stairs towards Jane's room and Selina shuffles into the hall, dragging a suitcase. Even from many feet away, I can see her trembling. I watch as she stands by the front door, staring up in the direction of her child. I think she's going to go upstairs to continue the fight until they tire themselves out as usual. Though this is more extreme, far more aggressive than I've seen them before. Instead, still shaking, Selina grabs her handbag from the hook, pulls on some shoes from a pile I've not long straightened and storms out. Seconds later, the front door opens again and she flings her keys onto the floor, then slams her way out.

William is still upstairs, guarding Jane, when Bob comes up into the hall. 'I can't do it anymore,' he says. 'Not today.'

'What about Alan?'

'He's already gone,' Bob says. 'We'd just started on the thing they used for Reflection. We got it down off the wall OK, but it left a big hole and it was ... it was hard for us to touch it ...' He rubs his wrists automatically, and I reach out and take his hands in mine. 'Alan made up some rubbish about tomatoes and went off to his shed ages ago. It's a right mess down there, but I can't ... not today.'

I tell Bob to wait in the car, put the cleaning things away and then rush out. It's my normal time to leave anyway, give or take. As we head down the drive, en route to the childminder, I try to ask more.

He just shakes his head. 'We shouldn't have gone down there,' he says. 'I'd forgotten what it was really like.'

It's heady today, but thick rather than hot. Still, I wouldn't like to be out in it. Not like whoever that is down the lane, struggling with something. As we get closer, I realise it's Selina and her suitcase. I didn't think she'd actually go this far, not with all her stuff. She's threatened so many times, but this looks different. And he had looked different. For the first time, I saw his genes in action. Saw a glimmer of what William might be capable of, when pushed. Selina's crying so hard that her face is puce and she's clattering away from the house, the case banging into her legs so she zigzags around like a dying wasp.

I pull up next to her and Bob jumps out, flipping the passenger seat forward so she can climb in the back.

'Are you sure?' she says, as Bob takes her suitcase and tries to stuff it in the boot.

'Of course,' I say. As she settles herself, I reach back and pat her arm, just quickly. I try not to picture William's face earlier, the way the tendons on his neck had bulged like they were ready to snap. 'You're with friends now.'

I feel like I'm harbouring a fugitive as I let her into our house while Bob walks to get the girls. If she's shocked by the size and chaos of our two-bed terrace, she doesn't let on. 'We don't have a spare room,' I say, 'but the sofa's quite comfy. If you want to stay.'

'Thank you,' she says. 'You're a real pal.'

Now she's wearing a big Hofmeister 'Follow the Bear' top as a nightie and I'm wearing my Stevie Nicks T-shirt and shorts. We look like we're at an overgrown sleepover. Rizzo and Sandy. The girls are finally in bed, Bob is in the pub and we're on the sofa, drinking the bottle of wine that I won in the school Christmas raffle last year. It's about the only booze Bob doesn't like and I'm not normally a wine drinker either, but Selina is. I can tell that from the way she swallows, trying not to show what she thinks of this cheap plonk.

She has just told me that she's going back for Jane. And I've just misunderstood.

'Yeah, you'll make it work,' I say, and she looks up from the glass she's staring into, twirling it in her palm like a crystal ball.

'No,' she says. 'I mean I'm going back to get her, and then we're *both* leaving.'

'He won't let you,' I say and she looks at me sharply. 'But you know he won't, Selina. He'll fight you, and he has the money and determination to do it.'

'He chose that house over me,' she says. 'He doesn't get to keep Jane too. I've told him that and it scares the crap out of him, he knows I mean it.'

'Where would you go? If you had Jane, I mean?'

'She's on my passport, so—'

'The States?'

She nods. 'Yeah, take her to Cedarville to see where her mom grew up. Show her all the sights – the churches, the lake, my daddy's tackle shop. Not forever, because it's boring as hell and

I'd never do that to Bill, but just for a little bit. To show him ... to make him realise, you know?'

She takes a big gulp of drink, grimaces just slightly.

'I just have to get my daughter, Rosemary.'

I have always liked the way she says my name, turning it from three clear syllables into a sloping Roh-s'm'rry. The wine has gone to my head, because I only just stop myself saying this out loud.

'I feel so dumb for throwing the keys back in,' she sighs, stretching her suntanned legs out like a cat about to clean itself. 'But if I show up banging on the door, there's no way he'll let me come in and just take her. He's as determined to stop me as I am to take her. I don't think there's anything he wouldn't do. You've not seen how he gets, not when he's really angry.'

I don't say anything, but I think of earlier. And I think of the Brigadier.

'I can't be apart from her,' Selina says. 'I just can't.'

'No,' I say, 'you can't. No mum can.'

'No,' she says slowly. 'No mom can.'

I look at her – how far is she willing to go? How far is any mother willing to go? All the way. Of course she is. And how well do I know William really? Is she right to be scared?

'Maybe you should try talking to him with someone there to keep you safe, someone neutral? If you knock on the door and—'

She shakes her head. 'There is no one neutral. If you or Bob did it, he'd fire you, Rosemary. And I don't really know anyone else. If I lawyer up, he'll do the same. And he has far deeper pockets. I just need to get her out.'

I stare at my glass and imagine it was one of my girls in that house, behind that locked door.

'I think I know how you can get in without him realising,' I say. 'But you can't ever, ever tell William that I helped you.'

*

We wait for Bob to crash home, stagger up the stairs and fall flat on the bed. I peel his shoes off for him, pop the window open to let the booze fumes out and then check on both the girls one last time, kissing their foreheads. It's a sticky night and their sweaty, pink skin coats my lips with the taste of salt.

No, no mother can be apart from her children.

Selina has changed into some jeans and a long-sleeved T-shirt and tucked her suitcase next to our sofa. I've already told her that she can take some of Lizzie's clothes for Jane, they're a similar age, so she doesn't have to waste time in her room. She can just grab Jane and go. I have to trust that she'll know how to keep her own child quiet on the way out.

I'm still wearing my T-shirt and shorts so I can just slip back into bed afterwards without any faffing, not that Bob's likely to wake up easily. And then, first thing tomorrow, I'll drive them both to the airport.

I switched my wine for tea as soon as we came up with this plan, but I'm glad that my senses are still slightly deadened. If I think about this too clearly, I don't know if I'll be able to go through with it. I only hope that I'm OK driving the car, it's still new. New to us. But when I sit in the driver's seat, window down, the fresh night air brings all my senses to the front. Adrenaline also helps me stay sharp as we rattle along the thin road from the village to the manor.

I have never been out here at night. The fields and hedges seem to be writhing with menace. A huddle of bats flap up towards the moon and the little stone walls that guard the road seem like sharp incisors, ready to swallow us up. 'Are you sure about this?' I say and Selina nods.

'Are you sure, Rosemary?'

Am I? Too late to back out now. 'Of course.'

I've told her everything I know about the passageway, but as I've never actually been in it, she's still going in blind. What I've gathered from Bob and Alan, and some of the boys over the years, is that it leads from the floor of the shed down to under the house, then, somewhere, there is a set of steps that lead up to the hallway cupboard. As long as she finds those steps, and goes up quietly, she'll be able to move around the house without anyone knowing. She just needs to get Jane, slip out of the front door and make it down the drive, where I'll be waiting in the car.

As she climbs out of the Mini, our flaky old torch in her hand, I think of something else. 'Don't put your torch on until you're fully in the passageway,' I whisper. 'And avoid Alan's tent. If he hears you, he'll raise the alarm or ...' I think of the gun he uses for rabbits, but I don't want to scare her. 'Just be really careful, OK?'

'OK,' she says quietly. 'Thank you so much for this, Rosemary.'

'Good luck, Selina.'

I've quietly turned the car around without putting the lights on. Now I'm ready to roll away down the drive as soon as the precious cargo is on board. I'm not thinking about William. I'm resolutely not imagining him finding Jane's bed empty tomorrow. Walking around that monstrous house, desperately looking for the people he loves. I'm not thinking about looking him in the eye knowing I helped squirrel them away. Instead, I'm thinking about how long Selina's been gone. I'm wearing my dad's old watch, the only watch I own, and wondering if it's keeping time correctly because it feels like Selina left the car hours ago, but apparently it was only thirty minutes. How long is this passageway?

An hour later and she's still not out. I've left the car where it is and walked up to the house. The lights are all off, at least at the front of the building, and I wonder if she ended up reconciling with William and they're curled up asleep while muggins stands out here, shivering. That doesn't feel likely though; I can't imagine her not coming out to tell me to go home. Maybe even William thanking me for bringing her back.

The moon is bright enough for me to see that all the curtains are closed, but Selina took our only torch, so I can't see much else. I pick up a tiny stone and weigh it in my hand... But if I'm wrong, and it's just taking her much longer to extract Jane, chipping William's window won't help her.

Oh God, I wish I knew what to do. It's cold now, my T-shirt and shorts ridiculously flimsy against the night air. I walk around the side of the house and follow the path she would have taken until I reach the shed. Alan's tent is just over there, but there's no light or movement from inside. I take a deep breath and open the shed door, not sure if I imagined the squeak. I can barely see the floor, and squat down, knees clicking from years of scrubbing on them, and gently pat the floor in front of me until I touch the rim of the entrance. As my eyes adjust, I can see that the hatch is still up. It's lucky I didn't fall.

There's nothing else for it, I take a deep breath and climb down.

The passageway itself is lit with dim bulbs and I can just about see all the way along. It's cold and slightly damp, as if the seasons can't reach down here, and I'm shivering as I walk along with my bare legs and tennis shoes. I can see cobwebs and mouse droppings, it smells ripe but somehow dead too. God, I don't want to be here.

I'm reminded of the stupid prayer my mum used to say when she put me to bed and whisper it to myself as I step carefully along the passageway. I can barely see Dad's watch in this dim light, but whatever it says, I feel like I'm running out of time.

I speed up and my urgent footsteps echo back to me, but there's a thin reedy sound too. A voice? A cry? I stop to listen, hoping it's my imagination. Then I hear it again. It could be her, or it could just be the whistle of old pipes, the wind trapped somewhere.

'Selina?'

There's no answer and I rush forward, emerging from the passageway into a kind of open hallway, with some doors off it. I'm punch-drunk, reeling that there is a whole other layer to the house. Bob has only described it in slivers, and in my head, I'd joined them together into some fractured thing that was nothing like this. This is huge. A full shadow version of Moirthwaite Manor was lying under my feet all these years.

There are three doors ahead of me – no, my mistake, there's one more round the L-shaped corner. She could be behind any of them. I look for the stairs, the ones she was supposed to go up, but there's bits of wood piled up and slabs of metal propped all around the walls. I can just make out a kind of dark enclave and I think the staircase might be in there, but there's a lot of detritus in the way. I'm briefly furious with Alan and Bob for leaving it like this, but that's hardly fair.

I think, from the little Bob said, the stairs must be there. One thing's certain, she can't have gone up there. But at least that means William can't come down and find me here, not through all that.

Selina probably couldn't even see the stairs. So she's either come back out the passageway and not told me, or she's still down here, devastated that the plan failed.

I hear the sound again. It must be her. But she can't just stay here crying and I can't stay out all night. I need to find her.

I try the first door, but it's just an old cupboard. A prehistoric mop and bucket, a broom that looks fit for a witch. The next door opens onto an empty bedroom, coated in dust. By the look of the bed, this hasn't been used since the boys left. I shudder, imagining having to spend the night here.

The next room is an old coal store full of creepy-crawlies. I shut that one quickly.

The sobbing has stopped, and I wonder if I just imagined it as I reach for the last door.

How I wish I'd imagined this.

82

ROSEMARY – 1987

'What did you do to her?' I cry.

Selina is splayed motionless on the floor, her head on Alan's lap. His hands are stroking her hair and he's sobbing quietly. Lying on the floor in front of them is a strange long ladder, with two straps at each end, tattered as if they've been slashed. Our old kitchen torch is on the floor next to Alan's knees and I reach for it, running the dim light over this… thing. When I do, a blade sticking through the bars near one end bounces the light back to me. It's covered in black blood.

'What the hell is …' I swing the light round to Selina. Her face looks pale and serene, but blood has pooled from her throat, soaking her hair and Alan's lap. There's so much of it that nausea suddenly sweeps through me and I battle not to vomit.

'I didn't do anything,' he sobs. 'I just found her. She was caught up and I tried to help her … I did, Rosemary, I promise.'

'Oh Christ, we need to get her to a hospital.' I slide onto the floor next to her, trying to find a pulse on her tattered red neck. I can see the damaged wall from where Bob and Alan must have pulled this contraption down. 'What the hell is that ladder thing?'

'Reflection,' he whispers. 'I found her caught in it. Her ankles and hands were in the straps and . . . he made it so you couldn't get out once you were in, not without—'

'The Brigadier?'

He looks behind him as if the dead man could yet appear, then nods. 'And she kept saying she thought it was the steps. I told her to stay still, but she didn't. She made it worse.'

'Oh Christ, Alan, I can't find a pulse, lay her down, we need to do mouth to mouth.'

He's not listening, he's still rambling as I brush the hair from her face and pull her from his lap onto the floor. My friend, my poor friend.

'We'd got it off the wall yesterday, but we just left it propped up. We didn't want to keep touching it.'

I put my hands on her chest, hoping to feel it moving, but it's not. Alan is still slumped on the floor, his hands in his lap as if she's still there.

'She was facing the wrong way, Rosemary. We had to stay upright on it or the blade would cut our backs, but she's short so the blade was by her neck . . . and she wouldn't stop panicking and moving and then it fell on the floor with her still caught in it.'

I've never done CPR, I've only ever seen it on *Casualty*, but I have no choice. I put my mouth over hers. She tastes of iron and wine. I close my eyes and blow everything I have into her. Once, twice, five times. I rise up, and Alan is still babbling about finding her. About hearing people in the grounds and going to his shed and hearing a cry.

I lattice my hands together and press onto her chest. She feels so fragile, like I might crack her open. I take a deep breath and then I push down, gently at first and then harder. There's a gurgling sound and more blood appears from her throat. No breath. And I know then that there's nothing I can do. Nothing I could have done. 'Alan,' I say. 'She's dead.'

*

I run up the passageway and down the drive so fast I think my lungs could genuinely rupture. I can't pump my legs fast enough, can't get the key in the ignition, can't work the handbrake with my shaking, sweaty hand. I have to get to Bob, have to get him back here to help. Alan is completely useless by himself. But everything seems insurmountable. My feet slip off the pedals. I can't risk the lights waking William, so I slide along in the dark, rolling without the engine, knocking the car into brambles and God knows what like a pinball.

When I hit the lane, I manage to get the engine started, flip the lights on and rattle back to the village. I slide into the usual parking spot outside our terrace and sit there, for just a moment, staring at the phone box. I could phone the police now, anonymously, and no one would know who I was. As far as anyone knows, I've been asleep in bed next to Bob like I have been every night for seven years and change.

Would they believe Alan if he said I was there? That she was trying to sneak into the house to the kidnap her own child, on my instruction, and got caught in a... bloody torture device that my own husband had left there? A device that those poor boys had once been strapped into. The fear they must have felt, having to stay rigid, knowing that going slack even once would have pushed their backs onto that blade. Those boys, like Bob and Alan, who both have police records from back along...

I slap my own face. A woman is dead. She's dead because of me, but all the cogs in my head are churning through ways to get *myself* out of this. A woman, a mother, a friend, a wife, a daughter, is dead. I climb out of the car and unlock the house. Inside, our own phone sits waiting. I could call 999 and confess. It was an accident. It wasn't anyone's fault and—

'Mummy?'

I look up at the stairs. Nina is at the top in her nightie, golden hair plastered all over her forehead and her tatty old dog teddy hanging from one hand.

'Are you OK, love?' I whisper, climbing halfway up the stairs and then realising my fingers are red with blood. I put them behind my back, lean forward to kiss Nina on the forehead and then shoo her back to bed. 'I'm just getting a glass of water, do you want one?'

'Yes please, Mummy.'

I go back downstairs and wash my hands until the water runs clear and my cuticles are shredded. Back at the manor right now, Alan is sitting on the floor next to her body, waiting for me and Bob to come back. To tell him what to do, to fix this. As I carry a beaker of water back through the living room, I spot Selina's suitcase. Everyone thinks she left. If no one finds her case... but could I really...

I take the beaker of water up to Nina and check on Lizzie. It's OK, they're both all right. They're safe. We're all OK, we're all safe. I repeat it like a prayer as I go in to wake Bob up. Yesterday, he couldn't finish the job. Now he has a far worse task to fulfil.

I put the suitcase back in the boot and we carry the girls to the car. It's too early really, but we can't wait and risk Alan running to wake William, or William coming down to inspect the work, maybe braving the passageway, and finding them like that. It's all too messy, each one of us involved. But it was my idea. I sent her into that tunnel, I gave her the loose, sloppy directions that sent her stumbling into the wrong room looking for steps. Bob and Alan left that contraption lying there, ready to snap its jaws one last time. And Alan, heavy-handed Alan, cutting the straps on her arms and legs with his hunting knife even though it was already too late, her throat had met the blade.

There's no other option.

We pull up to the house and Bob climbs out with his toolbox and waves to William, who is standing in the window of his bedroom, staring out. Bob walks as naturally as he can around the side of the house as William slides his window open and calls down to me, combing his fingers through his hair. He looks so benign now, but what would he do if he knew the truth?

'Bit early isn't it, Rosemary?'

I swallow and try to sound normal. 'Sorry, William, there's a lot more to do than they realised, so Bob wanted to get an early start on it.'

'Are you coming in too?'

I shake my head and desperately try to keep my voice level. 'Just dropping Bob off. I'm not in today, remember?'

'Oh,' he says, 'sorry. A lot on my mind. Don't know if I'm, you know...'

'Coming or going,' I say, my voice sounding screechy and frantic in my head.

He raises one hand in goodbye and closes the window with a bump. I lean on the car and wait for my heart to stop hammering.

The girls have already conked out again by the time I pull into the lay-by by Ullswater, alert for early hikers.

It's clear though, no one is watching as I pull the suitcase from the boot, pop it open and stuff it with extra stones from the side of the road on top of the carefully folded clothes.

My children and the mountains sleep, as I stagger down to the jetty, look around one more time, then let go.

83

JANE – 4:41 a.m.

'The skeleton,' Aisa says. 'Fuck.'

I stare at the fire, imagining how frightened my mother must have been, alone, injured, just trying to reach me. And then falling…

'Oh God, Jane, I'm so sorry about your mum.'

'Yeah, me too,' I say. 'Thirty years of wondering about her, but I never made the link. I thought I'd actually imagined them… those bones.'

'Me too,' Aisa says. 'After a while.'

'And honestly, we left this house soon after you moved and I didn't think about them much at all.'

I feel Aisa shift next to me. Have I lifted thirty years of weight from her, or given her a greater burden than ever? She didn't imagine it, but the reality was worse than she could have ever guessed.

'There's something else,' I say. Because I've learned it's better to know everything, however unpalatable. And I feel a frenzied need to unburden.

'Something other than my dad burying your mum in the wall of your childhood home?' Aisa says. 'Something besides that?'

I smile, I can't help myself. Then I start to laugh, and so does she. And I notice just how sharp her teeth are. I run my tongue along my own upper set, pointed, dangerous. Wolf teeth, my dad always called them. The two of us, the wolf pack.

I reach into my pocket, pull out the envelope and offer it to her. She fumbles and it drops to the floor, the scrawled name staring up at us.

As Aisa reaches down, she says, 'This is my mum's writing.'

I just nod. I know this hand so well, after thirty years of letters and cards, birthdays always remembered. First to Moirthwaite Manor and then to the new-build we moved to, not that long after the Kelseys left.

'What does it say?'

'You can read it, I don't mind.'

She swallows and carefully pulls out the card. A picture of a doll's house on the front, and a shaky version of Rosemary's looping writing on the inside. I watch as she reads. There are only a few paragraphs.

A confession. An apology. Finally, a suggestion.

I'm sorry I waited so long to tell you. I was a coward, yes, but I wanted to protect everyone. Once the truth is out, there's no going back. And I was so scared you would tell your dad, and he would come for her. So now you know you probably have a little sister out there, and I think you would be good for each other.

'Rosemary knew it was hitting me hard that I'd have no family left when Dad died,' I say, finding myself explaining, guilty at knowing about this for longer than her. Guilty that I'd not sought her out yet. 'He got ill around the time that she ... when she realised she wasn't going to get better.'

'So my mum cheated on Dad.' It's not a question. Aisa's voice is flat. Disgusted.

'Just once, according to the card. I wasn't sure whether to believe it, but I asked my dad if he'd had an affair with Rosemary when I was little. I just blurted it out last week and I could tell, just from the look on his face. He said it was just after my mum left. He was lonely and angry, and I guess your mum felt guilty. And I think Bob... I don't think he was coping at the time, that's me reading between the lines though.'

'But your dad—'

'He didn't know about you, no. And I didn't tell him, it was too late to do that to him.'

Aisa doesn't say anything. For a moment, I think she's angry, building up to storming off, but then she unzips her handbag and shoves her hand in, pulling out an identical envelope.

'I've not been able to,' she says. 'I knew there was something, deep down, you know, and I couldn't bring myself to look.'

'How about you do it now?'

She stares at it for a moment and then suddenly slides her thumb under the flap, opens it in one quick move and lets the card fall out. On the front, a picture of Liza Minelli from *Cabaret* stares out. Aisa rubs her thumb over Liza's face, takes a deep breath and flips the card open. 'Who are you, Aisa?' she whispers to herself.

It feels intrusive to watch, so I look at the fire. What's left of it.

I'd read my own card from Rosemary in my staffroom, while my assistant boiled the kettle and fussed around with biscuits, chatting away about nothing. It felt incongruous for life to be happening while I read this message from beyond the grave, but if anyone can handle that kind of dissonance, it's a funeral director.

'I don't know for sure,' Aisa reads from the card as Liza's cartoon kohl eyes bore into me, 'who your biological father is. But there's a very strong possibility that it's William Proctor. To get myself to pick up this pen, I convinced myself this was about health. That you need to know who you are so you can keep yourself safe and well. Things run in families, as you know. But it's not that. Not only that, anyway. Aisa, you are the most alive person I've ever met.'

Her voice cracks, but she doesn't look up and I watch in awe as she manages to keep reading.

'Having you as a daughter has been such a source of joy for me. You've brought me so much happiness, and a few near heart attacks, but mostly happiness. I know every part of you and I love every part of you, but if you don't know this... then I'm getting in the way of you, Aisa, knowing every part of yourself. I know that now. I'm sorry I didn't realise it before.' She pauses and takes a breath. 'The one person I haven't told is Bob. I understand if you can't keep this from him, but I hope you'll find a way to fit things together. He loves you so much that I couldn't bring myself to take that away when he was already losing me.'

Aisa looks up. She's not crying, she looks more shocked than upset. The dazed look I see on the loved ones' faces when people have died suddenly, like they just can't quite make it feel real. Right up until the service, anyway.

She looks at the card again, and finds her place. 'Whatever you decide, I hope you look up Jane, I think she could do with a sister. Her address is in my book. More than anything, I hope you'll forgive me, my little Ace.' Her voice breaks, but she reads the last line. 'Because I'm so, so sorry. I will love you forever and ever, Mum.'

'You don't have to believe it,' I say. 'No one has done tests; we can't know for sure.'

She nods and keeps staring at the card. She brushes her fingertips over the words, brings the envelope to her nose but seems disappointed. 'It just smells like my bag,' she says.

So this is my sister, I think. Do I need a sister, like Rosemary said? I don't know. I needed one when we lived here, when all I had was Dad but he was consumed with – *by* – the house, and all its ghosts. I was always so jealous of Lizzie, of her having two sisters, a mum. I was probably horrible to her because of it. Having someone else to absorb Dad's sadness back then would have been some relief. But that's not a sister, that's a human shield.

At first, it was worse after Rosemary left. He couldn't handle the house without her and none of the local women he got in to help understood what he really needed. None of them were her.

Once we left, moving to the Midlands where there was no memory of any one and it was all brand new – even a new-build house – Dad became a different person. It wasn't immediate, of course. At first, he kept coming back here to check on it, and then arriving home dragging his shadows with him. Then he set up some mad CCTV system that, back then, buzzed a pager if anyone broke in. They never did. And Alan was here anyway. I didn't know he'd ever updated it to his mobile number, right up until his chunk of a phone buzzed earlier tonight. Alan turned the system off years ago, but—

'Did you turn on that big switch by the front door earlier?' I say, and she looks up, blinking.

'What?'

'Don't worry, it doesn't matter.'

It wasn't exactly dark days followed by light, it was more that we slowly emerged through grey. Once we left Cumbria, I had a good childhood. And my dad loved me, I never doubted that.

He became a writer. Not a very good one, but a fulfilled one. I'm not sure he would have wanted anyone to actually read his grand works, he just liked writing them. I laugh, but Aisa doesn't look up from the card. The words must be scored into her retinas by now.

But I guess I'm not totally unaffected. I mean, I played with a skeleton as a child. *I played with my mother's skeleton.* And I stayed obsessed with death. With containing it. I'm a funeral director after all. I did an art degree, but I'm a funeral director. I don't think it would take a psychiatrist to unpick that.

I watch her as Aisa reads it all over again. She has his hair, I think. And his teeth. And the same shoulders as me. It's up to her if she chooses to see this though, so I say nothing.

To have a sister would have meant to share him. I'm not sure if I would have wanted to share my dad when he was alive, but, fuck, I wish I could share this grief.

I hold my hand out to Aisa and she takes it in hers, just briefly, and then lets it fall. 'Are you OK?' I say.

'I don't know,' she says.

'The car's fixed,' Lizzie says, as she barges through the door, brushing herself off.

84

JANE – 5:22 a.m.

Rafferty offers to take Lizzie home with him, but she shakes her head. 'Thank you, my love, but no. I need to sort some stuff out with my sisters,' she says, 'so I'll get the train back later.'

'Are you sure?' he asks.

'Yes, I'm definite. A hot chocolate and a flake,' she says, 'that's what I'm ready for.'

If he's put out, he doesn't show it. Instead, he grabs her by the waist like she's Elizabeth Taylor, not Lizzie Kelsey, dips her slightly and kisses her for so long that we all look away.

'Did Lizzie just *dismiss* that sweet maniac who drove three hours in a *Wacky Races* car to help her?' Aisa says quietly.

'Yeah,' I say. When I pictured what Lizzie might be like as an adult, I just pictured child Lizzie but stretched, not—

'An absolute queen,' Aisa says.

'Good for her,' Nina says. 'Thanks again!' she calls after Rafferty, pointing to the Mini.

'My pleasure,' he says, smoothing his collar and climbing into his car.

'There's something else we need to do,' I say to the Kelseys, although Aisa already knows what I've decided. 'It's not going to be nice but—'

'Jesus Christ, Jane,' Aisa interrupts. 'That's putting it mildly.'

'My mum,' I say. 'She's ... There was an accident when we were little and your parents and Alan were involved and they covered it up and—'

'The bones,' Nina says, rubbing her forehead. 'Is that what you're saying?'

I close my eyes and nod. 'We could go to the police,' I say. 'But I had a different idea.'

'But it's not going to be nice,' Aisa adds, quietly. 'Like she said.'

Nina rebuilds the fire and then lies on the nearest sofa, the shotgun next to her at her request.

'I get that Alan didn't know what he was doing, but he still did it,' she says. 'And he's still out there somewhere.'

She can't go back down with us, she's too hurt and we need her to be able to drive as soon as this is done. This. What a tiny, tiny word.

I open the hallway cupboard door, shine my torch around. I haven't been down here since I was a child. I don't know if I can do this, if I can really—

'Take my hand,' Lizzie says, shoving ahead of me. 'I'll lead you there.'

'And I'll be just behind,' Aisa says. 'We've got you.'

Epilogue

JANE – Six days later

The beautiful black coffin sits backstage, ready for its final performance. It's quite unique, made from black poplar wood. Dad chose it himself, one of the more amusing of our final conversations, me propped on the bed with the brochure I'd brought with me from work, him telling me to just chuck him in an old cardboard box. 'It's more ecological,' he'd said.

'It would definitely be a lot cheaper than the wooden one,' I said, 'but luckily I can get these at trade prices.'

Gallows humour, maybe, but the thought still makes me smile. It was all planned to a T, the poem I would read, the clothes he wanted to be buried in. He even showed me how to do his hair.

Preparing my father's body should have been the hardest thing I'd ever done. But I feel sorry for ordinary mourners, who don't have a hand in these preparations. Alone with their thoughts, treading water, no professional diversions. For me, I was able to use everything I'd learned. I was able to ride pillion on much more of his journey than a daughter normally could.

My assistant, Deb, offered to help, but this was one job I could only do alone. Even before … but especially then. I had worried

I might rush it, my heels snapped at by adrenaline, or fear. But I took as long, maybe longer, than usual. An almost blissful calm. Reunited, at the last moment.

He looked so small on the dressing table. All the time he'd been in hospital, his gown and blankets had hidden the changes. His neck was thinner, his skin looser, I knew that. But underneath, he'd become curled and hollowed, like an autumn leaf. I dressed him carefully, not easy to do alone, and wished I could remember the times that I was small enough to be dressed by him. Though more likely it was my mother and then Rosemary.

The suit he'd chosen was too big for his final body. I cut the jacket slowly along the back with surgical scissors, placed it on him gently and used my hands, and pins, to tailor it. He looked sharper than he had in years. It's always exhausting dressing a body, the dead weight and strange pivot points, but I've been doing this for so long that I was almost on autopilot. Until I placed his shoes. A smell of shoe polish from childhood rushed at me. The way he would buff the toes of my slip-ons, the concentration on his face. Those were easy tears.

And then, when I was sure that I was truly alone, I began the rest of the preparation. Removing the lining of the coffin, the careful latticing, the intricate placement. Hello, goodbye.

I chose my favourite celebrant and my favourite florist, who has filled the funeral chapel with white chrysanthemums for me. A flower that symbolises truth and loyal life. I'm not normally one for symbolism, but it felt right.

I would ordinarily watch this performance from the wings, but I stand at the head of the chapel, gazing at the twenty or so mourners, and clear my throat. 'My father chose a Wordsworth poem for me to read,' I say, my voice quiet and determined. I do not add that I have replaced it with a different Wordsworth poem, but I think he would approve of my choice. I think they both would.

> A slumber did my spirit seal;
> I had no human fears:
> She seemed a thing that could not feel
> The touch of earthly years.

> No motion has she now, no force;
> She neither hears nor sees;
> Rolled round in earth's diurnal course,
> With rocks, and stones, and trees.

It may seem left-field to almost everyone in the chapel, but not the three women on the front bench facing me – Nina, Lizzie and Aisa. And behind them, one man I was expecting and the other I never expected to see again. Alan and Bob.

The wake is held in a nearby village pub that my dad specified, even though I'd never known him visit it. Still, I've changed enough about his service without going against this. The main thing, he emphasised, was that he did not want to be buried in the family crypt in Moirthwaite. No matter what.

I flit between the small groups of people in a daze, not knowing what to say to any of them, not knowing which of Dad's different strands they knew. Only I knew the whole tapestry. I nod and smile at all of their stories, recognising him in almost none of them.

The women from the library are here. And the charity reps, hoping to get some hefty donation from the estate. A few staff from the hospice mill about. And the flotsam and jetsam of casual friendships from over the years. I recognise very few of them and am glad to have a couple of uni friends, my assistant Deb and, of course, Nina, Lizzie and Aisa.

People are curious to know what I'll do with the money, how much I've inherited. They don't ask that outright of course, they inch around it. Sipping from the edges of curiosity like it's hot soup.

'Will you be moving into the family home?' they ask. They mean, of course, my dad's house in the Midlands; I'm not sure anyone knows about Moirthwaite. Dad barely mentioned it, simply saying that he didn't care what I did with it. 'Burn it, for all I care.'

'Is there much to sort out with the solicitor?' That one skims closer to the bullseye. I smile my dumbest smile and respond only to the actual words they are using – 'Not too much, no' – and not the question they're really asking, then I drift off to do it all over again.

The truth is that I don't want to live in my dad's house and I sure as hell don't want to live in Moirthwaite. I can cancel the fee tail. The law changed when I was a teenager apparently, but we didn't find out until Dad was getting his affairs in order, while he still could. But there's something underwhelming about selling that monster off to be yet another hotel. I'd like to use it to help people, but my family doesn't have a great history of such endeavours. Maybe I really should burn it.

I would have let Alan stay on there, I suppose, but Bob has whisked him and his tent off to live with him in Cheshire, something he's apparently been trying to get him to agree to since Rosemary died. He'd been deteriorating for years, but what happened with Nina was the final straw, and Lizzie called Bob to tell him just that when she finally got reception on the way to my funeral parlour on that bleak, sleepless morning six days ago.

The Kelseys had helped me take everything inside and then, at my insistence, left me there. Nina needed to get her ankle checked over, and they all needed to sleep. I'd watched them leave, Nina in the middle, flanked by a sister on each side. They weren't speaking, we were all shell-shocked, after all. But there was a peace between them, an almost visible understanding.

I spot Nina now, standing next to her girlfriend Tessa at the bar. That was the first call Nina made once she got reception during the drive. Pulling into a lay-by and easing herself out to call in private. An apology, she said, though I don't know for what. And a proposal. They're going travelling, giving up their jobs and camping their way around Europe.

'Working out what we really want,' Nina said. Better them than me.

'I haven't told the others yet,' Aisa says, a plate of untouched sandwiches and cocktail sausages in her hand. I didn't realise she was standing next to me until she started to speak. 'And look,' she says, 'William was your dad, not mine. I'm really, genuinely, sorry for your loss. But the stories in that funeral service meant nothing to me. My dad didn't go to university, he isn't a rich man or a writer. The closest he gets to reading a book is circling the stuff he wants from the *Betterware* catalogue.'

We both look over. Bob is gripping a glass of lemonade so tightly I think it might shatter, Alan is next to him on a bar stool, reading things from a little bit of paper. A middle-aged woman I don't recognise stands awkwardly nearby, undoubtedly trapped by terrible small talk.

'That silly man over there is my dad,' Aisa says. 'That's who my mum chose for me, and I think she was right.'

'I understand,' I say, hoping to hide the disappointment in my voice. But what else could she say, really? She can't even remember Dad's face. 'Just legs,' she always says.

She reaches for my hand. Her nails are dark red, chipped and bitten, but underneath they're just like mine. Even the knuckles. I didn't know you could recognise knuckles.

'I could always do with an extra sister though,' she says. She smiles her pointy smile. 'If you'll have me.'

I flash my mirror teeth back and squeeze her hand, just quickly, as Lizzie and Nina look over and smile sympathetically.

'That's good enough for me,' I say.

I tentatively reach forward, but she hugs me back willingly.

Afterwards, we walk together back to the chapel's garden, wordless. Aisa looks at her wrist. No longer an Apple Watch – 'I was a slave to that thing' – but a bulky man's timepiece, a scuffed face, mottled leather strap, inherited from Rosemary. 'They should be finished, yeah?' I nod. We pass under ornate wrought iron gates, weaving along the little path through all the lives.

We reach the plot just as the men are packing up. Two opposites: fat/thin, old/young. Both look a little uneasy. I feel like they would take off their hats if they were wearing them, but instead they just hover.

'Family?' Old says and I nod.

'My parents,' I say, and feel Aisa's hand suddenly on mine, gripping it. I realise my mistake and my stomach flips right over like a decked fish, but neither man flinches.

'Sorry for your loss,' the younger one says. 'We'll get out of your way.'

The soil is as black and shiny as the coffin itself. The gravestone shines in the fading light. Black granite with perfectly precise white letters that could never say enough. Aisa reads them out, barely loud enough for me to hear, but I know the words off by heart anyway.

'Loving father, William Jonathan Proctor, 1953 to 2023.'

'And loving mother,' I add. 'Selina Mary Proctor, 1955 to 1987. Never forgotten.'

*

Top Google Search results for 'Moirthwaite Manor' in September 2023

Urbex Site Report – Moirthwaite Manor *WARNING*

Visited August 2023

Google Maps location here

Got chased off by gunman. Approach at your own risk.

Urbex Site Report – Moirthwaite Manor

Visited November 2022

Google Maps location here

Visited with Pete G. and Tamsin S. Vast grounds with outbuildings still sound. Furniture visible through windows. Could not get inside as angry man (looked like a vagrant, not a security guard) came running at us from behind the house. Avoid.

Acknowledgements

The dedication at the front nearly read, 'For Ribblestaff Manhattan'. A private joke that precisely one person (my sister) would get. I think that's what having siblings is about. A private universe spun together from jokes, memories and understanding.

My sister (and only my sister) will share the same memories of taking our dog Skipper through a mop-and-chair showjumping course. Of eating lardy cake and watching Saturday wrestling. Of radio shows recorded on my Alba tape recorder and renting *Grease* from the video shop every time we were given a quid. Of colluding against our parents. Of characters invented in the back of the car who are still referenced over thirty years later, like Ribblestaff Manhattan and Mr Delaware Chicken. I don't remember how they started, but that's not the point. I hope *The Short Straw* captures some sense of those private sibling universes.

I started *The Short Straw* in Amsterdam, finished it in Kent and everything in between was written in Hilversum, Henley on Thames, Camber Sands, the Kentish Weald and, most fittingly, Cumbria. It was written while my husband, our ridiculous dogs and youngest two children (making up their own private jokes in the back of the car and being amazingly good sports), picked up and moved five times while we waited for our new home to be ready. It was written as my beloved eldest two children moved out of the family home and into their shared flat. It was written, in other words, at some of the sharpest points of family life.

A time for considering everything I wished I could do over, those younger years when I was always so frantically busy; wishing I could slip back just for a day and hold hands a little longer, sod whatever deadline was breathing down my neck. Reflecting on the home we'd left behind, not quite as suddenly as the Kelseys, and the home we hoped to make.

It's all in there. It always is.

My amazing husband deserves a top slot in every book's acknowledgements, but he's earned some kind of crown this time. When I was in the final editing stage of *The Short Straw*, I broke my ankle (and came down with Covid the same day). Alongside working, parenting, doing all the dog walking and all the cleaning, he had to butler me food and drink, guide me up and down the stairs, help me sit in a garden chair in the shower, accompany me to X-rays (on one such trip, my name was read out as 'Holly Cheesedog', which almost made the break worthwhile) and turn a blind eye to the bizarre pyjamas I kept ordering for myself when I was high on painkillers. He's just the best.

Special thanks to my wonderful agent, Sophie Lambert, and my trailblazing editor, Sam Eades, who were so kind and understanding when I had to take all our Zoom calls in bed with my leg elevated on a cushion, looking half dead. I am so lucky to have such talented, hardworking and enthusiastic legends in my corner. On that note, I must also thank Francesca Pathak, Zoe Yang, Lucy Brem, Brittany Sankey, Ellen Turner and the whole team at Orion. My heartfelt thanks too to all at C&W, who work so hard for their authors.

Gillian McAllister, as always, has been my sounding board,

confidante and cheerleader. Our friendship is simply one of the greatest joys of my author life.

And final thanks to Richard Shepherd (and Robert Scragg, who introduced us) who gave me such insightful advice on urban exploring and decaying old buildings.

If I've forgotten anyone, I'm sorry. Please blame the pain-killers.

Credits

Holly Seddon and Orion Fiction would like to thank everyone at Orion who worked on the publication of *The Short Straw* in the UK.

Editorial
Sam Eades
Snigdha Koirala

Copyeditor
Francine Brody

Proofreader
Jade Craddock

Audio
Paul Stark
Jake Alderson

Contracts
Dan Herron
Ellie Bowker

Design
Charlotte Abrams-Simpson
Joanna Ridley
Zane Dabinett

Editorial Management
Charlie Panayiotou
Jane Hughes
Bartley Shaw
Tamara Morriss

Finance
Jasdip Nandra
Nick Gibson
Sue Baker

Marketing
Brittany Sankey

Publicity
Ellen Turner

Production
Ameenah Khan

Operations
Jo Jacobs
Sharon Willis

Sales
Jen Wilson
Esther Waters
Victoria Laws
Toluwalope Ayo-Ajala
Rachael Hum
Anna Egelstaff
Sinead White
Georgina Cutler

If you loved *The Short Straw*, don't miss Holly Seddon's electrifying previous novel...

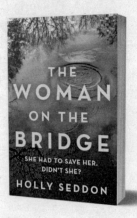

HOW FAR WOULD YOU GO TO SAVE A PERFECT STRANGER?

Maggie is trapped. Dumped on her wedding day, rejected by her family and hounded by a man determined to make her suffer.

Charlotte is desperate. Double-crossed by her only friend and facing total ruin, she will go to any lengths to save what matters.

Two women, one night. A decision that will change *everything*.

AVAILABLE TO BUY NOW

And be hooked from the first page with Holly Seddon's *The Hit List* ...

YOU LIVE AN ORDINARY LIFE. SO WHY DOES SOMEONE WANT YOU DEAD?

On the anniversary of her husband's accidental death, Marianne seeks comfort in everything Greg left behind. She wears his shirt and cologne, reads their love letters and emails. Soon she's following his footsteps across the web, but her desperation to cling to any trace of him leads her to the dark web.

And a hit list with her name on it.

To try to save herself from Sam, the assassin hired to kill her, Marianne must first unpick the wicked web in which Greg became tangled. Was Greg trying to protect her or did he want her dead?

AVAILABLE TO BUY NOW

Reader's Guide

1. What do you think the main themes of *The Short Straw* are?

2. What would you have done if you were the Kelsey sisters running out of petrol near Moirthwaite Manor? Would you have stayed together, split up or something else entirely?

3. Did you recognise the sibling dynamics at play and did they ring true in your experience?

4. Did you relate to one character in particular?

5. Do you think Rosemary did the right thing in telling Jane and Aisa her posthumous secret by letter? Should she have told Bob about Aisa's origins?

6. Which plot twist surprised you the most?

7. Of the surviving characters, who was the biggest present day victim of the events of the past?

8. Did you think Rafferty might be Lizzy's imaginary friend, like the imaginary friend she had as a child?

9. On balance, did Jane and the Kelsey sisters do the right thing in burying Selena with William?

10. Would you ever explore an abandoned building? Has *The Short Straw* changed your mind about this?